NOTHING TO LOSE

She rested her forehead against his and breathed in his scent, taking him deep into her lungs as she longed to do with her body.

She felt his smile beneath her fingertips, brief and a bit crooked. An endearing smile that made her feel special because it was so rare with him.

"What am I going to do with you?" he asked.

Love me! She bit back the words because she didn't want anything to shatter the moment, but the truth sang in her heart.

The first time she'd laid eyes on him, she'd fallen a bit in love. He was different than any man she'd ever met. Aloof. A drifter who made no apology for what he was.

She had so little experience with men, but she knew when she exchanged a shy glance with Trey that he wouldn't be a gentleman. He wouldn't stop at a few stolen kisses for fear her daddy would catch them.

"All my life I've bowed to a man's orders," she said, grazing his lips once, twice. "No more."

She settled her mouth over his, explored the seductive curve of his lips as she dragged her fingertips over the rasp of today's whiskers. He hadn't given anything of himself yet, just remained kneeling in front of the chair. But she sensed the tension rippling under his skin, felt his body shudder when she slipped her tongue under his upper lip.

The same tremor rocked her as she sucked on his mouth, his chin. Her secret lay between them like a sore. She should tell him. Tell him now and get it over with.

Books by Janette Kenny

One Real Cowboy

One Real Man

A Cowboy Christmas

In a Cowboy's Arms

Cowboy Come Home

COWBOY
COME HOME

JANETTE KENNY

ZEBRA BOOKS
KENSINGTON PUBLISHING CORP.

ZEBRA BOOKS are published by

Kensington Publishing Corp.
119 West 40th Street
New York, NY 10018

ISBN-13: 978-1-61793-166-6

Printed in the United States of America

Chapter 1

West Texas, 1895

Trey March had done the one thing that most cowpokes in West Texas had the good sense to avoid. He'd gotten on the wrong side of Jared Barton.

It hadn't been intentional, and he surely wasn't wholly to blame, but the end result had been the same. He had the scars, lingering pain, and burning anger from that lesson to remind him how badly he'd screwed up.

All because he'd thought with his dick. All because he'd stupidly trusted a woman to tell the truth.

Not just any woman.

Nope, he'd surrendered to the temptation that glistened in the big, innocent eyes of Barton's daughter. How damn dumb could a man get?

The reality that she'd played him for a fool was never far from his mind. It'd festered in his gut month after month while he was laid up hurting so damned bad he wanted to die.

Only one thing kept him going. Revenge.

But he wasn't about to waste any more time on the female object of his scorn, which was why he'd waited to come back until now. He didn't want to see her or hear her name mentioned.

He just wanted what he'd worked hard to achieve. He damned sure wasn't leaving until Barton squared with him.

Trey swung off the gray gelding he'd finagled in El Paso and looped the line through the fancy hitching post set in front of the big sprawling hacienda. It was as impressive as the hundreds of acres of land where Barton raised prime Herefords, but right now it looked as desolate as the West Texas soil.

Droughts had a way of reducing grandeur to nothing, just like this one was drying up creeks and wells and men's dreams. Good thing for him he'd given up on wishful thinking six months back.

His personal deadline to claim his shares of the only home he'd known was long past. Instead of going back to Wyoming, all he could do now was claim his money, his horses, and start over again.

Forget the woman and remember the lesson.

He rolled his shoulders to ease the tension cobbling him. Dun grit covered everything, even the scrubby rose struggling to survive in soil that had baked adobe hard. *Her* yellow rosebush.

His gut twisted a bit tighter as memories of Daisy laughing and smiling and moving under him galloped through his mind, a torment that he couldn't forget. He cursed his own weakness for her still. Not that it mattered.

She'd done her slumming with him last fall. By now she'd be married as her daddy had planned and living two counties away from here in another fine, big ranch house. A rich rancher's wife.

Yep, he'd timed his visit to the JDB just right. Wasn't it damned odd that these inhospitable conditions were a fitting welcome for him as he dared to brave Jared Barton's ire?

Trey strode through the white picket gate liberally covered with dust and up the walk to the front door, his spurs chinking in time to the steady clang of metal on metal echoing from the blacksmith's shack.

This time of day the hands would be busy doing chores, though with the drought that equated to hauling water. Barton would be alone in his office hunched over his books, likely trying to find a way to hold on to what he had until the drought broke.

If Ned Durant was with him . . .

His fingers grazed the sidearm resting easy on his left hip. That sonofabitch wouldn't catch Trey off guard a second time.

He gave the brass knocker three hard raps then waited. When a good minute passed and Ramona failed to answer, he smacked the knocker harder, letting off some of the old steam that continued to boil in him whenever he thought of how he'd let a woman play him for a damned fool.

He heard the housekeeper muttering a litany in Spanish long before she opened the big carved door. Ramona's soft brown eyes rounded and her mouth dropped open, clear signs that he was the last person she expected to come calling.

"Señor March! Where have you been?" Her black eyebrows snapped together as she looked him up and down. "You are too thin!"

Rangy, claimed one of the gals who worked at La Valera's Cantina where he'd been laid up. Like a wolf too long on the range hunting for easy prey. But that predator would tell you there was no such thing in nature or life.

He managed a smile for Ramona's sake, not the least bit surprised nobody had told the housekeeper what had happened to him. That kind of justice tended to be swept under the rug or buried six-feet deep. He'd come uncomfortably close to the latter.

"Spent the winter in El Paso." He had no time to waste

on idle talk, even though he'd have enjoyed visiting with Ramona. "I need to see Barton."

She clapped both hands over her mouth. "Ai, yi, yi, you don't know?"

"Know what?" he asked.

Hell, had Barton packed up and moved to his other ranch? No, he wouldn't have left Ramona here. So why did the older woman look distressed?

"Ramona, who's there?" came a sweetly feminine voice from deep in the house, a voice that haunted his nightmares.

The hair on his nape lifted and the skin burned. What the hell was Daisy doing here?

He heard her heels strike the tiled floor in that slow Southern cadence that set a man's thoughts to lustier images. Any second she'd step into the hall, the gentle sway of her hips in contrast with the quickened beat of his pulse.

Every nerve in his body tensed, the muscles bunching of their own accord. There was no avoiding it. No way to temper the fact he was a heartbeat away from laying eyes on the woman with an angel's smile and the cold calculating heart of a she-devil.

"Ramona, what's wrong?" Daisy Barton stepped into the hall, looked his way, and came to a dead stop.

He had the satisfaction of seeing her face leach of color. She even took one shaky step back. If she was smart she'd hightail it until he was gone, then he'd ride out of her life for good this time.

"Ai, yi, yi." The housekeeper shook her head, clearly distressed over the tension that was cracking in the air like sheet lightning between him and Daisy.

Hell's fire! She shouldn't be here. He shouldn't still feel that pull toward her like a bee to Texas bluebonnets.

She was married now. Not his. *Never his.*

Ramona mumbled a string of Holy Mothers. A waste of time. No amount of prayers would douse the rage blazing in his gut. Daisy had lied to him and betrayed him and damned near got him killed. Now she was looking at him as if he were the one who'd hurt her.

"Is Barton here or not?" he asked.

"*Por favor,* you must speak with Señorita Barton," Ramona said, and then she scurried off with a kerchief pressed to her mouth.

Señorita Barton? Daisy hadn't married.

He could lie and say he didn't give a damn, but he couldn't deny he was curious to know what had happened after he'd been dragged off. But the last person he aimed to talk to was Daisy.

By the way she was eyeing him from across the room, she was none too pleased to see or talk to him either. Well too damned bad.

He had no desire to tramp around the ranch to find a hand who'd tell him what the hell was going on with Barton or Daisy. He just wanted his due, and then he'd be gone.

"I don't know why you decided to come back now, but you can just turn around and take yourself off again," Daisy said, chin high and voice catching with that soft Southern pride that she wore like battle armor.

Despite her full skirt and the oversized puff on her sleeves, she looked no more than skin and bones. Haggard even. But then she was dressed in drab gray—a color he'd never seen her wear before.

From this distance he could see that dark crescents streaked under her big eyes. What the hell had happened to put her in this state? Had Kurt Leonard learned she was a lying bit of muslin who was loose with her wares? Had he broken off their engagement and sent Daisy back here in shame?

Served her right if the rancher had dumped her. If her pa had to suffer the shame of her actions along with her. He could care less. She was nothing to him now. Nothing but a bad memory.

He aimed to say his piece to Barton, collect his due, and vamoose. Whatever problems father and daughter were having here was none of his concern.

"I need to talk with Barton right now," he said.

"That's impossible—"

"Don't try stopping me, *ma'am*," he interrupted, putting undue emphasis on Daisy's address. "If he isn't here, I'll wait for him to come back."

She pushed back a strand of golden hair with a hand that trembled—a left hand that was missing her betrothal ring. "All right. Come back to Daddy's office."

She disappeared through the doorway like a thief, likely anxious to tell the old man that Trey had dared to come calling at the front door. He was tempted to wait here until she left Barton's office for he wasn't in any mood to discuss his business while she was in the room.

But maybe it was for the best that she was on hand. Maybe she should hear what he'd come back to retrieve, for then she'd see he hadn't been a drifter. He'd had plans for a better life for himself. For them once he felt worthy of her.

Maybe she'd feel a smidgeon of remorse once she learned that she'd killed every bit of respect he'd had for her.

If only he could've done the same about this intense desire for her, but it was still there. Another thorn in his side to bear. Reminding him how good it had felt to hold her, love her, make her his in the most elemental way.

He wasn't about to give her the satisfaction of knowing how badly he hurt—how much he still hurt—how much she crossed his mind when he least expected it.

Trey ambled down the hall, his spurs chinking on the tiles to beat out the annoyance that hammered in his blood. He'd never come in the front door before. He'd been one of the hands, and when he had business to discuss with Barton he'd used the back door.

A far cry from his life on the Crown Seven, but he'd

learned that too was just another bump in the road for him. A home and family given to him only to be snatched away just when he was starting to let down his guard—just when he was starting to trust.

He'd been born unwanted, and nothing much had changed of late. No sense dwelling on that simple fact.

Trey pushed into the office and came up short. Instead of Barton presiding over the room from his big leather chair, Daisy perched on it like a nervous bird about to take flight.

The man in question was nowhere to be seen.

"What the hell are you trying to pull?" he asked.

Her spine went stiff at that. "I am trying to manage this ranch in my daddy's stead, which isn't easy to do when his *trusted* hands take off without a by-your-leave and then return half a year later and act like the world owes them a living."

The realization that something was dead wrong here slipped past his anger. He took in the pile of papers on the desk, the tray holding a teapot and uneaten wedges of toast. Somebody had spent a considerable amount of time right here, and he knew it had to have been Daisy. But why?

"Where is Barton?"

She stared at him straight on with the same delicate strength as a bluebonnet defying the punishing West Texas sun. "Daddy's dead."

Her lips trembled, and she worried her hands again, a tell that told him she wasn't as strong as she was putting on. But somehow she surprised him and fought back the tears that were threatening to fall.

Damn, he hadn't expected that news. It was clear she was in dire straights here holding the ranch together. He wasn't going to feel a smidgeon of pity for her. Not one damned bit.

But he was curious, worried even, for Barton's fate could have a negative impact on his own.

"What happened?"

Her chin came up, and she fixed accusing eyes on him. "Daddy had a stroke a couple of months after you left. It took him right away."

"Damn! You've been managing the ranch since then?"

"Yes."

"Alone?" he asked, because she'd never had a lick of dealing with ranch business, never done anything but be her daddy's spoiled little girl, and she'd been engaged to marry one of the richest young ranchers in the state.

"I don't see where that's any of your business, Mr. March." Her features hardened like tempered porcelain, as if challenging him to ask more probing questions.

Oh, he had plenty of them to ask, but he wouldn't. That would be admitting to being curious, and he preferred her to think that she'd never crossed his mind these past six months.

"Now that you know, you can leave," she said.

"I'll gladly do just that after I collect what's owed me."

"You should've collected your pay before you left the JDB," she said, the heat back in her tone.

"Your daddy had other ideas, and you damned well know it."

"All I knew was that you'd packed up and left."

He'd been lassoed and dragged near to death, but maybe Barton hadn't shared the details with her. He sure as hell wasn't about to tell her the particulars.

"What's it going to be? You going to pay up?" he asked.

She leaned back then and stared at him. "I only have your word that Daddy owes you. For all I know you could be trying to bilk me out of more money."

He planted his fists on the desk and glared at her, taking small satisfaction when the pulse in her throat warbled to a nigh frantic beat. "I wouldn't do that, and you damn well know it."

"I've learned that I don't know you at all." She turned in the chair and stared at the window. "Not that it matters. If Daddy owes you, I still can't pay. I've spent everything on hauling water and doing what I could to keep the herd alive."

He took in the proud tilt of her head and knew she was telling the truth. Like hundreds of other ranches, the JDB was in poor financial straits due to the drought. Now he was shit out of luck.

"Paying to haul water is a losing proposition," he said. "Surprised Ned didn't balk at doing that."

"It was his idea."

"A piss-poor one."

"I suppose you have a better idea?"

He shrugged. "Barton would've moved the herd to his other ranch that wasn't hit so hard by the drought."

Barton would've sold off the excess as well. But the rancher was dead, and his daughter was calling the shots now.

Daisy didn't know a damned thing about ranching. She was relying on Ned to guide her, and the foreman was leading her down a path toward bankruptcy.

But why? What the hell did Ned hope to gain if the ranch bellied up? What would Daisy do if she lost the ranch?

Don't dwell on her problems. Don't dwell on her. Best thing he could do was cut his losses and ride out.

"I don't have any cash to speak of," she said again, "but you are welcome to take a cow and a calf to cover a month's pay."

"A month's pay? Sweetheart, your daddy owes me over two thousand dollars."

Far from a fortune, but it amounted to a year's worth of scrimping and saving. "That doesn't count the horses I won. Barton let me keep them at the Circle 46. Aim to go get them when I leave here."

You'd think he'd said ten times that amount, seeing as the color drained from her face. "Why would Daddy owe you so much money?"

It was a question that deserved an honest answer. "I agreed to take half my pay up front the whole time I worked here and let Barton hold the other half for me. Did a couple of drives for him on the side and had him apply the whole of that pay to my savings. Check his ledger. It's listed in that old battered trail log he kept in the back of the bottom drawer of his desk."

Trey had stood here month after month while Barton jotted down the amount he held on to for Trey before he collected his pay. He'd had dreams of claiming his share of the Crown Seven Ranch with that money.

Barton became the bank that wouldn't let him withdraw money without thinking things through first. For the first time in his life, he'd saved up a fair amount of money.

Yet as it stood now the end result was the same.

While he had been laid up in El Paso, the deadline to claim his shares passed. He'd lost the Crown Seven. And without the money he'd worked for, he wouldn't be able to buy a ranch either.

Hell, he didn't have any money. With the drought burning West Texas to a crisp, ranchers were laying off cowboys, so he could damn well forget about getting work in these parts either.

"I didn't know this was in here," Daisy said, as she brought the worn ledger out and laid it on the desk.

Had she just stepped in here and not given the papers a thorough inspection? Had she any idea of half the deals her old man had made with his hands, ranchers, and buyers?

Nope, he'd bet she left those details in Ned's hands.

That explained why she was losing money. Why she was clueless about the deal Trey was calling her on.

Her fingers fumbled to untie the worn leather thong holding the ledger together. She turned the pages slowly, scanning each one, her frown deepening as she went through the book.

Surprise and shock registered on her face. When she got to the pages that the old man had devoted to Trey's dealings with him, she downed her head and bowed her shoulders.

He started to reach for her again and just barely quelled the yearning. Damn if he'd let history repeat itself with her.

"The amount Daddy held for you matches what you're asking." She closed the book, and her hands fluttered nervously over the leather. "I don't have the cash, but I can give you the equal value in stock."

Prime stock too, or they had been before the weather took a toll on them. Still it was a tempting offer and likely would be his only chance to amass a sizable herd and recoup some of his losses.

"With the market as tight as it is and the cattle in poor condition, I'd need twice as many to get my price out of them," he said, not about to question why he was being straight with her. "I couldn't do that alone, and every man I hired would need to be paid. Fact is, I don't have a place to hold stock until the conditions get better."

She bit her lower lip, as if thinking something over. "You can keep them here."

He laughed at that notion. "Ain't no way I'd do that."

Her chin came up, and pure hurt shadowed her eyes. "Are you arguing just to be contrary? There are only two choices. Take your cattle or leave them here with JDB stock."

He wanted to think she was just being sassy, but it was clear she believed her own words. "Why didn't Ned move any of the herd to Barton's old homestead?"

"He told me the trail would be too hard on them in these conditions," she said.

"Harder than them dying of thirst here?" He shook his head that she'd caved to Ned so easily, but then Ned had been the old man's foreman for ten years. She'd likely not seen that Ned was out to gain control of the ranch little bit by little bit. "If money is so tight, how are you paying the hands?"

"They're working for room and board with a promise I'll pay them back wages plus bonuses once I get back on my feet. All except Ned. He wanted stock up front instead of money later."

"How many head has Ned taken off your hands?"

A frown pulled at Daisy's smooth brow as she opened a different ledger and ran a slender finger down the line of entries, her lips silently moving as she ciphered the sum. "A hundred and ten head."

"What'd he do with them?"

"Kept them here, I suppose," she said. "I didn't ask."

He settled his hat on more firmly. "Maybe you'd best find out what your foreman is doing with his herd and yours before he owns all of your daddy's stock. Hell, I doubt you have enough cattle to cover what's due me."

He turned to leave, knowing a losing hand when he'd been dealt one. He'd lost it all but the horses, and without land he'd have to drive them to San Angelo and put them up for auction.

"Wait!" She rounded the desk and crossed to him. "Do you really think we could save the herd by moving them to another ranch?"

"I surely do." He scraped a thumb over his chin, thinking. "Drought ain't near as bad up on the Concho River."

"I've heard Daddy talk about the old ranch, but he never took me there."

Trey wasn't surprised. He'd heard Barton lost his first

family at the Circle 46. He'd moved on, and for reasons that were solely Barton's, it appeared he didn't want his new family mingling with memories of the old.

God knew the house wasn't nothing to brag on.

He'd spent a week there last fall when Barton sent him and a couple of hands to San Angelo to buy thoroughbreds he'd had his eyes on. That's when Trey won his horses. They'd driven them all back to the old homestead and set about turning it into a stud farm. It wasn't much to look at then, but the foreman was a good man.

"Unless the river has suddenly gone dry, the old ranch will beat this dust bowl you're living in now," he said, stating the obvious as he turned to face her one last time. "You're the boss, Daisy. Tell your foreman you want that herd moved."

She stared at him, as if shocked by the idea of going against Ned. She'd transferred her allegiance to him now that her daddy was gone.

Tied her cart to a dead horse was more like it.

Trey turned and headed for the door, hating Ned more with each breath he took. Maybe revenge wasn't such a bad idea after all. God knew he'd gain satisfaction meting out just a portion of what the foreman had heaped on him months ago.

"Why don't you do it?" she asked.

Her words lassoed him and brought him up short again. He slammed a palm on the doorjamb and stared at the far wall, hating the thrill that hit him at that suggestion.

She couldn't mean it. He had to have misunderstood her, for Ned would pitch a shit fit if Trey stepped in now. Hell, he had to be loco for just considering it.

And yet wouldn't that sate a good deal of the desire for vengeance boiling in him? To get back at the man who'd left him for dead? To have the woman who'd shunned him crawl back and ask for his help?

No, he wasn't that way. Never had been. The best thing for him to do was to put this behind him and head out.

Instead, he found himself asking, "Just what are you suggesting?"

"You help me, and I'll help you," she said. "Drive the herd up to the Circle 46 and agree to be the foreman until the drought breaks."

"You've got Ned to do that for you."

"I don't trust him."

"You don't trust me either."

She didn't deny it, but she obviously placed him on a rung above Ned. He took no satisfaction in that, for when he'd needed her to step forward, she'd hid out.

That's what he ought to do now. But he couldn't seem to make his feet move, even though he heard the rustle of her skirt over the pounding of his heart and knew she was coming toward him.

"I know you don't want to stay around here," she said, her voice soft as velvet, "but I'm asking for your help. Just for a few months."

Trey didn't want to help her. This downfall was just punishment for the Bartons. He should walk out with a smug smile on his face just knowing that the mighty were tumbling. Yep, he should cut his losses and skedaddle.

But he'd be lying if he said he wasn't tempted by her offer. He could come out of this disaster ahead of the game and give Ned his comeuppance for damned near killing him.

"That's all you want from me then?" he asked. "Move the herd and take my due when we part ways in a few months?"

He heard her nervous sigh and caught the subtle scent of roses. She was right behind him. So close all he had to do was turn around and take her in his arms. Take her here and now and end the damned dreams that wouldn't die.

"Yes," she said.

Taking her up on the offer was worth the aggravation of working for her, for he'd gain cattle in the bargain. They'd be his start for his own spread.

But he still didn't have a place to run them, and the open range was over. What little remained had been eaten clean in this drought. So all he could do was sell them and bank his profits or do as she suggested.

"Sam Weber still the foreman on the Circle 46?" he asked.

"I'm not sure. Ned told me that daddy hadn't run much there but a small herd of longhorns and some mustangs," she said. "After Daddy died, Ned thought it best to have a couple of men there to keep vandals from running off with the stock. He said the foreman decided to move on."

She'd been fed a line of whitewash if she thought those horses were wild. It was mighty clear she hadn't had the inclination to visit the place herself to see what needed to be done. Clear too that Sam hadn't come down to discuss what should be done with the thoroughbreds, though he could see where the man wouldn't want to work for Ned.

"I want it in writing that I'm the new foreman at the Circle 46 for the next two months," he said.

Brittle silence cracked in the room, and for a heartbeat he suspected she'd refuse. "What if I don't find somebody to replace you by then?"

Not his problem. "One other thing. I won't work with Ned."

"No, you won't," she said. "He was Daddy's pick. Not mine. It's time to part ways."

"He won't go easy."

"I know," she said at last, but didn't say why.

Not that she needed to give him a reason. It was clear that Ned had been taking advantage of her naiveté. Just like that bastard had accused him of doing.

"I'll draw up the papers," she said.

He gave her time to return to her desk before turning around. But she hadn't moved.

She stood before him, chin high and big eyes full of worry and heartache. He stilled the urge to reach for her, to pull her into his heat and hardness and drink from her soft lips.

He'd hired on to do a job, and he aimed to put himself first this time. She'd soon find out he wouldn't bow to her every whim. He damn sure wouldn't be lured back into her bed again.

Now if he could just convince his body that he didn't want her . . .

Chapter 2

Daisy forced air into her lungs and hoped her knees wouldn't buckle as she made her way back to her daddy's big desk heaped with its monstrous responsibilities. My God, the last person she had expected to ever see again was Trey March.

But here he was, just inches from her. Bigger than she remembered.

Each breath she took drew him deeper into her and brought the memories that were never far from her mind to aching, pulsing life.

All she had to do was reach for him.

So tempting.

In his arms she could forget the hell she'd endured these past six months. Just once more she could lie beside him, skin on skin, with their hearts beating in tandem like she'd dreamed of doing night after lonely night.

Nobody could stop her now for giving herself to the cowboy she'd fallen in love with the first time she'd seen him. Nobody but her remaining strong, remembering the sad fact that the only love they'd shared had been physical. The only heart involved had been her own. That's all she'd ever have with him.

She'd given him all her love, and he'd taken it and her hopes and her dreams and then he'd ridden away.

Daisy couldn't go through that again, yet here she was sitting behind her daddy's desk staring at a blank piece of paper. Trey wanted proof that he'd be in charge. He didn't trust her.

But then she didn't trust him either. In fact she'd learned not to trust anyone save Ramona, her husband Fernando and their son Manuel.

She wasn't a starry-eyed innocent any longer. She saw men in a whole new light. She saw Trey for what he was instead of what she desperately had wanted him to be.

Yet right now she was poised to draw him back into her life for a few more months. Only because the plan that Ned had suggested—no, that he had insisted she agree to last week opened her eyes to what he wanted.

She had to cut all ties with Ned Durant. But she needed a strong man to run the JDB spread until she could find a man she could depend on to take Ned's place.

Trey could handle himself against Ned. She had no doubt about that.

The question was, could she handle herself around Trey?

He'd be at the Circle 46, and she'd be here. She wouldn't have to deal with him on a day-to-day basis.

She wouldn't be tempted to expect more from him. Not again. She'd barely survived the consequences the last time with this man. But she had proof that her daddy had cut a deal with him, and there wasn't one mention in the ledger of Trey taking his money when he'd left.

She owed him, and she damned well intended to use him like he'd used her so many months ago.

"Before you drive the herd to the Circle 46, I think you should ride over there and see that your plan is viable," she said, and took a break in drafting her agreement with Trey March to give herself another chance to change her mind.

Not that she would. It was just that being confined with him for this long had her nerves cracking like sheet lightning.

She wanted him to take his stock and leave. She wanted to go through this ledger and see what else needed to be done. See what she'd missed. See what other surprises awaited her.

"Aim to do that today," he said, confirming he'd thought this through. "Cattle are going for around fifteen bucks a head now. Reckon with what Barton owes me, that comes to about one hundred and fifty head."

She nodded, but tallied it up just to make sure. He was right, though on the shy side. She didn't take the lesser number as evidence of him being generous. Just the way things were done among cattlemen.

"Take your pick once you get there," she said.

He didn't answer right off, so she looked up at him. But he was staring out the window, and by the dark frown he wore she wondered what was going through his mind, if he even heard her.

Trey had never shared much about himself, claiming there wasn't much about him to tell. He'd spent much of his childhood in an orphanage and then ended up on a ranch in Wyoming. She never knew why or how that came about.

Asking had never netted her an answer, for when she'd gotten too curious, he'd taken her mind off his past by loving her. When she was in his arms, she thought of nothing but him.

A tremor raced through her at the thought, unbidden and uncontrollable. She went still and stared at the telling squiggle left by her pen, standing out just like the error she'd made in thinking with her heart.

This was a mistake, but a worse one would be accepting Ned's proposal. Her stomach lurched at the thought, but she ignored her unease and read the contract again, wanting to be sure she'd worded it right.

If Trey could find a loophole to claim more than agreed upon . . . If he turned out to be as dishonest as Ned . . . Hell, he could drive the entire herd off, and she'd not be the wiser.

"Take Ramona's son with you," she said.

"Manuel?"

He snorted and jammed both hands in his back pockets, and she wondered how he could look recalcitrant and manly at the same time. Wondered why her mind wandered in that direction after the hell he'd put her through.

"I'm not wet-nursing a boy on a cattle drive," he said.

"I'm not asking," she said, glad her voice didn't crack, glad she wasn't visibly giving away the turmoil boiling inside her. "He's seventeen, hardly a boy. If I recall, you said you were younger than that when you took up cowboying."

Trey's lips thinned, and his dark eyes turned cold and hard as his heart. She held her breath, and she wondered if he'd tell her to forget it and walk out. He was so difficult to read.

He didn't give of himself. He always held something back. He wasn't the staying type either. He'd already proven that to her. He'd left her to suffer shame and tragedy alone.

"All right. Manuel comes with me," he said at last.

He seemed accepting of her request. But then he'd always taken the younger hands' side in everything, which earned him more disfavor with Ned.

Ned. She still had him to deal with.

She took a breath but she still couldn't relax. She wondered if she'd ever be able to again.

Daisy slid the contract toward Trey. "If you'll just sign this, we will be set to go."

Trey stepped closer, and she fought the impulse to shrink back. He angled the paper toward him with two fingers, going still as a statue.

She noted the strength in his hands, remembering too

well how those long, blunt fingers had felt splayed against her bare skin. How she'd let her own hands skim up his muscled arms to find purchase on his broad shoulders.

Trey March had been the forbidden fruit. The man who was more exciting, more dangerous, more man than the one she'd been engaged to marry.

And just thinking of Trey's hands brought a new flush to her face. Dammit, she didn't want to think about what they'd shared. What they'd lost.

She'd convinced herself she had found true love with Trey and that what they did wasn't wrong. She'd been such a fool.

"Make two copies," Trey said and slid the paper back to her before ambling over to take a closer look at the books on the shelves.

"Of course."

She'd not thought of that. She'd have made one copy and given it to him. She wouldn't have had any record of their agreement. *Stupid, stupid!*

She took another paper and began making a duplicate, achingly aware that Trey was watching her every move. Watching and probably laughing at her ineptness.

And she was inept.

She could blame the headaches that came often, more so since her fall from the loft. But the truth was that she had holes in her memory. Like a child's puzzle scattered about, with pieces that just didn't fit.

Snippets of a mother she barely remembered. Of trains and cold dank rooms. Of a boy tugging her along and a fear that wouldn't leave her. Of being too afraid to even cry.

Nightmares, her mama had called them.

And soon after, her mama had become one of them.

From then on it'd been just her and her daddy. He'd raised her to be taken care of instead of teaching her how to take care of herself and this ranch. He'd kept her removed from his dealings because all she was destined to be was a rancher's wife. A rich rancher's wife.

She was supposed to have a life where those menial tasks were done for her. Where every thing she whimpered for would be granted.

She knew how to manage the house, knew how to ride a horse, and knew how to entertain. She knew how to look pretty and what to say to guests that would help her husband's status in the county.

As her daddy said, *she'd make a husband proud.*

Just thinking of that old saw made her anger bubble to the surface. She wasn't an ornament.

Dammit all, she owed it to her daddy to prove that he worked hard to amass this land only to have her lose it.

Right now she was mighty close to losing the empire that Jared Barton had built with his sweat, blood, and determination.

Please don't let this be a mistake I'll regret. She carefully signed and dated both contracts and passed them back to Trey, glad her hands didn't shake.

"This is a fair deal," she said, mimicking what she'd heard her daddy say and hoping it was true.

Trey returned to the desk—to her side actually. He was too close, too big, but she kept those thoughts to herself as he stood beside her and slowly read the contract that bound them together for the next two months.

He gave a curt nod, then signed his name on both documents with bold straight strokes that mirrored this no-nonsense man's attitude.

"If the Circle 46 is in good shape, I'll move the cattle up there as soon as possible. Then we'll come back for the remuda. Shouldn't take more than four or five days to get all the stock settled." He folded one paper and tucked it into his vest pocket.

"I'd like a weekly report on how things are going up there," she said, staring at her copy of their agreement because she refused to lean back in her chair to look up into his eyes.

"That's fair."

Trey took a step to leave just as the back door slammed shut. He stopped cold, and she did the same.

Dread washed over her as Ramona's voice took on a strained pitch. Too much so for the visitor to be her son.

The measured tread of boot heels striking the floor grew louder. Someone was on his way to the office and that could only be one man. Ned.

The headache that never seemed to leave her pounded harder when she thought of the coming confrontation between her and the foreman. The fact that Trey hadn't moved from her side, seeming to tower over the room and her, also kept her anxiety level high.

Every inch of him screamed fury, from the rigid line of his broad shoulders to the strong arms that hung deceptively loose at his sides. Like a rattler, he was ready to strike.

Daisy had no doubt he could be deadly if he so wished.

Ned stepped into the doorway of the office and stopped cold. He stared at Trey, his angular features taking on a honed edge.

She didn't like Ned, but keeping him on had been easy. She had intended to let him manage the ranch until she decided what to do—stay or sell. But she hadn't counted on a drought hitting them or on her foreman having an ulterior motive.

Yes, letting the ranch ride as it'd been doing had been easy. She hadn't had to think about what to do when she'd been crippled by grief. When she felt so alone that she wanted to die too.

Ned's shrewd gaze swung back to her, hard and assessing. "You need help getting rid of this unwanted visitor, Miss Daisy?"

As far as she knew Ned didn't know there'd been anything more between her and Trey than infatuation on her part. If she was wrong . . .

"Why would you assume Mr. March is unwelcome?" she asked, sensing more than seeing any hint of surprise in Trey.

"You saying he is?" Ned asked.

How to answer? Caution seemed the prudent approach, for the moment Ned sensed he was losing his position here, God only knew what he'd do in retaliation.

"According to Daddy's ledger, he owes Mr. March a substantial amount that I simply don't have," she said, opting for honesty as there were too damned many lies out there already.

"Why would Barton owe the likes of him anything?" Ned asked in a voice taut with poison.

"'Why' isn't the issue here," she said, not about to divulge anymore than she had. "I inherited daddy's holdings along with his debts. Since I am cash poor, I can only pay Mr. March in cattle. But he's land poor, so I've agreed to let him run his herd on the Circle 46 and act as foreman there until better times prevail."

Ned crossed his arms over his chest, and she was tempted to huddle up from the cold hard glint in his eyes. "Going to cost you to go back to having a foreman on both spreads when one man can handle it all."

"Very true," she said. "But I owe Mr. March cattle and—"

"Then give him his cattle and good riddance to him," Ned said.

She'd given him that option. Take his stock or take over as foreman. Time would tell if she'd made a strong pact or a huge mistake.

"Due to the declining conditions here, I've decided a major change is in order. We'll move the stock to the Circle 46. Mr. March will be the new foreman."

"You're making a mistake," Ned said.

"You're entitled to your opinion, but it won't change my mind," she said.

Ned visibly stiffened, head snapping back and shoulders racking taut. He didn't glance at Trey beyond the swift shifting of his eyes.

"You're giving me the boot?" Ned asked.

"It's for the best," she said.

"Don't look that way from where I'm standing," Ned said, sliding Trey a damning look before turning that same glower on her. "I'm betting if he hadn't dragged back here, you'd have taken me up on my offer."

She shook her head, feeling Trey's gaze on her, questioning, doubting. "You're wrong."

"Easy for you to say that now." Ned's light eyes sparked fire for a heartbeat, then narrowed into glacial slits. "The old man would roll over in his grave if he knew you were putting him in charge over me."

She shot to her feet. "That's enough. Daddy's holdings are mine, and I can damn well pick who I want managing them."

"Yes'm, you sure enough can." Ned scrubbed a hand over his mouth, his expression mellowing and his stance losing its brittle edge. A chameleon with a Stetson and spurs. "I've got a small herd I've got to get settled elsewhere now. How soon you want me to clear out?"

She was tempted to give him the same answer as he'd suggested for Trey. But she wouldn't put the cattle through more stress than they were already suffering with the drought.

"A week, but I'll be lenient on time," she said.

"I can do that. I'll also be taking a couple of extra head to cover this month's pay."

"Fine," she said, for whether she liked him or not, she still owed him that.

Without another word, the foreman strode out with the same surety he'd shown when he walked in.

Daisy waited until the back door closed. "I expected him to try working a deal where he could keep his stock here."

"Why the hell would he want to keep them in this dust bowl?" Trey asked.

She shook her head, simply surprised that Ned had agreed so easily. That he'd given in without a fight.

"What was his offer?"

She grimaced, loath to tell him. "Last week, Ned asked me to marry him."

Trey didn't say anything for the longest time. She wondered what was going through his mind. If he was wondering why she hadn't married the man she'd been betrothed to.

She hoped he didn't ask about that, because she saw no need to tell him the truth. She didn't intend to tell him anything about that awful time after he up and left. What had happened couldn't be changed, though it had changed her forever.

"I figured as much," he said. "While I'm gone, you need a man here in case Ned tries to force your hand."

That dragged a shiver of dread from her. But he was right. She needed to put up fences between her and Ned, and between her and Trey as well.

Some mistakes simply didn't bear repeating.

Trey's boots kicked up dust clouds as he made his way to the blacksmith's shop. The clanging of metal had stopped long ago, but the tang of hot metal still hung in the air.

He saw the older man when he rounded the cookshack. He picked up his pace, anxious to get answers from Ramona's husband—the one man he trusted to be square with him.

Fernando glanced up from repairing staves on barrels that had seen better days. But then hauling water day after day tended to take its wear and tear on the equipment and the men.

"How many miles are they hauling water?" Trey asked after giving the older man a nod in greeting.

"Too many for thirsty cattle, señor."

Trey imagined what didn't splash out en route evaporated. "Where's Ned holding his herd?"

Fernando shrugged. "I have heard the vaqueros speak of Señor Ned driving cattle to an old rancho on the Devil's River."

A fair piece from here. "Let me guess. Ned owns it."

"*Si.* He won it in a poker game last fall."

One man's bad luck was another's lucky charm. Hell, that's how he came to own four thoroughbreds.

But had Ned thought of leaving the JDB back then? Or was he setting up a place where he could rustle off a few head of JDB cattle with nobody the wiser?

If so, there'd have been hell to pay if Barton had found out. Damned shame the man dropped dead.

"You here the day Barton had his stroke?"

"*Si.*" The older man hung his head, seeming so intent on his work that Trey wondered if he'd tell him what had happened. "It was the señorita's birthday, and the señor had great plans for it."

Trey could well imagine. Birthdays were always celebrated large on the JDB, especially Daisy's.

"Barton died that day?"

Fernando nodded, his eyes bleak with sorrow. "Galen Patrick from the old homestead arrived that afternoon with

a fine mare he'd trained for Señor Barton. That is when the
señor and Ned had words. After that, Galen and the señor
talked in private before Galen left."

"What got Ned on Barton's bad side?"

"I don't know, but after the señor gave the señorita the
mare, she went riding. It was after that when I heard the
señor and Ned arguing again." Fernando shook his head.
"They were too far away for me to hear what was said, but
both were angry. It was then that the señor staggered back
and fell to the ground. I ran to help, but it was no use. The
señor was dead."

"Damn." Trey planned to get Galen's side of it when he
rode up to the Circle 46, if the man was still working
there. "Had Barton and Ned gotten into arguments before
that day?"

Fernando shook his head. "Señor Barton's temper had
been bad all winter, but it grew worse after Señorita
Barton's accident just a month before."

He was helpless to stop the cold stab of worry that hit
his gut. "Tell me about it," he asked, more than curious
how her mishap tied into Barton's sour mood.

"For weeks, she'd come to the barn every day around ten
in the morning and go up to the loft," Fernando said, and
slid him a look that hinted of disapproval.

Trey wasn't one who embarrassed easily, yet he felt
the burn of shame scorch his neck and cheeks now. Hell,
did the old man know he'd been meeting Daisy up there
last fall?

No, he could only guess. They'd been careful. So
who was she meeting up there this time? Who was her
new lover?

Those were questions a man didn't ask about a lady,
even if he had cause. Trey had lost the right to know details
of Daisy's private life the day he'd been waylaid.

But it shouldn't be hard to find out who had suddenly disappeared off the JDB a few months back. Right now a bigger question demanded to be asked.

"You going to tell me about Miss Barton's accident?"

Fernando treated him to another long stare, but this time Trey saw the worry banked in the old man's eyes. "She fell through an open trapdoor. By the grace of the Holy Mother, I'd taken Barton's *diablo* stallion from his stall in the barn earlier to get him shod and found her when I returned."

Trey set his teeth so hard that his jaw ached. Divine providence, indeed. Daisy would have been stomped to death by that spooked horse if she'd fallen in when he was in his stall.

And that bit about her just falling through an open trapdoor . . . Though Barton had joked that Daisy was a bit on the clumsy side, Trey had never seen a woman more poised and in control of herself whether she was riding sidesaddle, driving her fancy little buggy, or making love with him.

She knew every nook and cranny in that loft.

"She's lucky, all right," Trey said, thinking she looked no worse for wear to him. "Who left the trapdoor open?"

Fernando shrugged. "I fed the stallion last, and the door was shut. Señor Durant told me and Señor Barton that he hadn't seen anyone go into the loft since I'd left with the horse and the trapdoor above the stallion's stall was closed."

"Somebody opened it. Hell, she could've broken her neck."

"Perhaps that was the intention," Fernando said.

Trey's annoyance exploded as the old man stared at him with nothing short of accusation. "Just what are you getting at?"

"Señor Barton was with me when I brought the stallion back," Fernando said. "Barton carried her out after deciding she hadn't broken any bones. Before she drifted into the deep sleep, she called out for you. She told him she'd been pushed."

"By whom?"

"I don't know. She fell into a deep sleep then." Fernando treated him to a cool perusal. "But Señor Barton sent men out looking for you." Fernando's cold stare proved he suspected Trey had done it.

"I didn't push her. Hell, I was hundreds of miles from here."

"So you say."

Trey swept his hat off and exposed the scar cutting across his forehead and disappearing into his hair. "Two months ago I was still laid up in an El Paso cantina, nursing a broken arm, busted ribs, and what the doctor called a bruise on my brain. I wasn't able to walk without weaving like a drunk for another month. I'd been there since a few weeks before Christmas."

Fernando didn't break eye contact, staring at him as if trying to read the truth in his eyes. Finally, his brow furrowed, and he looked away.

"Who did this to you?"

It'd be easy to tell the truth, except he'd be obliged to explain why Barton had ordered him nearly beat to death. Not that it would take much imagination to figure out what Trey must have done to warrant the old man's ire.

Considering what she'd done to him, it'd serve Daisy good too to have her reputation dragged through the mud. To let this fine man know what kind of woman he was working for.

But he couldn't find any satisfaction in confessing what he and Daisy had done. Mutual consent. That's what it'd been. He could've walked away when tempted. He never would've gone as far as he had if she'd just said no.

He wasn't the type of man to brag over his amorous conquests. If Kirby Morris, his adopted father, had taught him one thing, it was to always respect women—all women.

"Don't matter much who did it," Trey said. "Fact remains I was waylaid and left for the vultures. I didn't much know what had happened for months."

"So this is why you disappeared," Fernando said.

Last chance to spill his guts. But Trey merely nodded and turned his gaze to the big barn where he'd awakened a fiery passion in the rancher's innocent daughter.

"What the hell was she doing up there?" Trey asked.

Fernando shook his head, his expression suddenly haggard. "I do not know. For weeks on end she would go to the hayloft and just sit there, looking out at the plains, looking so sad."

"You saying she was up there alone every time?" he asked, despite his determination not to ask how she'd spent her days after he was gone.

"Every day after *Navidad.*" Fernando's eyes met his, and Trey knew at that moment that the blacksmith was aware of his assignations with Daisy.

They'd been careful, but obviously not careful enough. Had Fernando been the one to spill the beans to Barton all those months ago?

No, he would've known that Barton would set out to punish him for daring to touch his princess. But someone else surely had. Someone who knew they'd met here. Had that same someone followed Daisy to the loft? Had that someone pushed her?

"Barton ever find out who hurt Daisy?" Trey asked.

"No. He told me later that he feared she'd tried to kill herself. That nobody had pushed her."

"Why would he think that?"

Again, Fernando's shoulders lifted in a weary shrug. "I would not know."

Trey let that news sink in. What had made Barton so angry at Ned that he'd had an apoplectic fit? And more troubling, had Daisy tried to kill herself?

Chapter 3

Trey had never seen such poor looking cattle in his life. He doubted all of them would make the drive to the Circle 46, but those same cattle could die here as well.

Several of the water troughs were bone dry, and the rest were close to empty. The stretch of hard pack dirt along the fence hinted that hay had been pitched there at one time.

"How often has Ned been feeding these beeves?" Trey asked.

"Every week at first," Manuel said. "But this month he told us to stretch out feeding them or we'd run out of hay."

Trey suspected Ned's cattle looked far better, but he'd yet to lay eyes on them. Same with most of the hands who'd worked here. When Ned had pulled out, Trey guessed the bulk of them had too.

Just as well. Last thing Trey needed was men working for him who'd just as soon stab him in the back. But he was left with an odd mix of cowboys who had little or no experience driving cattle.

He glanced at the trio of boys who'd ridden out to the far pasture with him and Manuel. Damn if they weren't like a flashback to when he'd first come West with Reid and Dade, his foster brothers.

Three boys who hadn't known a damn thing about ranching. But they'd learned. Of course Kirby had taken the time to teach them—time Trey had no intentions of investing in this crew.

All they needed to know were the basics of driving cattle. Once they reached the Circle 46, these young hands would be relegated to minding a fenced herd. But he feared that he'd find the place deserted of men and stock, that his horses were long gone.

If that were the case, he had nothing to hold him here except his word.

Yep, once they moved the herd to the old homestead, he would settle back and wait out his two months. He only hoped the fence was intact and the quarters livable. That there was a good supply of fresh water. That was most important.

If he could just shake the fear that Daisy might still be in real danger. It wasn't just that she'd been pushed from the hayloft. It was not knowing why anyone would want to kill her.

Not his problem. Not his responsibility.

Trey didn't have the patience to wet-nurse her.

He'd leave a man or two at the JDB to watch over her and Ramona. It was up to her to figure out where to go from there. The couple of months he'd be minding the herd should be plenty of time for her to realize she'd be better off selling out and moving to town.

But until she did, he had to keep the herd alive.

He took in the young cowhands who'd trailed him and Manuel out here. They were all good in the saddle, but he needed to know if they had the patience for droving. No time like the present to find out.

"I want these beeves herded up toward the house," Trey told Manuel. "The pasture to the east of the barn is big enough to hold them for now. Closer to water too."

"The only water there is the house well."

Trey nodded, well aware of that. "I don't aim to play it out; just make sure the herd is well watered before we head them north."

"*Si,* Señor March," Manuel said, and Trey hoped to God the boy could handle this chore.

"Get the men into position then and open the gates. And go easy," Trey said when he caught the boys' exuberance. "I don't want to run them."

He held back while Manuel gave the other cowhands instructions in clear, easy to understand commands. He liked the fact that the boy wasn't puffed up on himself. He was taking his job seriously, and that took a huge load off Trey right then and there.

Driving the cattle across the JDB wasn't exciting or difficult. He'd half expected Ned to show his face at some point to cause trouble, but he never did. That was likely for the best too, because the more Trey saw of the herd's poor condition, the angrier he became with Ned.

Daisy too? Yep, he wanted to nurse his anger at her. He really did, but her brush with death kept coming back to haunt him.

Ansel, the youngest of the hands riding drag with Trey, ventured closer as the herd spread out on the pasture that had been eaten to a nub. "If you want, I can ride to the house and get them troughs filled."

Trey grimaced at the boy's suggestion. "Worse thing you could do. If they catch a whiff of water, they'll stampede. Likely kill or cripple a good many beeves."

"I-I didn't know," Ansel said.

"Now you do," he said, careful there was no heat in his tone.

There'd been a time when he'd been that green too. How the hell had Kirby Morris put up with him and his foster brothers?

Patience. It was something he was in short supply of. Wouldn't be easy to cultivate it, but he'd damned sure try.

By the time they got the herd closed inside the pasture behind the barn, the day was pretty well spent. Cattle milled around the empty troughs and bellowed their displeasure, paying little attention to the hands who were dumping a small amount of hay on the ground.

They were too desperate for water, bawling more now than when they'd been herded into the pasture. Maybe he should've sent a few of the boys ahead of them to get some water in the troughs.

The thought barely crossed his mind when Manuel came running toward the fence. "Señor March. You must come quickly and see this."

Before Trey could ask what was wrong, the young man disappeared again. Trey was obliged to follow with dread dogging his every step.

He guessed he wasn't going to like this surprise long before he reached the clutch of men gathered around the well pump. As he got closer, he noticed the typically gray ground was black.

A lot of water had been pumped out onto the earth. From the dark stain that stretched to the barn, it was clear somebody had stood here a good long time and done nothing but man that pump.

The waste sickened him more than the fact that this was a malicious act. Water was life, and somebody had intentionally taken it here today.

"It is dry," Manuel said, and gave the pump handle several strong pulls to prove it.

Barely a trickle fell onto the saturated ground. They were out of water.

"Don't suppose anybody saw who did this," Trey said as he sidestepped the mire.

"We were all with you," Manuel said.

Trey glanced toward the blacksmith's shack. "Fernando was here."

"Dios!" Manuel ran to the shack with Trey fast on his heels.

Sweat popped from his pores the second he stepped into the shed. The smithy clearly hadn't worked for the fire pit was cold.

"Fernando!"

No answer beyond a scuffling sound deep in the shed.

Trey thumbed his hat off his brow and drew his Colt, pulling Manuel behind him and easing into the shadows. The skin on his nape tingled with warning, and his gut clutched with fear that he'd find the man dead.

He stepped to the back of the shed, the steady thump against wood raising his hopes. Right there alongside the workbench, he saw the shape of a man trussed up like a Christmas goose.

He holstered his gun and knelt beside the older man. Fernando was gagged with his own bandana and tied to the workbench with sturdy hemp.

Somebody had made damned sure he wasn't going anywhere.

"Who did this to you?" Trey asked once he worked the gag free.

Fernando sucked in a ragged breath. "I don't know, señor. I was laying a fire in the pit when I was hit from behind."

Trey severed the rope with his knife and helped the older man to his feet. "You're damned lucky you didn't get a bullet in your head."

"Si." Fernando pressed a hand to the back of his head and winced.

Yep, a gunshot would have drawn attention. Whoever had done this was careful to avoid that for he'd needed time. Lots of time to stand there manning that pump for hours.

The bellowing of cattle grew louder as the beeves protested the lack of water. Damn, they were in a worse fix than before.

He strode from the shadowy shed and stared at the cattle milling restlessly in the pasture. After that long drive they needed water, but that wouldn't be forthcoming here.

Manuel stood by his side with the other men behind him, all looking to him for orders. They weren't an experienced crew, but they damned sure had thrown their loyalty his way.

"Haul water in for tonight," Trey told them. "We'll drive the herd out in the morning."

"*Si,* señor," Manuel said, before leaving with the others to carry out his orders.

Fernando came up beside him, the top of his head barely reaching Trey's shoulders. "I heard and felt the ground moving as the cattle drew near. The stock will appreciate feed and water."

"Afraid that won't be happening like we'd planned." Trey pointed toward the blackened ground that was fast turning gray. "Somebody took time to pump the well dry today."

Fernando bit off several Spanish curses. "When I woke, I heard the pump working, but I thought the men had returned and were filling the trough."

"Whoever waylaid you did this," he said. "Ned?"

"It could have been anyone with a grudge or a dark heart. Though I didn't see who hit me, I am sure I spotted Durant out on the mesa earlier."

Had to be Ned's handiwork. Trey ached to hit something, to vent the anger boiling in him. But Kirby's words came back to him. *Cooler tempers always prevail.*

It was still a hard-learned lesson for Trey, especially after being waylaid by Ned. Anger at himself, Daisy, and the cruel foreman was what had given him the strength to fight past the pain as his body had slowly healed. As he'd forced his battered legs to carry his weight again. As he stood day after day and lassoed logs despite the agony ripping across his back and sizzling along his torn muscles.

He'd lived for revenge against Ned and Daisy.

Daisy!

Remembering that she'd been pushed from the loft before sent new fear crashing through him. He took off at a dead run toward the house, his legs throbbing from the punishment to remind him he wasn't entirely healed. That he'd never be a hundred percent whole again.

But that had been the idea behind dragging him for miles over rough ground until he couldn't hold on to consciousness any longer. And still Ned hadn't been done with him.

Trey shoved in the back door. "Daisy!"

No answer.

"Ramona!"

Silence pulsed around him.

He pushed through the rooms with his heart in his throat, throwing open doors. Terrified of what he'd find.

Nothing.

The house was empty.

He stood in Barton's office and scrubbed a hand over his mouth, a hand that trembled. He couldn't recall ever being this afraid in his life, and feeling that way for her rankled.

"She always does her shopping in town on Friday," Manuel said.

He swung on the older man. "What about Ramona?"

"My wife goes with the señorita," Fernando said.

Some of the tension knotting his shoulders eased, being replaced with the bite of anger that always came too swiftly. It was mighty clear to him that whoever drained the well knew Daisy's routine. Had to be Ned.

They'd made it easy for the bastard by leaving the ranch.

Only reason Fernando was alive was because he hadn't seen his attacker. What if the women had returned early? Would he have found them murdered?

The steady clip of hooves penetrated his anger. From the window in Barton's office, he watched a trim buggy pull up near the back door.

Trey exhaled heavily. The women had returned, none the wiser to what had happened here.

Daisy handled the reins while Ramona sat beside her. She was used to going and coming as she pleased, but how safe was she now that her daddy was gone? Hell, she hadn't been safe then, for she might have been pushed from the loft. Now this business with the well.

She wouldn't be able to stay out here alone. She could move into town. Stay with friends. She'd be around people and out of his hair. If he could just remove her from his memory as easily . . .

The heels on her dainty boots tapped out a rapid beat that matched his pulse. She strode into her daddy's office and came up hard, like she'd been short-reined.

"What are you doing in here?" she asked in a tone sharpened with obvious suspicion.

It was tinder tossed on his smoldering anger. "The well has been pumped dry."

Ramona stopped in the hall, as if shocked in place by that news. He tried to think of a way to soften the rest about Fernando, but he wasn't one to sugarcoat the truth no matter how painful.

The cattle chose that time to commence bellowing louder. Daisy looked to the window that afforded an expansive view of the outbuildings and pasture, then back to him.

"Did it play out before the cattle got their fill?" Daisy asked.

He shifted his stance and snorted. "Long before. My guess is someone manned that pumped continually the whole time we were gone, taking delight in letting the water run onto the ground."

"Why would anyone do such a malicious thing?" she asked.

"That ought to be obvious."

Her troubled gaze fixed on his. "Ned?" Then before he could voice his opinion, she asked, "Did Fernando see him?"

"No." He looked at Ramona standing still and tense in the hall. "He was coldcocked from behind and trussed up. But he's all right," he added when Ramona let out a gasp of distress.

The older woman ran to her husband's side, muttering a torrent of Spanish prayers. Fernando's gaze begged a moment alone, and Trey gave it, his heart aching as the old couple left the house arm in arm.

Trey hadn't expected her to take his word for it. He was one who had to see for himself as well.

"I shouldn't have left the house," Daisy said, rubbing her hands over and over her drab skirt until friction sparks crackled in the air.

"You couldn't have stopped him," he said, and if she'd tried she'd have been stopped. Likely permanently. "Whoever did this made sure there wasn't a witness. If Fernando had seen him, I bet he'd be dead now."

Her big eyes filled with distress and an emotion he'd never seen before. "Now what?"

He huffed a breath of annoyance that she hadn't grasped the obvious. Or maybe she did know what must happen next and was just testing him to see how he'd respond.

Without water, Daisy couldn't stay here.

He hoped to hell she had friends in town who'd take her in. Hoped she wouldn't insist on moving to the Circle 46 too, for the longer he was near her, the more those old memories and longings would torment him.

Right now he had enough aggravation to deal with.

"We continue hauling water for the cattle tonight," he said, and that earned him a shaky nod. "I'll head the herd out before dawn."

That dire news seemed to steal the strength from her. She moved to a stiff chair and eased onto it, looking frail and vulnerable again.

He took a step toward her and reined the urge to take another. Dammit, he wasn't going to let her get to him again. He'd been down that road once.

Never again.

Yet like it or not he'd cut a deal to work for her for two months. It was an uneasy alliance that he'd only agreed to because they'd be living apart. Because he wouldn't be tormented by having her at arm's reach from him. Because he wouldn't be tempted to pull her to him and ease the ache that had gnawed at him since he'd been dragged from here.

"Is there any chance the well will replenish itself soon?" she asked.

He shrugged. "A slim one, though I've heard of one that was usable a week after it'd been tapped out during the drought. But it'll take rain to bring the water level up to normal again."

There was no sign of a break in the punishing weather.

Until there was, the creek beds would remain cracked, and the wells would stay dry. Living in West Texas would be pure hell. Survival of the fittest.

A glance Daisy's way confirmed she didn't belong in that group. She needed to be taken care of. That damn sure wasn't going to fall on his shoulders.

"You had best head out tomorrow as well," he said.

She bobbed her head. "I'll be ready."

"Let me know where you'll be staying so I can send you reports every two weeks, and find you when my agreed-upon two months are due."

That statement seemed to be the string that jerked

Daisy up stiff. The back of his neck crawled as he read the determination in her eyes.

"I'm going with you to the Circle 46," she said.

"Not a good idea," he said, and cussed himself as he saw his reasoning for what it was. Weak.

That firm little chin of hers snapped up, and he knew that arguing with her was going to be a losing battle. But he couldn't give up either, not when having her close was going to drive him crazy with a smoldering combination of anger and desire.

"We have no way of knowing what condition the old homestead is in," he said, doggedly pursuing his line of reasoning. "The house wasn't much to look at the last time I was there. Primitive compared to this. The bunkhouse wasn't much better, but the men are prepared and able to bunk under the stars if they have to."

"I've slept under the stars before," she said.

Yeah, in his arms. Just what he didn't want to remember with aching clarity.

"Daisy, use your head. The house was built as shelter for a frontier family. There're three bedrooms upstairs and two rooms and a pantry down. Cooking is done on an old cook-stove, and there's an outhouse to see to your needs."

"I've lived in a cabin before," she said.

"Where?"

She opened her mouth, then frowned. "I don't remember right off. But even if I hadn't, I've read about how our ancestors had to live."

"Reading about it and doing it are two different things."

"My mind is set."

He looked her up and down, and would sooner have died than tell her how much she appealed to him. How much he wanted to be the man to take care of her. That dream had been killed.

"You're not fit for that life. You need Ramona to cook and care for you. You need your conveniences."

"I can learn to do for myself."

Dammit, she was digging in her heels and threatening to make this a challenge for him. Fine. Let her have her way.

It wouldn't take long for her to realize her mistake. Fernando and Ramona could make do in the room in back of the blacksmith's shop.

But Daisy living in that house, making do?

She'd never had to lift a finger her whole life. Wouldn't be easy for her to start now.

Nope, she'd head for town before one week was out. Hell, she'd be doing good to hold out overnight.

But no matter how long she stubbornly hung on, he'd keep his distance from her.

Daisy knew Trey didn't want her at the Circle 46.

That fact made her more determined to go there. His dogged insistence that she find lodging elsewhere actually eased some of the misgivings she had about living around Trey again.

What she couldn't be sure of was his reasoning.

She wanted to believe that he simply didn't want to be around her. But there was that other worry—the one that she'd exchanged one untrustworthy foreman for another.

She had to keep watch over him and her stock, and there was only one way to do that. Stick it out like her Daddy would've done.

It wasn't as if she had many choices anyway. She didn't have any money to her name, so she couldn't take a room at a boardinghouse.

As for friends . . . Well, she didn't have many. The one woman she considered her closest friend was married. Newly so. Daisy wasn't about to intrude on their honeymoon period.

So unless she was able to find a job in town to support

herself, her only option was moving to the Circle 46. Daisy had to admit to a good deal of curiosity about the place where her daddy had begun ranching.

She knew he'd lost his first wife and child there, but that was the extent of it. It was time she visited the place.

She was from strong stock. Trey's frank appraisal of the conditions there wasn't going to scare her off.

"Now that we have that settled," she said, with as much false bravado as she could muster, "I'll start packing for the move."

"Don't think you can take everything you own, because you won't have room for it in that house," he said.

She stared at him, growing more annoyed with his assessment of the grim conditions she'd face there. Yes, she was sure the Circle 46 was more primitive, and certainly it had fallen into neglect.

She was aware it wouldn't be a grand house—likely a step above the cabins she'd seen in the area. But it was hers, and she damned well had every right to go there.

Besides, if she was honest with herself, she found it ironic that she was starting over at her daddy's first holding.

She didn't recall seeing it before, but she had to have lived there early in her life. He hadn't moved to this spread until eight years after she'd been born.

Maybe seeing the place would jar loose some of the memories locked in her mind. Maybe it would ease the uncertainties that nagged at her.

Maybe like her daddy, she'd be able to bury her own past at the Circle 46 and finally move on with her life.

Chapter 4

Amazing what Daisy found she could live without when she had to load those things she prized or needed into one wagon. She'd certainly not need any of the fine gowns her daddy had commissioned for her. The fripperies her mother crowded on every surface had to remain here too.

She only needed the barest necessities and a few treasures she couldn't bear to part with—the cameo pictures of her mama and daddy along with his books and records on the stock.

Nothing else really mattered. God knew some memories generated here were best forgotten. Not that she ever would forget her biggest heartaches.

"You about ready?" Trey asked, startling her from cleaning out the last of her daddy's desk.

She closed a drawer and stuffed the last journal into an old satchel. "I think so. Is my mare tied to my buggy?"

"Yep. Now let's get a move on."

Trey hefted the satchel and marched from the room. She lit a candle then doused the lamp and followed, closing the office door in her wake.

She stood there a moment in the hallway in that flickering candlelight and let the memories crash over her, soaking up the details as best she could. Trey would be waiting outside, but she couldn't leave without taking another look at the house that her daddy had built for her mama.

Ramona had draped all the furniture with sheets to keep the West Texas grit from settling too heavily on every surface. With the drapes drawn, the coverings made the parlor look ghostly, like her memories.

"Daisy." Trey's voice was a mere hush of sound behind her that played over her skin and left her tingling.

"I don't want to forget it."

She thought she heard him sigh, but it could've easily been a curse. "You'll come back home in time."

Would she? She wondered if she'd ever see this house again or if it'd fade into her mishmash of memories. Wondered what she'd find at the Circle 46.

"Let's go," she said, blowing out the candle and leaving the house in the dark.

She'd walked this hall too many times to count in the dead of night. But those memories too were best left here. Not that she would.

Some things a woman never forgot. With Trey back in her life, she had to keep the memories fresh. She had to remember the pain and heartache.

She stepped outside into a morning that promised another scorching hot, dry day. Dawn was just beginning to color the horizon in swaths of pink and gold.

A glance at the pasture showed the hands mounted and ready to turn the stock out. Fernando and Ramona sat on a laden wagon by the house.

Daisy's trim buggy was hitched and ready for her. Her saddle mare was tied to the back.

"Follow Fernando," Trey said.

She nodded and started toward the vehicle that would carry her away from the only home she could remember.

An image of a rundown shack tapped her memory and was gone. It wasn't the first time she'd seen it, but it didn't fit with any clear memory she had.

Daisy put the confusing image from her mind. "How long will it take to get to the Circle 46?"

The anxious lowing of cattle answered her. She glanced back at Trey, but he was already halfway to the pasture and the men.

She wasn't about to feel offended that he hadn't helped her into the buggy. She didn't want his touch, for it'd make the memories that much stronger and that was the last thing she wanted to dwell on during this long journey.

No, all she wanted was for him to do his job for the next two months. Surely in that time the drought would end and she would find another man who could manage the ranch.

And she would manage her daddy's legacy.

Dusk was on them by the time they reached the western edge of the Circle 46's property line. Trey was relieved to see the fence intact here, but he still had no idea what awaited them further on.

He would've rested easier if Daisy had done as he'd asked of her when Fernando had taken a turn for the worse at the halfway point. He'd given Manuel leave to guide his folks on to San Angelo, for Ramona wouldn't have made that journey alone.

Trey had insisted that Daisy go with them. But she'd stubbornly refused, saying her place was with her daddy's herd and cowhands. He knew there was more to it than that.

"You still don't trust me," he'd said once the others had driven off.

"Can you blame me? I trusted you once, but you broke your promise when you left me without a by-your-leave."

He sieved air through his teeth. "Dammit! I told you

Ned roped me from behind, and then dragged me into the desert where he left me to die. I was lucky I didn't, though at times I hurt so damned bad I sure prayed I would."

The color drained from her flushed face. "If that's the truth—"

"It is," he said, and he had the scars to prove what had happened. But he wasn't about to show them to her, or tell her that his thirst for revenge had helped him live with the pain.

That would only make her distrust him more. He had enough to deal with already without adding to it.

"If you're going on to the Circle 46 with us, then get a move on," he said.

She'd flashed him a peevish glower before flicking the buggy lines and moving on down the trail.

Dammit, Trey had enough to worry over with greenhorn hands, and a herd of thirsty, near-starved cattle without fretting over having a lone woman in their midst. But Daisy was his boss.

So for the rest of the day, Trey took a position between her and the drovers behind him. With Manuel gone, he'd started relying more on Ansel. The young cowhand was proving to be a fast learner.

But Trey wasn't about to take anything for chance now.

Knowing they were getting close to the Circle 46, he left Ansel in charge of the herd and caught up with Daisy still holding the buggy at the same steady clip. He had to hand it to her that she had handled the lines with ease the entire day.

"I'm going to ride on to check things out before we drive the herd closer," he said to her.

"We're that close then?" There was no mistaking the weariness in her tone.

"Thirty minutes or less." He tipped his hat and rode on, relaying the same to the crew as he passed them.

Trey took off in an easy lope that'd eat up the last few miles without taxing his tired gelding. The rattle of wheels and hooves keeping pace with him had him looking back.

Daisy was right behind him, chin up and mouth pulled in a grim line. She was the picture of exhausted determination if he ever saw it, and his chest tightened with admiration and something he damned sure wasn't about to name, let alone dwell on.

He chewed out a curse and doubled back to her. "What the hell do you think you're doing?"

"Going with you," she said, the challenge in her voice clear as she kept the buggy moving forward at the same pace. "We've no idea who Ned left in charge, but they will likely believe my word over yours when they realize Ned is no longer the foreman of the JDB."

That was the idea behind having her sign the damned paper back at the ranch. Depending on who was here, having a contract could've taken some wrangling before he convinced anyone that it was real and he was managing Barton's holdings. But he was forced to admit having the boss's daughter here would carry more weight than a name on a paper.

"All right. But stay behind me," he said, and heeled his tired horse into an easy trot.

Less than a mile down the road they came to the lane leading to the ranch. A sign swinging from a gate post proclaimed this was the Circle 46, the brand burned into the weathered wood.

He reined into the lane without looking back and had the satisfaction of hearing Daisy wheel the buggy the same way.

Her thin arms had to be aching something fierce from handling the reins all day. Never mind she was adept at driving a buggy. It was a whole other thing to drive one in heat that would tempt stone to wither.

But she hadn't complained.

Not once.

He didn't want to admire anything about her. Didn't want to think kindly of her or commiserate over the aches and pains that would surely ride the devil over her tonight.

But he couldn't block her from his mind either.

She was her daddy's daughter after all, possessing the face of an angel and the courage of a she-cat. Not knowing how to do something didn't stop her.

It hadn't when he'd romanced her either, and just remembering how she'd come in his arms, how she'd clung to him and whispered her love twisted something inside him again.

He couldn't trust this woman. He sure wouldn't profess to like the way she walked and talked and smiled at him. But he wanted her still. With a deep, burning ache in his groin that he'd never felt with any woman except her.

"I smell smoke," she shouted, yanking him from thoughts of stroking her skin and hair and sex.

He sniffed the air and caught the telltale whiff of burning wood. Wind was in his face, so he scanned the horizon ahead of him.

It was neither impressive nor dilapidated. Just a simple homestead with a smattering of outbuildings.

"There." He pointed to the old stone ranch house in the near distance. Threads of gray smoke were rising from the chimney. "We're in time for supper."

"You think they'll see it that way?"

He smiled. "We'll soon find out. Come on, Miss Barton. Let's get you settled."

Trey urged his horse on, and the creak of wheels soon joined him. In the distance the cattle were starting to bawl their need for water again.

Their arrival wouldn't be quiet by any means. In twenty minutes or less, over six hundred head of registered

Hereford cattle would crowd down the lane that was flanked by three tight strands of barbed wire.

He couldn't see any stock in the pasture that rippled with a fair stand of buffalo grass. Couldn't see any sign of animals beyond the few horses grazing on the ridge, and those sure as hell weren't thoroughbreds.

Had Ned sold his horses along with the ones Barton had bought? He wouldn't be surprised.

Ned hadn't had any desire to run a stud farm. Cattle was his game, and he made no bones about it.

After Barton's death, who'd be the wiser if he sold off the horses and pocketed the money? Certainly not Daisy.

Before they reached the house, a short, stout man stepped out onto the porch. Trey didn't need sunlight to know the man was cradling a rifle.

He damn sure wished he could've paid a visit before they had to drive the cattle here. But a dry well had taken that choice from him. He just hoped they hadn't ridden into a trap.

"That's close enough," the man said in a gravelly tone that had Trey hauling back on the reins and had Daisy stopping as well. "State your business."

"Trey March. I'm the new foreman of the Barton ranches."

For a moment Trey wondered if that meant anything to the man. Hell, he wondered if the ranch was still in Barton's name or if Ned had pulled a fast one here as well.

"What happened to Ned?" the man asked.

"I fired him," Daisy said.

That grabbed the man's full attention. He ambled to the edge of the porch and peered out into the smoky dusk that was fast chasing away the lingering remnants of light.

Trey remembered him then. Hollis Feth, the ranch cook. He'd barely spoken to the man the last time he'd been here.

"As I live and breath," Hollis said. "What brings you up here, Miss Daisy?"

"Hollis? Thank God you're still here!"

She vaulted from the buggy like a farm urchin at the circus sideshow and ran across the dusty ground. The man hobbled down the three steps and swept her up in a bear hug.

Trey would put Hollis around Barton's age, only twice as shopworn. But somewhere along the way he'd gained Daisy's trust. Question was, did the man deserve it?

The bellowing of cattle sounded at the far end of the lane. The herd was nearly here.

"We need to get that buggy moved and those beeves turned into the main pasture," Trey said.

Hollis eyed him across the expanse, his expression nearly swallowed by shadows now. "What's going on?"

"I'll let Daisy explain it."

With that he rode to the stout wooden gate by the barn and got it open just as the herd rounded the bend. They were near loping now, likely scenting the water that glistened in the stock troughs.

A cowpoke came running from the darkened hulk of the bunkhouse. It was too dark now to see his face, and Trey was too busy swinging the gate back to bother with introductions or to give orders.

But the cowpoke seemed to know what to do, vaulting into the buggy and pulling it out of the way. Ansel rode into the yard ahead of the herd and took up a position alongside Trey.

In moments, thousands of pounds of bawling beeves crowded the yard before turning into the pasture. The promise of grass and water was enough enticement.

By the time they were all inside and the gate closed, the sun had sunk and a bloated moon illuminated their efforts. Trey heaved a weary sigh. They'd made the journey without losing one head.

It was down to just managing them and the ranch now, but how much opposition would he face?

Trey glanced back at the house and the pair standing on the porch. Mighty clear he was the outsider here. Outnumbered as well.

A dull ache tightened the muscles in his arms and bad leg, a reminder of how he got on Barton's bad side by seducing his daughter. The punishment of being dragged near to death.

He'd been betrayed by someone he trusted two times now. Never again. His brother Reid had looked him in the eye and had sworn everything would be all right. Told Trey to trust him.

He had.

And dammit all, he'd done it again with Daisy. He'd believed she was a rich rancher's daughter out for a bit of sexual adventure before she married the "proper man."

And knowing all that, Trey had baited the bear in her daddy by taking her into the loft, introducing her to the pleasures of lovemaking. She'd known he wasn't the sticking around kind, for he'd made no promises. She'd known and gone with him anyway.

When it was over, he'd promised he'd never divulge what had happened. That their affair was their secret. She'd promised the same, that it was just a one time thing.

But it wasn't. They couldn't get enough of each other. It lasted days. Weeks.

He was on the edge of rethinking his future with Daisy. Right up to the moment Ned lassoed him and dragged him into the desert.

A thousand thoughts went through his mind. Had Daisy tired of her cowboy lover? Had she feared that Trey would tell her fancy fiancé that she was a loose woman?

Then there was the question that had plagued his mind

all the time he'd been laid up in El Paso, wondering if he'd live. Had she wanted her *indiscretion* permanently silenced?

God knew, if she was out to skin him again, what chance would he have of getting out of here with his herd?

Mighty slim from his way of looking.

Fact remained that he needed an ally here. But friends were few in his world, and he hadn't seen anyone here that he remembered except the grizzled cook. All new men. Ned's pick? He damned sure would tread easy until he knew where their loyalty lay.

"You the ramrod of these beeves?" a man asked, his drawl as thick and dark as molasses.

Trey faced the man who was his height and packed twice the muscle and firepower. "Trey March, foreman. You are?"

"Cameron Ellsworth, Texas Ranger," he said. Trey's insides tightened with foreboding, because rangers didn't make a habit of visiting ranches and lending a hand unless they were chasing trouble. "Mind telling me who owns this herd?"

Trey was bone-weary, covered in West Texas grit and wary as a whore in church, rarely in any mood to talk to the law and surely not at all right now. But if he hoped to foster an ally in the lawman, it was best he appear as if he hadn't a care and hear him out.

"A hundred and fifty head are mine," Trey said. "The rest belong to Daisy Barton, owner of the JDB Ranch and the Circle 46."

"Jared Barton's daughter?"

"One and the same," he said. "The creeks at the JDB are running dust, and the well has been pumped dry— intentionally, we discovered. Since it's getting harder and harder to find water to haul in, Miss Barton elected to move the headquarters to the old homestead."

Ellsworth dipped his chin, as if stingy to give away

anything more. "Drought's playing hell on everyone. Now what's this about a dry well?"

Trey eyed the man swathed in shadows, wishing he could read his eyes, wishing he had a clue what brought him here to the Circle 46. "The JDB blacksmith was jumped from behind and trussed up, then the pump was manned 'til it ran dry."

The ranger made a sound of disgust and eased forward into a swath of moonlight, but the wide brim on his hat continued to shadow his face. "He claims he didn't see who attacked him?"

"Yep, and I believe him," Trey said. "Doubt the man would be breathing now if he'd so much as gotten a glimpse of who got the drop on him."

Ellsworth thumbed up his brim and a pair of glacial blue eyes speared Trey on the spot. "You got a hunch who did it?"

Trey snorted and jammed both thumbs under his gun belt, fighting the urge to look away from those probing eyes. "If I knew for sure, he'd be dead."

"No judge or jury would've hanged you considering the hell folks are going through trying to find water," the ranger said.

With anyone else, that comment might have lessened his tension, but the fact was it still pulsed hot and heavy between them. Those cool eyes of Ellsworth's were putting him on trial, and Trey feared the ranger would find him guilty in a blink.

"What brings you here?" Trey asked, damned tired of pussyfooting around.

"Been a steady trail of JDB cattle sold off in the last six months. The last hundred head were run through the auction block up in San Angelo and had fresh running brands." The ranger drew those last three words out, his emphasis alerting Trey that something wasn't right. "Whoever put the JDB brand on them did a sloppy job of it."

Rustlers. "You see this rogue brand?"

"Sure did. It was a JDB brand in size and all, but it'd been altered just enough to make it different from those used on the ranch."

Trey let what the ranger implied sink in and take root. If the lawman was right, somebody had gotten hold of a JDB branding iron. But if a rustler was set on stealing cattle, why bother with altering the brand so it would draw attention?

He didn't like the reasons tumbling in his head, for they all pointed to someone setting someone else up for a fall. Damned convenient that all this trouble started about the time he disappeared from the JDB.

"When did you see this altered brand again?" he asked.

"A few weeks back. Rancher west of San Saba bought them."

Yep, damned convenient that was when he was laid up, but then he suspected the man responsible had thought he was dead. "Ned Durant trail these beeves to market?"

"I didn't see the drover, but the listed seller was Trey March."

"Sonofabitch!" Trey stared at the ranger through a red haze of anger, but managed to hold a tight rein on it. "It damn sure wasn't me."

The ranger stared at him. "You could've ordered it done."

Trey's head pounded with the rage galloping through him. Altered brands. A rustler posing as him. What the hell had he ridden into this time?

A trap. That's why Ned hadn't kicked up a fuss when Daisy cut him free. He'd already stacked the deck against Trey.

No doubt Ned had used Trey's name to run his operation right down to selling JDB cattle, but the only way to prove it would be to wrest a confession from Ned or the men he'd hired. Damned slim chance of seeing either done, especially if Ned had been doing some rustling too.

It took every ounce of effort to tamp down his fury. He had to control that temper now. Texans meted out swift justice to rustlers, and he didn't aim to end up in jail or swinging from a rope.

"I had nothing to do with selling JDB cattle or any other stock during the past six months," Trey said at last.

"Can you prove it?"

"Yep," he said, but held off explaining until he knew what got the Texas Rangers looking into this. "You working on the auction house's behalf or for the JDB?"

"A bit of both," the ranger said. "I had a talk with Barton three months back when so many JDB cattle hit the market. He hadn't sanctioned a sale. In fact he wasn't missing more than a hundred head at the time."

So Barton knew he was being took. "You saying that Barton suspected I was rustling cattle and using the JDB brand."

"Made sense. Barton found it mighty interesting that his trouble started right after you lit out."

Lit out? Trey opened his mouth to protest, then thought better of it.

Barton knew damned well he wasn't rustling cattle. Hell, the man probably thought he was dead.

He suspected Barton had explained Trey's absence as desertion to cover his own hand in Trey's torture. Did it to protect Daisy's reputation as well if anyone had been privy to their dallying. And Ned surely had found out he'd been romancing Daisy.

Trey couldn't fault Barton for protecting his daughter. He couldn't find it in himself to spill the truth either, not when it could bring more grief on her. Besides, he doubted the ranger would just take his word for it.

"Six months back I was doing business for Barton when I got waylaid," Trey said. "I was dragged for miles then left for dead. If a drummer hadn't come along when he had and hauled me into El Paso, I'd have been food for the vultures."

"There anybody who can back up that claim?" the ranger asked.

"Pay a visit to La Valera's Cantina in El Paso. I was a guest at her establishment from before Christmas until about two weeks past."

The ranger smiled, but it wasn't a kindly one. "She could be your sweetheart and would be more than willing to lie for you."

It was a fact that he was aware of. "Call on Doc Ivy in El Paso. He patched me up and looked in on me the whole time I was there."

"I'll do that," the ranger said. "In the meantime I'm keeping a man here to watch you. You make one wrong move, and he'll be obliged to do his duty."

"Fair enough."

There wasn't a helluva lot else he could do but agree while Ellsworth checked out his story. Even then Trey didn't hold a lot of faith that his name would be cleared.

Chapter 5

Daisy sat at the kitchen table with a cup of steaming coffee cradled in her hands, relieved beyond words to be sitting on something that wasn't moving. She'd already explained to Hollis Feth why she'd moved the ranching operation here, earning her a dark scowl followed by a nod of approval for finally taking charge and firing Ned Durant.

Now she smiled and laughed as she listened to Hollis regale her with another story about her daddy. The man had worked for Jared Barton since the War of the Rebellion ended, in a variety of tasks, beginning with his being the chuckwagon cook in those early days of cowboying.

By his choice, he'd spent the past five years away from the JDB, then had come back to the Circle 46 a year ago to take over the job of ranch cook. It was a good job for a man his age, seeing as he had no desire to ever retire.

On sweltering days like these, he'd taken to cooking meals on the house stove. As he stated so succinctly, "No sense heating up the cookshack and the bunkhouse when this stove was just sitting here going to waste."

"I don't remember living here," she said.

"That's cause you never did."

"Are you certain?"

"Sure am. Your daddy had no desire to ever return to this ranch again."

"Why?"

Hollis gave a sad shake of his head. "Bad memories."

Yet Jared Barton had held onto the land just to run horses. A stud farm that she suspected her daddy would have left Trey in charge of one day.

This might have been the home Trey had brought her to if they'd married.

"Yessiree, I was mighty glad when your daddy up and moved from Colorado," Hollis said, as he forked over thick slabs of chicken fried steaks in the heavy frying pan. "These Southern bones of mine hated the cold and snow we got there."

She frowned at the scarred plank tabletop. "How long ago was that?"

Hollis's handlebar mustache twitched as he worked his mouth into a knot. "Reckon that was about sixteen or so years back."

She must've been born on the Colorado ranch then. "I don't remember living there either, but I do recall the snow and cold." Her mama had told her that her daddy promised to get them back home come spring. Home to Texas? Had to be. "Did he sell out?"

"Soon as he bought the JDB. We drove the cattle there, and the womenfolk took the train to West Texas."

Was that where she'd gotten those memories of being on a train? Maybe some of them, but she was certain she'd stayed with her mother and nanny on that trip. She hadn't huddled with a train full of other children. Scared. Cold. Alone.

As for the JDB, she had a clear memory of her eighth birthday there. Her mother had gone all-out to make it a day she would remember, but her daddy did one better when he gave her a spotted pony.

She could still hear her mother fussing that she was too young to ride, but the pony allowed her to form a tighter bond with her daddy. Maybe that was for the best, because before the next winter her mother caught a fever.

She'd died before Christmas.

Daisy felt bad that she had great trouble bringing her mother's image to mind. But she kept trying. All she ever got was vague pictures, no more than flashes of memory, before another woman's features blurred with her mother's to create another stranger in her life.

Her daddy explained it away as her being too young to separate her mother's likeness from that of the nanny who'd cared for her when she'd come into their lives. That's how he'd said it too. Not when she was born, but when she'd come into their lives.

"By the time me and the boys drove the cattle onto the JDB, your mama had settled into the new house." Hollis shook his head. "Damned shame she had such little time to enjoy it."

"Daddy told me that when Mother took sick with a fever, she'd feared that I'd contract it too," Daisy said. "She insisted that she move here to the Circle 46 to recuperate, and my nanny went with her as she had some of the same symptoms. But neither of them got better."

"I remember," Hollis said. "They're both buried in the old family plot alongside your daddy's first wife and only son."

Daisy cut the old man a sharp look. Her head throbbed just thinking about what her daddy had lost. "Daddy never talked about his first family."

"Can't blame him. Corinne Barton was a fine woman," Hollis said. "She went through hell during the war and after, same as the rest of the Feths."

That caught her attention. "Was she kin to you?"

"My sister. Only family I had living. We were both born on this ranch."

That explained why her daddy let Hollis do as he pleased at the Circle 46. It'd been his family's home. It still was in many ways, leaving Daisy to feel like a trespasser.

"The child that died. He was a boy?" she asked.

"Yep. Jared doted on that son of his. Damned shame."

A half-brother. Was it possible she'd heard about him and that had caused her to envision the boy who'd watched over her? Was that why she was troubled with the memory of a young boy from time to time? Why there were times she'd believed she had a brother?

That had to be the reason, for there'd been no young boy in her life. She'd just longed for a playmate. A sibling. Her mother had told her enough about it to fire her imagination.

She wanted to ask more about her daddy's first wife and son. Wanted to know every detail that Hollis Feth could remember about his sister and nephew. Wanted to know more about her own mother as well. But just forcing those few memories had her head pounding. If he told her more right now, she'd likely forget it or tangle it in her thoughts.

There would be time to visit with him later when she wasn't so tired and out of sorts. She could finally visit her mother's grave, and maybe just doing that would free her thoughts more.

Maybe if she sat there in peace at her mother's grave she'd be able to rid herself of the strange nightmares she'd had for as long as she could remember.

"Now your mama," Hollis began, yanking her thoughts back to him. "She wanted a child so. When you came along she was the happiest woman in Colorado. But I reckon you knew that."

When you came along. Odd that Hollis said nearly the same thing as her daddy had.

"Daddy told me, but it's good to hear."

She'd known that her mother had pined for a child—a girl if she could have her choice. Knowing that was the truth helped ease that empty feeling that had come over her out of the blue.

Hollis returned to the skillets sizzling on the stove. She felt comfortable around this man, even though she hadn't been near him for five years or so. Oh, he'd come to Daddy's funeral and talked to her some then, but she'd been too aggrieved to appreciate the visit.

Now in just an hour she'd found out he was her daddy's brother-in-law. This was his home, yet he'd left it too to go to Colorado with her daddy and mother. But when they came back to Texas, Hollis had moved to the JDB with them.

"Why didn't you come back here when you left the JDB five years ago?" she asked.

Hollis sighed. "It was time for me to move on and try my hand at something besides cooking and rounding up cattle. But last year, I was ready to come back home."

She thought to ask what he'd done during those years away, then changed her mind. He'd tell her when he was ready to, if ever.

"How many men did Ned let go here?" she asked.

"Six of them. All with horse experience." Hollis muttered something she couldn't catch; she suspected it was a ripe oath. "He had the gall to tell me that he wasn't paying me anymore for cooking, so I might as well clear out too."

"But you refused to budge."

"I wasn't about to let him run me off."

Thank God for that. "Trey asked if Sam Weber was still the foreman."

"Nope. He just took off without a word to anyone. Guess he had a bellyful of Ned telling him what to do and headed off to greener pastures."

"He wasn't fired then?"

"Nope. He'd been arguing with Ned over the horses, and I half thought Ned would send him packing. Wasn't surprised when Sam pulled up stakes."

Just like Trey had done.

She rubbed her brow. She'd been so sure that he'd tired of Ned's bossing too. That he'd tired of romancing her. That he'd just up and left so he wouldn't have to face her or her daddy.

Except Trey insisted that Ned had dragged him into the desert and left him to die. Trey hadn't left her of his own free will.

"Ned won't take kindly to having the tables turned on him. He bears watching," Hollis said.

That was much the same warning she'd gotten from Trey. "We all have to be vigilant."

Hollis forked the cooked meat into a big tin pan. "I heard March took off last year."

"He did," she said. "He came back yesterday claiming Daddy owed him."

"Don't know about that," Hollis said. "But he left four fine thoroughbreds here."

So he'd told her the truth. "Daddy must have trusted him."

"Believe so. Heard March was a hard worker. That he kept to himself for the most part. That he was a good man."

Good lover, too. But she wouldn't fall into his arms again. Trey was a tumbleweed. A seasoned cowboy who did fine for the short hauls.

He never professed to have roots, and he didn't seem inclined to put any down either. Soon as he found another place for his cattle and horses he'd be gone. Or maybe he'd just sell them and be free to roam. A tumbleweed.

"He only agreed to stay on for two months," she said.

Hollis stared at her, and for a moment she thought he saw through her bravado. That he knew about the history between her and Trey. That he was aware of her shame and heartache.

"Didn't peg him for the type who'd poke a rattler just to goad him to strike," Hollis said, bringing her worry swinging right back to Ned.

Pumping the well dry had been a cold, malicious act. But she knew that Ned was capable of far more brutal things. She knew it could turn deadly if Ned set his mind to it.

Trey had to be aware of that. He had to have known just what Ned was capable of before he'd agreed to stay on.

Hollis finished transferring the meat and fried potatoes into the tin pan. "Best get down to the mess hall and feed the men. I left enough for your supper."

"Thank you." She got the door for Hollis. "I'm glad you defied Ned and stayed on. As soon as we turn a profit, I'll pay you the lost wages."

Hollis pulled a face. "Ain't no need to do that. Man my age don't want for much more than a roof over his head."

Sadly that's all he'd had since her daddy died. How many other good men had Ned let go?

She closed the half glass door in his wake, then stood there for the longest time scanning the area between the corrals and the bunkhouse. Men milled around, but there was no sign of Ansel.

Her gaze flicked back to Hollis. Before he got halfway to the bunkhouse, a tall cowboy stepped into her line of vision.

His strides were long and unhurried. His shoulders broad and racked straight, as if he wasn't the least weary. Though his hat was pulled low over his brow, his head was up as if he was looking the world dead-on at an almost de-fiant angle.

A shiver of recognition tingled on her skin as the cowboy passed Hollis with a nod and kept right on walking toward the house. Trey. There wasn't enough light to see his face, but she knew it was him all the same. Knew he was coming to her.

Of course he would. He was obliged to report the day's events to her. Maybe even apprise her of what he intended to do tomorrow.

As he got closer, she noticed he carried his rifle in one hand. The other steadied the saddlebag slung over a shoulder.

Her stomach did a restless flutter, but she forced herself to stand tall in the doorway. She was the boss.

"Everyone settled in now?" she asked, holding her place in the doorway.

"Yep. Reckon they're chowing down about now."

Which is what he should be doing. With the men, not here staring at her.

He stopped, too close for her peace of mind. So close she had to tip her head back to look up and meet his eyes. Even then the shadow cast by his hat kept her from reading any emotion in them—not that she expected there was any.

They'd burned out all emotion and desire between them before. Or should have.

The hum of need that tormented her now wasn't welcome. If she wasn't so tired, she could've squelched it before it became something she even acknowledged.

"Has Manuel returned yet?" she asked, actually making a point of looking around him then, knowing it was rude and not caring.

She was too stressed from the ordeal at the JDB, the journey here, and having Trey back in her life to worry about manners.

"Don't expect him back until tomorrow."

He thumbed his hat up, and it was all she could do not to gasp at the intensity in those dark eyes. Midnight eyes that managed to capture just enough lamplight to make them spark a magnetic blue.

He didn't say anything for the longest time. "You're pretty much on your own here, Daisy. Can you handle that?"

For the first time in ages she felt her own anger boil deep inside her. She knew what he was getting at. She was the spoiled rancher's daughter.

Ramona had cooked her meals, cleaned her house, and helped her dress for as long as she could recall. Without the other woman, would she be able to function?

"Thank you for your concern, but I'll be just fine."

She stepped back to close the door but he thrust a boot forward and stopped it from shutting. "What do you think you're doing?" she asked.

"Coming inside."

"No!"

He slapped a palm on the door and pushed it open, forcing her to stumble back inside the kitchen. "You're not staying here alone, Daisy. No telling what Ned will get in his head to do next."

She opened her mouth to protest, but knew it was useless. She'd made an enemy of Ned and staying in this house by herself was risky. But how much greater danger was she facing by living here with Trey?

"You can have the bedroom on the south," she said.

That earned her a cocky grin. "Yes'm."

Trey strode to the stairs and mounted them with that same unhurried grace she'd admired earlier. The house was small, but the rooms seemed to shrink in on her with him sharing the same space.

She'd walked through the house as soon as she got here, which hadn't taken any time at all—it was only two rooms and a small pantry on the first level and three bedrooms upstairs reached by a steep staircase at the end of the fireplace. As Trey had warned her before they left, the house wasn't anything to brag on.

At one time someone had put paper on the walls and

hung curtains at the windows, but the paper had yellowed and peeled in places, and the flour-sack curtains at the windows were close to rags now. Daisy was sure if she had given them a smart tug they would have ripped in two.

Everything desperately needed a good cleaning, especially the windows. But it was a roof over her head, and it was her home.

She had felt a certain sense of rightness when she had carried her valise into the north bedroom. It had a good view of the ranch and had a lock on the door. Surely not a substantial one.

If Trey wanted in her room, he could bust down the door. But she knew he wouldn't do that.

He'd let her make the first move like she'd done before. He'd let her come to him.

Hell would freeze over first.

Now, as she stood alone in the kitchen, she wasn't nearly as sure. She dropped onto a chair and cradled her head with shaking hands. How could she possibly live here with him? How could she hate him and yet still desire him?

The answer continued to elude her. She'd been unable to shove him from her thoughts the past six months. Now those memories were as fresh as if they'd just happened.

Being his lover had been wonderful. She had thought that the next step would be marriage. She thought he was the man she'd love for the rest of her life.

Now that dream was shattered.

He worked for her now. They'd never be lovers again. She'd never allow it to happen, no matter how much her body craved his touch.

She'd not put herself through that hell again with him.

So for the next two months she'd avoid him as much as possible. Do her best not to get caught alone with him. And those times when they were alone, like now?

Daisy heard an upper door close, followed by his steady

tread on the stairs. She pushed from the chair and busied herself setting out tin plates for their supper.

She was obliged to hear out his report of the day. Then she could take her leave of his company.

That couldn't be soon enough, she thought, as he stepped into the kitchen. He'd taken off his chaps and gun belt, but he still looked big and dangerous.

"Hollis Feth left supper for us," she said.

For her more than likely and enough to last more than a day, but she knew she'd barely be able to hold food down. She was too nervous and too tired.

Still she'd try to eat something just to keep her strength up. She'd learned the importance of that two months ago when she'd nearly wasted away from grief.

I lost our baby, she was tempted to tell him.

But he hadn't known about the child. He hadn't known that she'd fallen from the loft and lost her baby and a bit more of her sanity.

There was no reason to tell him. No reason to strengthen that tie that had been severed six months ago.

"Are all the stock accounted for?" she asked, as she poured him coffee from the pot Hollis had left on the cooking range.

"Didn't lose a one." He forked thick slabs of meat onto his plate. "Your daddy's horses are still here. So are mine, bearing my brand."

She heard pride ring in his voice then and smiled. "I'm glad."

"Reckon the only reason they weren't sold off right away was that they were Ned's ace in the hole."

She frowned at that and cut off a small piece of steak. "To think Daddy trusted that snake."

Trey shrugged, but she sensed an underlying rage in him that she didn't understand. A rage that she felt was directed toward her as much as toward her daddy's foreman.

"Ned did what he was told," Trey said. "I'm guessing with Barton gone, he fancied that he'd get on your good side and move right on up until he was calling all the shots. Which it appeared he'd been doing since your daddy's passing."

She laid down the forkful of meat she'd just cut, insides twisting from the innuendoes that were arching between them. Or maybe she was misreading him, because her emotions couldn't be trusted around Trey.

"In my own defense," she began, choosing her words carefully so he would not twist them back on her, "I knew absolutely nothing about the business side of ranching when daddy died. So yes, I left those decisions up to Ned."

He bobbed his head as he ate, but he didn't comment further. In fact he seemed content to just ignore her troubles.

She wasn't so easily distracted. The food held little appeal to her now in the face of his disinterest.

How could she have been so totally wrong about this man? How could she have thought he cared for her?

"What? No chastisements for being a fool about the decisions I let Ned make regarding the ranch?" she asked, letting the lid fly off her smoldering anger now.

She was exhausted, but she shot to her feet and stalked to the back door, standing there and staring out over all that was hers. Wondering if she could trust anyone. Worried sick about Fernando and Ramona.

The responsibility of her daddy's legacy teetered precariously on her shoulders. She'd made mistake after mistake. She'd trusted Trey with her heart. She'd trusted Ned to carry on in the best interests of the ranch when it was all dumped on her.

Both men put their selfish needs first.

"What's done is done," Trey said at last. "If you aim to hold on to the land and cattle, then you'd best learn all you can about it. That way when you hire a new foreman, you'll know if he's doing right by you or just feathering his own nest."

She faced him then and knew by the sudden fire in his eyes and rigid set of his jaw that he was giving her sound advice. Didn't matter that it seemed to rankle him to do so. She knew he was right. Knew too that this was her chance to learn from the best.

"Then teach me," she said.

"I won't be around long enough to do you justice."

"Fine. Whatever you can show me will be far more than I know now."

A muscle ticked in his cheek, and his expression looked like it'd been carved from stone. "It'd be best if you hired someone else for that job."

"If there'd been anyone else with your qualifications, I wouldn't have hired you."

He gave her a halfhearted grin at that. "All right. We'll start on the basics and work up. That'll at least give you the ground work to understand how the cattle business is run."

"Good. The sooner we start, the better."

He didn't share her enthusiasm in word or expression, but then she hadn't expected him to. He was here under duress. Tacking on the duties of tutoring her about ranching would put more strain on their working relationship. But she wasn't going to back down.

He pushed to his feet, his mouth no more than a grim line as he looked from the dirty plates to her. "You need help cleaning up?"

"No, I'm fine." She didn't have to be instructed on housework to figure out how to wash the dishes.

Still it took her far longer than it would've taken Ramona to do the same job, all because the older woman knew how to take care of a house in short order.

Daisy blew out the lamp and climbed the stairs in the dark, feeling like the most helpless female on earth. She paused at the top of the stairs where moonlight filtered in through a small window.

The closed door to Trey's room was a few steps away. Was he already asleep? Did she cross his mind at all? Did any demons haunt his sleep?

She knew so little about him. Yet here she was sharing a house with him. It'd be so easy to do more. So easy.

Damning her own weakness, Daisy hurried down the narrow hall to her room and slipped inside. She closed the door soundlessly and turned the key.

She just hoped she was too tired to dream about a certain cowboy tonight.

Chapter 6

Trey hung his hat on the excuse that he had to inspect the ranch today. It was easier than voicing a truth that left him chaffing worse than a hard day's ride in a wet saddle.

He sure wasn't ready to sit down with Daisy and begin teaching her how to run a ranch. Hell, he wasn't even sure where to begin with a greenhorn.

That's just what she was, despite the fact that she'd been born and raised on a ranch. Her daddy had kept her apart from the business end of the operation.

Now, he didn't mind sharing what he knew with anyone. But the biggest thing bothering him was the fact he'd have to be close to Daisy for the whole two months he was here because it'd likely take her that long to grasp it all.

She'd slipped past his defenses before and got him thinking he could be more than he was to her. She got him believing he could win the hand of the rancher's daughter.

That's why he'd been set on keeping his distance from her.

He'd expected to sleep in the foreman's cabin and take all his meals in the mess hall. He'd see her once a day at best to keep her informed.

But they'd lost the bunkhouse to a fire that started in

the blacksmith's shack, and the men had converted the foreman's cabin into the bunkhouse.

Since his battered body would protest grabbing forty winks on a bedroll on a cabin floor, and Daisy was all alone in the house, he decided to sleep there. Now he was wondering if he should've just suffered the close confines of the cabin that would house ten men.

Not only had she invaded his sleep last night with memories of how it'd been between them, but she'd hobbled him into teaching her about ranching. It was going to be a long two months.

Hollis Feth was busy pumping water into a kettle when he reached the corral. "Don't know if you've ate yet, but breakfast is on in the mess hall in about five minutes."

Trey jumped at the offer. There'd been no supplies to speak of in the kitchen, and he didn't look forward to working without a belly full of grub and enough coffee to open his eyes this morning.

Besides this would give him a chance to talk again with the men. So why the hell did he keep thinking about the woman up at the house? Why did he give a care if she sat in the house waiting for Hollis to fetch breakfast to her?

"No supplies to speak of in the house," Trey said as he followed Feth to the mess hall.

He hadn't noticed it last night, but today he could see that the cook favored his left leg. Noticed too that the man packed a gun. There was an alertness about him too that hinted he was more than a cook.

The older man slid him a quizzing look. "You saying you didn't bring supplies with you?"

Trey damned the heat burning his neck, for who the hell would move to a new place and not bring provisions? "The housekeeper would've seen to that and likely did, but halfway here she was obliged to take her husband on in to San Angelo to a doctor."

Whatever was in Ramona's wagon had stayed with her.

"Reckon I'd best tote breakfast up to Miss Barton," Feth said.

Trey gave a nod and hunkered down at the table, putting Daisy and her needs from his mind for the moment. They'd gone with short rations yesterday on the trail, and his gut had protested mightily.

But then he'd just gotten back on his feet before trailing to the JDB for his money. So much for thinking he'd be on his way to Wyoming with a string of horses for a long overdue showdown with his foster brother Reid.

He just hoped to hell that Dade had returned to claim his shares. Hoped that one of them turned out to be half the man old Kirby Morris had been.

Water under the bridge.

He had cattle and horses and no land. No place that was his. Nobody who gave a shit whether he lived or died.

"Sounds like things have been going downhill on the JDB since Barton's death," Feth said.

Trey looked up from his plate and noted with surprise that the men had filed out of the mess hall. He hadn't expected Feth to take Daisy her breakfast that quickly. But he had. Now nobody was here but him and Feth and a river of old animosity that he instinctively dammed so nobody would get close again.

"Ned did what he wanted," Trey allowed.

The old man scowled and scraped out a pan that was as black as Ned's soul. "Why'd you let it go that far before you stepped in?"

So Feth wasn't aware of what had happened to him on the JDB? He wasn't surprised, but he wasn't inclined to spill his guts either.

He pushed his empty plate aside and leaned forward, cradling his tin cup between his hands. "Didn't know noth-

ing about how things were being run until I returned to the
ranch two days ago. Was a surprise to learn Barton was dead."

"A stroke took him," Feth said, going about his work
and not sparing Trey a glance.

"That's what Daisy told me," he said. "Hard to believe a
big hale man like Barton is dead."

"Yep, surprised the hell out of us too." Feth ambled back
to the table with the coffee pot, and Trey welcomed the
refill. "The day Barton keeled over, Galen took a fine mare
down to the JDB for him. She was a birthday present for
his daughter."

Trey nodded, relieved that so far Feth's story was following what Fernando had told him.

"Terrible that Daisy lost her pa on her birthday," Feth
said. "Heard that she took it mighty hard."

"Barton and Daisy were close," Trey said, and Feth nodded.

Now Trey understood why she had insisted that her
mare be tied to her buggy on the journey up here instead of
being driven with the remuda. She wasn't just being a
spoilt princess.

She prized the horse that her pa had likely picked out for
her and who Galen Patrick had trained because that mare
was the last gift from her pa.

"Damned fine horse," he said in honest appreciation.
"Had Barton been ailing?"

"Don't know about that," Feth said. "Galen told us that
the boss got into a helluva argument with Ned right before
Barton gave Daisy her mare."

His gaze locked on the old man's. "Any idea why?"

"Nope," Feth said, breaking eye contact. Trey knew he
was lying but didn't call him on it. He wanted to talk to
Galen first. "One of the hands rode up the next morning to
tell us Barton was dead."

Trey scrubbed his knuckles along his jaw, thinking. All the
time he'd worked at the JDB, he'd never heard Barton and

Ned exchange a cross word. To think that they'd had a fight shortly before Barton's stroke raked spurs over his curiosity.

Had the boss gotten so angry with his foreman that he'd brought on his own death? And what the hell had they fought about? The way Ned was managing the ranch? The disappearance of a couple of hundred beeves?

Whatever it was, it'd worked Barton into an apoplectic fit.

Wasn't that just in Ned's favor that Daisy was ailing at the same time. The foreman couldn't have planned it better. Or had he?

What else had Ned done on his own?

Memories of being waylaid thundered back into Trey's mind. Of the rope biting into his flesh before he'd seen Ned's horse take off at a gallop, kicking up dust and rocks that dug into him. Of the pain being so intense that he'd finally fallen into the black hole that promised reprieve. Of waking up deep into the night out on the mesa, bleeding and broken and hurting so bad he wanted to die.

Before he'd lost consciousness, Ned had told him straight up he was meting out the boss's punishment for trifling with Daisy. God knew Barton was a protective sonofabitch where his daughter was concerned. But did he order Trey nearly dragged to death?

Trey was second-guessing that now. If Barton had wanted him gone for good, then why keep that tally in the ledger of how much Barton owed Trey? Why not mark that page paid in full or just rip it out as he had other debts? Why hold it open as if he expected Trey to return for his due?

Several of the hands had been surprised he'd shown up again after hightailing it. Daisy believed he'd just up and left the outfit. Could Barton have been unaware of the near deadly beating Ned had given him?

Trey bracketed his hands on his hips and welcomed the

anger rolling through him. He'd believed what Ned had told him. Believed Barton wanted him dead.

But it was just as likely that Ned had found out he'd been romancing Daisy and took it upon himself to get rid of Trey. It was mighty clear everything had changed drastically on the JDB in the six months he had been gone.

When Barton died, Ned had just slipped in and taken over without anyone making a fuss. He sold off cattle, and Daisy let him do what he wanted.

Trey had been so sure she'd be married to Kurt Leonard now. Then he'd have stepped in to take over when Barton died.

But that hadn't happened.

He could guess why she hadn't married, but that's all it'd be. A guess.

There was just too much unknown to speculate on with any certainty. One thing was clear. Daisy was in way over her head, and it was up to him now to keep the ranch and her from going under.

He huffed out a resigned sigh as his agreement with her settled over him. Yep, he had his work cut out for him just teaching her the ropes of ranching.

And he wasn't convinced Ned was history.

Trey had best watch his back. The next time Ned might get lucky and kill him.

By mid morning Trey had taken stock of the remaining animals and the availability of supplies on the Circle 46. He credited Hollis with seeing that the storehouse remained stocked and Galen Patrick for keeping a vigilante eye on the horses.

The sixteen horses that Trey had herded up here from San Angelo last year were in their prime now. Reid would be pea-green with envy over these steeds, and that'd been on his mind when he'd won the four blooded horses.

Barton had a good eye for quality horseflesh too, and the thoroughbreds he'd bought at auction were coming into their own now.

The mare Barton had given Daisy for her birthday wasn't a fluke in the herd. If they continued with the breeding program Galen had lined out, Barton's dream here would sustain Daisy for years to come, as well as elevate the Barton name among Texas horse breeders. But it'd take longer than Trey had to teach her the ins and outs of raising thoroughbreds.

"We've had interest in the horses already," Galen said, as they stood at the pasture that confined the blooded stock.

Trey could well imagine. "Wonder why Ned didn't sell?"

Galen fell silent, but the sudden tension tightening his shoulders alerted Trey that he'd hit a nerve. "Wasn't his decision to make."

"That didn't stop Ned from cutting down the cattle herd on the JDB." Trey studied one of the stallions who stood out from the others, a big chestnut with impressive lines and alertness that he could appreciate. "I can't see him turning a blind eye on these horses, especially if he'd had offers."

Galen was clearly as nervous as a deer who'd just caught scent of a cougar. "Did Miss Barton give you the power to buy and sell without her consent?"

"Nope," he said, and it didn't bother him to be little more than a figurehead. "We worked a mutual agreement to see us both over a hump, nothing more."

The wrangler kicked at a clod of dirt, then gave a reluctant nod. "Ned never saw these horses."

Trey dipped his chin and let that news sink in. It was good to hear he wasn't the only one leery of Ned.

"How'd you manage that?" he asked, curious how straight the wrangler would be with him.

"That day I delivered that mare to Barton at the JDB, he took me aside and gave me orders I was to follow no matter what," Galen said. "When I got back here, I fired the three cowboys who were buddies of Ned's on the excuse that the herd was being sold off and they wouldn't be needed."

"But that wasn't the case at all," Trey said.

Galen shook his head. "Barton wanted Ned to believe he'd grown tired of raising thoroughbreds and was just going to keep a few mustangs here."

Trey's nerves twanged at that news. So Barton hadn't trusted Ned.

"Why the hell didn't Barton just up and fire him?" he asked, not expecting an answer.

"Don't know, but I had the feeling that Ned was holding something over the boss," Galen said.

Blackmail? What the hell had Barton done that he was desperate to keep secret?

"About these buyers," Trey began. "Was Barton aiming to deal with any of them?"

"Nope. Told me at the JDB that he'd said all he had to say to the gentleman from Kentucky when he'd outbid him in San Angelo."

Trey hadn't been aware of that. But then he'd been busy claiming his own horses.

"You remember the man's name?"

"Charlton. Owns land and thoroughbreds in Kentucky and Wyoming. Wanted to add these to his stock."

The name meant nothing to Trey, but then he'd never gotten involved in the horse world. That was Reid's dream.

Trey knew the value of a good horse and hoped to get into prime stock one day too. But at this point in his life, a saddle-broke mustang was more valuable than a fancy thoroughbred.

Kirby had raised him to be a cattleman. He understood beeves and enjoyed working with them, and he believed these white-faced Herefords he'd taken as back pay from Daisy would be the start of his own ranching dynasty.

Coupled with those thoroughbreds Barton had kept for him, he'd at last be equal to Reid when he claimed his share of the Crown Seven.

But with that dream gone, he had to figure out how to acquire land and keep his livestock. He let his gaze trail over the rolling pasture.

Maybe when the drought broke and Daisy returned to the JDB with her cattle, he could work a deal with her to let him stay on here. There was enough land for him to run his stock with hers.

If she even kept the thoroughbreds.

There was nothing saying she had an interest in them. As cash poor as she seemed to be now, she'd likely sell them in order to hold on to the JDB.

Yep, she might be willing to work a deal with Trey so he could buy this spread. He could stay on as foreman here for shorter wages, maybe sell off enough of his cattle to let him make a down payment on the land.

He wouldn't have to deal with her on a day-to-day basis as he did now. He'd finally own something of his own.

"Barton mention who else was interested in them?" Trey said.

Galen shook his head. "Nope, just said another man had his eye on the horses."

Ned would've likely known. If Barton hadn't convinced him that the horses were history, he'd have sold them already.

Galen scuffed a boot in the dirt again, clearly restless. "Miss Barton say what she aims to do with the stock?"

Trey snorted. "Don't think she rightly knows what to do. Barton kept her apart from the ranch, and Ned ran roughshod over the JDB."

The wrangler thumbed his hat back and fixed Trey with a steely look. "It's got to be mighty hard on her right now."

"Yep. Barton didn't do her any favor by keeping her ignorant of how things were run."

"Well, from my experience, ladies in her position usually marry a man who knows ranching inside and out, or they sell out completely and head on into town."

Just what Trey thought. "She claims she wants to learn the business from the ground up."

Teach me, she'd asked him.

Just as she'd asked him to teach her how to kiss. How to make love. How to please a man and tell him what pleased her.

"Reckon that'll keep you mighty busy then," Galen said.

"No doubt you're right."

It wouldn't be easy for her to start from scratch and learn the business. Wouldn't be easy for him to be near her and explain the workings of a ranch.

But he couldn't walk away. Not now.

Maybe being around a close working ranch would make it easier for her to understand. This old ranch had been the start of a dynasty before. There was nothing here to distract her. Nothing soft. Nothing done for her, even in the antiquated house.

Survival of the fittest.

Yet Daisy had already surprised him by making the journey here without complaint. She had grit—he'd give her that.

But did she have the drive her daddy had to rebuild the JDB? Time would surely tell.

Trey pushed away from the fence, casting a quick glance back at the house. "Guess I'd best see when the lady wants to start. I'll be at the house if you need me."

As he strode back that way, he saw in a new light just how neglected this place looked. It wasn't rundown by any means. Repairs had been made when needed—the fairly new sheets of tin on the roof proved that.

But there were patches in the yard that were overgrown—places that might've once held flowers. The whitewash on the house had dulled to the point that the whole thing blended in with the terrain.

Instead of fancy curtains at the windows, the men had used flour sacks, and they were in poor shape. Unlike the shiny glass panes at the JDB, these windows appeared to be covered with years worth of grime.

She'd always had someone else doing for her. How the hell was she going to survive on her own?

Galen was right. She'd likely marry a man who'd take the whole damned thing over.

Trey tried to ignore the spurt of jealousy that erupted in him at the thought. His romancing with Daisy was in the past. He'd not make the same mistake.

Nope, if he managed to work a deal with Daisy for the ranch, so be it. She'd still own the JDB with its fancy house and fancy outbuildings. She'd end up miles from him, which was for the best.

He stepped into the kitchen and helped himself to another cup of coffee. It was strong enough now to damned near stand on its own, but he needed the jolt to face an afternoon with her.

Trey stepped into the parlor and frowned. No Daisy. Damn, was she upstairs?

"Daisy?"

Just the sigh of the wind around the eaves answered him.

He swore under his breath and mounted the steps. Her bedroom door was open a crack, but he couldn't see anything. Didn't hear anything either, though that would've been hard over the sudden hammering of his heart.

The last place he wanted to find her was near a bed. Yet here he was at her bedroom door.

"Daisy?" he said, louder than before.

Still no reply. Was she sleeping?

He knocked on the door. When she still didn't answer,

he shoved it open and stepped inside. The bed was made. No sign of her here.

Where the hell was she?

He crossed to the window and looked out, his heart hammering from a far different emotion now. She should know better than to wander off without letting him or one of the men know.

His gaze swept over the land for a sign of her. He was about to give up when he saw a flash of white climbing the knoll. What was she doing way out there?

Trey retraced his steps in a matter of seconds. He left his untouched coffee on the table and strode outside, his long legs eating up the distance. But it seemed to take forever before he climbed the same rocky knoll.

He swallowed the ass-chewing he'd been mulling over and stared at her standing alone in a small, fenced cemetery plot that he hadn't known was even here.

The smart thing would've been to leave her in peace, but he couldn't walk away. Still he kept his thoughts to himself and just let his shadow fall over her, let her be the one to speak first if she wanted.

"This is Daddy's first wife," she said at last, her voice nearly lost in the wind. "He never talked about her or my half brother."

"Who told you about them?" he asked.

"Hollis Feth mentioned them yesterday. He told me that Daddy lost them both to a fever." She ran a slender finger over the carved stone. "I can barely read the inscription, but I know her name was Corinne."

He stepped closer and peered at the lichen-covered gravestone. Far as he could tell she was right about the name. He barely made out *Beloved Wife* below it.

Farther down was another name, the carvings far too small and nearly impossible to read from any distance. "What was his name?"

"I'm not sure. It starts with a *D,* but the rest of it's so worn down I can't make it out."

Trey didn't comment. In the year he'd worked for Barton, he'd never heard him mention his first family. But he was a bit surprised the man hadn't named a son after himself.

"A," she said, excitement in her voice now. *"D. A.* But the rest wasn't carved as deeply."

"Moss filled it in," he said, and fished in his pocket for the pearl-handled knife that Kirby had given him, one of the few possessions he cherished, for it tied him to the man who was the closest thing Trey had ever had to a father.

She sat back on her haunches and lifted her face to the sun, eyes closed and expression intent. *"D. A. D. A.* Da— *Dade!* That's it."

"I'll be. That's my foster brother's name too."

He crouched beside the stone and began chipping the lichen from the carving. Hard to say what unnerved him most. Daisy's nearness or the fact he felt her gaze on him.

"What happened to him?" she asked.

He swore to himself. This was why he never mentioned his past. Folks always wanted to know more, and he wasn't one to share the few good things that he guarded, any more than he shared the pain.

"Don't know. We drifted apart."

But there were many times he thought of his foster brothers and wondered if he ever crossed their minds. If Dade had made the deadline to buy back his shares of the Crown Seven. If Reid had gotten his comeuppance.

The faintest outline of the carving was visible now. *"D A V."* He ran the blade down the next letter. *"I."*

"Are you sure?" she asked, leaning over his shoulder now and tempting him with her sweet scent and velvet-soft voice.

"Positive. Last letter appears to be an *s.* Davis Barton."

Her sigh vibrated with disappointment. "I was so sure it was Dade. It felt right. It still does. How can that be?"

Trey hadn't a clue, but it was damned spooky that she'd plucked that name out of the air, because his foster brother Dade had a blood sister name of Daisy. Had he mentioned it before when they'd laid tangled in the loft in each other's arms? Had the name simply stuck in her head?

That had to be it. He turned to tell her as much, and his breath caught in his throat.

In less than a blink he had recognized an expression he'd seen countless times on Dade when he'd gotten lost in memories and worry over his blood sister.

She shook her head, and her confused gaze met his. Any resemblance vanished. Yep, it had to be a trick of the light.

"I wonder where I heard the name Dade?" she asked, though he suspected she'd aimed the question at herself.

"Reckon I told you about my foster brother Dade and his sister Daisy," he said.

She nodded and turned her attention back to the tombstone. "Yes, of course. That must be it."

Trey stood and fought the urge to pull her into his arms. She'd never looked so lost. So alone.

Feelings he knew well.

But he wasn't about to dally with her again.

"Thought today would be a good time to start teaching you about ranching," he said. "Unless there was something else you had to do."

"No, the sooner we start, the better it'll be."

Yep, all he had to do was keep his mind on business around her. That, he admitted, was going to take some doing.

Chapter 7

Daisy sat frozen on the tattered ladies' parlor chair and simply stared at Trey, stunned that he'd been talking and pacing for the better part of an hour. She'd never heard him string so many words together before. Never heard him speak with such authority and conviction. Never seen him show such passion for anything other than loving.

It was obvious that he knew the cattle business inside and out—the pitfalls and the rewards. He understood what it took to eek through those meager times and how to lay back in the fat ones.

He'd done it himself by having her daddy hold out part of his pay for a year. Shoring up for the lean times, he called it.

"Barton was the shrewdest rancher I've ever met," Trey said, and she smiled. "He didn't hold with no abuse of the stock."

"Daddy was a gentle giant."

"He was a mean sonofabitch when crossed," he said.

Her smile vanished, and she blinked, thunderstruck he'd say something like that to her. That he believed it of her daddy. And looking into his eyes told her he thought Jared Barton had a streak wider and meaner than the Colorado River.

"Daddy didn't suffer fools well."

"Or any man who dared to look too long at you."

Daisy eased forward on the cushion, sensing a charged energy in the air that had the skin at her nape burning with unease. "That's in the past. We'll do well to focus on the lesson of running a ranch."

"Yes'm," he said, his lean cheeks taking on a darker hue.

But he launched into the whys and wherefores of winter ranging of cattle, and her mind simply couldn't absorb it. She was still straddling that accusation he'd hurled out there about her daddy.

Yes, Jared Barton was overprotective. That was no secret.

In his eyes no man was good enough for his little girl. It didn't matter that she chaffed at the tight rein her daddy held on her.

She loved him. He was her daddy. Her only family. Her world.

He wanted her to marry a man worthy of her—not by her standards but by his. Wanted to leave everything he owned to her and her progeny. God, how she hated that word!

Though he professed to having reservations about Kurt, he had all but pushed her into the man's arms. She'd gone from Kurt stealing one chaste kiss at the county fair to being engaged to marry him one week later.

Her daddy surely had a hand in arranging that betrothal!

Yes, Trey was right. Her daddy *was* a mean sonofabitch when crossed, and poor Kurt tied himself to her with that stolen kiss made on a dare.

A dare meant to make Trey March jealous.

She liked Kurt. But she didn't love him.

Her heart had been lost to Trey March the first time she laid eyes on the rough and tumble cowboy with the crooked smile and hurt look. Those wounded eyes dared her to venture near. Dared her to tear down the barriers and get close to a man who craved love. Who desperately needed love.

Moth to the flame.

She'd reveled in the heat of him—the power he held a tight rein on. The unbridled passion he kept hidden from the world. The smoldering fury that drove him to give enough to please, enough to tempt a woman to want more if she was willing to dance in the fire.

Daisy had opened herself to all he was able to give her. She had trusted him with her heart and her soul. She'd found heaven in his arms and promise in his eyes. She'd found the man she wanted to spend eternity with.

But she'd ended up burned. Used and discarded.

He'd planted his seed in her and vanished.

And yes, her daddy had been enraged when he found out what she and Trey had done. He'd vowed Trey would be sorry for trifling with her affections.

"I'll drag his sorry ass back here and make him do right by you," he'd told her.

But soon after there'd been no need to force the issue. She'd barely come to grips with that loss when her daddy had dropped dead.

"You getting any of this?" Trey asked.

"I'm not sure," she said, flustered that she'd been caught woolgathering. If he only knew what had occupied her mind . . . "It's almost too much to take in at once."

He nodded, watching her closely. Too closely. "It's a start in the right direction."

They were good at starting. It was the staying that they'd failed at.

"There's much more to ranching than I had realized," she admitted. "How'd you come to know so much about it?"

"By doing it. Trial and error and a damned patient man to guide me."

"Who would that be?" she asked, speaking as softly as she would to a buck she'd happened upon so she wouldn't scare it off.

He frowned. Looked away. For a moment she was sure he was closing her off again. That he'd ignore her question.

"Kirby Morris, the man who took me and my foster brothers in off the street."

She hid her surprise over that news. He'd told her once he'd been in an orphanage, but she hadn't known that he'd gone from there to living on the street. Told her once that he had foster brothers but that he didn't care to talk about *them*. Told her he'd lived on a ranch in Wyoming but nothing more.

He'd never gone into detail about his life, and asking hadn't produced any answers. So she was hesitant to start now, because she feared that would signal an end to further talk.

"Is Kirby the Englishman who owned the Crown Seven?"

"That was him."

"Was?" she asked, coaxing him to say more.

He stared at the wall, his frown deepening, telling her more than words could that whatever had happened to the man troubled Trey still. "Kirby died a couple of years back."

A year later he'd come to work at the JDB. She could still picture that day clear as glass. He'd caught her eye the moment he'd ridden onto the ranch, seeming as tall and strong as her daddy.

She'd known him for a year, yet he was still so much a mystery to her. This rare give-and-take of conversation wouldn't last long with him. Nothing lasted long with Trey but lovemaking, and that he took his slow, sweet time with.

The memory of him moving with her, thrusting deep inside her, whispered over her, and she shivered. "You cold?"

She shook her head. "I'm sorry you lost Mr. Morris."

He shrugged, and she knew before he spoke that this interlude was over. "Nothing or nobody sticks around for long."

Perhaps it'd been that way for him. Perhaps that was what had made him hard. Perhaps that was why he seemed afraid to give too much of himself.

"It doesn't have to be that way, you know," she said. "The land will always be here, with strong men and women tending it."

"True, but ranching is a hard business made harder by the weather and the market." He shook his head, and one side of his mouth crooked in a rare smile. "But it's all I ever wanted to do or be. You have to want it too, Daisy, in order to hold on to the land and your sanity."

What she wanted . . . It'd changed so from the girlish dreams of having a family. Of being the rancher's wife. She'd never aspired to be the one in charge of such decisions or to have men dependent on her for their livelihood.

But the thought of moving into town terrified her more than sticking it out on the ranch. A hazy image of big, drafty buildings and long, dark halls tickled her memory, like a nightmare she'd been told about and could never forget. There were even times she heard crying, and would awaken to find her own eyes swimming in tears.

No, she didn't want to leave the wide-open spaces and the ranch her daddy had sweat blood to build. She'd learn this business if it was the last thing she ever did. Maybe if she was lucky, she'd learn to trust another man. She'd find love again. Maybe she'd forget Trey March in time.

"I'm not leaving my home," she said.

He nodded as if pleased with that answer. "Reckon we've got a lot of work ahead of us then. You got any questions?"

Did she ever! If Ned hadn't intervened, would Trey have

stayed with her? But she was tired of talking. Tired of being cooped up in the house in mourning.

She'd ridden all over the JDB and knew its beauty and its pitfalls. But this ranch was all new to her.

"I think it's time I got a better look at what I own," she said. "Care to give me a tour of the ranch?"

Again she was treated to a quick half grin before he sobered and tugged his hat brim lower, reminding her of a boy who was embarrassed to say more. "Sounds like a good idea. I'll have your mare saddled."

Daisy got to her feet, suddenly excited. "I'll change into riding clothes and meet you at the barn."

His curt nod was her reply, but she couldn't look away from his eyes. He was questioning and measuring her in turns with that mesmerizing gaze, and she caught herself from taking a step toward him.

Or maybe she did move, for he jerked his head back a smidgeon as if surprised by the hold they had on each other too. Whatever it was, the moment was broken. He turned and walked from the room without another word.

Daisy was finally able to draw a decent breath again. Still her legs quaked as she hiked her skirt to her knees and sprinted up the steps. She knew she was just kidding herself by thinking she'd ever find another man like Trey March.

The hesitancy bridling Trey over joining Daisy for a ride vanished as the ranch house and outbuildings blurred in the distance. He'd been itching to take a closer look at this spread, and now was the perfect opportunity.

Didn't matter that he was alone with Daisy. Didn't matter that this was all hers.

She'd soon find out that running the JDB would be more than enough to turn a profit with careful management.

Holding on to this ranch as well would mean she'd have to employ a second man she trusted to manage this one separately from the JDB.

He hoped to be that man. Yep, she could head back to the JDB when the drought broke, and he'd stay on here.

That's the way Barton had set the ranches up, though Ned had had other ideas. Did they mirror his own?

"This land is so different from the JDB," she said when they topped a rise and stopped to rest in the shade of an old pecan grove.

"Deeper draws and hilly," he said. "Helluva lot more water too, which means better grazing."

And trees. They were few and far between farther west with the land flattening out and getting sandier. The JDB had triple the acreage of this spread, but less than a fourth of it had water rights.

But in West Texas, a man was rich if his spread had good water rights. Barton had done well by himself there, but Trey couldn't help thinking he'd have done far better if he'd stayed here.

"Makes me wonder why Barton left this land," he said.

"Maybe it was the ghosts," she said, and he wondered if she'd gone loco on him to suggest such a thing.

"Ghosts, huh?"

She nodded, but her attention remained riveted on the acres of rolling land and the cattle that were grazing to their heart's content. "He lost his first family here. Maybe the memories were too much for him to bear."

Trey couldn't imagine big, gruff Jared Barton being haunted by the loss of a family. Yet the man had been overprotective of Daisy. Had he feared losing her?

His gaze flicked over to her again, and he felt a similar twang of worry vibrate through him. Daisy was small and delicate, the kind of woman a man naturally felt compelled to protect. But seeing her astride her horse with her back straight, taking in the vastness of the ranch through those big eyes, told him she had steel in her spine.

Yep, there were plenty of women ranchers in the west, but few who took it up when they knew only the soft side of that life.

"Would you consider selling this spread?" he asked.

"Maybe." She looked at him with eyes that probed deeply, but for once she gave nothing away of what she was thinking. "You interested, cowboy?"

He knew better than to tip his hand, but he couldn't stop his grin anymore than he could've stopped the sun from rising. She was handling herself like a seasoned horse trader, just like he'd told her to do back at the house.

"You're a quick learner, Daisy Barton."

This time she smiled, and he felt that old familiar kick of arousal that had gotten him in a fix with this woman in the first place. "I had a good teacher."

Dammit all, they were falling back into that easy routine, getting too comfortable with each other. At least he was.

He wasn't about to travel that road again, not out of pity or want. "You ready to see the rest of it or are you ready to turn back?"

She sobered, and he knew she'd picked up his withdrawal from her. "I'm just getting started."

With that she kicked her mare into a gallop and left him standing there eating her dust. He should let her go. Let her get her fill of inspecting the land. Get her out of his hair for the rest of the day.

But the fact remained that Ned could've followed them up here. He could be up to no good, waiting for a chance to strike.

No matter what his past differences were with Daisy, he wasn't about to let any harm come to her. Not if he could help it.

He took off at an easy trot after her, content to follow at a distance. To avoid any more talk at least for today. To just watch her.

He'd been uneasy telling as much as he had about himself, doling out a bit more for her to piece together. What would she say if she knew the truth? That he'd been dumped on the steps of the Guardian Angel's Orphan Asylum when he was a few days old. That the nurses at the asylum had named him because they figured he'd been born on the third of March and someone thought it was a fitting name.

That nobody had ever wanted him.

That he'd lived all his life with that hole in his identity, wondering if the next man or woman he passed was his blood kin. Wondering if he had any blood kin at all.

No, he didn't want Daisy getting any closer to him, for she was bound to ask more questions about his past. About his family. About his dreams.

He'd said enough. Too much really. Any more and she'd pity him, and that was the last thing he wanted.

She turned her horse south and rode less than a quarter mile before reining up sharply. Dust kicked up in a cloud as her spirited mare shied and scrambled back.

Visions of her riding hell-bent onto a rattler thundered through his mind. He spurred his gelding into a gallop, his body protesting the unnecessary jostling, his heart racing faster than the horse beneath him.

He pulled up beside her with his sidearm drawn, his gaze scouring the ground. Nothing coiled, rattled, or slithered off into the brush that he could see.

But something had sure spooked Daisy. Her face had

leached of color, and her eyes were wider than the big silver conchos on her fancy saddle.

He shifted closer and laid a hand on her thigh, jolting from the spark that arced from her to him. "What is it, Daisy?"

"There," she said, her voice trembling as she pointed to a rag caught in a tangle of brush near an outcropping.

His eyes narrowed on the spot, and his insides heaved, then knotted. It was a red plaid shirtsleeve with the decayed remains of a hand dangling from the cuff.

Trey swung from the saddle and ground reined his gelding, his gaze sweeping the area slowly before focusing on that arm again. Couldn't tell a damned thing from here. Doubted he'd know much more when he got closer.

But he couldn't just ride off. He had to see this to the gruesome end now.

He climbed through the barbed wire fence at the back edge of the property, and eased toward the body, still alert for rattlers. All was quiet save the wind whistling around the rocks, the sound low and mournful.

Being up close didn't give him any clearer idea of what had befallen the man. Scavengers had gotten to him. What remained wasn't recognizable, though the fancy silver buckle on his belt was oddly familiar.

Trey squatted beside the dead man, eyes narrowing and anger kicking up a notch. The back of the man's clothes was intact, but the shirtfront was shredded and stained red. The jeans from the knees down were damned near threadbare and ripped, and the leather toes of the boats were worn bare.

Memories of the excruciating pain of being dragged behind a galloping horse lanced through him. Made his stomach knot up tighter than a noose.

"Do you recognize him?" Daisy asked, intruding on his dark thoughts.

"Nope, but I'm guessing he didn't die of natural causes."

"You think he was killed?" she asked, her voice rising.

"Sure do."

Sun caught the hook on a watch fob still fastened to the dead man's vest. There were dark reddish stains on the vest as well.

Trey tugged on the chain. He could hardly believe a watch was still attached to it.

The gold was badly dented and scratched. On one side *CS* was stamped without flourish or embellishment, as if hundreds of such watches had been produced and doled out, which is exactly what had happened. On the other a *W* had been etched, proof that the owner wanted to personalize his watch.

As he recalled, Sam Weber had been a Confederate soldier. Sam had also favored big silver belt buckles and silver toe tips on his boots.

Trey had to use his pocketknife to pop open the badly dented watch cover. The timepiece was ruined, the ivory face shattered.

The back fell off on its own, and inside the back cover was another inscription. *To Sam, with deepest affection, Lydia.*

"Just what I feared," he said at last. "It's Sam Weber."

"My God. Poor man didn't get far at all."

If that wasn't the oddest damned thing to say he'd eat his Stetson. He stood to face her. She was still astride her fine horse and managed to look both regal and vulnerable.

It was that combination that had gotten him in trouble with her before. At least that's what he'd told himself.

"You know something about Sam that I don't?" he asked, wondering what she'd heard, wondering if she was an innocent about it all like she claimed to be.

She bit her lower lip as if unsure what to say or unsure

of how much to confide. "Hollis said that Sam went away one day without any good-byes or explanations."

"Weber just up and left?"

"Hollis assumed he grew weary working for Ned and quit."

"Like I did?"

Her face flushed a dirty red, proof he'd gotten through to her this time. "Well, apparently not the same if this poor man was dragged to death."

He swore and strode back to the fence, easing through it with care. "I was lucky."

She stared at him, not blinking, barely breathing. Even the wind seemed to lay by as she obviously mulled over the fact that he hadn't intended to leave the ranch and her.

"You're sure Ned did that terrible thing to you?"

"Damned sure. Bet he was the one who did this to Sam Weber too." He grabbed his gelding's reins but didn't gain the saddle yet. "Only difference is Barton likely told Ned to get rid of me for good for daring to romance you."

"Daddy wouldn't have done that."

He snorted and swung onto the saddle. "Like hell. I saw Barton horsewhip a hand once for running his mouth about how much he wanted to get cozy with you."

The man had been drunk and talking way out of turn. Hell, if Barton hadn't stepped in, Trey would have. It wasn't as if he'd scarred the man. Scared the hell out of him was more like it. Sent him packing then.

But that was Barton's way. Swift punishment followed by getting booted off the JDB, for Barton wouldn't condone any men looking at his daughter with anything but respect.

"Ned would've done this one on his own," he said.

"I'm sure Ned decided to do that to you as well without Daddy even being aware of it."

He pulled a wry grin. Shook his head. "The problem with putting somebody on a pedestal is that he will shatter when he eventually falls."

"Daddy wouldn't have had you dragged to death behind a horse," she said. "Horsewhipped, maybe. But he wouldn't have had you killed."

Trey heard the conviction in her voice. She'd never believe Jared Barton capable of meting out Western justice as he saw fit. Refused to even think that he'd order something as brutal as a hanging or a dragging.

"Barton would be proud of you for having such blind faith in him."

She jerked her head back as the truth in his words slapped her. "That wasn't my daddy's doing. I suggest you think back to who you crossed." A couple beats of silence drummed the stillness. "I'm sure I wasn't the only woman you seduced and left."

There had been damned few women he'd gotten tangled up with for any length of time. Daisy had been the only good girl. While he'd known he was playing with fire the longer he romanced her, he couldn't stop dancing in the fire of her desire either.

If Barton hadn't stepped in to put a stop to it, who else would have paid Ned to do him in? The man she was to marry? Or someone else on the JDB?

Someone took matters into his own hands. He was still banking that Ned was the culprit.

"Maybe Ned feared I'd end up married to you and he'd have to take orders from me," he said, thinking out loud. "What's funny is if he'd just waited another couple of months I'd have been gone."

She went still as death then, the color draining from

her face. But it was the hurt in her eyes that lashed him, laying his old wounds open.

"You never told me you planned to leave," she said.

He shrugged. "Told you I wasn't the putting-down-roots sort of man, that I had nothing to tie me down."

"I was just a diversion to you then?"

Hell, how to answer that? The memory of holding her, loving her, had robbed him of sleep far too many nights. It still did. But he was in no position to compete for her hand.

Even if he was, what kind of woman cheated on the one she was promised to? She could spout all the righteous chatter she wanted. She'd done her intended wrong by crawling into the hay with him.

"You were engaged to marry Kurt Leonard."

She shook her head. "I couldn't have gone through with it."

His eyebrows lifted, and he almost smiled. "You saying you'd have gone against your daddy?"

"I couldn't marry Kurt after what we'd done."

Strong words, but he read the hesitation in her eyes. She'd have been hard-pressed to go against Jared Barton's wishes.

As for him, he wouldn't have stood a chance of gaining her hand. Not that he ever thought he had a snowball's chance in hell of marrying her. Barton wouldn't have let a two-bit drifter like himself claim Daisy's hand, even if that cowpoke had a bit of jingle and prime horses. He'd known that going in.

That's what had convinced him to claim his shares of the Crown Seven by Christmas Eve.

If he'd just divested Barton of his savings and moved on sooner. If he'd ridden out months beforehand instead.

He'd have owned land. He could've returned sooner and asked for her hand.

If he just hadn't gotten so tangled up in Daisy's arms that he hadn't wanted to leave . . .

That he couldn't bring himself to walk away from her. To stop dreaming of her. To forget that she made him feel things he hadn't believed possible.

"Did you actually believe that I would go through with that marriage to Kurt after we'd made love?" she asked, her voice strained yet ringing with a note of anger.

"Sure I did," he said, and every time he'd thought of her in the arms of the other man he'd wanted to fight Leonard for her hand.

But he was a cowpoke without a home or a family or a name. Leonard had roots deep in Texas and a ranch to rival Barton's.

He'd have treated Daisy in the manner in which she'd been raised. She never would've had to want for anything.

"Didn't what we shared mean anything to you?" she asked, and this time he saw the glint of tears in her eyes.

Shit, she was fixing to start bawling. Though he'd do damned near anything to avoid being around a weeping woman, he wouldn't lie to her either.

She wanted flowery words, and he couldn't tell her something he didn't believe existed. "You know damned well I enjoyed making love with you, but I never promised anything more, Daisy."

She drew in a shaky breath, holding back her tears. "At least you're honest."

He was for the most part. How he truly felt about her was something he couldn't explain. Something he couldn't even figure out himself.

"Why didn't you marry Leonard?" he asked.

She looked at him then, and he cringed at the hurt banked in those glittering eyes. "For a cowboy who professes to know the cattle business, you sure are pitifully ignorant about the ways of the heart."

Before he could find a rejoinder for that verbal slap, she reined her mare around and took off back toward the ranch house.

Trey watched her, sorely tempted to follow. In the end he climbed back off his horse and untied his bedroll.

He had to let her go. Had to put her from his mind.

He had to gather up Weber's remains and bury them properly back at the ranch.

He'd cut a deal with her to see him by. A bit of dallying on the side would only complicate things.

Nope, he had to keep their roles separate now. She was the boss lady. He was her foreman.

This time he was going to do this right. This time he wasn't going to be swayed by a pair of soulful eyes, lips that begged to be kissed, and a ripe body made for loving him.

Chapter 8

It took Trey the better part of thirty minutes to make a travois to haul Sam Weber's remains back to the ranch. Cost him the blanket in his bedroll and a throbbing ache in muscles that weren't quite healed.

No matter his discomfort, he'd ended up better off than Sam. But it'd been a mighty close thing.

The steady drum of hooves had him looking up from lashing the blanket to the two saplings that served as poles. Daisy must've made it back and spread the news of their discovery.

Galen Patrick reined up beside his gelding and dismounted, crossing to Trey with an economy of movement. Was he the man the Texas Ranger had left behind to keep an eye on things? If so, Patrick was lax in his job.

"Damn," Patrick said, crouching beside the dead man, much like Trey had done when Daisy found the body. "I knew he wouldn't just walk off, not with the boss counting on him and me to keep them thoroughbreds hidden."

"Yet you didn't go looking for him."

Patrick glared up at him. "There you're wrong. I looked for the better part of a week, but we was hit with a freak snow and the ground was covered." He turned back to the dead foreman. "One of the men claimed to have searched up here. One of Ned's men. Dammit, I trusted him. Didn't ride up here at all."

The wrangler's voice held that angry tone that was typical of someone who was kicking his own ass for something he blamed himself for. With snow on the ground, it would've been easy to miss one dead man on the fringe of a twenty thousand–acre spread.

"Help me move him onto the travois," Trey said. "Man deserves a proper burial."

"Miss Barton was beside herself, but it sounded like she said that Sam had been murdered," Patrick said, after they'd maneuvered what was mainly rags, skin, and bones onto the blanket.

"Roped and dragged." Trey glanced at the other man, noted his confusion. Shock. Dare he trust him with more?

Patrick's eyes narrowed in suspicion, and Trey knew then the man hadn't had a hand in this. "How would you know that?"

"Because the same damned thing happened to me." Trey settled his hat low on his brow, as much to shade his eyes from the punishing sun as to prevent the other man from reading him. "I was roped from behind. Before I could turn I was yanked off my feet and dragged for miles."

The bandana Patrick had around his neck bobbed, and he swore. "You see who did it?"

"Ned Durant." The bastard did it with a smile that had needled Trey's memory the past six months. "He told everyone at the JDB that I pulled up stakes and moved on."

"He ought to get a taste of his own medicine," Patrick said.

Trey had felt the same as his body slowly mended. "Waste of rope and man hours. Better to string him from the highest tree and be done with it."

The other man nodded, his mouth pulled in a tight line.

In that instant Trey believed he'd finally found an ally on the ranch.

"What do we do now?" Patrick said.

"We get Sam buried, then we have a powwow and lay down a plan that'll protect the thoroughbreds, the cattle, and ourselves."

"You think Ned will try something?"

Trey squinted at the vast plains chiseled from rock and sprinkled with dirt, held tight by short grass, mesquite, and the sweat and blood of countless men. "I'd bet on it, which is why I want those thoroughbreds brought in from the canyon. We need them close so we can watch them."

"We'll drive them in this afternoon," Patrick said. "What about the mustangs?"

"Cull a dozen good mares from the remuda and run them with the thoroughbreds in that pasture closest to the barn. Turn the rest out to run with the cattle."

He was banking on those few mustangs to help conceal the blooded stock. Plus it'd be interesting to see what type of foal those wild mares would throw if one of those stallions caught them in season.

Unlike Reid, Trey wasn't opposed to throwing a mixed breed. He'd seen some damned fine stock with such combinations.

With Sam secured on the travois, both men gained their saddles and started back to the ranch at an easy walk. This was the first time that Trey had ever been in charge. That he'd given orders and had them obeyed. That another man had looked up to him for counsel.

The responsibility hit him hard, for he had to think beyond himself. He had to think in broader terms for the good of all.

And just doing that seemed to calm the anger that typically boiled deep in him. That feeling of never being wanted, never being trusted, never having anything much of his own vanished, replaced by a strong sense of purpose.

Though the Crown Seven had been the closest thing to a home that he'd ever had, it was clear from the start that Reid viewed that ranch as his own, that he was the boss and favored son.

That's the way it had ended up, with Dade and Trey accused of rustling when they'd done no such thing. Having family turn on him, toss him out, was the turning point.

A man just didn't forget something like that.

Oh, he reckoned he could've trailed along with Dade as he searched for the sister he hadn't seen in twenty years. A waste of time, if you asked him.

So he'd struck out on his own, swearing that he wouldn't miss the men he'd called brothers. That he wouldn't regret closing the door on his past.

Yet last year when he heard that he had until Christmas Eve to claim his shares of the Crown Seven or lose them forever, he decided to do just that. Head back home and have it out with Reid. Home . . .

Hell, he reckoned he'd always think of the Crown Seven that way. That part of him would always miss Reid and Dade. But going home wouldn't be a reunion, and he sure as hell wouldn't stay.

He wasn't about to try working side by side with Reid again, even if he was asked to stay on—even if he could have a parcel now for his own stock.

Trey just couldn't take orders from his oldest foster brother anymore. He wouldn't continue being the little brother sucking hind teat.

Nope, he aimed to stay in Texas. The land was as raw and as wild as he felt inside. As big as the dreams that he'd kept to himself all these years.

He had a chance to see them through now. From the

first time he'd driven Barton's thoroughbreds to the old homestead, he knew it was time he settled down in Texas.

But he'd never forget the past in a Pennsylvania orphanage that shaped him. Never forget the brotherhood forged in blood. Never forget those good years growing to manhood under Kirby Morris's tutelage.

For as long as he lived, he'd regard the two men he'd grown up with as his only family, even though they'd drifted apart.

He'd made plenty of mistakes along the way, but he had learned from them. He'd surely live longer if he was slow to trust. If he held a tight rein on his temper and thought things through first.

And most important, if he stopped baiting bears. He'd done that with Daisy, knowing she was spoken for but flirting with her anyway. That led to a few stolen kisses, and as if there were a fever in his blood he had wanted more of her. All of her.

He hadn't been strong enough to walk away from her when he'd known to stay was wrong. He'd never gotten his fill after one stolen kiss.

Hell, if he was honest, he still dreamed of getting lost in her arms. But he wouldn't go there again, no matter how much she tempted him. No matter how much he still wanted her.

"What're you going to do with Weber?" Patrick asked when they were nearing the ranch, breaking the silence that had settled over them on the ride back.

"Reckon that ranger would find his death mighty interesting," Trey said. "But it could be a spell before he comes around."

The lawman was likely in El Paso seeing if Trey had told him a lie. Trey wasn't of a mood to ride into San Angelo and look up the U.S. Marshal. Either way they'd end up waiting.

"In the state Weber's in, even keeping him in the barn will draw predators," Patrick said.

Trey damn sure couldn't dispute that fact. The poor bastard had been savaged enough by the elements and the worthless sonofabitch who put him through this torture. Trey's body throbbed at the memory of what he'd endured, not just from the dragging but for six long months afterward.

"You think we should bury Weber and forget calling the law?"

Patrick shifted uneasily in the saddle, and Trey wondered if the wrangler was fighting emotions or guilt. "Yep, I do. Don't know that anyone will be able to tell much from what's left of Weber. Burying him just seems the right thing to do."

He agreed with all that, but still he didn't want to bury the man until someone else who he trusted took a good long look at what had happened to Weber. He didn't want this being passed off as a cowboy who ended up accidentally dead. Weber had been murdered and brutally so.

Trey wanted the man responsible to pay. But who the hell did he trust here? He didn't know any of these men that well. As for trust . . . Well, it was rare when he doled that out.

I'll leave a man here, the ranger had told him. But had he? Did one of the hands wear a tin star too?

Hard to tell. That could've been a bluff to keep Trey in line. But he had nothing to lose by following the hunch that the ranger had been straight up with him.

"Gather all the men out by the barn," Trey said. "They need to see what happened to Weber."

Patrick cut him a shocked look. "Some of the hands are just boys."

As if that made any damned difference at all. He knew

all too well the hell that boys could get into, of their own accord or by the hand of a no-good.

He'd been there and seen the worst that mankind had to dish out when he was just twelve. Seeing that side of life had toughened him. Opened his eyes to how downright mean one man could be to another.

It'd formed the grit that made him into the man he was today. A survivor. If he hadn't been tempered early, he never would've lived after Ned's brutal attack.

Yep, he wanted all the men on this spread to see what had befallen Sam Weber. He wanted to watch each face as they took a look and then another. Hopefully he'd be able to tell which man viewed Sam Weber's remains with a lawman's shrewd eyes.

Patrick gave a jerky nod and rode off toward the ranch at a lope, leaving Trey to continue on at his slow pace with the travois scraping the ground. He was close enough to the cattle to draw their attention. The horses too lifted their heads and watched the somber procession toward the ranch.

By the time he drew aside the barn, all of the hands were milling around the area between the bunkhouse and the corral. And smack dab in the middle of them was Daisy, her straw hat perched at a jaunty angle and her wide eyes trained on him.

He felt that stare clear to his soul and something inside him shifted, softened against his will. Once again the hardest thing he had to do was tear his gaze away from her troubled one. But putting her from his mind was impossible.

Trey swung off his horse and strode to the travois. "Miss Barton found this man up on the north end of the property on the other side of the fence. I found a watch on him that belonged to Sam Weber." That dredged up grumblings among the men. "Take a look and see if you recognize anything."

The young hands from the JDB hung back, most turning

an unnatural shade of green at the sight of the remains. The older hands ventured closer, each face showing a fair amount of revulsion.

"Them's Sam's boots," one of the men said. "Recollect the day he got them fancy tips put on them, but they're sure gone now."

"That's his belt buckle," another man said, and the others nodded and grumbled a bit more.

One of the JDB hands heaved, then clapped a hand over his mouth and took off running behind the barn. Wasn't long before another young cowpoke followed, either in commiseration or struck with the same affliction.

All of the other men looked shocked, clearly sick at what had happened to one of their own. All except Hollis Feth, who took a gander and didn't blink.

The older man's poker face revealed nothing, but then Hollis had likely seen worse cases during the war. "Appears he took a beating. Dragged, maybe."

"Just what I thought," Trey said. He suspected he'd found the man Ellsworth left behind. "Any idea who had it in for Weber?"

Hollis worked his mouth, taking his time answering. "Seeing as he was the ramrod and didn't hold with no tom-foolery, I reckon he acquired a good deal of enemies."

"Was Ned Durant one of them?"

"They locked horns on several occasions," he said. "The last was after Galen left the JDB on Daisy's birthday. Durant made a trip up here a week later to tell us he'd be taking over."

"Did Durant want the thoroughbreds?" Trey asked.

Hollis dipped his chin. "He accused Weber of stealing them."

Trey looked to Patrick, whose face was hard as bedrock. "He corner you too?"

The wrangler nodded. "I told Weber what the boss

wanted done. He told me to tell anyone who asked that the horses were gone by the time I came back from the JDB."

So Sam Weber set himself up for that fall. Saved Galen Patrick's hide as well.

"I want to know what this is all about," Daisy said, looking from Galen Patrick to Hollis Feth before locking gazes with Trey.

He read the impatience in her eyes and was glad she wanted to know. That she wasn't just letting the men handle the ugly part of this business.

"I suggest Hollis and Patrick join us at the house while the men see to Sam Weber's burial," Trey said. "The ranch have a plot for the hands?"

"Up on the ridge, alongside the family plot. I'll put on coffee," Hollis said, and started toward the house with the wrangler following suit.

Trey turned to the hands remaining. All were young, and more than a few were green about ranching. All looked like they'd rather do anything than bury a man.

"I-I'll see to him," Ansel said, surely the youngest and scrawniest cowpoke Trey had ever seen.

The boy from the JDB had made plenty of mistakes on the drive up here, but he had owned up to them. He didn't back down.

Trey nodded. "I'll leave you in charge then."

That earned him a stiffening of bony shoulders. Might make a man out of the boy yet.

He turned to Daisy. "After you, boss lady."

She spared the dead man one last look, then headed for the house. Trey heaved a sigh and fell into step beside her.

"Am I right to guess that this all started after Mr. Patrick delivered my mare to Daddy?" she asked.

"That's the way it looks to me."

"Ned Durant again?"

"Yep." Trey grabbed her arm and stopped her, got her

looking up at him again. "He's dangerous, Daisy. Hard telling what he'll take in his mind to do."

"I can see that now."

"You might think of moving . . ."

"No! I'm not going anywhere." She jerked free of him and continued on to the house, her pace quick and her back painfully stiff.

He scrubbed a hand over his chin and sighed. Damned stubborn woman.

But he thought more of her for digging in her heels and staying than if she had hightailed it. Surprised him too.

The curious and protected Daisy he'd known had changed. She had a backbone of steel and treated him with cool regard most of the time.

That should have been enough to douse any desire for her. But it didn't.

As he trailed the inviting sway of her hips into the house, he admitted he liked and wanted her more than ever.

Daisy eased onto the big chair at the head of the kitchen table and waited for the men to file in and take their places. Hollis Feth went straight to the old cast iron stove and proceeded to make coffee. Galen Patrick hesitated a good spell before straddling a kitchen chair, looking uneasy about being in the house.

Trey had yet to walk through the door, which wasn't surprising to her. That man danced to his own drumbeat and damned anyone who tried to change the tempo.

Just keeping that in mind kept the fire on her annoyance with him burning steadily. She couldn't believe he'd planned to leave her all along. That he'd come back with a demand for his due and a brutal story of being nearly killed.

In the span of an hour she'd gone from being hopeful that she and Trey could work together to being outraged over his devil-may-care admission. She didn't doubt Ned had tried to kill him. But it infuriated her that he insinuated that her daddy had ordered it done. That her daddy could torture a man to death without batting an eye.

She'd been ready to sever her agreement with Trey then. Until Hollis Feth had all but confirmed that her daddy wasn't the gentle giant that she remembered. That he had a brutal side as well. That he could mete out Western justice to those who crossed him.

Hollis had been the first man she'd seen when she rode back to the ranch. When he asked her why she looked like she was hunting for bear, she told him. "I'm thoroughly disgusted with my foreman, who claims I've placed my daddy on a pedestal."

"Now what brought this on?" he'd asked.

"I spotted a dead man half hidden behind an outcropping and Trey suspects the man was dragged to death," she said, and right before her eyes Hollis changed from a laid-back ranch cook to a man who was as coiled and dangerous-looking as a rattler. "He insinuated that my daddy was capable of meting out such cruel punishment."

"Which you don't believe for a minute," Hollis said.

"Daddy wouldn't torture a man."

Hollis shook his head and stared at the far horizon, his smile disappearing faster than the taunting promise of rain. "War changes a man, Daisy. Hardens him. Brings out something deep inside him that can shame him. Scare him too in the deep of night when he's lying beside a good woman who's tried to gentle him."

A good bit of apprehension sank into her, for she'd never remembered her daddy being anything but gentle. Yet she'd known the men he employed feared him. That they walked the straight line he drew at the JDB. That none of them defied him.

None except Trey March when he tempted fate to romance her. Could her daddy have found out sooner than she knew about her and Trey? Had he ordered her lover punished? Who in the world was she to believe?

The scuff of boot heels at the doorway brought her gaze up to meet Trey's. The air seemed to crackle around her, and she fought the urge to draw back from his knowing stare. But he gave her no more than a passing glance before taking the chair at the opposite end of the table.

And wasn't that just what they were? Opposites whose lives had collided like two stars in the heavens, blazing with fire and energy before exploding apart.

The fire should've died. It should've withered in her heart for good, burning away the longing and the dreams.

Yet her body still remembered the passion. Still ached for his touch, even knowing now that given the chance he'd love her when it suited him then ride out of her life.

She couldn't deal with that now. Wouldn't give in to the wanting.

Her daddy owned two ranches that were different as night and day. His old life here seethed with memories of another family lost to him. A ranch rich with new thoroughbreds and old secrets.

His vast West Texas spread bore his brand. The only home she remembered. The fancy house he'd built for her mama, where Daisy had found love and loss. Where she'd grown from a little girl to a woman.

The JDB was Daisy's home. Though her mama died here, she'd been brought back to the JDB. Daddy rested in peace beside her. Or did he?

That ranch had dried up along with her dreams this spring. She couldn't hide behind her daddy any longer. She couldn't rely on strangers to take care of business for her.

"If any of you know about any friction between my daddy and Ned Durant, I want to hear about it," she said, determined to get the truth out on the table.

Trey hiked a thumb at Patrick. "Tell her what happened when you took the mare to Barton."

The wrangler squirmed on the chair, but he maneuvered the matchstick he'd been worrying to the corner of his mouth and looked up at her. She wasn't sure, but she thought she read a note of apology in his eyes.

"It was the damnedest thing," Galen Patrick began, his gnarled fingers curled around a tin cup and his head bent so she couldn't see his eyes. "Soon as I got to the JDB, Ned saw that I got the mare settled then fetched Barton. Your daddy was mighty pleased with the finish I put on that mare."

"So am I," she said, meaning it. "The mare is a joy to ride."

Patrick lifted his chin, and she read the sincerity in his eyes that were the color of worn leather. "First thing Ned wanted to know was how many more I had in that condition. Before I could give him an answer, Barton flat out told him that this mare was the last of the thoroughbreds."

"Daddy lied to him?"

"He sure did, and then he gave me a look that told me to keep my trap shut." He hunched his shoulders. Frowned. "Ned just fired questions at him about what the hell was he running up here. Barton told him mustangs and longhorns. That he'd tired of dealing with the blooded stock and sold the lot of them to the fellow he'd outbid at auction."

This was more confusing than before. "Why in the world would Daddy lie about the horses when Ned could've ridden up here any time and seen they were still here?"

"Barton had that covered," the wrangler said, and took a long drink of his coffee. "As soon as I got back to the Circle 46, I was to handpick the men to help me drive those thoroughbreds north, but instead of taking them to a buyer, we were to hide them in a box canyon. Even left a man up there to keep watch day and night."

It was just more proof that her daddy had lost trust in

Ned Durant. In fact it sounded as if he feared Ned would rustle the horses.

"Why didn't Daddy just fire that man?" she asked, not expecting an answer.

The chair creaked as Patrick leaned heavily on the back, flicking nervous glances at Hollis and Trey. Her stomach cramped, and her heart felt heavy. Troubled.

"Tell me the rest," she said, her voice more strident than she'd intended.

Patrick sighed. "I think Barton just might've done that."

"You aren't sure?"

"I heard them talking low and heated but couldn't make out what riled Barton so," Patrick said. "It was after Ned stomped off that Barton told me to get back to the Circle 46 and hide the horses. That he was through with Ned. Didn't say why. Didn't tell me what he and Ned had been arguing about."

My God, had Daddy fired Ned Durant?

She thought back to that day. A month had passed since her fall from the loft. She was still gripped with heartache over the loss of her baby, a crushing loss that was stronger than any shame she felt, worse than when she told her daddy the whole truth.

That month cooped up in the house gave her time to grieve and heal enough to function. So when he gifted her with the mare, she allowed herself to be a fanciful young girl again, if only for an hour.

She had ignored the prickle of unease that something bad troubled her daddy and the urge to ask what was wrong. He never would tell anyone. He'd never discussed the ranch business with her. Never.

Besides it was her birthday. She'd done as her daddy suggested and taken a quick ride on her new mare, no more than going out a couple of miles and back.

When she'd returned, Ned had met her at the barn, his

face solemn. He'd told her then that her daddy had suddenly taken ill. That he'd collapsed. That he was dead. That he'd sent a man to town to fetch the undertaker.

The rest of that day was a blur, as was the one after it. She had run to the house and lost herself to grief while Ned continued to do his duty as foreman.

"Do you think Daddy fired Ned?" she asked, looking from her daddy's oldest friend to the man who still took her breath away.

Trey thumbed his hat back and snared her gaze in his dark penetrating one. "Yep. I'm guessing he caught Ned up to no good."

"That'd be my guess," Hollis said. "Damned shame he didn't tell Patrick here what was going on, but there ain't nothing can be done about that now."

"There is if we can prove Ned had a hand in what happened to Sam Weber."

All eyes turned to Trey again.

Her thoughts tumbled back to his claim that Ned had dragged him near to death. That hateful act had been the reason he'd disappeared, even though he admittedly hadn't intended to stick around the JDB and her for long.

If Trey was telling the truth . . . If Sam Weber had died by Ned Durant's hand, then her daddy's old foreman was a far more dangerous man than she'd ever thought.

She'd fired him.

She'd put Trey March in his place. A man he'd tried to kill once before.

Ned would surely be out for blood this time. Their blood.

Chapter 9

A few hours later, Daisy gathered with the cowhands as they buried Sam Weber in a plot at the family cemetery. He hadn't been the first cowhand to die and find eternal rest here, but years had passed since the last burial had taken place, with her mama and nanny being the last interred.

Each man paid his silent respects before going about his chores again. Everyone but Trey.

On the walk up here, she'd paid more attention to his gait. The way he held himself. The stiff rack to his shoulders.

He'd always walked with slow, masculine pride, his long legs seeming to measure each step, with his lean hips rocking a slightly jarred cadence and his broad shoulders shifting just enough to draw a woman's attention.

She'd noted the change in him, but thought his movements were indicative of the anger bottled in him. That he was just holding himself in check around her. Now she wasn't so sure.

If he'd been dragged and laid up as long as he claimed, the slight hesitation in his gait and his stiffer stance could be attributed to a near life-ending injury. And lingering pain?

She touched her left temple where a dull headache had

begun to thrum. They always came when she concentrated too hard, like she'd been doing today.

A strong, warm hand splayed on her shoulder, and her head snapped up. Trey stared at her with dark eyes that had seen far too much agony in his young life.

"You all right?"

"A mild headache. I've been plagued by them all my life," she said. "Or rather the life I remember."

He canted his head to the side, those eyes of his probing hers now, tickling the fringe of a memory that was buried deep inside her. "How far back can you bring to mind?"

She frowned, testing her memory before speaking. "Eight. It was autumn and still hot, but my mother dressed me up in yards of petticoats and lace just the same for the harvest festival."

His mouth quirked in a smile. "Bet you were a fetching little girl."

"I've been told I was a spoilt child."

"No doubt in my mind."

Her cheeks warmed at his light teasing, the tension banding her slowly letting go and taking her headache with it. It'd been that way from the start with Trey. She'd felt drawn to him. Comfortable just being near him.

It was as if she'd known him all her life—loved him all her life. And that was pure craziness.

Just like of late when disjointed images flashed before her eyes of her huddling next to another little girl on the hard bench of a train filled with children. Of standing on a loading platform in the cold clutching each other's hands. Of a stern woman grabbing hold of her and dragging her away.

And the last one, of her breaking away and running. Crying. Falling.

"What's troubling you, Daisy?"

She shook her head, hesitant to voice her fears. He'd

never asked before. Never seemed concerned, and she'd not been of a mind to unburden herself to him, not when there was another diversion, something that she'd far rather do.

But today it seemed right to tell him. It was something she'd never done, not even with Ramona, for the older woman would always shake her head and tell her to speak with her papa when she tried to remember her childhood.

"I get memories of myself that make no sense at all," she said, and told him without embellishment about seeing herself on a train crowded with other girls. "Daddy said that I must've read a story and it stuck in my head."

Trey frowned, as if recalling something unpleasant. "You believe that?"

"I don't know what to think. I have never read a story where so many children were traveling together on a train, or heard tales about it either."

She'd looked high and low when she got old enough to question her own mind. Ramona never told her such stories, and she was sure that her mama hadn't either.

Her daddy must've tossed out that reasoning for lack of a better one. Yet, deep inside, that excuse bothered her on a whole other level.

"Sounds like those trains that carried unwanted orphans West," Trey said.

Her gaze drifted back to the headstones of her daddy's first family. He'd had a life here that he never talked about.

It was as if he was hiding something, maybe the pain of losing so much. Saying nothing about them was his way of keeping the past locked away where it wouldn't plague him.

Would he have done something similar to her, thinking he was protecting her? It had always left her uneasy when she'd ask him about events that had happened to her before she'd lost her memory. His answers were always vague.

Even Ramona, who would wax on about events that had involved everyone at the ranch, couldn't give her the details of her childhood. It was as if she was hiding Daisy's past from her.

"I don't know anything about the orphan trains."

"Somebody must have told you about them," he said, his voice oddly flat and his gaze far off now, as if he was caught in a memory that troubled him too.

She wanted to ask. Wanted to wrap her arms around him and just hug him, but that was too easy. And it brought back clear memories of them together that were best forgotten.

So she closed her mind to Trey and focused on carrying on a conversation, on getting past this awkward moment. "Those trains were horrible. The children had to cluster outside in the cold and rain and get picked over like cattle at market."

"So I heard," he said, and finally took his hand from her shoulder. "You just did it again."

"What?"

"Gave details about something that you claim to know nothing about," he said. "Only two ways you could know that. You either read about the trains and knew how things went. Or you saw it."

She closed her eyes and saw a flash of children getting off a train, of the hiss of smoke filling the cold air. Of feeling the bite of the wind. The fear of having strangers gawk at her.

"I saw it," she said. "My God, I was there."

But she didn't know how that could be. Didn't know why she saw herself on that platform clutching the hand of another girl. Saw herself being dragged away and breaking free. Running. Crying for help.

That's where the memories always ended and a new fear began.

Her daddy had told her she'd taken a bad fall when she was young. Nothing had been broken, but she'd cried for days.

Could the two be connected?

"Maybe you were in town once when the orphan train came through," Trey said.

That was the logical answer, but she didn't think it was true. There wasn't a reason for her daddy to hide that from her.

She shook her head and stared into his eyes again as if searching for an answer, for somebody to finally see how much this troubled her. She wanted to lift that veil on her childhood, to talk to someone about the unknown that troubled her. To have someone listen for once.

"I see the children leaving the train." She hugged herself, for the ideas swirling in her mind like a frigid, wet blizzard chilled her to the bone. "I can feel the cold and fear deep inside me. But I couldn't have been there. I couldn't have known what happened."

"You'd know if you were one of them."

She stared up at him again and shivered at the odd emotion banked in his eyes. "That's impossible. I'm Jared Barton's daughter. Everyone knows that."

He looked away, his body so tight she could almost hear his nerves twanging like discordant fiddle strings. Surely he thought her crazy. Surely he believed that she was weaving a tale that had the substance of smoke, because to her it did.

A name, a place, a face would pop into her mind, then vanish a heartbeat later. They'd come to her sporadically all her life and were impossible to dredge up again at will.

Yet after the fall from the loft they'd occurred more often, the images lingering to haunt her. She could even recall tiny details about two of the strangers now.

The first was a young boy with a wealth of unruly

brown hair and soulful brown eyes, a boy far too serious for his young age. The other was a girl her age. They slept together on a small cot in a huge, drafty building, and huddled together on a bench seat on a train. Clasping hands and crying silent tears together.

She clearly could hear the girl scream her name, scream "Daisy," then the memory faded to black. It was those times that she was nearly numbed with the confusion, the pain, the fear.

Of course she'd told her daddy about these visions. *That's some imagination you got, Daisy.*

And that's what they must be. These phantom vignettes had to be some quirk of her mind, perhaps something that was born from the accident that kept the first eight years of her life locked in her memory.

"As children, we tend to believe what we're told again and again, whether it's the truth or not," Trey said, drawing her attention to him and those memories of them that remained crisp and vivid.

She blinked, stunned that the man of few words was actually attempting to engage in more conversation. Had they finally found something in common?

"I suppose that's how we learn," she said.

He slid her a quick sideways look that startled her, for she read the disillusionment in his eyes and saw it in the taut set of his jaw. "Or how we're hoodwinked."

She stared at this tall cowboy who projected a devil-may-care attitude, yet who was clearly a pessimist. "What would make you think that way?"

He stared at his boots, and for a moment she thought he'd share some more of his past with her, more of the deeper thoughts that troubled him.

Instead he shrugged. Squinted at the horizon again. She knew before he spoke that he'd shut off a part of himself from her again.

"Why'd you think your brother's name was Dade?" he asked.

"I don't know," she said. "It felt right."

The name had popped into her head and settled in, like it'd always been there just waiting for her to open that door on her memory and let it out. Even knowing she'd been wrong hadn't made it go away.

"But I was wrong," she said. "I imagined it in my mind, just part of dreams that have no rhyme or reason."

"Such as?"

She shook her head and cast an apologetic glance at Davis's marker. "I dreamed about a boy holding me close when I cried in the dark, telling me everything would be all right. That he'd protect me."

"Sounds like something a brother would do," he said.

"Yes, if he'd lived," she said. "But Davis was dead years before I was born. Maybe this Dade who I imagined was just my guardian angel sent to watch over me."

He said nothing for the longest time, just stared at the graves with a frown pulling his brow. But she sensed the change in him—a tension that charged the air and set her nerves snapping like a flag caught in the wind.

Trey made a face that was as close to conveying guilt as she'd ever seen, then swiped a hand over his mouth as if erasing it, and cut her a curious look.

"How old were you when you took this fall that scrambled your memory?" he asked.

"I was told I was six or seven years old, but I don't remember it. I don't remember anything at that age or before."

"And you're how old now?"

"Twenty-four," she said, and frowned when he began quietly ciphering. "What are you doing?"

Again he fell silent, only this time her tension doubled. She'd never seen him act nervous. Never seen him be anything but assured. But right now he looked jittery as all get-out.

"You're scaring me, Trey. What's going through your mind?"

"Something I damned sure don't like thinking," he said. "I told you my foster brother had a sister. Daisy was her name."

"Yes, I remember. It's a common name."

"Maybe so. But how many Dades with sisters named Daisy do you reckon are out there? How many Dade and Daisy Logans could there be?"

Just hearing the names together felt right. But they always had in her head and her heart, as if they held special meaning just for her.

And then she realized what he was implying. His foster brother's sister bore her name.

She rolled the names over in her mind. Dade and Daisy. It sounded right. Familiar. Yet how could it?

A sudden chill whispered over her, as if a fierce storm was moving in from the mountains to trap her in its icy grip. "Dade and Daisy Logan? Your foster brother is my brother?"

He dipped his chin, his expression hard. Unreadable.

He thumbed his hat back and stared at her like she was a prime piece of horseflesh up for auction. "The orphanage had too many to care for, so they decided to send some west to find good homes."

She swallowed hard. "The orphan trains."

He nodded. "Dade's sister had just turned six when they sent her west. She was a little bit of a thing. He worried that he'd lose the only family he had forever."

"What happened to her?"

He shook his head, his expression scaring her now. "Don't know for sure. I'm guessing a rich Texan adopted her and claimed her as his own."

She reeled back, knowing he implied that's what had happened to her. "If so, I hope she is with a good family."

And if that rich Texan was Jared Barton?

Daisy's stomach quivered with unease. It made sense if she was the orphan. It explained part of the odd snatches of memory that plagued her.

Yet it hurt to think that her daddy wasn't really her father. That he'd lied to her all her life. Why would he do such a thing? Was he afraid that one day she'd go looking for her blood kin? That she'd leave him?

Did she have a brother looking for her? One that Trey March knew well and called his foster brother?

The possibility rocked her to her soul. If she was Dade Logan's sister, that bond between brothers would surely be tested if the whole truth about her and Trey ever came out.

The next morning, Trey walked Daisy back to the house after they'd laid Sam Weber to rest. He'd said no more about his suspicions that she was Dade's sister, but he was more certain than ever that she was.

It surely put him in a fix, for Dade wouldn't take kindly to knowing that he'd taken Daisy's innocence. That he was right now trying to work a deal with her to own this ranch.

Take kindly?

Hell, Dade would kick his ass ten ways to Sunday if he ever found out. Just like Trey was doing to himself right now.

A man was judged by his word, and there was a time when the three brothers had made a blood vow to protect one another and Daisy should they ever find her. Trey had done just the opposite.

Never mind that he hadn't known her identity at the time. When he'd first heard the big boss's daughter's name was Daisy, he'd been reminded of Dade, who constantly spoke of his lost sister. He hadn't looked beyond that, because he hadn't wanted to dredge up his own painful memories of his youth spent in an orphanage. Of folks coming by from time to time and looking past him. Of knowing he'd been unwanted by his own family.

He'd ignored any niggling in his mind when Daisy had told him she'd lost her memory of her earliest years. Or he'd tried to ignore it.

Fact was, once, when he was taking a rest from mucking out the stalls, he'd overheard Daisy ask her pa about the fall that had blotted her early memories from her mind. She had sounded desperate to know what had happened.

Barton had simply told her there was nothing to tell, that she'd taken a spill and hit her head. The doctors claimed there was nothing that could be done to bring back her memory. In fact telling her specifics about her early years could do more harm.

Trey couldn't imagine why, but he'd never heard the subject brought up again. At least Daisy hadn't commented on it. She didn't argue either, which was typical of her.

Daddy's girl. She did what he wanted.

Except where Trey was concerned. Their dalliance had remained secret. Or so he'd thought.

He'd seen her one more time before he'd been waylaid. And yep, she'd been on his mind then.

Hell, who was he kidding? She was always on his mind. He'd gone from lusty thoughts of her to thinking about getting back at her and Barton. Now?

Now was a whole other thing to consider, because he wasn't sure if Daisy Barton was really Daisy Logan. It was so much easier to think of her as Barton's daughter, but this business about her recalling a brother named Dade just wouldn't let go.

She couldn't have plucked that name out of thin air. It

had to have meaning for her, even if she didn't remember why. That left one logical thing.

She was his foster brother's sister. The girl that he and Reid had promised to help find. The girl sent west on an orphan train.

Trey sure as hell had done more than find her!

Now that he and Daisy had history together, it was anyone's guess what he should do with her.

He cast her a sideways look, noted the slump to her narrow shoulders, and let a stampede of curses gallop across his mind. There was only one thing he could do— get word to Dade.

Even that had to be thought out. He sure couldn't write, *Dear Dade: I think I found your sister. Didn't know it was her until after I'd had a roll in the hay with her . . .*

Yep, if he told his foster brother the truth, he'd likely find himself the guest of honor at a shotgun wedding. Didn't matter that he wasn't the marrying type. Dade would demand he do the honorable thing.

So why don't you? If he married Daisy, he'd own both ranches. He wouldn't have to scrimp and save and slave. Hell, that's what Ned had had in mind.

Just the idea of another man romancing Daisy piqued his temper. He didn't like that possessive streak in himself any more than he liked the idea that his and Daisy's destinies would twine together into something binding.

Of course, there was a good chance Dade would take one look at Daisy Barton and say she wasn't his sister. Then the only guilt eating at Trey would be his own for romancing Daisy in the first place.

Yep, he had to get word to Dade. Best chance he had of finding him was to send a letter to the Crown Seven. Hopefully Dade was there, holding on to his shares of their legacy.

If so, he'd hightail it down here. The rest would depend on if Daisy truly was Dade's sister.

"I'm going into San Angelo," he said when they reached the house. "Anything you need from there?"

She bit her lower lip, which was already fuller and redder from her worrying it at the grave. "It can wait until I can go to town myself for it."

He gave a curt nod, telling himself he should be glad she was letting him off the hook, that she wasn't insisting on tagging along with him. Except it annoyed him that she didn't want to find out about Fernando and his family firsthand. That she'd rather wait for him to come back with news.

Yep, he should be content to let her.

Instead he heard himself saying, "You can ride into town with me if you want."

"When are you leaving?"

He shrugged. "Soon as I get a letter written and then saddle the horses. We'll make better time with them than with a wagon."

She stared at him, as if stunned that the likes of him could write a letter, let alone that he'd have somebody to send one to. But then why would she think otherwise when he'd professed to have almost no kin and damned few friends?

Right now she was clearly debating the wisdom of riding off to town with him on horseback. But he wasn't changing his mind.

Taking a buckboard or her fancy buggy would give them too much time to talk. Too much temptation to stop the damned thing and take her in his arms like he'd ached to do since laying eyes on her again.

Yep, riding a horse to San Angelo put her beyond arm's reach and made talk less easy if he set a brisk pace. He damn sure intended to do just that.

He expected her to realize he was asking her along just to

be polite, that he didn't really want her company. He thought she'd thank him and stay right here where she belonged.

He should've known that Daisy wasn't an easy one to read. She smiled, big and wide and warmer than the sun, and something inside him just melted, because he'd seen that smile in his dreams countless nights and wondered if he'd ever see it again.

"I'll fetch my hat and gloves and join you in a minute," she said, before dashing into the house.

"Take your time." But he doubted she heard him.

He waited for his annoyance to kick up a notch, but he liked seeing her happy for a change.

Enjoy it while you can, buddy. It was a sure bet his life was bound to change yet again.

He headed into the parlor. Found a stationery box holding yellowed paper and envelopes and the stub of a pencil.

Then he wrote a short letter that would likely get him leg-shackled. And damn it all if he didn't find himself smiling over that prospect.

Chapter 10

On the ride into San Angelo, Daisy longed to ask Trey who he'd written to. But it was clear he wasn't in a mood to talk, and she didn't feel like prying.

No, she had bigger things on her mind—namely whether she was really Jared Barton's daughter.

"If Daddy took me off an orphan train, then he had to have traveled a goodly distance to find one back then," she said, as they rode down Clairbourne Street.

"Nothing saying he didn't meet one of those trains when he drove cattle to the railhead."

True, and there were many of them in operation back then. The question was which one would've been the closest to his Colorado ranch.

That information would have to come from somebody who knew the Bartons well. Like the housekeeper who'd worked for them for as long as Daisy could remember.

"I need to find Ramona," she said, nearly shaking from desperation to get to the truth.

"You got any idea where to start looking?"

"Ramona brought Fernando to San Angelo because her sister lives here. Chances are good they are in the Mexican community." It was just a matter of finding her.

"You know their name?"

She shook her head, feeling more anxious than before. More helpless. She couldn't go around knocking on doors.

"Maybe the local doctor has treated Fernando. He could direct me to the house."

"It's worth a try."

A good one at that, they found out when they called on the local doctor. "So it was your ranch where Fernando was attacked," the doctor said, as he placed items in his black leather satchel.

"Yes. It just sickens me to think how he was attacked," she said.

The doctor harrumphed. "I've seen worse."

She was sure the old doctor had, but this violence was all new to her, thanks to being sheltered from the brutal ways of men her whole life. Or at least the life she'd remembered as Jared Barton's daughter. So much of what men could do to each other shocked her. She'd already done a terrible disservice to her cowhands by not firing Ned Durant sooner.

"I'm very worried how Fernando's doing," she said, and Lordy, did she ever miss Ramona.

"Still plagued with bouts of dizziness, but that's to be expected with a brain bruise like he's got." The doctor turned his attention to Trey. "Reckon you're eager to know when he can return to work."

She and Trey exchanged a look before she spoke. "I'm certainly not rushing him to do so."

"I know for a fact that these things take time," Trey added.

She was reminded again of his claim to have been laid up in El Paso these past six months. Reminded too of the other cowboy Ned had dragged to death. How close Trey had come to meeting the same fate.

"That it will," the doctor said. "He's in no shape to suffer the stress of swinging a hammer. Can't imagine he'd be able to tolerate the racket either with his head aching most of the time."

"That poor man. I need to visit with him for a while," Daisy said.

And she needed to speak with Ramona in private, for she was the only person Daisy knew who'd been there when she'd lost her memory the first time. She had to know Daisy's past.

She'd insist the woman fill in those blanks and answer the questions whirling like a Texas tornado in her head.

"I'm headed out that way now," the doctor said. "You're welcome to follow."

"Thank you," Daisy said.

"I've got business to attend to first," Trey said, clearly intending to invite himself along. "Give me directions, and we'll be along directly."

The doctor proceeded to lay out a route, naming landmarks so they wouldn't get lost. Not that Daisy feared Trey would. But she wasn't about to stand around and twiddle her thumbs while he mailed a letter and tended to whatever other business he had to do.

Without money to her name or credit in a town where she wasn't known, she couldn't very well do any shopping for things needed or wanted. That was surely a first for her. But then her life had taken a complete turnaround since her daddy's death.

What else was in store for her?

"I'll follow the doctor, and you can meet me there later," she said.

Trey's frown said that idea didn't set well with him. "I don't like you going off alone."

"I'll be fine with the doctor."

Trey doubted that Ned was watching them here, waiting for a chance to cause more trouble. And she probably didn't want an audience when she had a heart-to-heart with Ramona.

It was very likely that the housekeeper would still hold loyalty to Jared Barton. If that was the case, it would take a lot of coaxing to get Ramona to talk.

The string of squat adobe houses looked no different than any other Mexican settlement Daisy had seen in Texas. There wasn't a thing to set one apart from the other, right down to the children squealing and playing among the chickens pecking around in the yards.

If she hadn't followed the doctor, she likely would have ended up going from door to door. And she still might not have found the house Ramona's sister owned.

Her daddy had warned her long ago. *Not all Mexicanos cotton to Gringos. They watch us and you'd be wise to do the same.*

Right now her nerves twitched, as if someone besides the children were watching her. An odd hush had fallen over the area as well, and Daisy was sure the doctor must hear her heart thundering.

Of course these people would be curious why she was with the doctor, why she was here at this house in the first place. They were surely curious to see what reception she'd receive here.

That answer came a heartbeat later when Ramona opened the door. Her gaze slid from the doctor to Daisy.

The woman's big brown eyes glittered with moisture and surprise. Daisy felt the same stab of tears as well, for Ramona was firmly entrenched in her heart.

"Señorita Barton! How good of you to come to San Angelo to see us," Ramona said, as the doctor pushed past them and went in search of his patient. "Are you all right?"

"I'm fine." Now that she was enveloped in a warm hug.

Now that she felt welcomed and loved by the woman who'd raised her after Daisy's mother's early death.

It was an emotion she craved and one she'd been given lavishly by her daddy and Ramona. If only Trey had cared for more than rolling in the hay with her. If he'd just loved her.

But he didn't.

A boy who'd grown up without tender affections now saw the world in hard angles. A cowboy who'd withdrawn from emotions was now holding his own close to the vest. A man she'd been drawn to from the start, whom she'd fallen in love with.

Ramona led her to a kitchen in the back of the house that held the scents of chilies, grilled corn, and cinnamon. "Are you hungry?"

She was starving for answers, but she knew she couldn't just blurt out questions. "For your empanadas? You should know that you don't have to ask."

Ramona's face split into a wide smile, and she shooed Daisy toward a chair, just like she had done when she was a child. "Then sit while I make hot cocoa. I know what you like, *niña*."

As well she should, since she was the only mother figure Daisy could recall clearly. Her own mother's face blurred often, as if she were becoming a stranger to her.

Other than a vague memory of her mama dressing her up as if she were a doll, she couldn't remember much else about her. Not so for Ramona.

She'd been the one to wipe her tears and cradle her when she had a bad dream. She'd seen that her clothes were clean and her hungers were met.

Like the hot cocoa and empanadas. Comfort foods. Treats that she associated with home. With someone who cared about her enough to put forth the effort to spoil her a bit instead of showing her off.

Were there other older memories trapped in her mind as

well? Memories that reached back before the fall that cloaked her mind in dark shadows that even she couldn't see through?

She rubbed her forehead, wondering if she'd ever have a clear recollection of her childhood. Her gaze flicked to the room the doctor had slipped into. She wondered if Fernando was plagued with the same ailment now after the crushing blow to his head.

"How are Fernando and Manuel?" she asked, genuinely concerned.

"Ai, ai, ai, there are days when Fernando is tormented by terrible pains in his head," Ramona said, as she busied herself at the hearth. "Manuel left this morning for the Circle 46."

How sad his path hadn't crossed hers and Trey's. "I've a feeling Fernando's headaches are far worse than what I've suffered since the fall."

Falls, really, but she held off saying that for now. This was about Fernando, not her.

Ramona slid the cocoa pot onto a heavy trivet and turned to Daisy, her eyes sad and banked with worry. "The pain in your head. Has it returned?"

"A time or two when I've tried to force my mind to remember things."

"What is so important that you want to dredge up the past?"

Daisy sat forward and captured the older woman's gaze with her own. "Who am I?"

Ramona's face went white as paper. "You've forgotten that?"

How to answer. "I know I'm Daisy, but I'm not sure that I am Jared Barton's daughter."

There. She'd voiced her fear. And judging by the resigned look that passed over Ramona's face, it was one she'd expected to eventually hear.

Yet it was just as clear that loyalty ran deep in the older woman. "What is this? Of course you are Jared Barton's daughter."

Daisy took a sip of the rich cocoa, but it failed to lull her as it had before. "I've remembered things that don't fit in with being a Barton."

Ramona paled, and her throat worked nervously. "I don't know what you mean."

"I've remembered my brother," she said. "Dade was his name. Dade Logan."

"I know nothing about him," Ramona said, and Daisy believed her.

"I've also remembered standing on a loading platform at the train station with the other orphans."

Ramona nodded and slumped a bit more in the chair. "Your memory has returned then?"

"Not fully, but I recall enough to know that I'm not Jared Barton's natural daughter." She reached across the table and laid her hand atop Ramona's. "Please. Tell me the truth."

A nervous sigh whispered from the older woman as she fidgeted with the plate of empanadas, putting the food between them like a temptation for Daisy to eat instead of talk. Or was it a barrier? A means of trying to keep at bay the inevitable.

"Please," Daisy said again.

Ramona looked to the doorway, her face lined with worry, as if she was afraid that Jared Barton would catch her revealing his secret. Such loyalty should have been rewarded.

"Señora Barton told me that she prayed and prayed for a child," Ramona said at last, her voice low and solemn. "Then one day her prayers were answered, and you came into her life."

That was in keeping with what Hollis Feth had told her. Her mama had desperately wanted her. Wanted a child.

Where there's a will, there's a way, her daddy said often.

He was a man who was used to getting what he wanted through hard work and determination. He'd wanted a cattle empire and had gotten one. He'd wanted a chance at a second family after losing his first wife and son. But it didn't look like he'd have a second child, not unless he took matters into his own hands.

"I think that Daddy and Mother decided to take in a child," Daisy said, sitting back to cradle her cup of cocoa, hoping the warmth of the crockery would thaw the deep cold that always stayed inside her. "Tell me the truth. Did they take me off an orphan train?"

"I do not know, *niña.* Señor hired us when he bought the rancho in Texas. I had never seen you or your mother until Señor Barton brought you both to the JDB."

So Ramona couldn't know if Daisy was an orphan. She'd taken over her care after they moved to the JDB. She would naturally have assumed that Daisy was the Bartons' child by blood.

Ramona had believed what she'd been told, that Daisy was their only child.

But Daisy knew that wasn't true.

She closed her eyes and willed the shadows to recede from the past, but the fog hovered like a specter at the end of the loading dock. She shivered. Cold. Afraid.

A big hand clamped over her arm and pulled her from the others. She remembered breaking free. Of running from the woman into the mist to hide. Of falling.

The rest was a blur of faces and fleeting memories of being gripped with pain and terror. That surely matched another memory stuck in her mind, of riding with a man on a horse and being too terrified to cry.

"Daddy told me I lost my memory after taking a bad fall. But was that before or after I came to be Daisy Barton?"

Ramona took Daisy's hands in both of hers and held

them tight, like a loved one would do in the face of despair. "What does it matter? You had parents who loved and cared for you."

She smiled at that, for though Jared Barton had a reputation for being tough and gruff, Daisy had always known he had this softer side. He was a good daddy.

But for all the love and comfort she had growing up on the JDB, she had had a void in her too. Of memory. Of sensing that she'd lost something and still mourned it deep inside her.

A brother?

Yes, if Trey could be believed. If what she felt in her heart was true. Dade Logan was her brother. Trey's foster brother. Had their lives been destined to intertwine long ago in a Pennsylvania orphanage?

She turned to Ramona. "Did I ever mention Dade Logan?"

The older woman sat back, her expression clouding. "*Si*, when you were little. You asked where he'd gone but I couldn't answer you."

"I doubt that even Daddy could have done that."

Ramona stiffened. "Ai, ai, ai! Señor would get angry when you asked about this boy, so I told you to never mention his name again."

Daisy had heeded Ramona's advice, though Dade's name had stuck in the far recesses of her mind to trouble her during those lonely hours deep in the night. She'd always wondered who the boy was. Why his name would pop into her head whenever she was scared.

Her daddy had carefully kept her past from her for reasons of his own. She wasn't much different than the remuda of wild mustangs he'd rounded up—not blooded but bearing the JDB brand anyway.

"Daddy was afraid I'd remember my past," she said,

certain of that now. "He wanted me to believe that I was Daisy Barton."

"But you are. It doesn't matter if you were born his daughter," Ramona said. "He raised you as his own. He loved you, *niña*."

She knew that.

The Bartons returned to West Texas with a daughter. Not long after that, her daddy was left to raise his child alone.

Jared Barton had lost two families. He likely wasn't about to tell Daisy the truth, for fear he'd lose her as well to her own kin. And Ramona was right. Her daddy was the only family she knew.

But he was gone now.

She had a brother. Dade.

"It troubles me that I left you alone on the ranch," Ramona said, her warm brown eyes swimming with regret. "But I could not leave Fernando, and my sister needs me now too."

"It's all right. I'm managing just fine," Daisy said, which was true. "Your place is here with your family."

Ramona smiled and bobbed her head. *"Gracias."*

Yes, deep in her heart Daisy longed to be with family too. She didn't want to be alone.

She had to find Dade. Surely Trey would know how to contact him. Maybe once she was reunited with kin, more of her memory would return.

She just hoped she didn't regret getting her memory back.

Trey collected Daisy from Ramona's sister's home, staying just long enough to be polite. "We have enough daylight to make it home before dark if we leave now."

She didn't argue with that. In fact she seemed more pensive than when she'd ridden into San Angelo with him.

"Ramona shed any light on your past?" he asked when they were back on the road.

"Not really. Daddy hired her as the housekeeper at the JDB, so she didn't meet Mother or my nanny until we arrived at the ranch." She frowned as if a thought struck her, then shook her head just as quickly, like she'd discarded whatever had come to mind. "Ramona said we'd taken the train from Colorado to San Angelo, then come by buggy to the ranch."

"You don't remember any of that?"

"I don't know." She heaved another sigh and stared off at the miles of land stretching as far as the eye could see. "Maybe you're right. My past doesn't make a lick of difference. But my future as a rancher sure does."

"Two spreads to run is a helluva big responsibility."

She nodded. "I guess that's why Daddy pretty much put men at the Circle 46 to manage things and stayed at the JDB."

"It's the larger of the two and was the one he built for you. Built it to last generations."

She smiled at that, a wistful smile that told him she was thinking of the JDB. Of home. He sure understood the longing, but where she had a place to return to, he didn't.

The ranch where Kirby Morris had raised him and that he had intended to leave to him, Reid, and Dade was no longer his. He had nothing now but a dream.

And a chance to make a stake.

"I'd like to buy the Circle 46," he said, feeling a might giddy for voicing what he wanted most.

She stared at him, saying nothing for the longest time. "I thought you were broke?"

"I am cash poor, but when I get my herd fattened up, I can sell a good deal of them at auction. Bet I could get a good price for the horses too."

"You still won't have enough money."

He smiled, amused by that bite of sarcasm in her voice.

It was one of the things he liked about her. That though she looked like a prim, little lady, she was no shrinking violet.

Shame Barton hadn't taught her how to run a ranch.

"The way I see it, you are going to be run ragged managing two ranches," he began, careful to keep the excitement that made his heart pound from his voice. "The JDB is your home. It's the larger of the two. If a few more wells were dug, you'd avoid this problem during dry years."

"You've had your eye on the Circle 46 all this time."

Since he first herded those horses onto the spread nearly a year ago. "It's perfect for me. Small house with just enough outbuildings to hold all I'd need to run the place."

She reined her horse around and stared at him with nothing short of disgust. "What if I don't want to sell the Circle 46?"

Damn, why couldn't she just make up her mind? Why did she have to dither over everything?

"You telling me you've grown attached to it more than you have the JDB?" he asked.

"Of course not. But I have the horses here."

"Drive them back to the JDB. Hire a damned good wrangler when you do."

"I don't know." She reined her mare around and started back down the road at a good clip.

He bit off a couple of ripe curses and followed. "It's a damned good deal, Daisy."

"I'll think about it."

"You do that." And he aimed to do all he could in the meantime to persuade her to sell to him.

Chapter 11

Trey had always felt responsible for Daisy, but after sending off that letter to Dade at the Crown Seven, he was more duty bound than ever to watch over her. Of course that was like watching the horse ride off after closing the barn door, but hindsight was a damned fine thing.

What had happened between him and Daisy couldn't be undone. And dammit all he didn't regret it either.

But he wasn't going to repeat past mistakes. That very first kiss he'd stolen from her was a fool's move, for once he'd tasted her desire, her hunger, there was no holding him back.

If she would've just slapped him for trying. If she'd done anything but bow into him, fitting that sweet little body of hers to his, like she was made just for him.

He scrubbed a hand over his face and took a good, long look at reality. His dalliance with Daisy was in the past, a part of his life that he'd tuck away to remember. Same as those years growing up on the Crown Seven under Kirby's guidance, being the youngest brother to Dade and Reid.

He'd had his rows with both brothers from time to time. But he'd trusted Reid and Dade with his deepest secrets. His worst fears. His life.

Reid had betrayed him and Dade in the worst possible way, using their trust to finagle them out of their shares of the ranch. Hell, Reid had come mighty close to getting him and Dade hanged when he'd sided with Kirby's rotten cousin, who accused him and Dade of rustling their own cattle.

Lesson learned.

Trey and Dade had gotten away with the shirts on their backs and their lives. Reid got his name cleared, and ended up with the ranch and the cattle. Or so Reid had thought.

Dade and Trey had still had one more shot at claiming their shares. Last fall Trey had aimed to head up to the Crown Seven and do just that, plus finally have it out with Reid for betraying him and Dade.

But Ned Durant, either by Barton's order or not, had other ideas. Instead of Trey getting what was due him, Durant had dragged him into the desert and left him for dead.

He shook his head, thinking it ironic that he'd lost his second chance to claim his stake in the Crown Seven. That Reid won it anyway by default, or hopefully was forced to share it with Dade.

Yep, he couldn't change the past. But he could hold up his promise to the closest thing he'd had to a family.

Which is why he'd written a short letter to his elder brother—the thing he'd vowed never to do after Reid had betrayed him and Dade. He wasn't ready to bury the hatchet, but he had to make sure that Dade knew he'd found Daisy.

In the event he wasn't at the ranch, Trey could only hope that Reid knew where Dade was at and would contact him. At the least forward on the letter.

And if Reid had no idea where Dade had gone?

Nothing Trey could do about that. Trey had found Daisy

and done his best to notify her brother, just like the three of them vowed to do nigh on twenty years ago.

He'd done a lot of things wrong since then, but unlike Reid, he wasn't one to go back on his word. And hell, didn't this qualify as him squaring things with his foster brothers?

Hell if he knew.

Trey was on his way to the house when he spied Cameron Ellsworth riding toward him, his back straight and his face giving away nothing that was on his mind. Having the lawman around so much made him nervous.

Trey braced a shoulder against the barn and waited for the lawman to rein up. "You coming by on business or is it a social call?"

"Business." The ranger shifted in the saddle and eyed him like one would a rattler. "I came by earlier but Feth told me you were in San Angelo."

He inclined his chin. "Spent the better part of the day there."

The ranger nodded. "Is there anybody who can vouch for that?"

It'd been years since a lawman had questioned his whereabouts on a given day, and the fact that he might need a witness to being where he said he was got his hackles up. But he bit back the smart-assed remark about it being none of the man's business and nodded.

"The hands here, and a few folks in San Angelo," he said. "Daisy went with me as well."

"I'd like to talk with her," the ranger said.

That was to be expected too, but he hated that his word was doubted, hated that his senses told him that whatever brought the ranger out here wasn't good news. "Mind telling me what's going on?"

The ranger shifted in the saddle, drawing the moment

and Trey's patience to the breaking point. "There's been trouble at the JDB."

Damn! "Such as?"

"It burned down last night."

Trey let all the ranger said sink in. Trouble at the ranch. Fire. Trey would bet the ranger was thinking this was intentional.

"You see it?"

The ranger dipped his chin. "Yep. Saw the smoke as I was coming back from El Paso."

That took Trey's mind off the fire. "You find what you were looking for there?"

"Yep. Folks remembered you. Said you were in mighty bad shape when you was brought in."

"Yet you still aren't convinced I'm innocent."

"My job is to get to the truth, no matter what. Like that fire. Reminded me of the days when the Comanche burned out the *rancheros*."

Trey had heard plenty of those bloody tales before, and thanked God he lived in more civilized times. Then he nearly laughed at that thought.

Leaving a newborn baby on a doorstep without any notion of his kith or kin wasn't civilized. Neither was dragging a man near to death behind a horse. Or burning out a ranch.

"Any idea who did it?" Trey asked, having a damned good idea who'd stoop to such a lowdown stunt.

"Could've been anyone."

True. But he'd bet Ned Durant had something to do with this. If he was lucky, he might just find proof of it.

"You'd best come on in the house and tell Daisy."

"What's wrong?" Daisy asked the ranger, showing amazing perception of trouble.

Trey stood back while Ellsworth told her the same story he'd told him a moment ago. Shock flickered in her eyes, then sadness rolled in like a dank fog, making her look so forlorn he had to stop himself from going to her and taking her in his arms.

That was always the problem with him and Daisy. She drew out that protective bent in him. Drew out other feelings he didn't care to look at either, for they were ones he'd learned long ago not to trust.

She dropped into a chair and swallowed hard. "Is it all gone?"

"Afraid so," Ellsworth said. "Barns and bunkhouse burned right to the ground. House is badly damaged and will likely cave in with the first strong wind we get."

She pressed a shaky hand to her forehead. "Was there a heat storm? Is that what started it?"

The same thought that had first hit Trey. As dry as it was down there, it wouldn't have taken much to start a blaze. One heat lightning strike could set the whole thing on fire. So could an untended campfire.

"I'd bet my star it wasn't any accident." The lawman shifted his stance and cast Trey a cool look before turning back to Daisy. "Where was you yesterday?"

"In San Angelo," she said without hesitation, and Trey was sure she didn't grasp what the lawman was trying to prove.

"Why?"

That brought her gaze up to the lawman's. If the frown pulling at her brow didn't prove she knew something was wrong, the stiffening of her spine did.

"I'll ask you the same thing," she said. "Why do you need to know that?"

Trey bit back a smile when the lawman braced both hands on his hips and stared at Daisy, likely stunned that she wasn't as meek as he'd thought.

"Just doing my job, ma'am," Ellsworth said. "Somebody burned the JDB to the ground, a ranch that was seeing mighty hard times. You and March were gone all day yesterday. I need to know if either of you had a hand in that fire."

She sat back and gripped the edge of the tabletop, keeping her eyes on the lawman instead of Trey. "Fair enough. Trey had business in San Angelo, and I needed to visit Ramona and Fernando."

"You and March together the whole time?" he asked.

This time she glanced at Trey, and worry flickered in her eyes. "No. There was about an hour or so that we were apart."

But even if they'd been separated for two hours, Trey would've killed his horse riding from San Angelo to the JDB and back in that short length of time.

"You're welcome to visit Ramona and Fernando and make sure I'm telling you the truth," she said.

The lawman actually let out a low chuckle. "Like I said, I'm just doing my job."

"I trust that means you're looking for the man who could have done such a thing," she said.

"That I am. If nobody else has trouble, I'm inclined to think this was a personal vendetta."

"Ned Durant," she said.

"I've got men on the lookout for him," the lawman said. "Best be on my way now. Sorry to be the bearer of bad news and all."

"Thank you for riding out to tell me," Daisy said.

But she wasn't looking at the lawman as he left. Nope, Trey could see that her courage had been sapped from her. She stared at her hands, shoulders bowing in, head down. Defeat.

It was mighty clear she was a blink away from bawling her eyes out. That was the time he'd always vamoose and let a woman to her tears. But this wasn't just any woman.

This was Daisy.

Possibly Dade's sister.

She was Jared Barton's little princess daughter and the woman Trey had lost his head to. Nothing more.

She was simply a driving desire beyond anything he'd known in his life.

Now he worked for her. Plain and simple.

So why did this feel so damned complicated? Why did knowing that she was close to tears have him squirming between hightailing it and taking her in his arms?

Dammit, he wasn't going to soften toward her again. They'd made their mistake. Time to move on.

Or try to. This was surely changing his plans to buy the Circle 46, for Daisy wouldn't be going back to the JDB when the drought broke. Hell, she might not return at all. She might hole up here at the place he'd had his eye on.

All because somebody burned her out just for the hell of it. Or for revenge. Didn't matter which. The end results were the same.

Except for him.

"I have to go there," she said, seeming to pull her courage up again before his eyes.

"Why?" Trey asked.

She gave him a look that said he was dense as an oak tree. "Everything I owned was left in the house. I need to see if I can salvage anything before somebody helps himself to it."

"I can do that for you," Trey said.

"Your help is welcome, but I'm going and don't you dare try to talk me out of it."

He brought up his hands, palms facing her, certain the woman was loco. Certain he was too for wanting to applaud her grit.

But reality was a bitch neither of them could avoid. He'd be a bigger fool if he didn't point the obvious out to her.

"You'll be safer here at the Circle 46. If this was done to even a score, there's no telling what else he'll try doing if you go there."

"The same could be said if I stay here," she said. "With you gone, anybody could get into the house."

That thought had his blood boiling. He'd kill anyone who dared harm her. Not that he expected anyone would. If Durant was responsible for torching the JDB, he'd be satisfied with the end result. He would've gotten his due just knowing the trouble he'd put Daisy to in returning there.

No, Trey's reasons for keeping her here were selfish. How damned safe was she going to be trailing down there with him? They'd be alone with a passel of memories and desire raging between them.

"The house is gone, Daisy. You'll have to camp out in the open." With him.

"I've done that before."

That surprised him. "When?"

She opened her mouth, then closed it and frowned. "I'm not sure, but I was very little. I remember sleeping on the ground, huddled in a blanket, yet being so cold I couldn't stop shaking."

That surely wasn't a memory of her time as Barton's daughter. He never would've put his child out like that.

But he recalled Dade telling him about when his pa took him and Daisy to the orphanage, how cold it'd been. How she'd cried silent tears long into the night. Was she starting to remember her past before she'd become Daisy Barton?

"I wrote to Dade," he said. "I reckon he'll head here as soon as he knows you're here."

"And if he's not my brother?"

"Then he'll be disappointed." And Trey would escape being the groom at a shotgun wedding.

She got to her feet and smoothed her hands down her skirt. "When do we leave for the JDB?"

He huffed out a breath. "Bright and early tomorrow morning."

He damned sure didn't want to get there and have to scout out a place to camp on the ranch right away. Didn't want to think of spending a night alone with her.

But that would likely be the one thing that stuck in his mind on that hard ride down to the JDB.

Daisy had defied him, and that should've pissed him off. He should find that bullheaded defiance so revolting that it'd kill off his desire for her.

But it hadn't.

Nope, seeing this side of her, this determination and courage, just made him want her more. For he could see she was more than a match for him. He could see that Daisy knew how to give as well as she got.

Problem was he didn't have a damned thing to give a woman like her but a good roll in the hay and a vague promise that he'd amount to something. It wasn't enough.

Not for her.

And it sure as hell wasn't enough for him anymore.

Daisy's heart ached as she stared at the charred remains of the JDB ranch house. She'd seen the damage done to ranches before due to cyclones and fire, but the JDB had always been spared.

Not this time. Like the ranger had said, very little remained of the house beyond a shell, which was more than could be said about the outbuildings.

If not for part of the corral remaining, she'd be hard pressed to pinpoint where the barn had stood. Fire must have started there. Burned outward. Burned fast.

Even a day and a half after the fire, the stench of scorched wood filled the air to burn her nose and make her eyes water. Made her mare skittish as well, forcing her to hold a shorter rein.

A gust of dry wind stirred the ashes and blew the charred odor right in her face. Her mare whickered and sidestepped.

Daisy automatically stroked the horse's neck, feeling the animal's restive quiver through her gloves, feeling a similar tremor stir deep inside her. Gone. All gone.

"Can't be anything inside that didn't get burned to a crisp," Trey said, leaning forward in his saddle, looking and sounding solemn.

"Probably so."

Pictures, letters, clothes. Memories that she barely could hold in mind were now lost forever.

Inside she was bawling over the loss, but outwardly she refused to shed a tear. *Crying don't solve nothing, girl.*

She shook her head, unsure who to attribute that saying to. Unsure of everything now that the only home she'd known had been destroyed. She'd lost so much. How much more could she stand?

Trey shifted in the saddle, the creak of leather loud in the eerie silence that roared between them. "We could leave now and get back to the Circle—"

"You're not rushing me off."

She dismounted and gave her riding skirt a shake to rid it of trail dust. The fine gray powder fell onto the charred remains of grass that crunched underfoot.

She ground reined the mare and started toward the house. A muffled curse sounded behind her, but she didn't turn around. Didn't stop. Didn't even slow.

Before she got halfway to the black arch that had been the front door, a tall shadow fell into step beside her. The briefest smile pulled at her mouth, and a sense of relief settled over her that he wasn't intent on trying to change her mind anymore.

Still, she paused a heartbeat when she reached the front step and thought back to how inviting it had always looked.

"I always admired that rose of yours," he said, surprising her with that bit of news.

A yellow rose that had always made her smile. That was supposed to bring good luck. That she had tended with loving care.

"Daddy said Mother had that yellow rose planted the day we moved in here," she said.

There was nothing left of it now but black brittle canes. So much for good luck.

She looked up at him, and her heart seized up again. He'd thumbed back his hat to let the full sun fall over the chiseled lines of his face.

He didn't look quite as pale as he had a few days ago, but his skin still wasn't as deeply tanned as before. Not as full either.

Trey was leaner all over now. Not rangy so much as having that on the prowl hungry look. What would sate his appetite? What would erase the hard lines around his eyes and mouth? What would lighten his heart, for the man was surely carrying around some heavy woes?

She shook off those thoughts. That was a road she didn't want to travel with him again.

Liar! She did ache for his touch, for his kiss, for his brand of love that surely was hotter than the flames that had licked over the JDB.

Even the memory of it left her hot and thirsting for what they'd had. And her foolish heart was telling her they could have it again.

"Best let me go in first," Trey said. "See if it's safe for you to poke around."

She nodded and tore her gaze from his, hating that he could hide his emotions so well while hers were hung out like laundry for all the world to see.

He stepped into the blackened hull of what had been the entry and moved into the parlor. His steps sounded hollow, like he was walking on eggshells.

A moment later she knew why when wood cracked and he dropped through the floorboards.

"Trey!" She rushed into the entry.

"Get out of here," he said, but she didn't move. "You could fall through anywhere just like I did."

He hoisted himself up onto the floor and tested for a stronger place to hold him. "Fire must've started here."

In the middle of the parlor floor? Of course. Someone had broken into the house and intentionally set a fire, using Mother's furniture for kindling.

Most of the interior walls had been reduced to ash, leaving only the adobe exterior walls. One of them was crumbling, likely because the rafters were gone.

She moved toward the bedrooms. Hers was destroyed.

"Daisy, get out of there," Trey said, but she ignored him.

She stepped into her daddy's room, and stared at the burned remains of a massive bed.

The dresser on the far wall was charred but intact.

She moved to it, her steps cautious, her heart hammering wildly. This was his private domain. The one room she'd been run out of as a child.

She hadn't ventured in here since, even after her daddy's death. She'd even instructed Ramona to leave her daddy's things where he had left them instead of cleaning out the room.

"Daisy," Trey said, his tone sharp and holding a strong measure of annoyance.

"Shh."

She felt like a trespasser in fear that the owner would catch her, as if her daddy would holler at her to scat. If only it was him behind her instead of Trey!

A small case sat on the dresser, one edge of it half

burned black. It'd been her mother's jewelry box and clearly something her daddy couldn't part with either.

She lifted the lid, but it broke off and fell on the dresser top. Ashes scattered and released their oily scent again.

Inside were a few pieces of jewelry. A ring. Ear bobs.

Her fingers closed over the broach buried deep in the case. A memory stirred to life of seeing a similar one pinned at a woman's throat, the details on the bone relief of a woman and child so delicate that she could see the expression of love on the mother's face.

Yet this one was simply a cameo of a woman. Why had she thought it was a mother and child?

"I remember crying for this when I was little," she said. "Mother stopped wearing it. In fact I thought that it had been buried with her."

"Reckon your pa kept it for you."

A lightning flash memory of a broach being pinned on her dress came and went, too quickly for her to grasp. Yet the sadness that seeped into her and left her weak in the knees convinced her the fleeting image was real. When had Daddy done that? Why hadn't he let her keep the broach?

"Maybe he was afraid I'd lose it," she said, staring at the beautiful piece of jewelry cradled in her palm.

Her fingers tightened around the delicate face of the broach, the ivory cool against her skin. But though it was beautiful and stirred sweet memories, something about it troubled her. Something wasn't quite right.

The pounding of hooves stampeded over that thought. She whipped around to find Trey's broad back to her, blocking her from seeing who was approaching. His right hand hovered near the six-shooter strapped to his hips, and his gaze fixed on the crumbling southern wall, giving a clear view of the mounted men.

A chill feathered down her spine. "Who are they?"

"Can't tell."

She felt his tension pulse in the air and hum along her already taut nerves. She'd never felt so exposed. So vulnerable. So afraid in the house that had been her safe haven for years.

Correction. Make that a shell of a house.

They had nowhere to hide here. No way to reach their horses before the riders were upon them.

Her gaze darted to the men approaching at a steady clip. Six cowboys.

They were too far away to see their faces. They'd have to ride much closer before she and Trey knew if they were friend or foe.

Close enough to greet them with a smile. Or a bullet.

Chapter 12

Daisy recognized the tall man riding in front of the others at the same instant that Trey went for his gun. A moment's panic knifed through her.

She stepped forward and curled her fingers around Trey's right hand. He jolted, and she shivered as she felt his rage and some other emotion arc from him into her and leave her struggling for breath.

The intensity was just too much. It was as if she'd reached into a dark place to find him, a place where a battle of wills was going on. Again she realized she didn't know him at all, not the man buried deep inside.

"It's Kurt Leonard," she said.

"So it is." He dropped his hand from his gun and helped her from the ruins. Then he took a stand a few feet from her, not shaking her off, but the distancing felt the same.

That invisible barrier he threw up was deceiving, for even when she'd been in his arms, she'd been miles away from the heart of this man.

There was still so much unsaid between them. So much uncertainty over what she should tell him.

All along she'd decided he didn't have a right to know. He'd been the one to leave her.

Except now she knew that's not what had happened.

She took a breath. Held it. Rolled the truth and lies over and over in her mind until one fact stood out from the others.

Nothing would be accomplished by telling him her darkest secret. Nothing but more hurt. It was over. Done with. She couldn't repeat that mistake.

But even knowing that, she had to fight the urge to move closer to him. She pressed her other hand over her pounding heart and realized she still held her mother's broach so tightly that the delicate design was digging into her palm.

Her earlier tingle of memory failed to resurface. Like smoke caught in the wind, it was gone.

Just as well. This wasn't the time to get caught woolgathering. The man she'd promised to marry was just about upon them. And the Romeo cowboy who'd ridden into her life and lassoed her heart looked ready to tear him limb from limb.

She shook her head, certain Trey's anger had nothing to do with Kurt. Yet the thought persisted that he acted like he owned the place and didn't want Kurt setting foot on the JDB.

The cowboys reined up back where the bunkhouse had been, but Kurt rode on. Slower now. Taking his time. No doubt noting the big man beside her and taking Trey's measure.

Those broad shoulders and the gunfighter stance were mighty intimidating, even in a country where most men and their dreams were impressive.

Trey was a throwback, a man others respected if not feared. He possessed the grit and guts that most men just dreamed about.

She hadn't seen Kurt since Daddy's funeral, and then he had been a blur in the crowd. He hadn't done more than extend his clipped condolences and move on.

That was to be expected. He'd been angry with her when she'd called off the wedding, and equally furious with her daddy for letting her do as she pleased.

She'd been certain Kurt's anger with her and her daddy would ebb in time. She was sure he would forget her when the right woman came along. A woman who loved only him.

He was a handsome rancher. A good quiet man. Or so she'd thought.

But he'd clearly changed. Had those deep lines around his eyes been there at Daddy's funeral? When had that hard glint begun to burn in his eyes?

Kurt reined up across from them and gave her the barest dip of his chin, his eyes shadowed by the wide brim of his hat. "Afternoon, Daisy."

"Hello," she said.

It was difficult for her to remember courting Kurt. There'd been nothing memorable about all those weeks of seeing him. Nothing that had tempted her to toss up her skirts and have her way with him.

She'd simply been captivated by Kurt's handsome face, charming smile, and undemanding ways. He was nice. Safe.

He'd been the first man who ever called on her. They'd gone riding. Gone to church. Gone to barn dances.

They'd kissed that first time on a dare. Later they'd shared no more than chaste pecks on the cheek and one light brush of lips on lips. He'd never forced more on her. She'd never craved more, because at that point she hadn't known there was more for a woman to want.

She'd thought she'd be happy being his wife. Thought she'd make her daddy happy. Thought she'd find peace in his arms.

But she hadn't.

Maybe she would have if Trey March hadn't ridden into her life and stolen her heart. If his arms hadn't been the ones that made her feel safe from a past she couldn't remember.

She wanted Trey. Desired him. Had known passion with him that blazed hotter than the sun before it was snuffed out.

There was no going back. No making amends. She'd hurt Kurt. Shamed him. Used him. And now here she was with Trey by her side and feeling every inch the jezebel.

"What brings you by?" Trey asked.

Kurt shifted his gaze to Trey, and his eyes went hard and his mouth pulled into a flat line. "I could ask the same of you, seeing as you moved the herd and left the JDB."

"Somebody pumped the well dry," Trey said. "Only choice was to move the herd to the Circle 46."

"Here I thought Daisy had up and sold out."

She'd feared she'd have to do just that. "Even if I'd wanted to, I'd never have gotten a decent price for the herd or the ranch during a drought."

She'd get even less now that the house and outbuildings had been destroyed.

"Didn't know you'd had trouble before the fire," Kurt said.

Trouble had been her constant companion since her daddy's death. No, since Trey had disappeared. But Kurt wouldn't have known that, because he hadn't come around.

"Why are you here?" she asked, realizing that he'd never answered Trey's question.

"I've had a man watching the JDB," Kurt said. "Feared whoever had done this to your spread would get it in his head to burn out another ranch. When he saw a couple of folks poking around, he let me know."

"Any idea who did this?" Trey asked, taking charge. Asking what she should have asked.

"Nope. Reckon it was either done for the hell of it," Kurt stared at her, "or somebody had a grudge with the JDB."

"Ned Durant," she said, the name instantly springing to mind. "He was none too happy when I fired him."

"Did you now?" Kurt flicked a glance at Trey. "That before or after March came back?"

"After," she said and damned the heat that stole up her neck and blazed on her face.

Kurt had to know that there was something between her and Trey. *Had been* something, she amended.

She'd surely never admit that she still ached for him, still dreamed of him holding her, kissing her, moving deep, deep inside her. If not for the nightmare of losing Trey, of losing their baby, she'd be sorely tempted to toss aside the thin veil of propriety she clung to and welcome him back in her bed.

Heat burned her cheeks at that inner admission, but she held her head high. "Trey found out that Durant had been cheating Daddy with the cattle. Cheating me even more."

"I suspect Durant was selling off fifty or more head at a time," Trey said.

That drew a frown from Kurt. "You might be right. He approached me about two months back, offering up close to a hundred head of JDB cattle. Good stock, but I was ready to decline until he told me that Daisy was forced to sell them to make ends meet."

"How good of you to help me out in a pinch," she said, stiff with anger that he'd offer that type of charity yet he'd never come by to see how badly she was struggling.

"I did it out of respect for Barton," Kurt said, putting emphasis on *respect*. "He was a damned good man."

He didn't add that she wasn't a damn good woman, and he wouldn't. Daisy knew she'd hurt him. Or maybe just humiliated him. Kicked dirt on his pride. But better now than after they were married and both were miserable.

She hoped he'd realize that one day. Hope that she'd find a damned good man to love.

She thought she had with Trey.

Her brow furrowed. He *was* good, just not that cubby-hole good her daddy wanted for her. Like Kurt.

She felt Trey shift his stance beside her, felt his tension and anger. "Is that the only time he offered you cattle?"

"Nope. Durant came to me just a few weeks back with another fifty head. I declined. Doing good to hang on to what I had with this drought worsening," Kurt said.

Ned could've sold them to another rancher, could've driven them to market, or added them to the cattle he'd been buying off her. She could just scream in frustration when she thought how much that man had swindled out of her.

"You see Durant hanging around?" Trey asked.

"Nope. But he could be holed up on one of the ranches that went bust." Kurt shifted in the saddle and squinted at the remains of the house. "Nothing left here but the land. Are you going to hang on to it or are you ready to sell out?"

"I'm keeping it," she said.

For as long as she could, anyway. How long would that be once Trey rode off again?

Kurt dipped his chin. Eyed her like she was a bug on the wall. "If you change your mind, let me know. I'll give you fair value for the land. Any stock you want to get rid of too."

That would double Kurt's holdings as well as increase his water source. He'd be a cattle baron to be reckoned with. He'd own what he would've gained if she'd married him.

"Just think about it," he said.

She nodded, unable to say more. For though her heart stubbornly wanted to hang on to the JDB, she knew the reality of her running two ranches wasn't promising.

* * *

Trey stood still as stone as Kurt Leonard and his men rode off. He was between a rock and a hard place and didn't like the feeling one damned bit.

Before it had dawned on him that Daisy could be Dade's sister, he'd aimed to buy the Circle 46 and sever all ties to her and the JDB. He hadn't rightly given a damn what happened to her.

At least that's what he kept telling himself. But he did care. He cared too damned much.

The whole time he'd been laid up fighting to live, he'd thought of her. He'd hated her, or he had tried to. The only constant was that he hadn't been able to get her out of his mind. Out of his blood.

Each time he'd thought of her in another man's arms, rage had exploded inside him. Now when the real possibility of her losing everything Barton had owned kicked up like a cyclone on the plains, he was thinking up ways how he could help her hold on to it.

With the JDB rendered to ashes, she'd have to rebuild. That would take time and money. She had plenty of the first, for she could continue living at the Circle 46. But she was as close to dead broke as he was.

And with Kurt offering for the JDB . . . Hell, he was going to have to act fast here or risk ending up on the outside looking in.

He needed land. If she wouldn't sell the Circle 46, then all or a damned good portion of the JDB would do.

It was the thought of convincing her to go along with his plan that gave him heartburn. Right now she was holding on to everything her daddy owned like a bur on wool.

Then there was Dade to figure into this.

When Dade realized what he'd done to Daisy, the shit would hit the fan. His brother wouldn't be forgiving, not when he'd spent years looking for Daisy.

Claiming ignorance of her identity wouldn't wash. She'd

mentioned having memory voids before, but he'd never given them much heed. But then he'd been intent on one thing—seducing the big boss's daughter.

That had proved mighty easy. At times it'd been hard to tell which excited him more—the risk of playing footsie behind Barton's back or the pure pleasure he'd felt each time he'd taken Daisy in his arms.

Now he knew which one set his blood on fire. Wouldn't take much encouragement from her and they'd be right back in bed.

Problem was he couldn't dally with her now that he knew who she really was. He'd written to Dade, and he suspected he'd head here as soon as he got that letter.

Trey surely didn't look forward to the battle that would ensue. Didn't like thinking that Dade might put a bullet in his heart instead of a shotgun in his back.

Yep, the only sure way he could own the land he coveted was to marry Daisy. Might not take more than a few words and sweet loving to get her to agree.

Long as she didn't know he was marrying her to get his hands on the land, all would be fine. He'd just have to find a way to live with the fact that he'd deceived her. Lied to her.

And damn it all but he just couldn't do it. Yep, he was a born bastard. He could be a mean sonofabitch when crossed. He'd never had a problem loving a woman and walking away.

Except this was Daisy, and she stirred something inside him that scared the ever-living shit out of him.

Then there was the fact she'd been hurt enough. By thinking he'd abandoned her. By Barton's death. And now this—seeing her home burned clean to the ground.

Dammit! He wanted the land. Wanted the woman. So why was he dithering over taking both?

Don't cheat a man, and don't break a woman's heart,
Kirby had told them time and again.

Words to live by.

He flicked a glance at Daisy and grimaced, for her emotions were right there for anyone to see. Grief. Defeat. Fear. And sometimes when she looked at him, he caught that glow of warmth and longing before anger distorted it.

She cared for him. Maybe fancied herself in love with him still. Long as she never knew there wasn't any love in him to give to her or anyone, she wouldn't get hurt.

But Dade knew his shortcomings.

Trey wouldn't be able to fool him.

"We'd best head back," he said, steering her toward their horses.

She nodded, looking around. Looking sad. "I want to visit Daddy's grave before I leave."

He nodded and let her lead the way.

They could see for miles, and nothing was stirring, not even a breeze. Her small boots kicked up very little dust, but most of her skirt was covered in West Texas grit all the same.

He could taste the same on his tongue. Feel a fine layer coat his skin.

A man could bake to death out here. He'd come damned close to doing just that.

Because of Daisy. Because of lies and half-truths. Because he'd wanted her. And had taken her.

He'd known the risks and defied them anyway. That was the simple truth.

He could bitch and moan all he wanted. If a randy cowpoke used his daughter, he'd kill the sonofabitch too.

"Daddy told me about the time when Comanches terrorized much of Texas," she said, her breath coming hard as they started up the knoll. "He was a young boy, living on his family's homestead outside San Antonio, but he remembered Indians whooping and hollering. He said his daddy and his uncle stood their ground and fired back. How they were afraid that the house would be torched."

He shaded his eyes and looked over at her and went still, for she looked like those fancy paintings of angels at that moment, with the sun hitting her full in the back and casting a bright aura around her.

"That's what most of the early settlers faced."

"I know." She turned and started back up the slope. "Daddy said that they'd have likely died if the Texas Rangers hadn't ridden in."

"There aren't that many men who can say they survived such," he said.

"So why did they stay? Why face that risk for a place like this?"

He looked at the baked landscape and smiled. "Reckon they were a bit like me. It was their land that they either had claimed or homesteaded. They fought to make a living. Fought the elements and the Indians and the market that tended to fall more than rise. They were willing to die to hold onto it."

She stopped again, her back stiff. "I always thought Daddy was the strongest man I ever knew. I didn't think anything could kill him."

"Barton was a fighter to the core," he agreed.

"I always thought so too," she said. "I thought nothing could make Daddy give up, but that's what happened after he lost his first family. Hollis told me that when the War of the Rebellion ended, Daddy left Texas and moved to Colorado. Why would he leave his home?"

That was something only Barton could answer. But Trey suspected it had a whole lot to do with what the man had been put through in the army, coupled with the deaths of his wife and son at the Circle 46. That he'd tired of killing and fighting to hold on to what was his. That it looked easier to start over all new.

Trey understood that better than most. He'd lived most of his life on the Crown Seven. It was home, yet it had never been solely his. Never would've been, for Kirby had divided what he'd owned between Reid, Dade, and him.

"Sometimes leaving is the best choice a man can make," he said, thinking back to the day when he and Dade had been accused of rustling. "There's a big difference between what a man will risk when he's fighting for his family or his country, and when he's fighting for what is his and his alone," he said.

"But the Circle 46 was his."

"Maybe the title was, but the ghosts of his wife and son were still calling the shots," he said. "A man will either find something better, something that he can call his own, or find what he'd left was better for him and head back home."

For him, there was no going back. What he'd had on the Crown Seven was over, and he was content to hold those good memories and move on. To make his own way.

Holding sole title to a ranch was his dream.

She stopped again at the top of the slope, but this time she glanced back, looking down on him, looking far too troubled. "You think that's why Daddy came back to Texas? Why he bought the JDB?"

"Could be. He made this his home, Daisy," he said. "From what I knew of him, it was a good decision, for he was a damned happy man here on the JDB."

She gave a jerky nod, then started walking again.

It wasn't much farther to the fenced cemetery, but by the time they got there his back was slick with sweat. He felt rivers of it running down his face and neck, felt his hat settle down more with his hair soaked.

The sun was riding high and punished the earth again, as if trying to burn out every blemish, every infraction. He wet dry lips and wished he was somewhere cool. Wished he'd thought to bring a canteen along.

Daisy knelt by Barton's grave, looking as wilted as the plains that stretched out around her. She was a tiny thing, but bending over a grave made her seem even more small and defenseless.

She picked at the dried brush near the tombstone. "I planted bluebonnets in the spring so his grave wouldn't look so bleak, but the drought took them."

"He'd understand, Daisy."

"I know, but it makes me feel that much more of a failure," she said. "I couldn't keep flowers blooming on a grave. How in the hell am I going to run the ranches?"

He sensed her grief, her fear, and remembered the sharp stab of pain that he'd felt once in his life. That'd been when Kirby died.

Though Trey had tried damned hard never to get close to another person, Kirby had breached those defenses. He'd been his pa, and his death had left Trey's heart bleeding.

"You'll do what you have to do," he said.

She made a sound. A muffled snort. A sob maybe. He couldn't tell with the hot wind buffeting his back.

"I suppose so," she said and bowed her head.

He reckoned she was praying, but he didn't understand why. He'd never understood what folks got out of standing over a grave reliving the past. Why the hell did they put themselves through that pain again?

The dead were dead. Best thing to do was move on with life.

That's what Trey had done when Kirby had died. It's what he'd done too when Reid betrayed them and he was cast out of the only home he'd ever known.

Until he'd landed here.

"This is an unforgiving land where only the strongest survive," he said. "Don't take much muscle and brawn. Just strength of will. You've got to want this bad enough to fight for it, for every day there's a new struggle."

Daisy didn't reply as she got to her feet. She swayed a bit and rested her small, gloved hands on the stone.

His eyes narrowed on her, thinking he'd never seen her look so forlorn. He wanted to go to her. Take her in his arms and take her away.

This was her ranch. Her daddy. Her moment of grief. He'd give her a few minutes of privacy.

"We'd best find some shade soon," he said.

"Yes," she said, her voice weak.

He walked to the edge of the knoll to wait. He reckoned she'd shed more than a few tears before this was over, and he wasn't prepared to deal with that emotion.

To the west the plains stretched for miles with not a tree in sight, just a great dun river of land that had baked dry. But if a man stared long enough he saw a sea of inviting water. A mirage. Trick of land and elements that lured many a man to his death.

Yep, this was the kind of weather that separated ranchers into those that had the guts and wherewithal to stick it out and the ones who packed it in and headed back east. He landed square in the first camp even though he didn't have a dime to spare.

He had guts and the burning desire to have his name on a tract of land. And he had nowhere else to go.

This was his best bet.

He knew it. Had known it those longs months he'd been laid up in El Paso.

The question was, what the hell was he going to do about it?

Damned if he knew. He squinted at the horizon where the burned out remains of the ranch stood. He'd come a long way in miles, but no closer to finding any kind of peace.

Maybe that wasn't in the cards for him. Maybe fate took

pleasure in tormenting a bastard like him, giving him a taste of a normal life before snatching it away. Tempting him to let down his guard around a woman and then showing him just how stupid he'd been to do so.

The only thing a man like him could count on was the land and his own courage. He wanted this land. Wanted this woman.

But down deep he was afraid of getting too close to her again. Afraid of the emotions he struggled to hold at bay. Afraid to trust Dade, Daisy—anyone again.

He'd been betrayed twice by those who'd found a way to slip past his defenses. The next time might be the death of him.

He untied his kerchief and mopped his face, certain he'd sweat every drop of moisture from his body in the time he'd been standing here.

"Come on, Daisy," he said, turning to face her.

She lifted bleak eyes to his, her smile sad. Then she crumbled in a heap on the grave.

Chapter 13

Fear slammed into his gut like a mule's kick, driving the air from his lungs. "Daisy!"

He rushed to her and gathered her in his arms, his heart pounding like a smith's hammer. She was burning hot. Her head lolled back against his shoulder, her lips white, her face florid. Her eyes were glassy.

"Why didn't you tell me you were getting woozy?" he asked, but she couldn't answer. "You know better."

But so did he. He'd suffered heat exhaustion six months back, and it took the longest time to recover from it and his other injuries.

He cradled her in his arms and started back down the knoll, damning himself for letting her stay out here this long, for not taking a good look at her earlier. If anything happened to her . . .

That black thought drove a knife through his heart, drawing blood, drawing out the truth he didn't want to face. He could allow himself to care for her on a safe level as his boss's daughter. As Dade's sister.

He could lust after her for the rest of his days and give her all the passion a woman could ever want for. But anything beyond that was shoving him right out there onto thin ice.

With a curse, he blocked those soft thoughts that eroded a man's will from his head and viewed her like he would any hand who'd suffered heat exhaustion. Get her out of the sun. Cool her down outside and in.

It took forever to walk back to the house. Further still to reach the old adobe hut that had escaped the fire.

The horses were ground tethered to an old hitching post beside the hut and whickered softly at his approach. They were content with the little bit of shade offered by the adobe.

He kicked open the door and pushed inside. The dim interior was a welcome relief after suffering the punishing sun.

He stopped dead in his tracks, eyes narrowed to take in his surroundings. Something scurried in a corner. A mouse, likely.

"Where are we?" she asked, voice halting, eyes closed.

"The old adobe."

Barton had used the old house to store barrels of grain, but those had been moved to the Circle 46. Nothing was left inside but the beehive fireplace in the corner. Only furniture was a chair made of interlocking cattle horns with the seat covered in cowhide.

He sat her down gently on the chair that was nearly big enough for two. It was certainly large enough for her to rest against the curved bowl made by the horns.

"How can a woman who's lived her life in West Texas not realize when the sun was getting to her?" he asked, his big fingers fumbling to untie her bonnet.

"Don't. Know," she whispered, still not opening her eyes.

Dammit, she was limp as a dishrag. He cupped her shoulders and bent close to her.

"Daisy, look at me." He waited until her eyelids fluttered open, but the vague look she cast him didn't ease his mind one damned bit. "I want you to unbutton your bodice so we can cool your body down. You hear me?"

She swallowed. "Okay."

He removed her bonnet that was covered in dust. Hell, everything was covered in grit.

He hooked the bonnet on a bit of horn tip protruding on the chair back and went outside to fetch the canteens. Both horses lifted their heads. His gelding whickered.

They'd hit the worst part of the day now, and the sun was bearing down on the animals again. He'd hoped to be miles from here by now. Back to where a man could find a few trees and water. Back to being around people so he wasn't reminded how good it'd felt to be alone with her.

The saddles needed to come off. The horses rubbed down and watered. But he didn't want to risk taking time for them with Daisy so bad off.

"If she doesn't respond soon I don't know what I'll do," he told the gelding as he lifted the canteens off the saddle horns.

Exposing her to more sun was too great a risk. Hell, it wouldn't do either of them any good now. That meant they'd have to stay here, and he had very few provisions.

Bemoaning the fact wouldn't help a thing. He was as much to blame as her for being in this state, because he'd let her tarry. He'd stood beside her woolgathering and baking like a fresh-made adobe brick.

Now she was the one suffering for them both being fools.

He was back inside in no time. She hadn't moved. Hadn't even attempted to undress.

It dawned on him that she didn't have the strength. He'd have to do it for her.

He set the canteens aside and fumbled to undo the tiny buttons on her bodice, a task he'd had no trouble doing when they'd met in the hayloft. When he'd been anxious to shuck her from her clothes and kiss every silken inch of her. Sink into her and feel that rightness that he'd never felt with another woman. With anyone.

But there was no seduction or lust driving his moves now. Just hope that she'd snap out of this in time.

Her eyelids inched open again, and those big eyes fixed on his. "Sorry."

"So am I," he said as he peeled her shirt from her.

Sorry for all he'd put her through. Sorry he couldn't be the kind of man she deserved.

He tugged off his bandana and snapped the dust from it before he wet it down, using care not to waste their water. He draped it over her fine chemise, and she sucked in air.

"Better?"

"Umm."

He found a fancy handkerchief in her pocket and did the same with it, then laid it over her forehead. That earned him another sigh, which he took as a good sign. At least she hadn't passed out, but it'd been close. Too close.

"Take a few sips. No more or you'll get sick." He held the canteen to her mouth.

She did as asked. "Tastes good."

He nodded and eased her back down, acutely aware this was a slow process. He sat back on his haunches and took a long swig of water. It wasn't cold by any means, but it was wet and eased his parched throat.

Problem was they didn't have much water. One look at Daisy's pale face and bleary eyes convinced him she'd need rest and water before she could ride.

They'd have to spend the night here.

"I'm gonna see to the horses," he said.

She mouthed, "Okay."

The kerchief he'd laid on her chest was drying, the edges losing the dark color of moisture. He wondered if there was any water to be had in the well now. If he could just get enough for the horses and keep her cool, they could manage with the rest.

As for food, he had a can of beans in his saddlebag. Maybe one of peaches. It'd be pure luck if he could scare up a rabbit to add to it.

Minutes seemed to crawl by as he dragged the saddles from both horses and set them in the shade of the adobe to dry. He slipped inside to check her before seeing if he could find water. Her breathing was even, but her face was still on the red side.

He cursed the way everything had turned out and lead the horses toward the remains of the barn. The wooden corrals had burnt along with everything else, but the old pen where Barton had kept his prize Hereford bull was intact.

The well-strung barbed wire would do well for the horses. That old mesquite standing in the center would provide a bit of shade, even though the tree had dropped most of its leaves in order to survive the drought.

He cracked a smile. The tree was the only one of any size on the JDB, an old spreading native that many ranchers cursed more than a weed. But Barton had kept it to shade his bull, and that old bull had gotten fat off the leaves and bean pods of that tree.

He turned the horses into the pen, then headed over to the well. The handle let out a god-awful screech as he manned it, going slow, hoping to hell something besides dust would fall into the tin pail.

Sweat streamed from him, soaking his shirt and jeans. But the intense sun dried him off almost as quickly.

He was about to give up when the barest stream of water splashed into the pail. It wasn't dry. But it wasn't enough to sustain life for long either.

So he went slow, pumping a bit at a time, careful not to spill a drop.

When that pail was full, he carried it into the pen and toward the short trough set up under the tree. Maybe in shade the water wouldn't evaporate as fast, though he suspected the horses would drink this up.

"Enjoy it," he said as he filled the trough. "Might be a spell before you get more.

He headed straight back to the well and began the process all over again. It took longer this time to get another pail filled and carried to the adobe.

She'd somehow curled into a corner of the big chair, her head resting against a knot of horns and her legs tucked under her skirt. Her eyes were closed, but then she hadn't been able to keep them open since she keeled over on Barton's grave.

"Feel any better?" he asked as he toted the bucket inside and found a crock that would hold the water.

"So tired," she said, her voice weary.

"That's to be expected."

He carried the crock outside and upended it to give the bottom a good pounding. Last thing he wanted to do was dump their precious water into a crock that could just as easily be home to a rattler.

Nothing fell out but dust and the finest bit of chaff off grain.

He took it back inside and carefully poured most of the water into the crock. "This will have to do for cooling you down. Ain't the cleanest, but you're covered in grit anyway."

That earned him a fleeting grin. He returned it, but she didn't see. Just as well. Her chest was still rising and falling too quickly, and her face was still pink.

He took the dried bandana off her chest and doused it in water. A whiff of her scent rose from the wet cloth, mingling with the smell of his sweat.

It stirred to life the memory that was never far from his mind. Of the two of them back in that hayloft, arms and legs entwined and bodies writhing as one.

Dammit, he shouldn't be thinking about sex now. But seeing her lying there tempted him to claim what he'd been denied the past six months.

The wet bandana had plastered her chemise to her bosom and rendered it nigh on transparent. Not that he needed to see her naked to remember that the tips of her breasts were the color of a ripe peach. That her nipples would bud under his thumb and forefinger or his tongue.

That her skin smelled of roses and tasted like honey, warm and sweet and smooth.

That despite his desire for revenge and big talk, he was hard with wanting her in his arms again.

"This will be a shock," he said.

He squeezed a little water from the bandana then plopped it on her chest. She sucked in a sharp breath, her back arching, small hands clamping onto his wrists so hard he knew her nails scored half-moons on his skin.

Just as quickly she relaxed; her hands slipped off his to fall in her lap. "Mmm."

"Rest." He doused her handkerchief in the pail, wrung it out, and laid the cool folded cloth back on her forehead. "I'll be back as soon as I tend to the horses."

She didn't reply, but he hadn't expected her to. He grabbed the pail and headed back out into the blistering heat, unnerved by the new emotions playing hell inside him.

He managed to pump another pail of water before the well played out. Just as well because he was about spent too.

Today seemed a helluva lot hotter to him. He was sweating like hell, but it evaporated long before it could cool him down.

Thank God the adobe was still standing. Otherwise they'd be huddled with the horses under the thin shade of the old mesquite.

After he filled their canteens, he carried the pail into the pen and poured the rest of the water into the small trough. It'd be enough to see the horses through the rest of the day, and what they didn't use in the adobe would give the animals a drink before they headed out in the morning.

Morning. Damned, they'd have to spend the night together in the adobe. Just the two of them with her half dressed.

"If this ain't one helluva fix," he said.

His gelding whickering softly, as if agreeing. Daisy's mare tossed her head once, as if moving away from the few long bean pods was too damned much to ask.

Trey kicked at the baked ground, cussing roundly that there was little for the horses to eat except leaves and mesquite pods. He hated leaving them here where they could pick up a damned thorn. Hated that he'd tarried too long with Daisy, his thoughts centered on getting his hands on a land title instead of on getting the hell out of here when they could.

Now they'd be obliged to wait until she was fit to ride. He could hope that would be tonight, but he wasn't going to bet on it.

He squinted at the hazy horizon. Nothing out there. At least nothing he could see. But he knew this land. He knew there were plenty of arroyos and draws a person could hide in. Was Ned out there watching? Had he moved on?

Trey suspected the latter. Torching the JDB was nothing more than revenge against Daisy. He'd already conned her out of countless head of cattle. Nothing was left for Ned to gain.

It made his own quest for vengeance seem small and mean. Hell, what was the point now?

She'd lost damned near everything. Because he'd trusted Barton, he'd lost all the money he'd saved back.

For once he and Daisy were in the same fix. They needed each other to survive.

Considering who she was and what they'd done, it was damned near a given that he couldn't leave her. He'd surely sever all ties forever with Dade if he didn't make things right by Daisy. But hadn't he done that already?

Nope, whatever happened here had to be because he and Daisy wanted it. Nobody else mattered. Not Barton. Not Dade. Not any law.

They'd have to find a way to make this work. For now he'd mull on it. When they got back to the Circle 46, he'd have a long talk with her.

He trudged from the pen and up the slope to the adobe, anxious to get back to it. Back to Daisy. No sense denying it.

The sun pounded his back as if trying to fry his skin through his clothes. He wouldn't be surprised if it could.

Inside the adobe, Daisy hadn't moved from when he'd left her. But her eyes were mostly open now. Open and wary.

"Feeling better?" he asked.

Her small hands fluttered over her belly, as if unsure what to shield from his eyes. "Some. My head still hurts."

"It will for a while. Need to get water in you now."

"I'm parched." She grasped the canteen he handed her and took a greedy drink.

He pulled the canteen away from her mouth. "Just sip at it. You drink too much and it'll come right back up."

She nodded and did as he said, then passed the canteen to him. He too wanted to guzzle it, but he went slow, letting the water trickle down his parched throat. A man appreciated water more this way.

"How are the horses?" she asked.

"I put them in the pen where we'd kept the bull," he said and cracked a smile. "That old mesquite doesn't cast much shade, but it beats standing out in a full sun."

A smile trembled on her mouth. "When it was hot, that bull wouldn't move away from that tree."

Food, water, and shade. Creature comforts.

He took the dry cloth from her forehead and noted the worst of the red was fading now. "Still hot?"

"Inside and out."

"It'll take a bit to get the heat out of you."

He went through the ritual of soaking her handkerchief and his bandana again, staring at his hands instead of her lying there in barely anything. She had no idea just how inviting she was to him.

"Tell me about Dade," she said.

He wrung the cloths out and frowned, thinking it was mighty strange for her to be asking him about her brother. But then he'd known Dade far longer and had been as close to him as any blood kin could be. Closer as far as Trey was concerned.

"What do you want to know?" he asked as he draped the bandana over her chest then laid the other on her forehead.

Her eyelids fluttered shut on a sigh. She didn't say anything for so long he thought she'd dozed off.

"What kind of man is he?" she asked.

He grabbed his bedroll and knelt in the corner to lay it out, giving him time to pull his thoughts of Dade together. "He's a good man. Reckon a good bit of that came from Kirby taking us in and teaching us right from wrong."

A good deal came from Dade's disgust over his old man being an outlaw. He'd always cringe when news of the Logan Gang reached the ranch.

"I'm glad," she said.

So was he, though he hadn't always been that way.

He'd been mighty jealous that Dade and Reid had a tie to family. Didn't matter that their families weren't worth two hoops in hell. They knew who they were.

They knew their damned names.

Trey shook off the old resentment that had dogged him most of his life and settled back on the bedroll, drawing one bent leg up and hanging his wrist over his knee.

It felt good to rest his back against the cool adobe walls. Felt good to relax here with Daisy, sharing sparse talk. Sharing the same air.

It had taken a whole year for him to feel that kind of contentment on the Crown Seven. He'd always been expecting to get tossed out on his ear. For the whole dream of having a makeshift family to fall apart on him.

Damned if it didn't happen when he least expected it.

"I suppose he's a rancher too," she said, breaking the silence.

"That's what we were growing up, but Dade always talked about having a farm. Maybe run a few head of cattle too."

She wrinkled her pert nose. "A sodbuster."

"You sound like Barton."

"That's all I know," she said. "All I remember."

They'd never talked much before, but then the stolen moments they'd had were spent in each other's arms. Yep, they hadn't talked much at all, at least not about things that mattered.

"What about you, Daisy? Are you going to keep both ranches?"

Her deep sigh filled the silence. "I don't know if I can."

An honest answer and one he admired her for making. "You don't have to do it alone."

Her eyes popped open at that, wide and searching his across the room. "Who's going to stand by me? Dade?

Because if you're insinuating that he'll come in and take over for me . . ."

"I didn't mean that at all." Damn, he was handling this badly again.

He shifted on the bedroll, feeling suddenly big and clumsy and unsure of himself around her. "Dade can't take over anything unless you let him."

"But he'll try."

He bit off a curse and got to his feet. "Both ranches are yours, Daisy. You can do whatever the hell you want with them. Sell out. Hire a foreman to manage for you." His gaze caught and held hers. "You could marry and work with your husband to run both spreads."

She sat up a bit straighter in the chair, the handkerchief and bandana falling into her lap. "You want to buy the Circle 46. Is that it?"

He shifted from one foot to the other. "It's no secret I want the land. But I want you too."

"Are you angling to marry me because you want to get your hands on the land?" Her eyes bored into his, as if searching his soul. "Or do you love me?"

He sure couldn't admit to the first without looking like a money-grubber. And he damned sure wouldn't lie about the second.

"We were good together, Daisy."

She jerked her head away like he'd insulted her and crossed her arms over her breasts. Dammit, he couldn't understand how her mind worked.

"That's not the same as love," she said.

No, it wasn't. But it was the best he could give her. The best he could give anyone.

He took the discarded bandana and handkerchief and wet them again. She curled back against the chair, eyes closed. Shutting him out.

He felt the distancing as sharply as when he'd been laid up in El Paso. Without a word, he draped the cooling cloths on her then strode over to his saddlebags.

"I've got a can of beans and one of tomatoes. Not much in the way of dinner—"

"I'm not hungry."

"You should eat something."

She didn't answer. Fine.

He'd fill his own void and settle in for the night. But the food didn't sit well in his gut and neither did the silence pulsing in the adobe.

It promised to be a damned long night.

Daisy laid her hands on her stomach and suffered through another cramp. Her body was wrapped in pain, her insides twisting.

There is nothing we can do to stop it, Ramona had told her.

She was losing the baby. The fall had been too much.

Silent tears streamed down her cheeks and the pain . . . Oh, God, she ached for the loss. For the death of the one thing that still tied her to Trey.

Gone. All gone.

"Daisy! What's wrong?"

"It hurts," she said, caught between dream and reality since he'd not come before. "I'm sorry."

"You've nothing to be sorry for," he said and gently pulled her against him.

She fit against him so well. Her palms splayed on his chest, so muscular and bare. Just like she remembered from the time in the hayloft. Just them together. Only they lost the baby.

The tears fell faster now, even though the cramping in her stomach had eased.

"Daisy, wake up!"

She did with a start and blinked, confused to see Trey here before she realized she'd confused her nightmare with reality. She'd relived the agony of losing her baby too many times, but this time she wasn't imagining his arms around her. Holding her. Comforting her. He was really here.

My God, had she talked in her sleep? Could he know?

"You were having a nightmare," he said, no censure in his voice.

She nodded woodenly. He didn't know. Her secret was still safe. Still her grief to hold close to her heart until she knew what was in his.

The velvet night wrapped around them like a protective cocoon. She breathed in his scent. Felt the tension stiffening his muscles as he pulled back from her.

"What's hurting?" he asked, and she was glad he couldn't read the truth that must surely be reflected in her eyes.

Her heart. God, her heart ached for what they'd lost. What he couldn't give her then and wouldn't give her now.

Oh, he'd marry her. But there'd be no love.

She'd be nothing more than his lover. And God, she even craved that with a hunger that should have shamed her.

"My stomach cramped some," she said.

The sudden stabs of pain had been just enough to plague her mind in sleep and stir awake memories that wouldn't die. Just enough to make her relive that nightmare again, making it seem too real this time.

"It's the heat," he said, one big hand moving slowly up and down her back, comforting her, rousing other memories that were just as strong as her grief. "You need to take in a bit more water."

She nodded and sipped at the canteen he handed her,

knowing he was right. But she also admitted that what she wanted was right here holding her. That she wanted to feel that deep connection to him again.

That she loved him still.

Nothing was stopping her from taking what she desired most. Nothing but her pride.

Chapter 14

Daisy cupped his jaw and leaned close, her own eyes drifting shut. She pressed a light kiss at the corner of his mouth. Another on his chin. Then beneath it.

"I've missed you," she said, her voice so soft it was nearly a sigh on the wind.

Her mind registered his quick, indrawn breath, the stilling of his hands on her back. "Daisy?"

She didn't want to talk. Didn't want to admit that she wanted this. Needed this. It made no sense after the cold-shoulder she'd given him.

Her desire for him was stronger than her pride. Stronger than reason.

"We have nothing to lose," she said against his lips.

His only response was the slightest tremor shaking his big body. "Dade would nail my hide on the barn if he knew I'd taken you before. That I'd come back and fallen into your bed again."

"I don't care what he thinks," she said. "He's my brother, not my keeper."

"He might not see it that way."

"Then he's in for a surprise." She rested her forehead

against his and breathed in his scent, taking him deep into her lungs as she longed to do with her body.

She felt his smile beneath her fingertips, brief and a bit crooked. An endearing smile that made her feel special because it was so rare with him.

"What am I going to do with you?" he asked.

Love me! She bit back the words because she didn't want anything to shatter the moment, but the truth sang in her heart.

The first time she'd laid eyes on him, she'd fallen a bit in love. He was different than any man she'd ever met. Aloof. A drifter who made no apology for what he was.

She had so little experience with men, but she knew when she exchanged a shy glance with Trey that he wouldn't be a gentleman. He wouldn't stop at a few stolen kisses for fear her daddy would catch them.

Like Kurt, who never went a step beyond propriety, even though they were engaged to marry. She'd tried to feel something deep for him, but it wasn't there. She knew it never would be.

But Trey March was the forbidden. He didn't fawn over her. He made her come to him. And when she did, he didn't shy away from showing her the pleasure to be found in a man's arms.

"All my life I've bowed to a man's orders," she said, grazing his lips once, twice. "No more."

She settled her mouth over his, explored the seductive curve of his lips as she dragged her fingertips over the rasp of today's whiskers. He hadn't given anything of himself yet, just remained kneeling in front of the chair. But she sensed the tension rippling under his skin, felt his body shudder when she slipped her tongue under his upper lip.

The same tremor rocked her as she sucked on his mouth, his chin. Her secret lay between them like a sore. She should tell him. Tell him now and get it over with. And if he pulled away from her? If he denied her this moment's passion?

She pulled back and damned the fact she couldn't see his face in the darkness. But maybe that was better. Then she wouldn't see the emotions in his eyes.

"We've been through hell together," she began.

A deep groan tore from him. His arms banded around her and he pulled her flush against him.

"I can show you heaven, Daisy. I did before and I can again," he said, shoving her chemise up to bare her breasts to him. "If you want me."

If she wanted him? "Of course I do," she said, trailing gentle fingers down the steely line of his jaw. "But after you left I found out . . ."

The words died in her throat as his mouth closed over one breast and suckled hard. Her back bowed and her fingers threaded through his hair, holding him, holding words back that had no place here.

She couldn't let anything interfere with this moment, not when she'd relived it countless times. She'd convinced herself that the memory was better than reality, but she had been wrong.

She could almost convince herself that he cared deeply for her. Loved her. But he didn't.

Don't think about it. Just feel.

Don't spoil the moment with the truth, for nothing can be gained by it now. It didn't matter how it happened. Whose fault it was. It was over. Over.

"So good, so good," she said as the pressure inside her built until she thought her skin would split.

"It gets better," he said, his fingers tugging her drawers down and his mouth following.

Her skin burned but from a different fire than before. He grasped her bare hips and pulled her forward.

His palms skimmed up her bared legs to the place that wept for his possession. "We've never done this in the dark."

No, it'd always been light or twilight, stolen moments when she sneaked to the barn, when her daddy was busy or away. She'd been embarrassed to tears the first time, but the intense pleasure overrode modesty.

And then he was kissing her there, his tongue a blade of fire that shot heat through her. Her back bowed and her hands dropped to his shoulders, her fingers digging in tight. If she lost her hold on him, she might splinter off into the sky.

Each thrust of his tongue and intimate stroke of his fingers pushed her to the pinnacle, a bright orb that was warm and welcoming and promised an end to her confusion, her turmoil.

He'd taught her this, made her mourn the loss of him, this wickedly intimate closeness. In this she surrendered to him.

The admission struck like lightning and was gone, for she simply couldn't think any longer. Just feel his incredible mouth and fingers playing her.

She arched her back, desperate to get closer, to touch his heart as he had hers. Brilliant lights flared behind her eyes as she drifted upward on a tight, hot spiral. Her entire body convulsed in delicious release.

His name exploded from her, her fingers clutching at him, trying to pull him closer. She held on, for it had never been this intense before.

Strong arms banded around her and crushed her to his bare chest as she surrendered to the last tremors of her release. This press of bare skin to bare skin was what she'd dreamed about, what she wanted.

He dropped backward, falling onto the bedroll, taking her down with him. She sprawled on top of him, her mouth seeking his in a kiss that went on and on until they both gasped for breath.

"Now I have you where I want you," she said between kisses, as her hands skimmed down his slick chest to the buttons on his jeans.

"Want me how?" he asked in a lazy drawl that made her smile. "Naked? On my back?"

"Yes." She slipped open the first button with ease, then fumbled a bit on the second. *"Yes!"*

He groaned and stiffened. "Easy, darlin'. I'm full to bursting from wanting you."

She smiled at that and pressed a kiss on his throat before levering herself up to straddle him. She scraped her fingernails down his chest and under his waistband.

"I'll be gentle with you," she said.

That dredged a chuckle from him until her knuckles brushed against his arousal. The ache deep inside her doubled, making her tremble.

It'd be easy to let him have his way now. To make love with him and end this torture.

But this was her chance to do what she'd been too shy to do before. To make him yield to her. To be the aggressor. To force him to surrender his body to her even though he kept his heart locked.

She couldn't think about that now, for it would only cast a pall over this moment with him. She'd waited too long for him to return. To have him like this again.

"You taste good," she said as she dropped kisses on his hard nipples, making his breath hiss between his teeth. She shimmied down his body, kissing him, reveling in his salty taste. "Shuck your jeans, cowboy."

He lifted his hips and gave them a shove. She rocked back on her heels and pulled them and his drawers down his long legs.

She pushed the clothes aside and ran her hands up his

calves sprinkled with crisp hair, wishing again it wasn't so dark. Not that she needed light.

She knew the hair was black. Knew it grew sparse on his chest and arrowed down to a thatch at his groin.

Her palms skimmed up the insides of his thighs, hesitating as she felt the ridge of scars that hadn't been there before. The torture of being dragged, she reasoned, sliding up his long, powerful legs, fitting between his thighs, hoping this would take away his pain.

She'd known what to expect when they'd made love the first time, for she'd found a book of her mother's and read it cover to cover. But the author of *Eve's Daughter* warned that sex was for procreation. That seeking orgasms would lead to a nervous disorder.

The book was too vague and full of misconceptions to be any further use to her. So she was only going on instinct here. Instinct and strong desire.

"If I do something wrong—"

"You know there is no right or wrong in this," he said, his voice thick now. "But you don't have to do this."

"I want to." And before he could talk her out of it, she took him in hand and guided him to her mouth.

Her hands stroked down his hardened length and found the soft sack. She cupped it gently with one hand, stroking it with her thumb.

Her tongue laved the tip of his shaft, marveling at the velvety folds that became more rigid in her hands. The salty essence of him that left her thirsting for more.

He sucked in a sharp breath and bucked. "Good God, woman, you'll be the death of me yet. But I couldn't think of a better way to die."

She understood that completely, for when he'd loved her with his mouth, she'd thought she'd splinter apart from the overwhelming pleasure exploding in her.

That's what she wanted him to feel. That this moment

with her was special. That if he looked deep enough within his heart he'd find that he loved her.

"I can't take any more," he rasped, trying to pull her back up his chest.

But she held tight, emboldened by the power she had over this strong man who always held a part of himself back. She was determined to expose him, to get him to let down his guard if only this once.

She felt his body tense even more, felt a tremor rip through him, and gained satisfaction knowing she'd given him this. His fingers tightened in her hair, holding her to him, clinging like she had when she feared she'd be flung into the sky beyond the stars.

She took him in, surprised at the workings of his body as well. Her heart warmed, for in that spate of time when he was caught in his climax, she held him in her arms, protecting him, loving him.

When it was over and his big body relaxed, she kissed her way up his chest. Her head rested over his heart, and she smiled at the strong, sure beat that kept time with her own.

"Come here," he said, dragging her up until their mouths met.

This kiss was unlike any they'd had. Tender. Passionate.

It was as if his kiss was saying what was in his heart, saying words that she feared she'd never hear from him. Yes, she was likely deluding herself, but she held fast to the fantasy because she wanted it so very much.

Then the kiss changed again, becoming bolder, stroking her until she writhed atop him. "Yes," she moaned against his mouth, groping for his length.

She wanted him in her now, but he seemed in no hurry to oblige her. "Slow down," he said. "We've got all night."

That was certainly true, yet she felt a desperation to make love to him now. "I want this more than once. I want to make love with you throughout the night so I can remember every second."

"I'm not leaving again. Not unless you boot me out." He stroked a hand down her spine to cup her bottom, fingers splayed to hold her, caress her. "Is that what you're fixing to do because I won't tell you pretty words that mean nothing?"

She pressed her palm over his heart. "I know you feel something for me. Something good."

His big hands cupped her hips and yanked her against his hot, hard length. "That's what I feel. Lust. I want you, and you want me."

"Yes, but love is stronger. You're in my heart—"

His mouth captured hers again, smothering the words. She struggled to pull free, to hold on to her thought, to tell him she loved him, to tell him about the child they'd created in love and lost. But his sensual assault on her was too powerful for her to resist.

There was no urgency. She could tell him tomorrow or the next day.

With her mind free of that worry, she succumbed with a groan, kissing him back. His hands coaxed her legs apart though she needed little urging.

A stroke of his fingers over the moist, sensitive cleft between her legs made her buck against him. "Don't make me wait."

He didn't. His hands lifted her hips. "Guide me home."

Home. She smiled, for when they connected as only a man and woman could, she felt at home too. Protected. Safe. She felt the rightness of it seep into her soul.

Another groan ripped from him as he held her there, making her take him in slowly when she wanted all of him now. Wanted everything he had to give her.

"So good," she said as her body stretched to take all of him.

"I ain't complaining," he said, voice choked now.

Then he started moving in her, deep, strong thrusts that set every nerve in her on fire. Coherent thought skittered away on an exhaled breath.

She held onto him as he took her into the place only they'd been together. A place where fear didn't exist. Where he was her anchor in this world and beyond.

"Trey," she gasped as she soared past the stars to that place of contentment that only he could take her to.

Distantly she heard her name on his breath, a reverent whisper that touched her more deeply than anything ever could. She jerked once more as stars exploded around her, clinging to him, feeling his heart thundering against hers.

She collapsed on him, spent in body and mind. Her last thought before she drifted off to sleep was that she never wanted this moment with this man to end.

Trey had always banked on two things that would knock him out. Getting sloppy-assed drunk and sex.

The first had never failed him, though as he'd gotten older and wiser, he'd refrained from that particular endeavor. Sex, though, he could count on every time.

Or had been able to until he'd met Daisy Barton.

He had attributed his inability to doze off after he made love with her the first time to an innate sense of survival. He sure as hell hadn't wanted to get caught buck naked with the boss's equally naked daughter in his arms.

All the stolen moments with her after that he painted with the same excuse. Getting nookie on the side did have its risks.

But there was no accounting for why he was lying here with her snuggled up against him while he was wide awake.

No reason except the bald fact that she wanted something from him that he didn't think he'd be able to give. He didn't know what love was. Didn't understand how a man felt if afflicted with the emotion.

He'd shared a strong bond with his foster brothers, but he'd never loved them. He respected Reid and Dade. He knew he could count on them to be there for him through thick and thin.

At least it'd been that way for a dozen or more years until Reid had turned on them.

How the hell could he make her understand that he'd be there for her until she drew her last breath? That she could depend on him to protect her and pleasure her?

He didn't know. She wanted those flowery words. He could promise her anything tangible. He'd be at her side always. But he couldn't tell her something that didn't exist—at least for him.

He skimmed his palm down her bare back to the inviting curve of her hip, certain he'd never known a more perfectly formed woman. Never met one who fit him like a glove until Daisy.

A contented sound escaped her in sleep to torment him, for that pleased rest she enjoyed was eluding him now. She had him between a rock and a hard place.

He gathered her close and buried his face in her silken hair. She needed him. Needed a man to guard her back.

She surely didn't want Dade telling her what to do. And wouldn't that be one helluva row when he learned Daisy had grit?

Nope, she wanted Trey to be her husband, the man she leaned on in hard times, the one she clung to when wounds needed to be salved. The man who would show her pleasure the best he knew how for as long as he drew breath.

But she didn't want him unless he loved her. Shit, he couldn't lie to her. But the truth would have her walking away, and he couldn't let that happen either.

She was his. Had been his since the first time he took

her innocence. Why couldn't she see that? Why couldn't she be happy with what he could give her?

Women! Hellfire, what was he going to do with Daisy Barton?

Daisy woke with the first pale fingers of dawn that stretched into the smoky sky and filled the adobe with a warm glow. She loved this time of morning when the air was cool.

She loved this morning more because she finally awoke with Trey beside her. He looked younger in sleep. Untroubled. Handsome.

His body was honed. Lean. And horribly scarred.

Whitish strips banded his hips and thighs, though the left side looked worse. The marks from being dragged behind a horse. Left for dead.

Like Sam Weber. That man had died, but somehow Trey had survived.

My God, how he must have suffered!

She eased from the bedroll and quietly dressed. Everything between them was still so much of a jumble.

She loved him. Always would.

He wouldn't admit to any tender feelings, yet every kiss, every caress, left her feeling wanted. Cherished.

Now he wanted to marry her.

If only he'd proposed to her instead of suggesting in a roundabout way that they marry.

If only it was for love, but she knew his offer was based on two reasons. He wanted the land that passed to her. And he likely felt duty bound to marry her because she was Dade Logan's sister.

His loyalty to her brother was admirable but misplaced in this. Trey had to want her more than anything. Not because of the land. Not because of who she was.

Not even because the world stopped twirling when they made love.

She slipped from the cabin and attended to her needs behind the sage nearest the adobe. This land was unforgiving, never bending. She'd grown up here knowing no different, yet the past few days living at the Circle 46 had been a welcome change.

"What am I going to do, Daddy?"

Like she had all the mornings spent at the JDB since his death, she walked toward the fenced cemetery on the knoll. Without the barn and the house, the land looked more bleak than ever.

The sun sat on the horizon like an arc of white fire by the time she reached the cemetery. She dropped to her knees at his tombstone and stared at the inscription.

Beloved husband to Corinne and loving father to Daisy.

She hadn't realized how true those words were until she had learned her daddy's secret. Jared Barton had taken in an orphan and raised her as his own, all because his wife pined so for a child.

Her lost memory had been an asset to him as well, for Daisy had never questioned her paternity. She never had a reason to do so.

She'd had a good life as the Bartons' daughter. Spoilt. Her daddy coddled her. Protected her the best he could.

She'd had a carefree life. She'd been loved. God only knew what would have become of her if Jared Barton hadn't come into her life.

An image of cowering in a carriage with an austere man flashed in and out of her memory. She tried to catch it, to examine it, but it was gone.

She shook her head, wondering what mysteries her memory still held. Wondering if there'd be more secrets that would come to life and send her world tipping on its end again.

"Oh, Daddy, why didn't you teach me how to run this ranch?" she asked and then laughed wryly. "I know. There was no need. You aimed to marry me off to Kurt. He'd pick up where you left off. He'd take care of me."

But she couldn't marry a man she didn't love. Wouldn't marry a man when she was carrying another's baby.

Her hand stole to her belly, and her eyes drifted shut. She'd never been afraid of her daddy, but she'd feared telling him the truth about her and Trey. But even before she'd known she was with child, she'd known she had to tell him the truth because she couldn't go through with a loveless marriage.

"I rehearsed how to tell you so many times," she said. "There just wasn't any easy way."

So she had just told him straight out that she wouldn't marry Kurt. That she loved Trey. That they'd become lovers and she wanted to marry the cowboy. And then she had braced herself for his explosion of anger.

It'd been a terrible thing to witness. She'd never been afraid of her daddy before, but she'd cowered that day as he ranted and raved and heaped invectives on Trey March.

Later, her daddy had been her silent supporter when she'd told Kurt that she didn't want to marry him. Kurt had begged her to reconsider, begged her father to force her to do as promised, but her daddy had remained her champion.

"Sorry, my friend. It's Daisy's choice," her daddy had said, and Kurt had left the house in a red-faced huff.

Then her daddy had vowed to find Trey and drag his ass back here. A shotgun wedding had loomed in her future then, weeks before she'd known she was pregnant.

But Trey had vanished. Day after day, she had gone to the hayloft and clung to bittersweet memories.

Months later, a shotgun wedding was no longer necessary, for she'd stepped wrong in the loft and took that awful fall.

She rubbed her brow and looked up into the now full sun, wishing it would burn off the fog that swirled around that heartbreaking event. As many times as she'd been in that hayloft, how could she not have noticed that a feeding door had been left open?

She closed her eyes, seeing herself stumble. Fall.

But she forced herself to relive that scene again and again. She'd been near blinded by tears. Weak with heartache over Trey abandoning her when she needed him most. Her heart hurt too over disappointing her daddy so.

She'd stumbled. Fell.

An accident. She'd simply lost her footing as she walked across the thick hay in the loft.

No! She went still as a biting chill swept over her.

She hadn't been alone. Someone had been waiting for her in the loft. Laying a trap.

But she hadn't realized it until she was walking toward the haymow. Until she'd heard the scuff of a boot. Until she turned and saw the shadowy form of a man reaching out for her.

"Oh, my God," she'd said, pressing a trembling hand to her mouth and feeling strong hands yank her against him. "Let me go!"

"I'll make you forget March." His voice was a rumble of sound. Threatening. Distorted and terrifying as the memory.

"No!" But a hand over her mouth stifled her scream.

She had clawed at the hands that tried to lift her skirt, hands that were pulling her down to the bed of hay. Panic choked her, but the sweet memories she'd made here with Trey gave her strength.

She shoved hard and heard him fall, felt his grip loosen just enough for her to break free. She ran to the mow, drawing in air to scream her lungs out.

And fell through the trap door that had been left open. Her scream died in her throat as she hit her head going down. Pain blinded her, then exploded within her as she lay on the hard ground below. Then blackness. Blessed blackness that stayed with her for days and that had shrouded her already shaky memory for over six months.

"It wasn't an accident, Daddy," she said. "I was running from a man in the loft. Oh, God, he was going to rape me."

"Wondered when you'd remember that," Ned drawled, his voice too close, too similar to what was going through her mind.

She shot to her feet and whipped around, shocked that he'd sneaked up on her now and furious that he'd robbed her of her baby. Hers and Trey's baby. "Why did you do it?"

He flashed her an oily smile that made her skin crawl. "I didn't."

"I don't believe you."

He shrugged. "Makes no never mind to me. I wasn't the only one who knew you'd been sneaking off for a roll in the hay with March. Knew it was just a matter of time before Barton found out and arranged a quick wedding, whether March knocked you up or not. Then I'd be out on my ass."

She saw the truth in his dark eyes and cringed. "So you had to get rid of Trey first."

A cruel smile pulled at Ned's mouth. "Thought I had, but when your old man said he aimed to find March, I went back to look for his carcass and haul it back here, but there wasn't nothing there. Knew if varmints had gotten to him, I'd have found parts of him scattered about. So I figured the chances were good he was alive. That he'd recover and come back gunning for me."

Which is exactly what had happened. Her fingers bunched into tight fists when she thought of what this man had put her through. What he'd put Trey through.

"So you decided to kill me instead?"

He affected an indolent shrug that made her want to wretch. "Hell, no. I wanted you alive. Didn't even care if you was carrying that bastard's brat. Your old man would have been more desperate to marry you off to hide the shame. Then Barton would've doted on the heir to his dynasty."

"Which was his right!"

He took a step toward her. "Yep, whoever won you won both ranches. You passed old Kurt over for March. With him gone, I stood a chance of being the next in line."

How could he think that she would've married him? But looking into his mean eyes she knew that's exactly what he had thought. Why he had tried to eliminate Trey.

He was the reason she had lost her baby. And now he was back.

Despite the temperature that steadily climbed with the rising sun, a deadly chill slithered over her skin.

"Get off my land," she said, barely able to stand the sight of the man who'd cost her so much grief.

"Aim to do just that." Ned pulled his gun and leveled it on her, his eyes cold and filled with malice. "With you."

"No," she said, filling her lungs with air, ready to scream.

"Go on and holler," he said. "I'd just as soon plug March now than later."

And that silenced her as nothing else could. Because she knew Ned wouldn't hesitate to kill Trey.

"Damn you," she said.

He laughed and came toward her, his gun leveled on her. "I'll have you begging before this is over."

She kept backing up. "I'd sooner die first."

"Fine. I'll shoot you," he said. "But know that when you're dead, I'll go after March. I'll stake him out on the desert this time. Skin the sonofabitch. I ain't leaving until I know he's dead."

Defeat sucked the steel from her spine. He'd do it. Maybe not exactly like he said, but he'd make Trey suffer.

Trey had already come close to dying because of her. She wouldn't put him through it again.

"Daisy!"

Her gaze jerked to the adobe and the tall cowboy standing outside it. He was looking up toward the knoll, right at her and Ned. She didn't want to guess what was going through his mind.

Trey started toward them, his long legs eating up the distance. The click of a hammer being cocked snapped her gaze back to Ned.

"Get on your horse," Ned said, aiming his revolver at Trey. "Do it now or I shoot him."

"You kill him now and I have nothing to lose," she said, knowing the risk she took calling his bluff. "Holster your gun and let's ride."

He stared at her a long moment, then cracked a smile and holstered his gun. "All right. He lives. For now, anyway."

She turned and walked down the other side of the knoll to where two horses waited. Ned's gelding and her mare. He'd planned this well, just as he had in the hayloft.

Yes, she'd ride off with him now. And she'd wait for her chance to kill Ned Durant for robbing her of so much.

Chapter 15

Trey spent three grueling hours walking over JDB land searching for his gelding. Every damned step he relived the moment when Daisy had turned and walked away with Durant following her. Heard the thunder of hooves pound in his head as they rode away.

It pissed him off that she'd gone to the cemetery alone, that she'd put herself in danger. That he hadn't been able to do a damned thing to save her. Didn't she know the risk she put herself in?

On the heels of that guilt came the unsettling thought that Durant had watched them yesterday as well. The bastard had known they were holed up in the adobe.

The fact he'd taken the horses from the pen before dawn proved he'd planned to leave Trey on foot again. Daisy too?

Hard to tell what Durant had in mind. She had surely made it easy for him by leaving Trey's side.

He found his gelding tied to a fence post on the far eastern property line. Without water or shade, the horse would've died in a day.

But seeing the rider approaching from the south relieved that worry. Somebody would've come along and let the horse go.

Durant had put thought into this, knowing how much time Trey would waste looking for his gelding. Knew too that Trey could get here only to find the horse had been freed.

Either way precious time would be lost. The miles between him and Daisy would grow even more.

Anger nearly blinded him when he thought of what Durant had in mind for her. Dammit, how was he going to find them? It'd be nearly impossible to pick up their trail with the ground baked to rock.

Trey reached his horse and gained a weary nicker in greeting. He removed his hat and used it as a makeshift bowl, pouring water in for the gelding.

All the while he kept his eye on the rider who was nearly upon them. He shifted the hat into his left hand and let his right drift toward his sidearm.

The cowboy stopped six feet from him and pushed back his hat. He didn't recall the man's name, but he knew he was one of Leonard's hands.

"Mighty odd place for a man to tether his horse," the cowhand said.

"Wasn't my idea." Trey put his hat on and slipped the bridle on his gelding. "You see Ned Durant today?"

"Can't say that I have. He have something to do with your horse being out here?"

Trey swore as he untied the lead line and looped it around his gelding's neck. "Yep. This was Durant's work." He swung onto the gelding's bare back and eyed the cowhand. "Durant has taken Daisy Barton. I'd be obliged if you'd get word to Hollis Feth at the Circle 46. Tell him I'm going after Durant and her."

"You want me to alert the rangers too?"

"Fine by me," he said. "Just make sure Hollis knows."

He brushed two fingers over his hat brim and turned the horse back toward the adobe. As soon as he filled his

canteens and saddled his gelding, he aimed to ride hard.
Ride west.

Ride to hell if he had to. He wasn't going to stop until he
found Daisy and dispatched Ned Durant to hell for good.

Daisy struggled to keep her seat on her mare, the day
passing from blazing hell into twilight in a blur of worry
and fear. And heat. My God, she'd never been so hot and
miserable in her life.

Even now with the sun ebbing, her head pounded. Her
throat was parched. Her legs had grown numb from hours
of relentless riding.

The fact she'd been forced to ride hard after making
slow sweet love with Trey caused its own misery, both in
body and mind. What was he thinking? Had he picked up
their trail?

She longed to rant and rave, to complain about being
treated so poorly, but she wouldn't give Durant the satisfaction of knowing how much pain he caused her. So
she suffered in silence and prayed that Trey would find
her soon.

The land had gotten harsher. Dryer. Bleaker. All the dangers she'd heard about being in the desert came rushing
back to her, some just as terrifying as the man who held her
captive.

She surely didn't want to think about the night to come
alone with Ned. Didn't want to imagine what horrors lay in
wait for her. But she'd likely find out soon, for she doubted
he'd push on through the night.

Even a lowlife like him had to rest some time. Maybe
when he did, she'd find a way to escape.

Beyond the barren landscape, she saw a river flowed
like a thin, pale snake for as far as she could see. Across it
on the horizon rose a hazy ridge. Mountains? It had to be.

She'd never thought she'd come this far west to actually see them. Now that she was here, any excitement their beauty might have stirred was tempered by the fact that Ned was taking her to an isolated place. There'd be less chance to escape. To get back to Trey.

"We'll camp up ahead on the Pecos River," Durant said. "There's water and grass there for the horses."

Her mare whickered, scenting water already.

Daisy wet her own parched lips. What she wouldn't give for a long drink of water. Or a bath to soak the West Texas grit off her skin.

Even though she dreaded the night to come, she was relieved when Ned found a place along the river that suited him.

When he dismounted, she did the same. The last thing she wanted to do was encourage him to come closer to her. Just fearing that was in the offing made her sick inside.

She'd have a battle to endure tonight, for she wouldn't surrender to him. He'd have to take what he wanted.

By sheer will she forced her numb legs to support her. Still she had to lean against her mare a moment to gain her footing. Don't show any weakness, she told herself.

"See to your needs," Ned told her as he lead both horses to the river to drink.

She surely wouldn't argue the point as she sought out the cover of a greasewood bush. Too soon she had nothing to do but stand nervously and wait for Ned to make his next move. Even if she could force her wobbly legs to run, there was nowhere to go. Nowhere to hide.

Her thoughts turned to Trey. Where was he now? Was he searching for her? Had he given up the effort and returned to the Circle 46?

No, he wouldn't do that. He might not love her, but he wouldn't leave her to Ned's devices either. He'd look for her.

But even if he didn't find her, she couldn't be a victim either. Somehow she had to overpower Ned.

If she could get on her mare and have control, she'd ride for her life. And she knew that's exactly what she'd be doing.

She returned to the area Ned had chosen to find he'd unsaddled both horses and staked them nearby. So much for making a quick escape. Though she could ride bareback, she couldn't manage without a bridle.

He cast her a cool look that made her stomach churn with dread. "You know how to cook?"

"No," she said, which was a partial truth.

Ramona had taught her the basics, but she was nowhere near accomplished or comfortable in the kitchen. But then that held true for most anything.

"Then make yourself useful and gather greasewood for a fire," he said. "And keep your eyes peeled for rattlers."

She went about that task without complaining. At least this kept her from being in his close company.

Still it took no time at all before she had a good stack of brush for his fire. The setting sun made digging around much longer a danger, even though she morosely thought that getting bit by a snake was preferable to enduring his attention.

She eased down on a flat rock upwind from Ned and watched him build the fire and light it. "What do you hope to gain by doing this?"

"My just due." He stripped her to the bone with his beady gaze. "With you and Barton gone, both ranches will go up on the block for back taxes. I got enough saved to take it all over."

"You're going to kill me?"

"When I'm done with you."

She didn't ask what he meant. She knew.

Ned had stolen enough JDB stock to fall right back into

the cattle business. The only person who knew Ned had abducted her and likely would be her death would be Trey, and she had no doubt that Ned would lie in wait for him and shoot him in the back.

Ned had wanted the ranches from the start, and he was willing to do anything to get them. How could her daddy have been so blind to him? Or had he seen through Ned at the last?

She rubbed her forehead and tried to think back to those dark days after Trey had left. When she'd finally told her daddy the truth, he'd vowed to track Trey March down. Swore he'd drag that cowboy back here and make him do right by her.

Then the fall from the loft ended that need. The trapdoor had been left open for a reason. Her attacker meant to push her from the loft, either to kill or cripple her. But she'd fallen through on her own in her haste to escape.

Ned had murdered her baby. He had planned to do the same to her. Had he had a hand in her daddy's death as well?

The disgusting breadth of Ned's treachery set her insides churning. He'd abused her daddy's trust and hers, and hid it all under a guise of willing servitude.

"Daddy guessed you had a hand in Trey's disappearance," she said, certain of it now. "He confronted you. What happened? Did you threaten to kill him? Me?"

Ned flopped back on his bedroll and laughed, kicking at the rocks with what looked to be custom-made boots. Yes, he'd already started living the good life off his ill-gotten gains.

His upper lip lifted in a silent snarl, and his eyes went black and cold. "The old man couldn't see that I'd done him a favor. That I was the better choice."

"Daddy knew that no man could trust a rattler."

Ned sprang forward and crouched before her, his hands

like manacles on her arms. "Don't go blaming me for what happened. Things would've gone on like they were if you hadn't crawled into bed with March."

She tried to break free but he held fast, his grip punishing and the fires of hell blazing in his eyes. "I don't believe you. You had designs on the land and me for a long time. You wouldn't have stood by and let me marry Kurt."

"Ranch accidents happen all the time."

"I hate you!"

She hated him for taking everything she loved from her. If she found a way, she'd kill him. Even if it was the last thing she did.

"Don't rightly give a shit how you feel about me."

Ned rocked forward and pushed her back on the flat rock, her fisted hands between them little barrier. But her knee connected with his groin.

He grunted, off balance just enough for her to shove him off her. But his hold on her wrists remained tight, even when she tried to knee him again.

He spat out a vile curse and dropped her left wrist. She jutted her hand toward his face to claw him just as his fist slammed into her jaw.

Pain shot through her head and left her disoriented, seeing double. Too soon he was straddling her again, holding both of her hands in one of his.

She just managed to turn her head and avoid his mouth covering hers. But she could do nothing as he ripped open her blouse. The hot blast of his breath on her neck sickened her even as panic welled inside her.

She pinched her eyes shut, going cold inside, pulling apart from the horror that was about to happen. She locked those precious memories of making love with Trey aside, becoming someone else, someone who couldn't feel.

It took her a moment to realize Ned was shoving away

from her. She looked up at him, standing now with his gun drawn.

He's going to shoot me instead.

But he wasn't aiming the gun at her. He wasn't even looking at her any longer, but was staring at some point behind her.

The unknown sank new fear into her, but a thread of hope bloomed too. *Please let it be Trey!*

She pulled her torn blouse over her chemise and scrambled to her feet, putting distance between her and Ned. Only then did she turn around.

Not Trey. Not her hero.

Her gaze widened on the four riders who stood at the edge of their camp. Even in the dim light she could see all of them were armed, though none had drawn a weapon. But if looks could kill, Ned Durant would be a dead man.

She took a step backward, then another. These men weren't here to rescue her. No, they were of the same ilk as Ned. Maybe worse. Good God . . .

"Little lady, you'd best stop where you're at," said the man who sat tallest in the saddle, his wide-brimmed hat blocking out all firelight that would have let her see his face.

She froze in her tracks and swallowed hard.

"Run," Ned told her.

She felt the calculating stare of four pairs of eyes daring her to try. She knew before she cleared camp she'd be shot. And maybe that would be for the best.

The leader of the men spoke up. "You got five seconds to holster that Colt or the man behind you is going to blow you to hell."

She glanced back, seeing moonlight glint off a gun instead of the man holding it. Again, Ned was the target.

Ned didn't bother turning. He just swore and shoved his revolver in the holster.

"You with him?" the man asked her.

Tell the truth or lie? Either could be the death of her.

"No," she said and earned a ripe curse from Ned. "He forced me to ride with him."

The leader of the riders chuckled, a rusty sound that scraped over her nerves. "What's in it for you, Durant?"

So this man knew Ned. Still, she didn't hold any hope that this would work out better for her. She was still in danger.

"Just a woman to warm my bed," Ned said.

"You should've picked a more obliging one." The man's demeanor shifted like a winter wind, growing cold and biting. "You owe me, Durant."

"Told you I'd make it good in a month or so."

The man snorted and nodded to one of his men. "I'm tired of waiting."

She caught the nervous tick along Ned's jaw as the cowboy rode over to where Ned's gelding and her mare were staked. "The mare is worth a pretty penny, but you won't get much off that old plug I'm riding. Leave it so we can ride out of here."

But the cowpoke led both horses away anyway. A sick feeling settled in her gut when she realized she'd be stranded here in the middle of the desert with Ned. They were miles from civilization with little to eat or drink. They surely wouldn't live long.

"Damn you!" Ned said. "I said I'd pay you back."

"You've been saying that for months. Your time has run out."

Ned inched backward, his body coiled with tension like a snake ready to strike. But the riders were just as on edge, just as deadly looking.

"Take her," Ned said. "She'll fetch a pretty penny in Mexico."

She felt their gazes on her again, assessing her worth. She

hated Ned for drawing their attention to her, for suggesting that she be sold like a slave.

"Those golden-haired ones always did bring a good price," the man said. "But I'm not about to tempt banditos and a revolution for a chance to peddle her to the highest bidder."

"So it comes down to this," Ned said, his tone flat.

"You reap what you sow. Get a rope," the man said, still staring at Ned whose eyes were darting nervously around now.

A cowboy unfastened his lasso from the saddle and began whirling it over his head. It whistled in the deadly silence, a lonesome sough that left her trembling, left her wondering what would happen next. Nothing good, she was sure.

Was that how Trey had looked when Ned had cornered him? When he knew he'd be dragged to death behind a horse?

She saw the rope sailing through the air toward Ned. He stepped back, but instead of bolting, he drew his revolver. But he never got the chance to fire it.

Shots exploded in the air, leaving a cloud of gunsmoke that burned her nostrils. Ned's body jolted three times, seeming suspended in midair.

He collapsed on the ground, shirtfront bloody, body limp. He'd chosen this way to die over being dragged to death. He'd left her alone with these men.

Her heart pounded so fast she was lightheaded. Her stomach roiled with dread of what was to come.

Nobody gave the order to bury Ned. She was too afraid to voice the suggestion.

"Saddle the mare and help the lady mount her horse," the leader said.

The man in the shadows jumped to obey, leaving her standing in the wash of the campfire. Alone. Terrified.

"Please. Take my horse and his. Just leave me here," she said. "There are people looking for me and—"

"Afraid I can't do that, ma'am," the leader drawled. "We've got a U.S. Marshal on our trail, and we can't have you telling him you saw us in these parts."

Outlaws. She'd known they must be, but hearing that they were wanted doused her in renewed fear.

"I don't even know who you are," she said. "Even if I did, I wouldn't say anything."

Though she couldn't see his eyes, she felt his gaze bore into her—cold, hard, impatient. "Ma'am, if you want to live, you'll set your mare and be quick about it."

She stifled a hysterical sob and wiped the telling moisture from her eyes. No, she didn't want to die, but surely going with these men would be the death of her if the law caught up to them and guns started blazing.

All because she was riding on the wrong side of the law. In the company of outlaws.

As always, that word scraped over a brief memory of three other outlaws, their faces lean and scraggly, their eyes cold and unforgiving. Wanted posters she'd seen once when a posse of Texas Rangers had paid Daddy a visit on the chance one of the gang was working for them.

She'd never understood why those posters had made her feel so sad. Why their faces and names had seemed familiar to her since Daddy told the rangers that the trio had never set foot on the JDB.

But as that memory of them flared in her mind again, she knew why. The Logan Gang. Three brothers who chose to live by their guns.

She knew in her soul that she was the daughter of one of them. Clete? Yes.

"You're trying my patience, ma'am," the outlaw said. "I ain't a patient man."

She could balk like Ned and end up shot to death here,

or take her chances with the men. She surely wasn't fooled by their manners toward her. But she wasn't ready to die. There was still the chance she could escape. That she'd find her way back to Trey.

Find her way.

That seemed to be the sum of her life. Searching for what she couldn't find in her lost memory. Stumbling across the truth when it wouldn't do her any good.

Daisy crossed to the men without looking at them, refusing to give them the satisfaction of knowing she was terrified. She waved aside the cowboy's help and gained her saddle alone, dismayed to realize they hadn't put a bridle on her horse.

The dangers that Ned had described to her about traveling at night seemed inconsequential now. These men were used to moving in shadows. Evading the law.

"Let's ride," the leader said.

The others fell into place as well, riding in a loose group, setting a fast pace. Heading north.

Another chapter of her life began, this one threatening to be brutal if not short. Would she ever have a normal life?

The days of being a rancher's pampered daughter seemed a lifetime away. But her memories of Trey sharpened with each mile that took her farther from him.

Because of Ned, he'd gone through hell, yet he had survived and returned to her. She had to be just that strong.

Trey rode as fast as he dared to push his gelding, but there were too many times he had to stop and search for the trail. Too many times when memories of being dragged over this hard, arid ground tormented him. Too many when his fear damned near brought him to his knees.

He'd failed Daisy. Didn't matter that she'd sneaked off to her daddy's grave alone.

After seeing the ranch burnt to the ground, he should have expected more trouble. He should've suspected that Ned had done this to bring him here to finish what he'd failed to do six months ago.

But he'd gotten wrapped up in Daisy's arms. That adoring glow in her eyes had muddled his mind. He'd gotten caught up in lust. He'd been sure that she'd accept his suit. But she wanted more. She wanted his heart, and he didn't have that in him to give. At least not like she deserved.

He crouched and pressed his fingers into the tracks he'd been trailing. Ned was headed for Pope's Crossing.

It didn't seem possible that one week ago Trey had left El Paso and come through here on his way to the JDB. Now he was heading back. Or not.

Hard telling where Ned was taking her, but he suspected they were camped for the night somewhere before Pope's Crossing, somewhere isolated. He recalled a place just a mile ahead.

Darkness had settled over West Texas hours ago and gave much needed relief from the punishing sun. He was riding on instinct now, taking a chance that Ned had camped this side of the Pecos River tonight.

His horse blew softly and tossed his head, begging for water. But the banks were too steep here. Up ahead there used to be a pole and bucket that settlers used to haul water from the river to the campground. That's where he expected to find Ned and Daisy.

He shifted in the saddle, sniffing the air for smoke. The barest whiff of it drifted to him.

The last thing he wanted to do was alert Ned he was near. So he kept the pace slow, inching his way over the rugged terrain, using care so his horse didn't stumble.

He reached his destination at last and stopped on the edge of the area. At first glance it looked deserted, leaving him to think they'd stopped here but moved on, riding into the night.

Then his gaze spied the form lying prone near a mesquite bush. The man wasn't sleeping, not sprawled like that.

Trey dismounted and walked into the camp, heart thundering with fear of what he'd turn up. The prone cowboy was Ned, shot to death.

Had she gotten the jump on Ned? Or had someone else killed the bastard?

He hoped it was the first and she was simply hiding now. Hoped she wasn't injured or worse.

"Daisy?"

Nothing answered him but a hot, dry wind that rattled the creosote bushes and his patience.

He broke off a branchy limb and stuck the splintered end into the campfire embers. The makeshift torch flared to life and cast a yellow glow over the sandy ground, the pungent scent masking that of death.

He found where two horses had been staked out, likely Ned's gelding and her mare. Two sets of men's boot prints churned up the sand. One headed back into the camp. The other skirted it.

Yet another set inched around the perimeter. They'd been surrounded by at least two men.

He held the torch overhead and followed the tracks, noting different boot prints. Spotting small footprints. Dainty ones mingling with the multitude of hooves. Daisy.

His blood ran cold. There were tracks of five more horses at the far perimeter. Only two men had dismounted.

Couldn't have been lawmen, or they would've taken Ned's body back toward Odessa or on to Pecos. Instead the tracks went north toward Pope's Crossing.

There were two main roads beyond the Pecos River. The Texas Road leading north into New Mexico and the El Paso Road.

He doused the flame in the burned out fire pit and forked the saddle, fearing the worst. Any manner of men could've taken her. His only choice was to ride on and find their trail.

He wasn't going to stop until he found her.

Chapter 16

Daisy was close to falling from the saddle when the first rays of sun shot pink and gold arcs into a cloudless sky. They'd ridden steadily all night with few stops.

The last time the leader—Egan Jarvis, she'd discovered, though the name meant nothing to her—had ordered her tied to the saddle when she'd refused to ride with him. He was a handsome man and not much older than Trey, but she didn't want his hands on her. Having him watch her so closely was enough to make her skin crawl.

As for the others, they deferred to Jarvis with as much loyalty as her daddy had earned from his hands. At least most of the men.

She swallowed hard and tried not to relive that moment when Ned was gunned down. When she'd stood there frozen and terrified, wondering if a bullet would find her next.

"Welcome to the Lazy 8, Miss Daisy," Jarvis said, his soft-spoken drawl drifting back to her.

She refused to comment, but she did stare in surprise at the ranch spread out in the valley ahead. All along she'd painted Egan Jarvis and his men as outlaws, wanted for God knew how many crimes.

But his show of good manners and educated speech was at odds with the swift way he'd killed Ned Durant and threatened to do the same to her unless she went with him. Ned must have owed him. But why did he feel he had to abduct her?

She doubted the answers would ease her mind. As she got closer, she could see that the adobe home was large and seemed well kept. So were the corral and barn.

The long, low bunkhouse where cowboys milled about was large enough to hold a small army. Judging by the well-armed men she saw everywhere, that's exactly what Jarvis had here on his ranch.

Sun glinted off barbed wire that went on for miles to fence in an odd mix of Black Angus, white-faced Here-fords, and horses of every description.

It wouldn't be easy to get in or out of this ranch that sat in the middle of nowhere. The sense of being trapped crawled over her. She had no idea which direction would take her to a town and help and which would lead her out into the desert.

Except for the ridge of dark mountains that rose to the west, the land looked much the same as what she'd always known. Miles of mesquite and creosote bushes with sparse grass for cattle to graze.

Not that she or her mare had the strength to travel any-more this day. She needed sleep, but she wondered if that would even be afforded to her here.

Jarvis swung off his big stallion and strode back to her, looking no worse for wear after their grueling ride across New Mexico. "I'll get you settled in the house and have your mare tended to. Ava will see that everything you need is provided for."

So there was a woman here. That afforded her a bit of

relief as his big hands made quick work of untying the rope that bound her to the saddle.

He lifted her off the horse and set her on her feet until she steadied herself. Though she wanted to protest his touch, she knew she couldn't have done either without his help.

"Thank you," she said when the numbness left her legs enough that she could move out of his hold.

A young woman stood on the porch with a little boy clinging to her skirts. "I didn't expect company."

"This wasn't planned," he told the woman.

The brittle silence told Daisy that the lady of the house wasn't pleased that he'd brought another woman home. Well, she wasn't happy about it either.

"Your wife and son?" Daisy asked him.

"Ava is my sister. The boy is hers."

So this was a family compound. That still didn't ease her mind a bit.

The big hand on her elbow signaled her to move. She did in silence, climbing the steps and giving Ava a tight smile. It wasn't returned. Neither was the one she favored the child with.

"Uncle Egan!" The little boy ran into Jarvis's arms.

He scooped the boy up, but not a bit of happiness or relief showed on his ruggedly handsome face. The face of a fallen angel, she thought.

"Miss Daisy will be our guest for a while," he told his sister.

"Not for long," Daisy rushed to add when Ava frowned. "I'd like to return to Texas as soon as possible."

Jarvis heaved a sigh. "It was unfortunate that you were in Ned Durant's company when our paths finally crossed."

"I won't tell anyone that you shot him," Daisy said. "After what he did to me"—and her daddy, Sam Weber, and Trey—"he deserved it."

"Forgive me for being slow to trust," Jarvis said, as he set his nephew down. "Please, go with Ava and get some rest. It's been a trying journey for you."

Daisy suspected life would get more trying as the days wore on. Though Jarvis appeared genteel now, she knew a killer lurked under that polished façade. But she knew there was no use pleading her case now, especially since she was too exhausted to think rationally with her emotions on edge.

Brother and sister shared an odd look before Ava led Daisy inside. A deep sadness wrapped icy arms around Daisy. She missed Trey so much. Missed her home.

"My brother means no harm," Ava said as she led Daisy down a hall, the heels on her smart half boots clinking on the tiled floor. "He doesn't trust you."

"I don't trust him either."

Ava smiled as she opened the door to a room midway down the hall. It was large and airy with a beautiful woven spread on the four-poster bed. But to Daisy it was still a prison that she'd be hard-pressed to escape.

"I can draw a bath for you now if you'd like," Ava said.

Daisy would have loved to soak in a tub, but it was an effort to keep her eyes open now. "I'll wait until I've rested."

"Do you need my help?" Ava asked.

A choked laugh, or maybe it was a sob, escaped her. "Convince your brother to let me go home."

Ava didn't answer, but Daisy hadn't expected she would.

She was barely aware of the door closing, of being alone in the room. She managed to remove her boots and jacket, but that took the last of her strength.

She crawled onto the clean bed, too tired to be shamed that she'd dirty it with her clothes on. Too depressed to do more than curl in a ball and surrender to sleep.

* * *

Daisy jolted awake and sat up in the bed, forcing her bleary eyes to focus on her surroundings. She frowned, disoriented in the darkening room.

Her gaze flicked to the windows, the curtains pulled back. Dusk had fallen and washed the barren landscape in a burnished hue. Not the Circle 46. Not her room at the JDB.

She pinched her eyes shut and hung her head as the past day's events came rushing back. Just yesterday morning she'd slipped from Trey's arms so she could have a few moments alone at her daddy's grave.

Her intentions had seemed so harmless then. Her decision whether to marry Trey so great.

He didn't love her. That hadn't changed. But her feelings for him were far stronger. However, he'd never know as long as she was being held on the Lazy 8.

She had to get out of here. If Jarvis wouldn't let her go, she'd have to take her chances and escape.

Daisy crawled from the bed and padded to the window, the tiles cool on her feet. There was nothing on the horizon but a vast expanse of mesquite and scrub. Which way should she run?

The knock on her door startled her. She whirled and stared at the carved wood, but it remained closed.

"Yes," she said at last.

"I've drawn you a bath," Ava said. "I laid out clean clothes for you as well."

The gesture touched her. She did want to get clean, but she was still leery of stripping to the skin.

Daisy ran a hand over her knotted hair and crossed to the door. She opened it to find Ava standing there, her face serene. The little boy hid behind her skirts again.

"The bathing chamber is this way." Ava started down the hall and Daisy hesitated a moment before following.

The house was quiet except for the clack of heels on the tiles again. But the scent of meat roasting drifted on the air, teasing her appetite awake.

She'd eaten little the past twenty-four hours. When she left, she'd have another long stretch with little to nothing in her stomach. So she'd better get her fill now and shore up her strength.

"Will you need help?" Ava asked after she led Daisy into the small room set off for bathing.

"I can manage fine."

This room was as antiquated as the one at the Circle 46, with only a copper tub and water hauled in. But the door had a lock, and Ava had scented the water with roses.

"Supper will be ready in an hour," Ava said.

She closed the door and Daisy quickly turned the key. An extra bucket of hot water sat on a stool near the tub, likely for her to rinse her hair. In this drought that was an extravagance she looked forward to enjoying.

Though she would've liked nothing better than to soak her aching body for an hour, she made quick work of her bath. She couldn't afford to get too comfortable here. Couldn't let herself be lulled into thinking she was a guest at this ranch.

When she was clean and dressed in Ava's gaily woven skirt and peasant blouse, she returned to her room. She crossed to the windows and sat in the dappled light to brush her hair dry, then wound it in a knot.

The smells coming from the kitchen were more intense, so she knew supper must be ready. Might as well play along with this charade for now. Her time for escape would come later.

Besides, she needed to know exactly where this ranch was so she'd know which way to flee.

She found Ava in the dining room setting colorful plates on the trestle table. The clatter coming from the kitchen confirmed they had a cook who was busy at work.

"It smells wonderful," Daisy said. "Is there anything I can do to help?"

Ava smiled and shook her head. "I'm done here, and Manuela is ready to serve."

Daisy noted places set for three people. "Who will join us?"

"Just you, me, and Egan. Might as well take your seat. He'll be in directly."

"Oh, I just thought . . ." She bit back the words and shook her head, not wishing to cause Ava embarrassment. "I didn't mean to pry."

"You didn't," Ava said. "I'm not married. In fact my son's father is dead."

"I'm sorry." And she was for broaching this subject no matter how lightly.

The less she knew about their personal lives the better. She took the chair on the side of the table and eased onto it.

Ava slid onto the chair beside her and looked at her then, but instead of lingering grief, anger darkened the young woman's eyes. "He died the month before I found out I was with child, but he'd have married me. Egan would've seen that he did."

Just like her daddy would've jabbed a shotgun in Trey's back and made him do right by her and the baby she'd carried. In his stead, she feared Dade would try to do the same thing.

She shook her head, because much had gone wrong from the start for her and Trey.

If she hadn't lost her child—if Ned had succeeded in killing Trey—she'd have been just like Ava. A single mother living under a relative's protection.

"Have you ever lost someone you loved?" Ava asked.

Daisy nodded. "My daddy just died this spring." She toyed with the linen and blinked at the sudden moisture stinging her eyes. "I lost my baby the month before."

"What about your man?" Ava asked.

She shook her head. "I thought he was lost to me thanks to Ned's treachery. But he survived and came back." She lifted her gaze to Ava's and the anger had been replaced with empathy. "He doesn't know about the baby. I meant to tell him yesterday morning but . . ."

Ned had abducted her. And now she was in the hands of his killer. A mysterious rancher with a dark past, she feared.

Ava slid her hand toward Daisy's, her touch comforting as nothing else had been in ages. She turned her hand over and accepted the younger woman's friendship, commiseration. Bond.

That was it. They shared a bond that only they understood. That sparked another memory of her being on a train, clasping hands with another girl. Was her name Maggie? Yes! She was sure of it, just as sure as the name Dade had felt right to her.

"How did you end up with Egan?" Ava asked, popping the fleeting memory that had come close to forming this time.

Daisy blew out a shaky breath. "It's a long story."

"We've got time."

And so she told Ava a shortened version of waking early. Of her decision to visit her daddy's grave and of Ned surprising her. The rest was a blur of fear and agony rolled together.

Ava didn't comment about her brother's actions. Didn't bat an eye that he'd killed a man.

"I wish that I could have visited my man's grave," Ava said. "But he died outside of Cimarron and was buried there."

"He's gone, Ava," Jarvis said, startling them both. "Best thing you can do is put it from your mind and move on."

He pulled back the chair at the head of the table and sat. Daisy found it difficult to look away from him. Gone was the growth of black whiskers that had made him look like a desperado.

Clean-shaven and wearing a suit coat and trousers, he looked every inch the gentleman rancher. He'd even donned a bolo tie fashioned with silver bobs and a large turquoise set in silver.

"He'd still be here if you hadn't hired on as detective cowboys for that big outfit. And for what? You didn't even get paid in the end."

"Enough, Ava," Egan said. "Miss Daisy doesn't need to know every detail of our lives. However, now that you've apprised her on your personal life, perhaps she'd be good enough to tell us about herself. Starting with her real name."

He was right. It was only fair that she divulge that.

"I was raised in an orphanage," she said.

"What happened to your kin?" Ava asked.

She thought back to the story Trey had told her. It still seemed as if it had happened to someone else.

"After my mother and her baby died in childbirth, my father couldn't care for me and my brother, so he took us to the orphanage." Daisy worried her hands and frowned, Trey's rendition casting a window on her own failed memory of the big brick building that always seemed cold.

"The Guardian Angel's Orphan Asylum. That's where my brother and I got separated," she said.

"Never heard of it before," Egan said.

She looked at him, expecting to see doubt instead of interest. "It's in Pennsylvania, not far from our home in Kentucky."

That explanation tumbled out, surprising her. Could it be true? Had she remembered more about her past?

Maybe that was the shack she sometimes saw herself huddled in, scared and crying.

"Were you one of the children sent west on the orphan train?" Egan asked, his knowledge of such another surprise.

"Yes."

She pressed her fingertips to her temples, trying to focus on that memory. If only she was alone . . .

"What was your birth name?" Egan asked.

"Logan," she said, trying to hold on to that old memory.

To her surprise, Ava's gesture of friendship had jogged that memory buried deep in her. She remembered Maggie. Remembered their girlhood vow that when they each held their own hands tight together when they were alone, it was like holding onto a friend.

Whatever happened to her? Had Maggie ever thought of her? Or had she forgotten Daisy?

The cook bustled into the dining room with platters laden with food. Yet Egan continued to stare at her.

"That brother of yours in Texas?" Egan asked.

She shook her head, feeling sad that her life continued to be a series of upsets. That she'd been removed from the one she loved again.

"I haven't seen Dade since I was six or seven." And sadly she still couldn't bring his face to mind.

Egan pushed back in his chair, a dark scowl drifting over his features. "Dade Logan. I've heard of him. Crossed paths with your father and his gang once."

She wasn't surprised, since he was in that deadly brotherhood of outlaws as well. But she kept that opinion to herself. Insulting him would get her nowhere.

"What do you know of Dade?"

He commenced filling his plate, saying nothing. Ignoring her, she thought. He'd found out what he wanted to know and nothing else mattered to him.

"Heard he's the sheriff up in a little town in Colorado."

"Is that far from here?" she asked, hoping her curiosity came off as just that instead of an attempt at judging which distance was shorter—returning to Texas and Trey or running to her brother for help.

He rocked back in his chair and stared at her—looked through her, really. "It's a good day's ride from here over rugged country."

"Where is here?" she asked, wanting him to pinpoint it, to give her an idea where she was at.

His mouth pulled into an amused smile. Even his dark eyes gleamed.

"New Mexico, Miss Logan," he said. "You don't know about your real father, then?"

"I've been told he's an outlaw," she said. "I've no interest in the man."

He bobbed his head. "Just as well. A bounty hunter rounded up his gang a while back. Clete Logan got away, but not for long."

So her real father was dead. She went still, waiting a moment for some emotion to touch her. But she couldn't feel anything for him, not even pity.

Her only living blood kin was Dade, and he was a stranger.

"Must you be so callous?" Ava said, breaking the tense silence. "Daisy has suffered enough without you adding to her woes."

"Life is full of suffering," he said. "You ought to know that."

Ava glared at her brother, clearly at odds with him. Would she have had to deal with something similar if she'd not been separated from Dade?

"Daisy recently lost the father who raised her. She's been ailing too," she added, sliding Daisy a knowing look.

He turned to Daisy. "What's wrong with you?"

She was not about to tell this man that she'd lost her

baby. She wasn't going to tell him anything of her personal life, for he'd be the type to use it against her.

But Ava seemed intent on standing on her own soapbox of discontent. "She's pining away for the man she was taken from. He'll be looking for her, Egan. Mark my words he won't give up on her."

"Shit! Is that the truth?"

Daisy nodded, her eyes watering and her throat thick with emotion. "I was with my beau when Ned Durant abducted me."

"You have to let her go," Ava said.

Egan shook his head. "Can't risk it. She knows too much."

"I'll never tell a soul," Daisy vowed. "Please, let me go home."

But the rigid set of his jaw told her he wasn't about to relent.

"What will you do when he tracks her here?" Ava asked. "Shoot him? Is that what our lives have come down to?"

"Would you rather see me hang?" Egan asked her. "Would you want your son taken from you because the law decided you were an outlaw as well?"

"No," Ava said, then more softly, "I'd never do anything to harm you or Cory."

Nor would Daisy want her to. But the helplessness of her situation sparked anger deep inside her.

She'd always been the one put upon. Taken from her home, her family, from her loved ones. Shuffled amongst strangers who looked her over like an item the storekeeper would put on sale. Something to get rid of, that had outlived its time. Something—someone that nobody else wanted.

They'd even taken her memory so her past was a dark fog that she couldn't see through.

A black cloud of doom shrouded her when she thought of Trey losing his life trying to rescue her. She'd sooner get shot herself escaping than witness his murder.

Which would likely be the case, because it wouldn't be easy to escape this prison.

"What you do away from the ranch is one thing," Ava said, her voice surprisingly strong. "But I don't want Cory seeing bloodshed. I don't want him knowing what you do."

A ruddy flush streaked across Egan's cheeks. "You move into town and people will ask questions."

"Then I'll take Manuela and go to her village."

"You would choose to live in squalor because you want to coddle your son?"

"I'm protecting him from men like you. As for squalor, they live honestly, Egan."

"Fine. I'll have the buggy hitched in the morning. When it's over, I'll send a man to the village."

"Thank you," Ava said, her features emotionless.

Daisy wanted to protest, but there was no use. She didn't even blame Ava for wanting to get her child out of here. Didn't fault her for not wanting to see her brother kill a man and maybe a woman as well.

If Trey was dead, killed because of her, she didn't know if she could go on.

With Ava leaving the ranch, it would be twice as hard for her to escape. That left her one choice. She'd have to risk it tonight and hope she found Trey before he tracked her here.

Daisy sat in her room in the dark, waiting for the house to go silent. Even when the lights were all out and Ava and Egan had taken to their rooms, she continued her vigil by the window.

She couldn't make a mistake now. She had to leave soon, before Trey tracked her here. Before he walked into certain death.

The first rumble of Egan's snoring brought a smile to

her face. He was finally asleep. She could slip out the window and disappear into the night. But before she could make a move, her door opened, and a slender, shadowy figure slipped inside.

Ava. If she'd come a moment later, she'd have discovered Daisy gone.

"We have to talk," Ava said in a voice barely above a whisper.

"Is something wrong?" she asked, keeping her voice pitched low as well.

"Yes, my brother's way of thinking," Ava said. "Tomorrow morning, you'll leave with my son and Manuela. Her family's village is south of here up in the mountains. But once you get to the village, you are free to head to Texas and your home."

The plan sounded like a godsend with one exception. "Everyone on the ranch will know it's me instead of you leaving."

"No, they won't. My buggy will be waiting outside with one of the younger Mexicans tending it. Manuela will take Cory and get in, and you'll take my place." Ava grabbed her upper arms. "You do know how to drive a buggy?"

"Yes, that's no problem." It could work. She could get out of here with relative ease. "Manuela knows the way?"

Ava nodded. "She'll guide you. All you have to do is drive the buggy."

The troubled snoring next door ceased, and both women went silent. Time seemed to stand still before Egan resumed the discordant snoring.

"I've packed a valise with the outfit you had on when you arrived and a few items to make do until you get back to your home."

Daisy took Ava's hands in hers. "Thank you for doing this. Your brother will be furious when he discovers what you've done."

"That he will, but I won't feel as if I betrayed a friendship. You'll be safe and with your man soon."

And right back to trying to decide what to do. Marry him on his terms or walk away.

"As soon as Egan leaves in the morning, I'll hurry in here so we can exchange clothes. All right?"

Daisy nodded. "Yes, I'll do exactly as you say."

Chapter 17

Trey crouched on the rocky bluff overlooking the Lazy 8 and studied the layout of the ranch. The first tracks had petered out on him, and he had ended up on a ranch in the next county.

When he'd told the old rancher he was tracking a good half dozen men who'd taken a woman, the man had told him about this place tucked back here in this valley. Warned him to be careful too if he decided to pay the owner a visit.

According to him, Egan Jarvis wasn't at all sociable. The place was well guarded. Too guarded for a run of the mill cattle operation.

The ranch was a fine spread, but the mix of beeves was a sure sign that the owner wasn't choosy about what breed he ran. Or maybe it was because he acquired them by less than legal means.

That would explain why the men were well armed.

Still, Trey saw nothing at first glance that indicated Daisy was here until the horses in the far corral shifted. That's when he spied her mare. She was here.

He didn't kid himself into thinking it'd be easy getting her out of here. For one thing his gelding had come up lame. That'd keep him from riding as hard as he would have to do to get out of here.

The sheer number of guards on the place would make it impossible for him to ease Daisy's mare and another horse from the remuda. But the heat of the day was on them now, and the Mexicans clung to their midday siestas.

Trey eased from his hiding place. As much as he'd like to ready the horses first, he couldn't take the chance of being discovered then. Finding Daisy came first.

Getting into the house proved easy. Too easy for a place this heavily guarded.

The quiet scraped over his nerves as he made his way from room to room. He found Jarvis in his study bent over his desk.

Trey whispered his Colt from its holster and eased up behind the big man. He pressed the gun barrel to his back. "Unhook your gun belt with your left hand."

Jarvis stiffened, his palms flattening on the map he'd been studying. "How'd you get in here?"

"Walked right in." He pressed the gun more firmly in the man's back. "Your gun belt?"

The man complied. "What do you want?"

"Daisy, the woman you took from Texas."

"What makes you think she's here?"

"Followed the tracks from the Pecos River here. Her mare is in the corral. Now where is she?"

"Miss Logan is in her room. My sister said the lady took ill after breakfast. She's been in there resting ever since."

"Show me. Real easy. Hands up where I can see them. I've been riding hard to get here, and I'm a bit twitchy."

Jarvis did as ordered and moved down the cool hallway with a lazy cadence. "Who are you?"

"Trey March. Her"—he stumbled over a title and finally settled on the one thing he'd agreed to be—"foreman."

A rusty laugh rumbled from Jarvis. "I'll be damned. Never figured she owned land."

Jarvis opened the door and stepped inside with Trey on his heels. A slender woman rested on the huge bed, taking her siesta as well.

He'd expected the room would be locked. That she'd be tied up. But it was obvious that she was free to roam the house.

"Daisy!" And when she continued snoozing, he raised his voice a bit more. "Daisy, wake up! Time to ride."

The woman sat up with a start and blinked at him, then at Jarvis. Not Daisy, but a pretty woman about her size and with hair just a shade darker.

"Who are you?" Trey asked.

"Ava Jarvis, Egan's sister," she said. "You must be Daisy's beau."

He dipped his chin, still uncomfortable owning up to what he and Daisy shared. Emotions like that had no place here.

"What the hell are you doing in here?" Jarvis asked the woman. "Where's Daisy?"

"With Manuela," she said and received a string of vile curses from Jarvis.

It was mighty clear that the women had figured a way to get Daisy out of here. Exactly what Trey aimed to do once he knew where to find her.

"Mind telling me where that'd be?" Trey asked her.

"A village in the mountains south of here. Los Azul." She pressed a hand to her mouth and stared at him wide-eyed. "You must have just crossed paths."

"Reckon so." Though he'd have been tempted in any case to ride back here and have it out with Jarvis for abducting her in the first place.

"Why'd you do this?" Jarvis asked her. "Why defy me?"

The young woman slipped off the bed and stood tall

before the big man. "Because it was the right thing to do. Because she wanted to go home to him. Now let him go too."

Jarvis shook his head, his body coiling as if to strike. "You know that can't be."

In the blink of an eye, Jarvis pulled a Bowie knife from his boot and swung at Trey. The blade scored his leather vest and sliced through his sleeve and skin.

Trey sieved air between his teeth, his left arm burning like hellfire. But Jarvis was quick with a knife and came at him again.

The blade hummed by his face, missing his cheek by a breath.

Trey aimed at the big man and squeezed the trigger, but nothing happened. Fine damned time for his gun to jam!

A sick sensation washed over him, but he shook it off and circled the big man, knowing he was in for the fight of his life. There'd been a time he was damn good using and evading a blade, but being laid up in El Paso for months had robbed him of a lot of his strength.

The cut on his arm was bleeding freely, and his fingers were starting to go numb.

"Stop it!" Ava shouted.

But her brother ignored her and stalked Trey.

The world shrank to just the two of them, circling each other like feral cats. His blood roared through his veins and pounded in his head.

"Just so you know, I don't give a shit what you do here on your ranch as long as you leave what's mine alone," Trey said.

"You expect me to believe that?"

Trey snorted. "I ain't telling you just so I can hear myself talk."

A flicker of uncertainty lit the big man's eyes, but was

banked under that cool mask of a killer a moment later. "I can't take that chance."

"Let him go," Ava said again, a distraction fluttering on the perimeter.

But though Trey was aware of her, it was clear that her presence here bothered Jarvis more. That was the edge Trey needed.

"Get out of here, Ava," Jarvis said.

"Keep trying to talk sense into him," Trey told her.

And she did, throwing up a lecture that'd do a preacher proud. Begging him to think of them as a family. To stop the violence.

Though Trey didn't know the particulars, he suspected that Jarvis hadn't always been bad. He surely cared for his sister. Protected her.

"It's not too late to do the right thing," she said at last. "Please! For me and Cory, let's live a good, honest life."

Jarvis took his eyes off Trey for a split second. That hesitation was all the time Trey needed.

He brought the butt of his gun down on Jarvis's knife hand. The big man grappled to hold on to the blade but it clattered to the floor.

Trey kicked it away and drove his fist into Jarvis's jaw. It was like driving his hand into granite, but he still managed to stagger the man.

Not long enough to get the best of him though.

Jarvis sent a ham-sized fist flying at Trey. Trey ducked, but his left eye still caught the worst of it.

He shook off the buzzing in his head and swung at Jarvis with both fists clamped together, catching him under his chin. The big man's head snapped back.

Jarvis stumbled back to the wall, slamming into it so hard a picture jumped off its hook. His sister gasped, and Trey just hoped to hell she didn't take a mind to defend her brother.

But she didn't move.

The big man's arms flailed to the side as he slid down the wall, landing in a heap on the floor. Out cold.

Pain laced through Trey as he took stock of his own wounds. He could barely see out of his left eye. His left arm was numb.

"There's a coil of rope in his office," Ava said.

He cut her a look, unsure if he should trust her to fetch it or leave her here to revive her brother. His own ebbing strength decided it for him.

"Can you get it?"

She gave a quick nod and dashed out the door. He hoped he could trust her as Daisy must have. Hoped that Daisy was safe in this village he'd have to search for.

Dammit, a lame horse and now he was bleeding like a stuck hog. But he didn't have time to tend to his wounds now. It'd have to wait until he'd ensured that Jarvis wouldn't come after him. Until he'd put as many miles as he could between himself and this big man sprawled at his feet.

Ava returned with the rope. "This was all I could find."

"It'll do."

He made short work of tying the big man's hands and feet, the effort taxing what strength he had. Jarvis's bandana made a fine gag—couldn't have the man bellowing for help, not with a ranch full of armed men.

Armed men. Hell, how was he going to steal a horse and get out of here?

He glanced at Ava, hating the thought going through his head. Using a woman as a shield didn't set well with him, but that might be his only choice.

With Jarvis tied up tighter than a tick, he pushed to his feet. Too fast. The room spun, and his vision blurred.

He grabbed the bedpost to keep from falling on his face.

"I need to tend that wound," Ava said. Her hand on his

arm was so light he hadn't even felt it until she gave him a gentle tug. "Please, let me help you to the window where I have good light."

The fact that he was edging into being helpless and dependent on this woman bothered him. He'd just tied her brother up. What was to say she wouldn't finish the job her brother hadn't been able to?

"Thank you, ma'am, but I need to get to that village."

Her hold on his arm tightened. "You won't make it to the ranch gate in the shape you're in. That wound is deep and needs stitches."

He sucked in a breath, knowing she was right. Knowing this was out of his hands and into hers.

Damn! He gave a sharp nod and staggered from bedpost to bedpost with her holding him with strength that surprised him, a hold that said she was sure of what she was doing.

"You've done this before," he said as she herded him across the distance to the chair by the window.

"More times than I care to remember." She saw him settled and walked away. "I'll get my supplies."

He cast a glance at the big man still sleeping like the dead. Did he have any idea of the grief that he caused his sister? Hell, did any man truly realize what he put his woman through?

Trey sure as hell hadn't, and that was an admission hard won. He'd been raised mainly around men with the exception of the housekeeper on the Crown Seven. That fine lady had worked in a bordello, so she knew how to deal with rowdy men and boys who thought they were too big for their britches.

A slow smile tugged at his mouth. That lady didn't know it, but she was the closest he'd come to having a mother.

His smile vanished. The woman who had given birth to him hadn't given a shit if he lived or died.

Ava returned with a basket that he was sure had been well used over the years. "Have you ever been stitched up before?"

"More than my share."

"Then you know what to expect. You've got your choice of taking your shirt off or having me cut the sleeve off so I can get to the wound." She looked at him, a steady gaze that told him that she knew in this she was in charge. "Seems a waste of clothes to ruin it."

"You bully your brother this way?" he asked as he set to undoing the buttons on his shirt.

She favored him with a quick smile. "Every chance I get."

Trey accepted her help getting out of the shirt—at least freeing his wounded arm. He eyed the bottle of whiskey.

"That rotgut for show or are you going to give me a taste?"

"If it will keep you still I'll gladly give you a glass." She produced one from her pack and poured a generous portion into it. After wetting a cloth in the dark, amber liquor, she passed the glass to him. "You're going to need this."

And with that she laid the whiskey-soaked cloth over the cut on his arm. Fire licked through his blood.

He bit back the stampede of curses that strained to burst free and downed the amber firewater in two gulps. A new inferno roared through his blood, as fierce and unfettered as a flooded river.

He tipped his head back against the chair and let the force carry him away. Let the years of pain and longing drown before his eyes.

As always his thoughts turned to Daisy. Her sweet scent spun a web of rightness around him, trapping him in her silken arms. But the love in her eyes terrified him, threw him back to being a young boy. Unloved. Unwanted.

He didn't understand those tender feelings. Didn't trust them.

"I hope you understand that my brother believed taking Daisy was his only choice," she said as she threaded a needle.

"Everybody has choices," he said.

He'd sure made some bad ones of late, but he hoped to change that. Hoped to herd his life in a new direction with Daisy at his side.

"I suppose so." She took the cloth from his wound, her brow furrowed in thought. "This will hurt."

He nodded, figuring the pain would be minimal compared to the mental hell he'd gone through the past three days tracking Daisy. "How long have you lived here with your brother?"

"All my life."

That earned him a smile that made her look very young and untroubled, but it vanished the moment she started to close the gash in his arm. "I know it's hard to believe, but there's good in Egan."

"I hope you're right," he said between clenched teeth. "But when a man heads down the wrong road, it's damned hard to do right after that."

"I know. Five years ago he wouldn't have dreamed of causing you or your lady harm." She finished her last stitch and tied off the ends, then cut the thread. "We came from a good, law-abiding family. I'm glad our folks didn't live to see what's become of both of us."

It surprised him that she included herself in whatever bad dealings her brother was into. But what did he expect? That she'd turn her brother into the law? See him hanged?

That would be an impossible choice to make. He couldn't do that to his foster brothers, even given that Reid had done them wrong.

"Daisy loves you," she said, wrapping a white strip of cloth around his arm and tying it off. "I hope you know that. Hope that you feel the same toward her."

He frowned, not about to share his feelings with a woman he barely knew. "She's a good woman and has been through a lot in her short life."

"Why is it so hard for a man to say what's in his heart?"

He understood loyalty. But love? "A man can't trust something he can't see, touch, or taste."

Yet all he had to do was close his eyes, and Daisy was right there. He trembled at the memory of her touch. Hungered for the sweet taste of her skin, her kiss.

He grit his teeth as he shrugged into his shirt and buttoned the front flap. "My horse came up lame. He'll be fine in time, but he's useless to me now. I'll leave him for one of your brother's horses and take Daisy's with me as well."

"I'll go with you to the corral and have a man ready them for you," she said. "He'll escort you to the gate. From there you're on your own."

"Sounds good." He got to his feet, the worst of the light-headedness gone now. "You think you can talk sense into your brother and get him to see that I'm not his enemy?"

"I can try, but he's a stubborn cuss."

He could be that way at times too. "As far as I'm concerned, your brother did the world a favor by killing Ned Durant. You tell him that. Tell him I'm grateful."

She nodded, looking sad and lonely. Made him wonder if Daisy would've ended up in a similar fix if her old man had kept her and Dade with him, if they'd grown up thinking wrong was right.

Ava put her supplies back in the basket. "Siesta is almost over. We'd better get you on a horse before the whole ranch is wide awake and asking for Egan."

"Lead the way, ma'am." The sooner he was on his way, the closer he'd be to finding Daisy.

He trailed Ava from the house and across ground that was baked hard. The heat of the day had passed its zenith, leaving the ranch scorched in a blazing, full sun.

One cowboy lazed in the shade of the barn, his hat pulled low and his boots crossed at the ankles. But before they got close, he shot to his feet with his gun drawn.

"It's just me," Ava said.

The cowboy hesitated a moment before he holstered his gun. "Who's he?"

"An old friend. He was riding close to here when his horse pulled up lame," she said.

Trey inclined his head toward the woods. "I left him tied just inside the tree line."

"Seems to me an old friend would've ridden him on in," the cowboy said.

"Wasn't about to ruin a horse," Trey said. "Besides, I recalled that riding onto the Lazy 8 unannounced wasn't the wisest thing to do, and I didn't want to get shot."

The cowboy eyed his bloody shirtsleeve, and Trey read the man's doubt as clear as day. "Appears you've been in a ruckus."

"Had a disagreement with a man over a lady."

That earned him a nod. "Where's the boss?"

"In the house snoozing," Ava said. "Before siesta, Egan decided to give him a fresh mount and the mare that the woman rode in on in exchange for his lame horse."

The cowboy gave him a flash of teeth. "I heard him and brought the gelding in about thirty minutes ago. Men are looking for you, mister."

"Call them off," she said in a voice that rang with authority.

It was clear the man wasn't keen on obeying, but he finally gave a reluctant nod. "Your tack is inside the barn. Tell me which horse you got your eye on, and I'll saddle it for you."

"Thanks for the offer but I'll do it myself." That way Trey would be assured that this ruffian hadn't slipped a spider under the saddle.

He had enough to worry about just trying to ride out without getting a bullet in his back.

"Please saddle my mare," Ava said. "I'll ride with him to the gate."

The cowboy didn't make a move to comply, but a glance at Ava proved she wasn't backing down either. Trey's respect for her climbed a bit higher.

"Yes'm," the cowboy said at last.

Trey followed the man as he grabbed a rope and stepped into the corral. Several horses perked up, Daisy's mare being one of them.

This close he could see the altered brands on most of the horses. One animal stood out among the others, a chestnut stallion with a crooked white star that put him in mind of Caelte, one of Reid's prize thoroughbreds.

As soon as the horse shifted his rump, he got a good look at the brand. Dammit to hell and back! He set his teeth as an altered version of the brand he'd rode under most of his life glared back at him.

This was Caelte. The old Crown Seven brand had been changed to a Rocking Crown 77. That'd been partly burned out with crossed rods, and the Lazy 8 brand burned close to it.

There were other scars that hadn't been there before too. Likely a man who didn't have a strong enough hand to ride him had beaten the stallion once. But he looked well tended to. He looked at home.

Still, Trey bet if he whistled like he used to do to coax this horse to him, Caelte would come trotting right over. He could ride out of here on this stallion now. Hold him for Reid.

Trey's fingers twitched into fists then relaxed. Doing that would surely bring Egan Jarvis gunning for him just for spite.

Let it go, the voice in his head said. The stallion would do Jarvis more good than Reid now.

He sure as hell didn't want to bring more trouble down on Daisy. She'd had too much, including what he'd put her through by seducing her when he had no intentions of being honorable.

That was a hard admission to make. It didn't say much for the man he was, but it was the truth he'd finally owned up to. He wanted her. He'd always want her.

But he wasn't ready to give her what she wanted. Hell, he didn't know if he'd ever be ready.

"Fine stallion," he said at last.

"He is the boss's favorite," the cowboy said. "Won him in a card game a year ago."

Trey cracked a smile. He supposed that could be true, that the outlaw had won the horse fair and square. He damned sure wasn't going to tweak the man's pride anymore.

He scanned the rest of the horses in the corral. Most were fine stock.

"That gelding of mine will do fine after he's rested up. Which one of the hands would want to trade horses?"

The cowboy straightened. "That calico gelding over there in the corner? He's mine. Raised him from a colt. But around here I have to have eyes like an eagle to keep the Indians up in the mountains from claiming him."

Trey gave the paint a good, hard look. His lines were smooth, and he was likely younger than the gelding he'd finagled in El Paso weeks ago.

"He'll do," he said. "Mind tossing my saddle on him?"

"I'll have the boy see to it."

Trey was thankful for that. Though Ava had stitched him up, he'd likely rip something open if he hoisted that much weight.

"Don't forget to saddle the lady's mare too," Ava said. She earned a quick wave and nod from the young man who'd ambled over.

That cowpoke had a shine for Ava, and if Trey wasn't mistaken, she was returning it. Shy attraction. He'd seen it, but he'd never played that role. Even with Daisy he'd made her come to him. And she had.

"I don't suppose if I warn you to take it slow and easy that you'll do it," Ava said as he cinched his saddle.

He scrubbed a hand over his mouth and smiled. "I want to put as many miles as I can between me and this place."

She nodded. "I'll try to talk sense into Egan while he's tied up. I wish there were more I could do to help you."

"There is," he said. "Tell me how to get to this village as fast as possible. Sooner I can collect Daisy, the sooner we can be heading home."

Home. Just saying it sounded so right. He hadn't felt that way about a place since he'd left Wyoming.

"I know a shortcut."

And from there, Ava went into detail so well that he could almost see Los Azul tucked in a mountain valley. By the time she'd finished and he'd committed the route to memory, the cowboy had saddled her horse and Daisy's mare.

"Much obliged to you for helping Daisy and me," he said once he gained the saddle.

"Take care of her," she said as they rode down the lane toward the gate. "You two have something special, if you'll just open your eyes and your hearts."

He dipped his chin and rode off, mulling that over. He could give Daisy his name and his protection. But the one thing he wasn't sure he could give her was his heart. And that was the one thing that she wanted from him.

Chapter 18

Dusk had fallen, and Daisy was still at the mountain village, unsure which way would take her back to Texas. When they'd arrived in the afternoon, she couldn't beg directions because it was siesta time, and those in the village who'd be of help were dozing while the others were away working.

Manuela had been no help at all, for she only knew her way from the ranch to the village. "You have missed the trail," she'd said when Daisy intentionally drove past it, hoping this was the route Egan had taken from Texas.

Daisy had gone on, traveling slowly down the narrow road until it widened enough for her to turn around. Even there she stopped and waited, her hopes of intercepting Trey withering under the heat of the sun.

Would this road take her back home? She didn't know. It'd been too dark for her to pick out landmarks.

Manuela patted her arm. "We go back to the trail now."

No! She wanted to wait here. She didn't want to admit that she'd made a mistake leaving the ranch, that she could wait here for the rest of the day and never see Trey.

But it was the truth. After giving the empty road ahead

a longing look, Daisy had backtracked to the worn trail that wound into the mountains. Her plan had failed.

"Maybe we should go back to the ranch," Daisy said.

"No! Señorita Jarvis wants her son to stay here where it is quiet."

Daisy looked at the small boy tucked between them, and her heart ached for him. Ached for what she'd lost as well. He'd huddled against Manuela all morning.

How different her own life would've been if Ned had killed Trey. If she'd given birth to their baby.

She could be living a near-mirror of Ava's life right now.

It could've been her. If she hadn't lost her baby, she'd have been alone with just Ramona and her hands to help her.

"Señorita," Manuela had begged. "*Por favor,* we go now."

Daisy was torn. "Will someone in the village be able to tell me how to get to Texas?"

"*Si,* my son Emilio."

So she'd followed the trail that took her to Los Azul. The sleepy mountain settlement was home to a handful of mixed Mexicans and Indians. She had no idea how far they were from a town of any size.

No idea where the village was situated in New Mexico, though Daisy would swear it was in the middle of nowhere. They hadn't passed a soul driving here!

For all she knew she could be closer to Colorado and Dade. She was still too close to the Lazy 8 Ranch and Egan Jarvis! Still too far away from Trey March and Texas.

And Manuela's son wouldn't return until evening! So she was stuck here.

"You will stay, *si*?" Manuela asked.

As if she had another choice . . . "I will spend the night and leave in the morning."

The kind lady beamed at her, putting her in the mind of

Ramona so much that she did feel at ease here. "I will prepare a bed for you," Manuela said.

"*Gracias.*"

Daisy stood in the open doorway and watched the heat of the day pass into a velvet dusk. The setting sun painted the mountains in shades of magenta and crimson and stole the variegated greens from the forest, leaving stands of black shadows to encircle the valley.

The men of the village returned in a cluster. They must all work at a nearby ranch or town. Maybe she could find help there. But without funds, she couldn't secure train passage. She couldn't afford a night in a hotel either.

Manuela's family's home was warm and welcoming, but desperation kept Daisy's nerves tight. Staying here was dangerous.

Egan was sure to come after her once he learned of Ava's deception. And there was Trey to consider.

He'd never find her here. And if he went to the Lazy 8? She shivered, terrified to think of him confronting Jarvis.

Where are you, Trey?

A man trudged toward the adobe, his shoulders bent and his face haggard. She stepped back as he drew near.

"*Hola,*" the man said, casting Daisy a questioning look before turning to Manuela.

"*Buenas tardes,*" Manuela said and embraced the man. "*Por favor,* you must help Señorita Barton. Señor Jarvis brought her home but his sister sent us here."

Emilio frowned as if concerned over that news. "How can I help you, señorita?"

"I need to get back to Texas but I don't know which way to go."

"To El Paso?" he asked.

She shook her head, bringing to mind as much as she could remember of the place where Ned had died by

Jarvis's hand. "We camped on the river in Texas. Not far from a town. Pecos, I think."

"You crossed the river there?"

"No, we followed it for miles and miles before going across it."

"Perhaps it is the old Texas Trail you seek," Emilio said.

Daisy didn't have a clue, but if he could direct her to Texas, she was halfway home. "That is probably the one. Tell me precisely which way to go."

"*Si,* but I could draw you a map."

"*Gracias!*" She'd be less apt to get lost that way. "How long will it take for me to drive there?"

"In the buggy? A day to reach the Pecos River," he said. "From there, it depends on where in Texas you want to go, señorita."

"To San Angelo," she said, hesitant to mention the ranch by name.

He shrugged his narrow shoulders. "I do not know where that is."

"That's all right. A map to the Pecos River will be fine."

She couldn't have pinpointed San Angelo on a map either, but surely once she reached Pecos, Texas, somebody there could better direct her.

"Come inside. Eat first," Manuela said.

Daisy did, only because she knew that Emilio was likely hungry after working all day.

They sat down to a simple meal of beans and tortillas. It was hot and warm and filling, yet Daisy felt cold inside.

Where was Trey? How could she possibly think of heading back to Texas without him? What made her think that he'd bothered to look for her?

Doubt and fear roiled within her all that night. She slept fitfully again, troubled by old memories and new fears.

She couldn't leave without knowing if he'd picked up her trail and gone to the Lazy 8 Ranch.

To be sure, she'd have to go back. She couldn't leave without knowing if he'd come after her. If he and Egan Jarvis had had a run-in and one or both were dead.

Dawn had just broken the horizon when Emilio hitched the horse to the buggy. She got up as well, exhausted from tossing on the cot and worrying about Trey. She feared what she'd find when she returned to Jarvis's ranch.

The majority of the men in the village were saddling their horses and mules for their treks to various ranches and towns to work for the day. Yet the accompanying sound was no more than a low hum that wouldn't have woken the children.

Emilio pressed his crude map into her hands. "This is the best I can do, señorita. It has been over a year since I traveled that way."

She took a good look at his endeavor and forced a smile. The writing was in Spanish. While she could speak it, she'd never learned to write it. Likely Emilio was the opposite.

"Thank you," she said and tucked the map in her pocket.

"Going somewhere?" Trey asked, his voice clear and deep and so very close.

She whirled around, startled to find him sitting on a paint horse not ten feet from her, holding a rope to her saddled mare. He'd been to the Lazy 8. Been there and left.

But one look at him told her it hadn't been easy. His face was battered, and one eye was nearly swollen shut. But what terrified her was that blood stained much of one shirtsleeve.

"Señorita?" Emilio asked, alarm in his voice.

She turned back to the young man and smiled. "It's all right. He's a friend. I won't need the buggy after all."

Emilio glanced at Trey and back to her. "You will leave with him?"

"Yes." As soon as possible, she thought, as she turned and walked toward Trey on shaky legs.

He was alive. He'd found her. Everything would be all right.

"Did Jarvis do this to you?" she asked.

He dipped his chin. "I got the better of him, though it wasn't easy."

She was glad she hadn't witnessed that scrape. "Did Ava tell you that I was here?"

"She did," he said. "I found the village after midnight, too late to look for you then."

She took the rope from his hands, her fingers lingering a moment on his. "Should we expect company?"

His swollen mouth pulled into a grim line. "I'd bet on it."

She looped the rope around her mare's neck, gathered the reins, and gained her saddle without help. She was glad she'd donned her split skirt again. It'd been necessary to wear Ava's dress when she left the ranch, but she felt more comfortable in her own things.

Now she was glad of that decision. She was grateful too that Manuela had set out food for her to take with her this morning.

She hooked the woven handle of the cloth bag over the saddle horn on the opposite side of the canteen. Food and water, enough for today at least.

"Adios," she told Emilio, and she gained the same reply.

Trey set a steady pace down the mountain trail, seeming sure which way to go. She was content to follow and get as far from here as possible.

"What happened to your horse?" she asked.

"Came up lame yesterday about ten miles from the Lazy 8. Left him at the ranch in exchange for this one."

She was glad he'd gotten her mare as well, though she'd have been more relieved if they'd crossed paths yesterday after she'd left the ranch. They could've taken the buggy and gone on. Gone home together.

"You found Ned then?"

"Yep. Told Jarvis I thought he did the world a favor."

"Did Jarvis believe you?"

"Reckon we'll find out in due time."

They reached the valley far sooner than it'd taken her to travel this route the first time. Trey set a fast pace and headed across the plains instead of taking the trail that wound south.

She sensed his urgency as their horses ate up the miles in silence. Yet it seemed like an hour passed before they reached a well-traveled road.

Trey never broke stride as he turned them south. Talk was out of the question at this pace, but she didn't complain. She just stored up the questions eating away at her. And she wondered again what went through the mind of the tall man who'd ridden to her rescue.

Even when they slowed their pace to rest the horses, talk seemed vulgar. She understood his reason for being more guarded out here in the open. Knew he was alert to danger swooping down on them.

But the silence played on her mind, and her future seemed more uncertain than ever before. Part of that was because of seeing how Jarvis had treated his sister.

She wasn't about to let that happen to her with Dade, though she did want to meet her brother. She wanted to build a closeness with him.

He was likely as hardheaded as Trey. She might side with him because of their close bond. But she was determined to make him understand that she could stand on her own.

First step toward that would be finding Dade and inviting him to visit the ranch. "How far are we from Colorado?"

"Helluva long way. Why?"

"Jarvis said that Dade was a sheriff in a small town there."

"He say where?"

"No, he was very vague."

He glanced back at her. "How'd that come up?"

"I told him I was a Logan," she said. "I thought it'd raise less questions if he knew I was the daughter of an outlaw and not a prominent Texas rancher."

Not that there'd been anyone left to ransom her to if that had been Jarvis's intention. But she'd learned the hard way that some men wanted her for the land and the cattle.

Kurt was willing to pay for the land, knowing she was over a barrel in debt with her daddy gone. Ned would have done anything to get his hands on the land, including murder. And what about Trey?

She wanted to believe that she'd won a piece of his heart, but that might not be the case at all. He wanted the ranches too.

He had suggested they marry. Not for love. No, because he felt guilty for taking her innocence when she was the one who'd chosen to give it to him.

She stared at the back of Trey's hard head and felt her heart break all over again. Before Ned had abducted her, she had thought she'd reached a decision she could live with. She believed that Trey might fall in love with her in time.

Now she wasn't so sure that would happen. Even if it did, she deserved more than a marriage of convenience.

"Why did you come after me?" she asked.

"What kind of a question is that?"

"A fairly simple one." If he loved her. Even if he just cared for her.

He shifted in the saddle, and even from this distance she could see his shoulders rack up tight. "I wasn't going to sit by and let Ned steal my woman."

"You make me sound like a possession," she said. "My horse, my woman."

He reined his mount around and trotted back until they were side by side. "Don't go getting prickly on me now. I was your first lover, and I aim to be your only one."

The sheer arrogance of that statement had her seeing red. "Why? Because we're good in bed? Because I own two ranches and, silly me, I need a strong man to run them?"

His eyes narrowed to slits. "You've damned near bankrupted yourself."

"The drought and Ned were against me," she said. "And yes, I didn't know what to do, but I intend to learn."

"What are you saying, Daisy?"

What she'd been trying to tell this thick-headed man all along if only he'd listen. "If we marry, it'll be because we are in love. There's no other reason."

"The hell there is." He leaned forward and splayed a hand over her flat belly, shocking her, yet stirring the embers of desire too. "You could be in the family way, and I'm not about to let a child of mine grow up a bastard."

"Do you think I couldn't take care of a child by myself? Is that it? Are you afraid I won't be able to be a mother any better than I was a ranch owner?"

He sighed long and loud, his fingers curling just the slightest bit on her belly so she felt the seductive pull of this man clear to her womb. My God, how could she love a man who was so dominating? How could she even want a man who was so set on taking everything she could give him yet giving so little of himself in return?

"Dammit, Daisy. I know the hell that being a bastard causes. What it does to a man inside when he's growing up and knowing nobody gives a shit if he lives or dies."

She flinched, her heart bleeding for the little boy he'd been, tossed out at birth and unloved by family. Unwanted by the folks who'd visited the orphanage looking for a child to adopt.

A bit of her own resolve crumbled right then and there.

Trey didn't know about the child they'd created before. How she'd grieved over the loss. How she still woke at night clutching her belly and reliving that personal hell. How she blamed herself for losing that precious gift.

"You have to know it wouldn't be like that," she began, thinking of what she'd rehearsed to say to the life within her months ago.

Your daddy was a good man but there was no future for us. Doesn't mean he didn't love you. For he never knew you existed.

"Damned right it wouldn't have. I'm not going to walk away and let you raise my child alone. I won't give in on this, Daisy."

And she knew he was telling the truth. That he'd never have left her before if he'd known she was in the family way. She suspected he might even grieve with her for that life they'd created in passion—she couldn't call it love, for she was the only one who'd given her heart.

But it confirmed that Trey March was a good man. An honorable man. A man who accepted his responsibilities without complaint. Who had way too much pride and way too little forgiveness inside him.

"We'll know if I am pregnant before long," she said.

"Good. Just remember we also struck a separate deal regarding what Barton owed me. I'm not going anywhere."

She shoved his hand from her, hurt that he'd bring that up now. "Of course we come back to what I owe you. Doesn't really matter what I say, how I feel. My daddy owed you and I can't pay up, so we are stuck together."

He sat back in the saddle, his face as hard as the sun-baked desert that yawned forever around them. "I can't change what was done. Your daddy made that deal with me. You agreed to honor it. You want me to forget about it?"

No! She wanted him to look inside his heart. To find that a part of him burned just for her. That she was more than the rich boss's daughter.

She had to know she was more than a convenient lover. She had to know he couldn't walk away from her. Not for money. Not for the land. Not for any past agreements.

She wanted to know he loved her. It was so simple.

So necessary to a woman who had been denied that special bond just like he had.

"No, but I won't be the woman you *had* to marry," she said. "I want as much respect and trust as you'd have afforded my brother."

He visibly flinched at that. "I've got history with Dade. Long-standing history."

She had history with him too, a life lost far too soon. A love in her heart that just wouldn't die.

"Then marry my brother," she said.

He smiled. An arrogant tilt of the lips that curved just enough to tempt her to follow suit, lips that she hungered to taste. It was hard not to lean forward. To hold herself back. Damned hard.

"You want to guess what your brother will say or do if he finds out we're lovers?"

Her chin came up at that question. Yes, she had a brother. But he was apart from who she was now. He had no say in what she did or didn't do.

"What I do with you is our business, not his."

"You think he's gonna see it that way?" he asked.

She got a firmer hold on her reins and backed up, just enough to let him know she could, just to distance herself a bit from the strong urge to give in to this cowboy. "Dade Logan has no say over what I do or don't do. Remember that."

His smile grew wider, almost like he was holding back a laugh that would rock the mountains. "Oh, I'll remember it all right. You'll learn that your brother is mighty protective of you."

An image of her being in the same fix as Ava flashed through her mind again. Yes, she had no doubt that Dade would be just as overbearing as Egan Jarvis was to Ava. But unlike Ava, she didn't have to bow to her brother's demands.

"You'll learn that I'm not about to take orders from him or you," she said.

"That'll only hold so far," Trey said, his amusement disappearing in a blink. "If you're pregnant, we're going to get married right off. No haggling. No demands that I can't make. You hear?"

Yes, she heard. And though she wanted to argue the point, she knew that in this she couldn't. She wouldn't put that burden on her child. She couldn't push Trey out of their child's life either.

"All right," she said at last. "If I'm with child, I'll marry you."

He stared at her so hard she swore he was trying to read her thoughts. "You'll tell me if you are. You won't lie to me about this."

Not questions, but she heard the pain and doubt in his voice, and it hurt knowing that he didn't trust her. "I'll tell the truth. I wouldn't—"

She tore her gaze from his, unable to say it, for though she hadn't lied to him before, she'd failed to tell him she'd missed her cycle. By the time she knew for sure, he was gone. And now . . .

He nudged her chin up. "Daisy?"

She caught the glint of fear in his eyes and felt that kindred tug of emotion in her soul. She could voice what was in her heart. He couldn't.

"I wouldn't lie to you," she said.

His smile was quick and brief. "Now that that's settled, let's get the hell out of here."

He reined his horse around and broke into a trot. She urged her mare to do the same and vowed that when the time was right and they weren't at each other's throats, she'd tell him about the first life they had created together.

Chapter 19

The punishing sun was setting when the whistle from a train echoed over the vast plains, drawing nervous whickers from both horses. "Not much farther and we can rest for the night."

Sweat slicked his back and his hatband was saturated. Daisy looked just as wilted, but she'd never voiced a complaint.

"Are we camping along the river?" she asked, a note of panic in her voice.

"Nope."

"Thank God," she said so softly he almost didn't hear her.

He supposed she was haunted by Ned's murder at Jarvis's hand. She likely was afraid the same would happen again.

The same thought had crossed his mind with every mile he put between the Lazy 8 and them. He'd pushed hard all afternoon and kept close watch in case Jarvis and his men set upon them.

Though they'd ridden in peace this far, there was the chance that Jarvis would track them anyway and strike at night. He damned sure didn't want to go out the way Ned Durant had.

"Pecos is just over this ridge," he said as the plume of black smoke from the locomotive lifted like a flag on a red-gold sunset. "We'll take a room there tonight. It's best we pass ourselves off as married in case Jarvis comes looking for us."

She was silent for too long. "Won't he suspect we'll do that and look for Mr. and Mrs. March?"

"Maybe, but he damned sure won't be looking for Mr. and Mrs. Morris."

"But he'll know we're here by the horses."

"I've got an old friend who will help us out there."

An hour later, he'd left his horses with a man who'd worked for Kirby up until they were all run off the Crown Seven. Trey trusted the man to tell anyone who asked that he'd bought the horses from a cowpoke. That he didn't know what had happened to him after that.

With any luck Jarvis would suspect that Trey and Daisy had boarded the train and were long gone. It was a damned tempting thought, but he knew she wouldn't want to lose that mare, and the only way he could afford passage for them was to sell the horses.

Hell, maybe they'd be really lucky. Maybe Ava had talked sense into her brother and Jarvis had let them go as lost causes.

He hoped so, because he was tired of watching his back. Tired of worrying about how he could keep Daisy safe. Hell, he was worried now about how he could keep Daisy.

She wanted him to profess his love.

His insides cramped at the thought of spouting such words that held no meaning. Of flat-out lying to her.

Dammit, why did women have to wrap everything up in hearts and flowers? Why couldn't they just take a man like he was?

He thought back to when he first met Daisy. She'd been

a cute little flirt, casting shy eyes at him. But once they were alone, her shyness had evaporated.

Yep, she'd been a virgin. She hadn't known anything about sex or how to please a man. She hadn't known how he could pleasure her.

But she had learned damned fast. *Teach me,* she'd whispered in his ear.

The same tone she'd used when she'd asked him to teach her how to run a ranch. She'd thrown out a hoop twice, and he'd stepped into it both times.

The hell of it was he was obliged to marry her now, but she was holding out on him. This standoff couldn't end well.

He dragged in a deep breath and blew it out. What the hell was he going to do with her?

The lady of the hotel stopped before a door on the second floor, seeming more than a bit uncertain about them. "I trust you will find the accommodations suitable. As my husband likely told you, meals are available in the hotel restaurant for another hour. If you prefer to take your meals in your room, I can have a tray brought up."

"We'll eat here," Trey said. "My wife and I are mighty weary from our journey. Steaks if you have them. Anything on the side will do fine."

The innkeeper's wife turned to Daisy. "Toilet is down the hall. With this drought and all, hip baths are three dollars extra, payable in advance."

"I'll pass on the bath," Trey said.

"So will I," Daisy said, surprising him, though he was glad since he was nearly broke. "But I'd like to borrow a needle and thread to mend his shirt."

"I can spare that." She looked from Trey's bloody sleeve to his battered face. "We run a quiet place here. Don't stand for no tomfoolery. Mind if I ask what happened to you?"

"Got in a scuffle with a thief while we were traveling," he said.

"There are still too many of them running wild in these parts," the woman said.

He just nodded, not about to embellish his story. Daisy held her tongue as well.

"Dinner will be brought up directly." The woman turned to Daisy. "I'll find needle and thread for you as well."

"Thank you."

The woman left, closing the door quietly behind her. Daisy dropped onto the bed. "I'm so tired I could fall asleep standing up."

"It was a long, hard ride." One that was made more tiring by the fact that they hadn't exchanged a dozen words since that standoff outside the village.

His ultimatum had played over and over in his head, sounding more domineering each time it crossed his mind. But he wouldn't back down, even though she was more troubled now than before. Could she be with child?

Her gaze fixed on his arm. "Did he shoot you?"

"Got me with his knife," Trey said. "Ava stitched it up."

He saw her throat work and her face leach of color. "I imagine she's had a good deal of experience tending such wounds."

"Reckon so." But not so for Daisy.

She'd never been exposed to the ugly side of life. Barton had pampered her. Treated her like a princess.

She'd been easy pickings for a man like Durant.

Easy pickings for a randy cowpoke to seduce. To tempt her to toss aside her morals.

Yep, she was too trusting.

Too nice for her own good, even now when she'd been put through hell.

A knock sounded at the door. He pulled his gun and crossed to it slowly. "Yes?"

"I've brought up your dinner," the lady said.

He holstered his revolver and opened the door a crack. It was the lady. Behind her was a robust man bearing a tray covered with a linen. The aroma of fried steak wafting under Trey's nose was proof the man was carrying their dinner.

"Smells mighty fine," Trey said, and his guts rumbled in agreement.

"I hope you enjoy," the lady said, coming inside the room.

The man followed her inside and headed straight for the lone table. He set the tray down, gave a nod and shuffled out.

"Here's my sewing basket for your wife," the lady said as she handed Trey a small wicker basket.

"Thank you, ma'am," he said.

"Yes, thank you," Daisy said.

"If you need anything, let me know," the lady said.

"We will." He closed the door in the woman's wake and carried the basket to Daisy. "Let's eat."

To his relief, Daisy joined him at the small table. Nothing more was said as they both dug into the meal.

"Take off your shirt," she said when he'd finished shoveling in his meal. "I want to mend it tonight."

They'd been as intimate as a man and woman could be, but he hesitated having her do something this domestic for him. "You don't have to do this."

"I know, but I want to."

He shucked his shirt and handed it to her. Her brow furrowed as her gaze flitted from the dried blood that had turned his blue cambric black to the dirty red bandage on his upper arm.

"You lost a lot of blood," she said.

"A fair amount."

"I'll see to that wound when I'm done."

He nodded, unnerved by how domestic this all seemed

with her stitching up his torn shirt and fretting over his wound. It'd been different when Ava saw to him.

"Just so you know, I don't aim to make a habit of getting in scrapes," he said, hoping to lighten the mood.

A tiny smile pulled at her mouth as she poked thread through a needle and set to sewing, her fingers sure and the stitches small and neat. "I suspect you've made that promise before to no avail."

"Not intentionally."

"Tell me about the others."

He shifted from one foot to the other and jabbed his hands under his armpits. He'd never been one to talk about himself. Didn't intend to start now. Yet he sensed this was important for her to know. For them to share.

"First time I used my fists was in the orphanage," he said, the memory as clear as if it had happened yesterday. "One of the older boys took a dislike to Dade the day you and him arrived. Dade put up a helluva fuss when they took you away. But then you bawled the ceiling down as well."

She stopped what she was doing and met his steady gaze. "I don't remember any of that."

"Just as well. This older boy, Hank was his name, was always picking on somebody and causing trouble."

"On you as well?"

He nodded and walked to the window to draw the curtains and block out the world. "Hank pulled some mighty damned rotten tricks on me. Always was needling me because the orphanage had hung this name on me."

"What was your real name?"

"Don't know as I had one." And when she just stared at him, he added, "I was left on the orphanage steps when I was a day old. Nobody claimed to have seen who brought me there."

"How could a mother do that to her baby?" she asked, her face ghostly white in the dim light.

He shrugged, having asked himself that question too many times. The answer was always the same. "I wasn't wanted. Hell, none of us in the orphanage were, but all of them knew why they'd ended up there. All of them knew their mothers' names at least. I know it's hard for you to understand—"

"Oh, but I do understand. I have so few memories of my own early life and all of those start when I was seven years old. Even then there are holes." She bent and set to working the stitches through the bloody cloth. "Go on with what you were saying about this bully who taunted my brother."

He scrubbed a hand over his mouth and thought back to that day when his life had changed for the better. "All the orphans took their meals in this big mess hall, but they kept the boys and girls on opposite sides of the room."

"Why?"

"Don't know." There were a lot of rules that had made no sense to him then or now. "We were in line to get our trays. Christmas Day, though all that amounted to was getting an apple and a piece of hard candy on our tray. Reid was first, then Dade behind him. Hank was after him, and I was at the end."

He snorted. Hell, he was always pulling drag.

"Dade saw you, and you cried out for him. So he stepped out of line to go to you, which was likely natural for him. Hank got riled because when one boy misbehaved, all those nearest him got punished. So he jerked Dade back in line, but instead of falling into place, he knocked him right into Reid. The tray Reid had just got filled along with the poor fare flew everywhere."

"So you all got reprimanded for that?"

He laughed, a deep release that he hadn't let go in years. Damn odd that this was a cherished memory for him.

"Nope, we got punished for the ruckus that commenced then and there. Reid saw this head butting as the last straw.

He whirled and threw the first punch. Knocked Hank into me, which pissed off the boys behind me. So they shoved me into Hank. After that it was a free-for-all."

She frowned and finished the last few stitches, the silence lending a crackle of tension to the room. Did she believe him? Was she troubled that her brother got whipped good for trying to protect her?

"What did I do while all this was going on?" she asked, genuine worry in her tone.

"Don't know, Daisy. Those matrons herded the girls out mighty fast. Next thing I knew Reid, Dade, and I were locked in the shed out back."

"But it was winter!"

Colder than biddy-blue hell. "That was part of the punishment. Missing out on dinner, the rare treat of candy and fruit, and a warm place to sleep."

"All because of me," she said, tears swimming in her eyes.

His grin vanished, and that hard veneer he had built around himself cracked a bit more. Shit, the last thing he wanted her to feel was guilt.

He knelt in front of her and took her small hands in his. "Daisy, you did us a favor."

"How?" she asked, her voice trembling. "You all ended up hurt and segregated because I was such a baby."

He couldn't help it. He laughed, and that surely made her stiffen up on him.

"There is nothing funny about what happened," she said.

"No, there isn't." He cupped her delicate jaw in his palms and stared into her gamine face. Such a beautiful woman. So open. So good. He didn't deserve her.

"What happened that day did something good," he said, swiping tears from her cheeks. "It forged a bond among Reid, Dade, and I that lasted for years. We became brothers that day, and even now after all that has happened, I still look on them as my only family."

She curled her hands over his. "I'm scared, Trey. That fall I took from the loft? It wasn't an accident."

He recalled what Fernando had told him. That she'd been in the habit of going to the loft every day. That she'd seemed sad. Despondent.

And the most damning of all, Fernando was sure that the trapdoor had been shut when he had left the barn. Ned had backed up that claim soon after. So that left one way it could have been opened. She'd done it herself.

Dammit, had she wanted to end her life?

He let his hands drop to her lap and twined his fingers with hers. "What happened that day, Daisy?"

She shook her head and bit her lower lip, looking at their hands instead of his face. "I can't remember more than bits and pieces of it, and at times it gets jumbled in my mind."

That's the way it'd been since he'd known her. He'd learned to tell when she was lost in a memory and when something triggered one. But he'd yet to find a way for her to unlock the things that troubled her most.

"Give yourself time and bring it to mind."

Her eyes drifted shut on a shiver, and he fought the urge to pull her into his arms and hold her. Time ticked away, as slow as a trickle of sweat streaking down his back.

Horse's hooves struck the hard ground in the street below in a slow, easy cadence. From the saloon in the near distance, shouts and raucous laughs mingled with the tinny notes from a piano.

In the hotel, a door slammed shut, and voices murmured in the room next to theirs. A feminine giggle confirmed there were a man and a woman seeking comfort in each other's arms.

That old familiar ache of longing stirred in him. He'd hoped to do just that tonight with Daisy. He'd even gotten the wild notion that if she wasn't with child yet, he'd damned sure do his best to see that happened. Anything that would make her his. That would convince her he'd be a good husband to her, even if he couldn't say the words she insisted on hearing.

She heaved a sigh and looked up at him with eyes that were so blue and troubled he could drown in them. "Kurt came to the ranch that day. Daddy had sent word that we had to talk."

"What about?"

She swallowed hard, and her lower lip trembled, and he knew that whatever she was about to say had tormented her. "I'd told Daddy the night before that I wouldn't marry Kurt. I couldn't do it. I thought Daddy would be furious with me, and he was. But when he finished fuming, he said we had to tell Kurt right away. That it was only right that we end the engagement immediately and let it be known it was my choice."

"Barton was right."

She nodded and clutched at his hands. "I know. That's the way it had to be. I should've done it sooner, but I was afraid. Always afraid."

"Daisy, everybody knew Barton would have hung the moon in a different place if you'd wanted it that way."

That brought an endearing smile to her lush lips, but they thinned too soon into a grim line again. "That's what plagues me the most. I never meant to hurt anyone. Not Kurt. Not Daddy. I just—"

Tears streamed down her face in hot rivers as she lifted her head and stared straight at him, like he wasn't there at all, like she was looking at something in the past. And oh, God, but she looked on the verge of collapsing on him.

He slid both hands up her arms and felt another shiver rip through her. "What is it, Daisy?"

She blinked, her gaze still on him, but this time he knew she was aware he was inches from her, that they were alone in the deep, velvet night, that he was on his knees before her, touching her, aching to hold her.

"I just fell in love with you," she said. "I'd never felt that way before. Never met a man and just knew I should be with him no matter what. I thought"—she swallowed and looked away—"I thought you felt the same."

He tipped his head back and stared at the ceiling, hating himself for being such an unfeeling bastard, for not being able to give her what she needed most.

She was his foster brother's sister. The girl Dade had risked his neck as a child to protect. The sister he'd made the pact with Reid and Dade to find one day. And what did he do? He took her innocence.

He hadn't connected the name with Dade Logan at all. He'd seen a fetching rancher's daughter cast him a longing eye, and he had wanted her. He had thought she was shallow. That she played around. Even when he knew she'd been a virgin, he tried to make her look like the seducer when it was him all along, egging her on, forcing her to come to him. And she had. God help them both, she had.

"How did Leonard take it?" he asked.

"Badly. He guessed that my refusal to marry him was because of you." She sniffled loudly and cleared her throat. "I tried to tell him it wouldn't have mattered, that I didn't love him. I couldn't be his wife because it would be wrong for him and me. But he didn't want to let go."

Annoyance danced along his nerves when he thought of the man confronting her. No wonder he'd given Trey a cold glare when they crossed paths at the remains of the JDB just days ago. Leonard saw him as his rival for Daisy's affections. He was the man who stood in the way of him gaining title to all of Barton's holdings.

"The man had gall to pressure you like that," he said.

"That's what Daddy said. 'Enough is enough.'" She gave a nervous laugh that sounded cold and brittle. "Kurt couldn't understand why Daddy didn't force me to go through with it. He kept spouting that we'd have built a dynasty in West Texas. That nobody would be able to compete with us once the ranches were combined."

Yep, old Leonard saw his dream snatched away from him—all because Daisy Barton wouldn't marry a man she didn't love. Trey heaved a troubled sigh, knowing how the man felt, for he was in the same damned boat.

With one exception—if she came up in the family way, she'd agreed to marry him. He'd hold her to that one.

"I just felt drained when he left," she said. "And so sad that I'd hurt him. But I was hurting myself. I was scared."

He shifted closer and laid a hand on her back, rubbing her gently, feeling the tremors ricochet through her like lightning. "Why? You didn't have to marry Leonard. That was behind you."

She shook her head, her eyes misting over again. "There was a bigger problem that came to light later on. I was pregnant with your child."

The words slammed into him, rocking him to his soul. A baby. They'd created a life together in that loft.

"When did you know that?"

"Right after Christmas. I was sick for weeks. Ramona figured out what was ailing me."

"Barton knew?"

"I told him. It was the hardest thing I'd ever done, but he didn't holler. Didn't fuss. He just said he'd make it right and sent a man out to find you. But one week turned into three, and he couldn't find a trace of you."

Trey pulled her to him and soaked up the fear that careened through her, knowing he was the cause and knowing there was nothing he could do to make this right. He'd thought he'd been careful with her. But he'd been wrong.

My God, they'd made a baby. No wonder she was scared

and angry at him when he disappeared. She thought he'd left her high and dry after knocking her up.

But she sure wasn't with child now. What had happened?

She must have lost it. Her fall from the loft. Fernando had hinted that she'd been out of sorts.

His heart was hammering in his chest and his head spun, like he'd had too much sun. Accident or intentional?

Trey felt sick inside at the thought that she'd tried to rid herself of her bastard. But before he could ask, her watery gaze lifted to his, and the words died in his throat.

"Ned knew about us," she said. "That's why he tried to kill you. That day he dragged me from Daddy's grave, he bragged to me about how he thought he'd gotten rid of you. That he'd have a chance with me if you were gone. When Daddy told Ned that he aimed to find you, Ned went to look for your body. Nothing was there, and he knew you'd somehow gotten away. He said if I didn't go with him, he'd shoot you dead. I knew he would. He'd already hurt you enough. I couldn't let him do more."

"You did the only thing you could do," he said.

She dabbed at her flushed cheeks, looking small and weary to her soul. "I went to the loft to think over what to do. Daddy said he'd send me away to a friend in Austin if I wanted, but I didn't want to leave home. I kept thinking you'd come back, and I wanted to be there."

He winced at the shame and pain he'd put her through, even though he'd been powerless to stop it. If Durant hadn't been dead, he'd have killed the sonofabitch for the hell he'd put them both through.

"I came back soon as I was able." To get what was owed him from Barton. But down deep he admitted he'd come back to have it out with her too. What a helluva surprise had awaited him.

"The baby?" he asked again, fearing she'd been so

distraught she'd jumped from the loft to avoid the scandal of having a child outside of marriage.

She inched forward on the chair and rested her hands on his chest, clearly grieving herself sick. "Someone was in the loft and grabbed me from behind. He tried to drag me into the hay, but I fought him off. I ran to the mow and didn't see the trapdoor was open until I fell through it."

She broke down then and gave in to big wrenching sobs. He held her close, feeling helpless, feeling responsible for the suffering she'd gone through, for the torment she still endured. Held her until she'd cried herself out and her breathing evened.

"You still have nightmares about it," he said.

Her head moved against his chest. "I wake out of a sound sleep, remembering the awful cramps. I can hear Daddy telling me again that I lost the baby, but that I was going to be all right."

"You will in time." At least he hoped to hell so. "Who grabbed you, Daisy?"

"I don't know," she said and levered herself away from him. "I remember looking back, but I fell at the same time."

"Had to be Durant."

"I don't think so," she said. "I accused him of lying in wait for me too, but he swore it wasn't him. He said he wasn't the only person who knew we were lovers."

"Fernando and Ramona knew, but they sure as hell wouldn't have done this. Can't see them telling anyone either."

"Even if they had, who besides Durant would want to hurt me?"

"Nobody that I can think of." Though one of Barton's enemies could have chosen to make the big man suffer by hurting Daisy, it was still a long shot. "I say Durant lied. That he was waiting for you in the loft."

"I hope you're right," she said, her fingers curling

against his chest, her breath warm on his neck. "Because I'm scared to death that I might end up alone with the person who tried to kill me."

"I'll be there to protect you this time," he said.

A smile trembled on her lips. "And I'll be there to watch out for you."

He leaned forward to press a light kiss on her mouth, but she met him with a hunger that surprised him. Her hands cupped his face as she bowed into him. He gathered her closer on a moan and kissed her with all the need bottled up inside him, taking all she had to give.

He'd intended to make love with her tonight, to plant his seed in her, to bind her to him. Now after hearing what had happened to her before, he just wanted to hold her, kiss her, love her.

In moments he had carried her to the bed and peeled off her clothes and his own. Then he stretched out beside her and gathered her close.

"I feared I'd lost you again," she said.

"Not nearly as much as it terrified me to see you in Durant's clutches."

Their lips met again in a long, lusty kiss that went on and on. He understood this need, this wild drive to be with her that pumped through his blood, that made him feel alive.

No woman had ever had this effect on him. He knew now that none ever would.

She made him a better man. Made him care more than he thought possible.

All he could do in return was vow to protect her with his last breath. To worship her with drugging kisses and sultry caresses and let his body say what he couldn't put into words.

Chapter 20

They left Pecos at dawn, and by midday Trey felt sure Jarvis had given up chasing them. Even so, they kept pushing to get home before dark.

Dusk had fallen by the time they reached the Circle 46. Daisy had never felt so spent in her life, yet a spark of hope bloomed in her that hadn't been there before.

Trey had treated her with more tenderness than he'd ever shown before. And last night, she'd believed he cared deeply for her just because of the intense way they'd made love and how he'd held her close to him throughout the night.

"We've had men scouring West Texas for you two," Hollis said by way of greeting. "They found Durant shot dead, but no sign of you or Daisy."

She shared a look with Trey that begged him not to divulge the whole truth. "Men that were gunning for Ned found our camp. They killed him, but I got away. Unfortunately it was dark and I rode the wrong way."

"I finally found her in a small village up in the mountains," Trey said, following her lead to her relief. "They found her wandering and took her in."

Hollis stared at her through narrowed eyes. "You was

mighty lucky to escape the man who killed Durant. Couldn't have been easy."

"I guess I was just lucky it was dark," she said, knowing the less she added to her lie the better it'd be.

For though she'd have liked to see Egan Jarvis get his comeuppance for holding her at his ranch against her will, she didn't want any harm to come to Ava. Maybe, just maybe, that woman could reform her outlaw brother before it was too late.

Her gaze flicked to Trey. Maybe she'd be lucky too and would convince this cowboy to open his heart at last.

"You two ate supper yet?" Hollis asked.

"Nope," Trey said just as Daisy's stomach protested its hunger. "Was hoping to get here before you'd fed the hands."

"You missed that, but I've got something laid out that I can whip up," Hollis said, looking to Daisy. "That okay by you?"

After what she'd been through, she vowed never to be picky about a meal again. "Anything would be welcome."

"I'll put it on," Hollis said, then stopped after he'd taken two steps toward the cookshack. "Had a visitor while you was gone. Said he bought half interest in the Crown Seven Ranch last Christmas."

Trey perked up at that. "What was his name?"

"Charlton. Said a letter arrived at the ranch about you finding Daisy. Don't know what the hell that was about."

"It's a long story," she told Hollis, who was ignorant of her true identity as far as she knew. She turned to Trey. "Do you know him?"

He shook his head. "Never heard of him before. I sent that letter to Reid, thinking he'd know how to get word to Dade. Sounds like this Charlton opened it. Why he thought it was of any interest to him is anyone's guess."

Hollis pointed up the lane. "Reckon you'll find out soon enough. He said he'd be back today. That's him coming now."

Daisy handed her reins to Hollis and moved to stand beside Trey. The stranger sat tall in the saddle, and he looked more gentleman than rancher.

"You want me to stick around?" Hollis asked.

She shook her head. "We'll be fine. Could you take the horses to the stable for us?"

"Sure enough," Hollis said. He ambled off with the weary mounts trailing him.

"Maybe you'd best go inside," Trey told her.

"My ranch. I'm staying right here."

He shook his head. "You sure are a stubborn woman."

"I've refined that trait from being around you."

He slid her a quick grin before turning back to fix a poker face on Charlton.

The man reined up before them but didn't relax his stiff pose one bit. "May I assume you are Trey March?"

"That's me," he said. "Who are you?"

"Shelby Charlton. I purchased the lion's share of the Crown Seven last Christmas."

"That's what Hollis tells me," Trey said. "You ride that horse all the way from Wyoming?"

Charlton's grim mouth twitched in the barest smile. This man saw little humor in life.

"I took the train, but the ride to and from San Angelo is rather long." He cut a sharp glance at Trey. "I need to speak with you in private, Mr. March."

"Sounds serious," Trey drawled, and Daisy knew he was digging in his heels, drawing out the moment just to keep Charlton on edge.

And he had the nerve to call her stubborn!

"It is very important that we talk," Charlton said, impatience making his tone sharp.

"This have to do with the Crown Seven?"

"Partly," Charlton said. "I'd prefer discussing this inside."

Daisy knew if she didn't take a hand in this now, these

two would be in a standoff out here half the night. "Please, do come in, Mr. Charlton."

"Thank you," the gentleman said and dismounted. "Am I to assume you are Daisy Logan?"

"Yes," she said, leading the way to the house and hoping she could make a decent pot of coffee. "Though I didn't realize it until recently."

"I'm sure the man isn't interested in your personal business," Trey said, dogging Charlton's steps and looking annoyed as all get out.

She guided Charlton to the small parlor. "Make yourself at home. Would you like coffee?"

"That would be most welcome." Charlton removed his hat and hung it on a hook before taking a seat by the window.

Trey pulled the chair from the desk and turned it around, straddling it so he could prop his arms on the back. She shook her head, wondering why he was struck with these bouts of defiance around anyone with authority.

"I'll be back in a bit with coffee," she said, sending Trey a warning look to be civil before she scurried off and let these two strong men alone.

Trey had had a real bad hunch he wasn't going to like anything this dandy said from the moment he laid eyes on him. For one thing, he'd bought their ranch out from under them. Never mind that Trey had thought he'd lost his shares last year.

Then there was the fact that this man opened a letter intended for Reid and had the gall to ride down here to confront Trey. Yep, he didn't have a good feeling about this at all.

"Get on with why you're here," he said.

Charlton's mouth thinned into a line of disapproval. "My reasons are twofold. First, you should know that I purchased the Crown Seven from Erston."

"Congratulations," he managed. "It's a fine ranch."

"That it is, though my wife and I have no intentions of living there."

He wasn't surprised. Charlton looked the city type to him, not a man who'd be comfortable living out on the wild Wyoming high plains.

"You buy it as an investment or are you running stock on it?" he asked.

Charlton showed the first signs of nervousness, rolling his shoulders and fidgeting with the knot in his tie. "Actually, I bought it because of you."

That surprised the hell out of him, but he was careful not to show it mattered one way or the other. "I can't imagine why."

"Yes, I'm sure this is all rather confusing to you," Charlton said.

"That's putting it mildly."

Charlton heaved a sigh. "If you'll just hear me out, my reasons will all be quite clear when I'm finished."

Trey nodded. "Fair enough."

"Reid Barclay has told us much about your life in the orphanage and how you came to be there."

"Us?"

"My wife and myself spent the holidays with the Barclays."

Barclays? Just what was going on at the Crown Seven?

"That so?" Trey said, struggling to hold on to his patience.

If Charlton picked up on his annoyance, he hid it well. "Mr. Barclay told us that you grew up in the same orphanage."

"The Guardian Angel's Orphan Asylum. I was left like a basket of kittens on the doorstep."

The man muttered something under his breath, a name or maybe just a curse. "You've no idea how my wife grieved that her son had been treated so cruelly."

Trey leaned back and tapped his fists on the chair back, his nerves snapping with the anger that simmered in him whenever he thought of how little his mother must have cared for him. How she hadn't even bothered to name him.

"Sounds like she didn't know what became of him."

"She didn't." Charlton's features hardened like stone, and his eyes blazed with fury. "Disposing of the baby was her father's choice, not hers. She nearly died giving birth to her son. When she recovered and learned he'd been taken away, she nearly grieved to death."

Trey scrubbed a hand over his mouth, reluctant to believe this man's story, that the young mother had been just as much a victim as the child she'd birthed. "Why'd her father do it?"

"He was a bitter man, filled with hate over the fall of the South. Over going bankrupt and losing his plantation. Having his daughter lose her heart to a Yankee was intolerable."

"Mighty sad tale," Trey said. "What's that got to do with me?"

"There really is no easy way to broach this subject. So I'll get right to the point. My wife is convinced that you are the son who was taken from her at birth."

Of all the things he thought this gentleman would say, that had never crossed his mind. He studied Charlton, looking for some resemblance they shared. But he found nothing.

In fact, the man didn't look one damned bit happy about revealing his reason for being here. That old sense of being unwanted loomed large inside him.

"I take it you don't share your wife's belief," Trey said.

"I am a skeptic by nature," Charlton said. "I've allowed her this fantasy of finding her son for years."

Her son. Not his. "You're not the father then?"

"No. Jeremy was a cousin of mine, a Union officer who

was charged with maintaining law and order in Atlanta while the South was undergoing the Reconstruction. He was shot dead as he was leaving his Army post."

Trey went still, feeling an odd connection to the man who might have fathered him, for he'd nearly suffered the same fate at Durant's hands. All because Daisy was with child.

If you're the son this woman's been looking for, you have a mother. You have kin, and they now own your home.

Nope, he wasn't going to believe it. He needed proof. If he guessed right, so did Charlton.

"So after you read the letter intended for Reid, you came down here to check me out first," he said.

Charlton pinned him with a dark glower. "Let me clarify one thing. Reid read the letter first, then passed it to his wife. She in turn gave it to me while he made plans to travel to Colorado in hopes of finding Dade."

Reid was married? Well that explained why he'd said Barclays.

"Wait a minute. I thought you said you owned the Crown Seven now. What's Reid doing there? When did he get hitched?"

"They exchanged vows last Christmas and continue to live on the Crown Seven. As for the shares of the ranch, we mutually decided to extend the deadline until we were sure if you were my wife's son."

"If I'm not?"

He exhaled heavily. "I've left that decision up to my wife. She's woven quite the touching story about three orphans finding a benefactor to create a family."

"It was more than that," he said. "As children, we were of a like mind to escape the fate planned for us. We knew there was power in numbers. The bond we made then was forged stronger after we were on our own. That's what made us closer than brothers."

"So Reid told me. It couldn't have been easy for any of you living on the streets."

It was hell, but they had stuck together. Cold. Starving. Yet being free was a better fate than being shuffled off to apprentice in some factory.

"Happening on Kirby Morris was the godsend we hadn't anticipated," he said. "He gave us what we'd never had in our lives. A home. Nothing's going to bring that back."

"You don't believe you're my wife's lost son?"

He shook his head. "Sounds farfetched to me."

"Perhaps, but your birth date and age match his."

Trey read the doubt in the other man's eyes and smiled. "Nothing saying that I was really born on that day. Hell, maybe that's when they found me."

"I'm of a like mind." Charlton pushed to his feet and paced the room, clearly not anxious to suddenly have a stepson. "We've visited many orphanages and found several young men who lifted my wife's hopes. I certainly wouldn't say for certain that you are her son just by what we know now."

Trey nodded, admiring the man's honesty. Hell, sounded like he was just trying to protect his wife. Trey would do the same with Daisy.

"That all you're going on then? My birth date and age?"

Charlton shook his head. "There is more to it. Phoebe swears she'll know her son on sight, and then there's the birthmark that he had inherited from his father, passed down generation to generation. It's never failed to show up, so, naturally, I place more stock in that."

Trey relaxed at that. "Afraid I'm not the man she's looking for then. Got plenty of scars, but I don't have any birthmarks."

"Yes, you do," Daisy said from the doorway. "There's one on the back of your neck."

Silence boomed in the room while tension sparked the air.

If that was so, then why hadn't he known about it before now? "That can't be," he said.

"Are you sure?" Charlton asked at the same time.

She nodded, looking from the older man to Trey and jiggling the tray of cups and coffee pot she clutched. He got out of his chair and took the tray from her, his legs feeling stiff and his mind a jumble of questions.

"I'm positive," she said in answer to Charlton's question, then she looked at Trey and added. "Just the edge of it shows on your nape."

He set the tray on the table with hands that shook, afraid to believe it could be true. That he did have a mother who'd wanted him. And a grandfather who despised him so much that he had him taken away.

Before he stepped back, Daisy quickly filled cups with coffee. She pressed one in his hand before turning to Charlton, a surprise for she was a stickler for serving guests first.

"Cream or sugar?" she asked Charlton.

If Charlton noticed the slight, he didn't mention it. "Black is fine."

Trey took a sip of his coffee and welcomed the strong jolt from the brew. He found it hard to believe nobody had ever remarked about the birthmark before. But then again, he'd always worn his hair long.

He set his empty cup down and caught the older man staring at him, his expression pensive. "So what happens next?"

"My wife will query me on your birthmark. May I see it?"

"Sure, why not." He couldn't very well refuse, not when this could just as easily disprove that he was this lost son.

He dragged his hat off and gave his back to the man. He felt the slight tug on his hair as Charlton pulled the strands apart, barely drawing a breath as time crawled by.

Finally Charlton grunted and let go of Trey's hair. He

faced the man again, impatiently waiting while he drank his coffee, noting Charlton looked more unsettled than pleased by his discovery.

"Well?" Trey asked when Charlton just stared at him.

"It looks the same as my cousin's, though his was more visible. Phoebe will know for sure."

"This is a lot to swallow," Trey said.

"Very much so," Charlton said, staring hard at Trey and likely still searching for more family traits.

By his guarded expression, Trey guessed that he didn't favor Charlton's cousin Jeremy at all.

"We'll return by the end of the week. I trust that is agreeable to you both?"

Hell, what could he say? That he was tickled to have found kin? That he could hardly wait to see the woman who'd given birth to him?

The bottom line remained that he wasn't about to open his arms to a stranger, whether they were kin or not. In that regard, he and Daisy agreed, for she wasn't about to bow down to a brother she didn't remember.

Trust had come hard for him all his life. He wasn't about to change now.

"Makes no never mind to me," Trey said.

That sparked a deeper scowl from Charlton. "Young man, I can understand that this is a shock. I certainly don't expect you to fawn over Phoebe either. But she has searched for you for nearly thirty years and finding you will be extremely emotional for her. I ask that you afford her the utmost courtesy and hear her out."

Trey nodded, holding his deepest fears close to his vest as well. He hadn't a clue how a man acted around a mother. Couldn't imagine what kind of woman she'd be. Didn't see any way that he could have anything more than a polite relationship with her at this stage of his life.

"I'll polish up my manners," he said. He was surprised when Charlton nodded.

"Very well. Now if you'll excuse me, I'll be on my way." Charlton stopped before Daisy and gave a brief bow. "Thank you for your hospitality, Miss Logan."

"Please, stay the night," she said, her smile tight.

"I don't wish to inconvenience you," Charlton said, glancing from Trey to her.

"You won't be," she said. "There's a small bedroom right at the top of the stairs."

Between their rooms, Trey thought with a wry grin. Having a guest would keep Trey in his room this night.

"Very well," Charlton said. "I promise to leave before daybreak."

"Hollis will have breakfast on in the cookshack by then. Help yourself," she said.

Charlton dipped his chin. "Thank you, Miss Logan."

She watched Charlton leave for his room, then turned to Trey. Her mouth was pinched in a tight knot, but it was the disappointment in her eyes that made him edgy.

"Why do you push people away?" she asked.

He rubbed his nape, but touching his neck only reminded him of the damned birthmark that would tie him to Mrs. Charlton. Phoebe, he'd called her.

A stranger to him.

"I don't push them away," he said. "I'm just careful who I let get close to me."

"Don't delude yourself," she said. "You've put up a wall around your feelings, and nobody can touch you."

He strode to her and slid his hands around her narrow waist. "I let you touch me all you want."

She shook her head and gave him a pitying look. "No, you don't. Not emotionally at least. That makes me wonder if you feel anything at all when we make love, or if it's just a physical release for you."

"I feel plenty when we're together."

"Like what?"

He scrambled for words to describe the riot of emotions that erupted in him when he kissed her, held her, drove into her and absorbed her tremors and little cries into his soul. "It just feels good. Right."

"My God." She pushed his hands from her and stepped back, eyeing him as if he were a stranger to her. "You've closed yourself off from everyone and everything for so long you're incapable of normal emotions anymore."

He swore loud and long, not liking the picture of a cold, unfeeling bastard that she painted of him one damned bit. But it was so close to the truth that he couldn't voice a denial.

"I don't know any better because I wasn't offered much kindness when I was a child," he said.

"Why?"

"There were a lot of kids in need of comfort. Reckon I'd gotten what little there was to give when I was a baby, but once I got age on me, I became just another mouth to feed."

"What age would that have been?"

He shrugged. "Four or five."

"You were still just a child," she said.

"Like I said, I was one of many, Daisy. The lucky ones got chosen by families when they were babies. Next to them were those who were just walking. Once we got past four or five, folks looked past us and we learned to exist."

She dropped onto the sofa, seeming deflated by that unvarnished fact. "That's horrible. Don't you remember any times when you were shown affection?"

He shrugged and forced himself to sift through those early memories of growing up in the Guardian Angel's Orphan Asylum. "I have a fleeting image of an older woman rocking and singing to me. Mrs. Peach. I can't recall her face clearly, but I always feel warm inside when I hear that lullaby."

"What else?" she asked, watching him closely, like she expected him to recite a list of similar instances.

He frowned, thinking hard now. "I took sick once. They put me in the infirmary for a week. Mrs. Peach sat by my bed, talking softly to me and keeping my head cool with damp cloths."

"She sounds like she was a very good woman," she said.

"She was. But one day she wasn't around anymore," he said. "I remember asking about her and being told she'd died."

"You must have grieved for her," she said.

He shrugged. "Guess so."

He'd cried in silence that night in bed, but he didn't tell Daisy. He'd never told anyone, though Reid had heard.

She crossed to him and cupped his face with her small hands. Warmth flowed into him, as if he were sitting beside a fire on a cold night, thawing the ice from his feet and his heart.

"See, you're not incapable of feeling," she said. "You just don't know how to express it. Why, I bet there were other instances of someone comforting you. Befriending you."

Damned few, but he nodded just the same. "Hank caught me outside once bringing in wood. Shoved me down. That's where I got this scar on my forehead."

She glided a gentle finger over the old wound and damned if he didn't feel healed. Feel whole. But what the hell did a man call that sensation?

"I hope he was reprimanded," she said.

"Nobody saw but Reid, and we all knew telling on Hank did no good," he said. "Reid grabbed Hank by the collar and slammed him up against the shed until Hank begged him to stop. He did, and warned him if he ever laid a hand on me again or did me harm, he'd have Reid to answer to."

"Was that the first time he stood up for you?"

"Yep, and I knew then that I finally had a friend." For the first time in his life he hadn't felt alone. He had been part of something he didn't understand, but that made him feel good. Feel wanted.

She smiled at him, and he found his lips twitching in kind. "Will you promise me one thing?"

His smile faded. "Depends on what that is."

"Stop closing yourself off to everything that tugs at your heart," she said. "Let yourself feel. Let yourself live. Let yourself go like you do in bed."

Damned if his ears didn't burn like fire at the thought. "Can't see a reason why I'd do that."

She dropped a soft kiss on the old scar on his forehead. "I'm going to say this once more, then no more. I love you. I loved you from the first moment I saw you. But unless you return it and mean it, there's no future for us."

"If you're with child—"

She covered his mouth with her hand, her eyes bright with moisture. "As of an hour ago, I'm sure I'm not. What happens to us is up to you now, cowboy."

Chapter 21

The next morning, Daisy woke in an irritable mood. She'd heard Trey leave his bedroom before dawn. Charlton had done the same a bit later.

When the house was quiet, she'd gotten out of bed, dressed and ventured downstairs. Though a pot of coffee had been set on the stove for her, her mood remained on the prickly.

That wasn't like her, but then she'd become a different woman since her daddy died. Since Trey returned to her life.

For one, she disliked sleeping alone. Even having him in the house was a comfort. But since this last ordeal with Ned Durant, she wanted Trey March in her bed every night.

She could have that wish come true if she'd toss out the ultimatum she'd given Trey as they traveled home from that mountain village. But she couldn't do that.

She deserved more, and so did Trey.

Yet the thing that had robbed her of sleep last night was the fact she wasn't with child. How sad was that?

She surely didn't want to be forced to marry a man who didn't love her, yet down deep she'd hoped that choice would be taken from her. But the start of her cycle just as they'd arrived yesterday had ended that hope.

Now she was right back to sticking to her demand and taking the risk that she'd forever lose the man she loved. Yet she couldn't endure a loveless marriage either.

As if to add insult to injury, she'd learned from Hollis that Trey and several of the cowboys had set out at dawn to tend to the calves that were birthing. With the drought and the stocks' condition in moving them here, he'd feared the cows could have trouble.

She couldn't fault him for his diligence, but she could complain that she'd been the last to know.

So with a cup of coffee in hand, she walked to the front door intending to sit on the porch and ruminate on what to do. The last person she expected to come calling was Kurt Leonard.

Just like before, she was gripped with the unsettling urge to run. But before panic engulfed her, Kurt sent her a boyish smile, and her odd unease around him evaporated like morning mist.

"Morning, Daisy." He held a wilted bouquet of wildflowers, but his grip on the poor stems was so tight his knuckles had turned white. Finally, he thrust the flowers at her. "These are for you."

She opened her mouth but nothing came out. Good grief, was he trying to court her?

With effort, she found her voice. "Thank you."

She almost had to pry the flowers from his fingers. He'd never been this nervous around her before. What put him on tenterhooks now?

"Nothing has changed, Kurt," she said.

She didn't love him, and she never would. So she certainly wouldn't encourage him, give him the least bit of hope that they could be anything now but neighboring ranchers.

He scuffed a boot on the porch much like a petulant little boy would do. "Can't you just give us another chance? I can bail you out. Save both the ranches."

But at what price?

She heaved a frustrated sigh. He was clearly a man used to having his way. A man who'd grown up knowing he could have everything he wanted. Anything he could buy.

Well, she was one thing he couldn't have. The sooner he realized it, the better off they'd both be.

"There's no point in trying," she said. "I meant it when I said it was over between us."

"I suppose I knew it that day I saw you with March at the JDB. But I just had to try once more." He stared at her with sad puppy-dog eyes. "Can I at least come in and talk to you one last time?"

"If this is about us courting . . ."

"No. It's not that at all." He scrubbed a hand over his nape. "There's something I need to tell you. Please."

She dreaded listening to his appeals again, but the fact that she'd humiliated him by breaking their engagement was all the reason she needed to hear him out once more. It was what she'd afford any man she might have to do business with in the future.

"Very well," she said and stepped back. "Come on in the parlor."

Kurt squeezed past her and strode inside, then stood in the middle of the room looking like he was lost. Such a nervous man, she thought as she closed the front door.

Of course, her turning him down before could be cause for him to feel awkward around her now. She certainly was ill at ease with him, which was something she'd never felt before. But then what had she felt for him?

He'd been kind. The gentleman who'd called on her and seemed content to sit on the porch sipping lemonade. The only man she'd ever been courted by. The only man who'd ever asked for her hand.

She'd accepted because her daddy had all but insisted on it after he caught her kissing Kurt. Just that one kiss made on a dare. But she hadn't wanted to disappoint her daddy more, so she'd agreed to marry Kurt.

That had been wrong. She'd realized it soon afterward. But she hadn't known how to end it without hurting Kurt and her daddy.

Then Trey had stormed into her life like a West Texas twister and swept her up in his passion. And in the end she hurt three good men.

She stared at the bouquet. Trey had never brought her flowers. She doubted he ever would. Yet Kurt had made the effort, even after she'd hurt him so badly.

"Have a seat while I fetch a vase for the flowers," she told him.

Not that a bit of water would help the poor things. He'd crushed the stems, and the blooms were already wilting from the heat that had begun to build with the rising sun.

Still, she went through the motions for his sake and to bide time. When she returned to the parlor, he was standing in the middle of the room right where she'd left him.

That bizarre unease pulsed around her, and she was beset by the irrational urge to run again. Sweat dotted his upper lip, and his Adam's apple was bobbing like a cork on water, signs that he was equally nervous or coming down with something.

"Are you all right?" she asked.

"I heard about Ned Durant kidnapping you." He looked at her, his gaze wary. "I suppose March was the one who rescued you."

"Yes. We didn't get back home until late yesterday." And that was all she intended to tell him about her misadventure.

He stared at his feet, a frown pulling at his brow. "Did you know Durant told me you'd been seeing March?"

I'm not the only one who knows, Ned had told her. "When was this?"

"The day your daddy summoned me over for that last talk. I didn't want to believe it. Even when you broke our engagement, I still wanted to believe I had a chance with you, that what you had with March was just a passing thing that you'd get out of your system."

As if love was something she could get over.

She pressed her fingers to the bridge of her nose and suffered another pang of guilt for hurting this man. She'd wronged him when she accepted his suit because she hadn't loved him then. When she did come to her senses, it only hurt him more.

"I'm sorry it turned out the way it did," she said, and for lack of a better explanation, she repeated what she'd told him that day. "I shouldn't have waited so long to break our engagement. In fact, I am sorry I led you on to start with."

That unnerving silence hummed around them again. This time the hairs on her nape lifted. It was the strangest sensation, for this only happened to her when she felt threatened, and Kurt certainly hadn't done anything the least bit hostile.

"The day you fell from the loft," he said. "Do you remember what happened?"

Why in the world would he bring that up now? "Vaguely."

"I tried to forget it too, but I can't," he said. "You've got to know I never meant to hurt you."

She set the vase down near the window and stared at him, nearly overcome by a sudden, deadly chill. "What are you talking about?"

He grabbed her upper arm, his hold firm yet unyielding. Just that strong hold sent memories tumbling like weeds in her head, too fast for her to focus on anything. But every nerve in her body screamed at her to run.

"I thought if you had to marry me, you'd come to love me in time," Kurt said. "That we'd have a family. You never would've wanted for anything."

If she had to marry him? Oh, God, oh, God . . .

Heat built in the room, and she felt woozy. Sick at heart as those snippets of memory that haunted her deep in the night blazed anew.

Strong arms tightened around her. Tried to pull her down in the hay.

She'd clawed and twisted until she broke his hold. Until she faced her attacker. And just like fog lifting over the creek, their eyes clashed for a heartbeat.

Not Ned, as she'd thought, but this quiet rancher.

Kurt had been waiting for her in the loft! Waiting to force himself on her in the hope he could plant his seed in her.

He hadn't known she was carrying Trey's child.

Hadn't known, or likely cared, that she couldn't bear to suffer Kurt's touch.

So she broke free and ran. Filled her lungs to scream for help, not seeing the trapdoor was open until she was falling through it.

"Damn you," she said. "Daddy never would have forced me to marry you."

He shook his head in denial. "He would have. You'd have been mine then. But you fought me. And then you fell." He swiped a hand over his mouth. "I thought you were dead and it was my fault. I knew your daddy would skin me alive. So I ran."

She clutched her middle, feeling sick inside as she realized why he'd done what he had. He hadn't meant to kill her, just trap her in marriage. But his selfishness had taken her baby from her.

"Get off my ranch, Kurt," she said, unable to hate him but unwilling to tolerate his presence in her life.

"It was an accident," he said.

She surely wouldn't reveal her secret to this man. "What we had is over and can't be brought back."

And even if it could, she still didn't want him. Wanted him less now that she knew he'd do anything to get his way.

Kurt nodded and backed to the door. "I'm sorry, Daisy."

So was she, but she wasn't about to give him the satisfaction of forgiveness, not after what he'd taken from her, not after he had the gall to come here and think that he stood a chance with her again.

So she simply stood there and stared at him until he finally turned and walked out the door. She moved fast then and turned the lock, heart pounding and heavy with grief.

She stood at the window and watched as he mounted his horse and trotted down the lane. Stood there until she couldn't see him any longer, until she couldn't hear the drum of hooves fading into silence.

Only then did her emotions get the better of her. She pushed away from the window and moved through the parlor into the kitchen with an awful emptiness ballooning inside her.

So much loss. So much heartache.

She collapsed on a chair when her legs refused to carry her any farther. There were no tears. She'd spent them all long ago when she thought Trey was lost to her forever. When she lost the precious life they'd created.

The sadness had stayed with her, aching like a muscle worked too hard. She'd never thought she'd have to deal with such matters and run the ranch, but she had.

After her daddy died, she'd been tempted to give in. But she'd fought back. Fought off Ned's attentions. Fought off Kurt's, not once but twice now. And she'd been prepared to fight Egan Jarvis with her last breath.

Now she was emotionally spent. Alone.

She had to busy herself. She couldn't just sit here and wait for Trey to return. She wouldn't crawl into a shell and cry over what had been.

So she pushed from the chair and set to work. There was

laundry to do. She'd helped Ramona a time or two. She could surely manage alone.

But she ended up needing Hollis's help to fill the wash-tubs with water. She'd insisted she could manage from there, heating the water and doing her laundry.

"Let me know when you're done," he said. "Can't waste water."

"I will."

Three hours later, she hung the last of her clean clothes as well as Trey's on the line in back of the house. Just tending to his things made her feel better. Made her feel like a wife instead of his lover.

But mercy, her back did ache, and she was soaked to the skin. She'd never felt this tired in her life.

Hollis ambled toward her. "Looks like you're done in."

"I won't lie," she said. "I'm bushed. In this heat the clothes ought to dry fast."

"Yep, getting too hot out now for man or beast," he said. "You best go on in the house and rest. I'll tend to my duds and dump the water in the garden patch."

"Thank you." Still she hesitated over leaving just yet, as Hollis set to dumping his clothes in the washtub. "When do you think Trey will be back?"

Hollis shrugged. "Hard to say. Could be any time. Could be late."

She hoped it would be sooner instead of later. "The man who called on me today. If you see him come back here before Trey returns, please come up to the house."

The old man stopped scrubbing his dungarees and stared at her. "You afraid of this fellow?"

The memory of what he'd planned to do in the loft sickened her. "I don't want to be alone with him."

Hollis gave a curt nod. "I'll keep an eye peeled for him then."

"Thank you."

She left him to his work and trudged into the house. With the heat of the day on them, she longed for a siesta. But she refused to rest until she'd washed the sweat from her body, donned fresh clothes, and cleaned the ones she'd worked in.

A quick scrubbing in the house took a bit longer than she'd hoped. She stepped outside to hang those garments too.

Hollis had finished his chore and had dumped the tubs, leaning them against the shed to dry. Nobody else was around.

That cold sense of loneliness swept over her again. Why did it bother her now when it never had before?

She had no answers as she returned to the house and slipped up to her room. With the shades drawn and a breeze drifting through the windows, it was relatively cool.

She curled on the bed, intending to nap for an hour at the most. But time was a thief.

She woke with a start, reliving that scene with Kurt in the loft again. Her breath came too fast and tears still blurred her eyes.

Just a dream, she told herself. There was nothing to fear.

The scuff of a boot on her bedroom floor debunked that thought. She lurched up in bed just as it dipped with a man's weight.

"It's just me," Trey said as he sat at the foot of her bed.

"You scared me."

She swiped the tears from her face and launched herself into his arms. He was safe. Home. Everything would be all right now.

"Didn't mean to frighten you," he said. "I wasn't going to bother you, but I heard you sobbing."

"I had a bad dream again."

He said nothing to that but rubbed her back in long, slow strokes, for he knew her nightmares came with more frequency now. More times than not a bit more of her memory returned as well. But not this time. This nightmare was simply of the tragedy that would plague her for a very long time.

"Heard you had a caller today," he said.

She pulled from him and drew her bare feet under her. "Kurt came by."

"What did he want?"

She tried to read his expression, but his wide-brimmed hat cast his handsome face in shadow. Not that it mattered.

Trey was an expert at hiding any emotion that dared to touch him, especially those he feared. And because of the austere manner in which he'd grown up, he had learned at a young age to closet his feelings.

Yet he wasn't a cold man. Just horribly reserved when it came to matters of the heart.

He had no difficulty showing his rage when it came to wrongs done her. If she told him what Kurt had done, he'd go gunning for him.

Maybe if she had thought Kurt would be a threat to her, she'd encourage Trey's intervention. But Kurt was choking in guilt already, and this time she believed she'd finally made him understand that there was no future for them.

"He asked if he could court me," she said, which was a partial truth.

Trey bit off a ripe curse. "He just doesn't want to give up. Maybe if I paid him a visit—"

"You'll do no such thing. Kurt knows it's over between us this time. Let it go."

"You sure as hell can't." He scooted closer to her. "I know when you're hiding something, when you're hurting inside. And right now you're silently crying a river. Why? Did Kurt do or say something? Did you remember more of the past?"

"Nothing important." Nothing she could share with him.

"I've faced the awful reality that men want me for what I own, but none love me."

He leaned close, not touching her, but she felt his strong presence wrap around her just the same. But it wasn't enough. It never was with him.

"Is love that important to you?" he asked.

"It means everything." Yet even now when they were at loggerheads over this, she ached to lean into him. "I wish you could understand that. Wish you could let yourself go and just feel what I do."

He heaved out a breath and hung his head. "I'm trying, Daisy. But I can't change nigh on thirty years of thinking one way for another overnight."

"I don't expect you too. There's no rush." Nor would there be, for she couldn't welcome him into her bed and risk entrapment again.

"Isn't there?"

"No. Any decision we make is ours now. All we can do is wait out the drought." Both the one drying up the land and the emotional one that could dry up her heart if Trey couldn't find it in his to love her.

But he was shaking his head as if disagreeing with her. "Dade could show up any day out of the blue."

"I don't see what that has to do with the way you and I run this ranch," she said, her anger building because she knew what he meant. "I won't hold for Dade Logan coming in here and telling me how to run this ranch."

"It's not the ranch he'll take exception to. It's me living here with you," he said. "It makes it look like we're not just business partners but bed partners as well."

Which they were. They had been from the start, and he hadn't batted an eye then. So why all the fuss now?

It was because of Dade. He was more worried about

what her brother would think than about sullying her reputation.

He cared more for her brother than her.

The thought of having a stranger here instead of Trey rankled. "I'm beginning to dread this reunion with my brother."

"Don't. You'll do fine once you get to know him again." He trailed a finger down her cheek, and she was powerless to stop the moan that escaped her. "I just don't care to get in a fight with him."

She grabbed his hand, her fingers curling around his. But instead of pulling him from her, she held him close.

"There will be no fighting," she said. "He's got to see that you're my partner in this ranch. It's up to us if we tell him any more than that. As for you sleeping in the house, you have every right to stay here with me."

He leaned closer to her, so close she could almost taste him on her tongue. "Dammit, Daisy. I'm trying to protect your reputation."

"A little late for that."

"What would you rather do? Flaunt that we're lovers in front of your brother?"

"Of course not. That's nobody's business but ours." She curled her fingers around his arms and felt his strength seep into her, chasing away her fears. "It's just that there's no need for you to move out yet, especially this time of day."

His hold on her gentled. "Hell, you're afraid to be alone."

She was, but she didn't like admitting it. "I'm not used to living in a house by myself, especially after all that's happened of late."

He cupped her chin and lifted her face to his, his kiss no more than the brush of lips. But she felt the burn of desire clear to her toes.

"If you marry me, you'll never have to sleep alone again."

She smiled and rested her forehead against his, for if

nothing else he was persistent. "Do you have something to tell me, Trey March?"

She felt the tension stiffen his body, and she went still as well. Even the wind whistling around the eaves died too, as if holding its breath for his answer.

He said nothing for so long she almost believed he was gathering his courage to reveal what was in his heart.

"No."

And that one word told her either he'd lost his nerve or she was just trapped in wishful thinking again.

"Then you'd better find your own bed," she said.

"I will," he said, yet he stole another kiss.

"Have you forgotten I'm indisposed?" she asked, thankful that her time had visited her now, because it'd be so easy to surrender to passion.

She had to be strong. For as much as she wanted him and his child, he had to come to her with love in his heart.

"Nope. I remember. But that don't mean we can't enjoy a bit of necking." His lips found hers in a long, drugging kiss that left her breathless, left her trembling with longing. "Just for a minute or two."

"All right."

But like all the other times, a minute or two of kissing turned into five. Then they were both lost in the passion that raged through them.

He pushed her back on the bed, and she threaded her fingers through his hair, holding fast to him. His hands weren't idle either, gliding over the curve of her hip before meandering back to her breasts.

It amazed her how quickly his big fingers could work the buttons on her bodice, but in moments he'd pushed that garment off her shoulders. Her corset hooks gave next, and then his big palms were cupping her bared breasts that were left damp from the heat of the day and the desire burning within her.

"You're so fine," he said, before his tongue swirled around one hardened nipple.

Her back arched on a pleading moan. He answered by drawing hard on one breast while toying with the pebbled tip of the other one, then kneading the soft flesh until she was sure she'd die from the pleasure.

Distantly she heard the back door open and close. Trey paused too, his big body going stiff.

"Hollis," she whispered.

The old cook brought up supper every day around this time. He'd set it on the stove and leave.

Still Trey remained frozen over her, his head canted, her breasts forgotten. The door shut a moment later, so softly she wouldn't have heard it if she hadn't been listening.

She vowed then to learn to cook for herself. In time she wouldn't want even this slight interruption.

He tossed her a crooked grin. "Where was I?"

She threaded her fingers through his tousled hair and pulled him back to her. "In my arms."

And a heartbeat later he returned to kissing her with wild abandon before lowering his head to pay her breasts homage again. She swept her hands down his back, annoyed that he'd left his shirt on and denied her the feel of his warm skin beneath her fingers.

But she marveled at the band of muscles that flexed beneath her palms. At the tremor that shot through him when she raked his back with her nails.

She'd been sure they'd made love every way imaginable, but this bout of necking took her back to that first time she'd gone to him. It'd been hot like this then, but a bigger fire had burned in her all day.

Daddy had had hay delivered from San Angelo, and Trey had been up in the loft to fork it from the conveyor and stack it to the rafters. Once or twice she'd caught a glimpse of him taking a breath at the haymow, shirtless, his beautifully toned body glistening with sweat.

Oddly enough he'd seen her as well standing near the well. The you-want-it-then-come-take-it look that he fixed on her shocked her to her core. But in the end she'd gone to him.

He lifted his head, his eyes glazed with passion, his breath sawing fast and hard in the silence. "We'd best stop while I still can."

"Are you denying me the pleasure of having my way with you?" she asked as she tugged his shirt from his jeans and slipped her hands up his bare chest.

He tossed his head back and pinched his eyes shut. "A man can only hold out so long."

"Then give in." *Stop fighting the emotions that surely must be crowding your heart. Tell me you love me as much as I love you.*

She got his belt unbuckled and the top button popped free on his jeans before he captured her hands. He pulled them above her head and grinned down at her.

"No fair," she protested.

"You should talk." He shifted and lowered his weight on her, letting her feel the hard ridge of his cock press against her belly. "I'm in control now, and I say that can wait."

She bucked against him, not to throw him off but to settle him more firmly between her legs. But the man wouldn't budge.

"Get off me."

"Nope. I finally got you where I want you—"

"What the hell's going on here?" said a deep, masculine voice, a stranger's voice, a voice laced with raw fury.

Chapter 22

"Get out," Trey said, not about to shift one inch and expose Daisy, especially to her brother, who was likely holding on to his temper by a thread.

The only thing saving Trey at this moment was that Dade Logan wasn't sure if the woman under him was Daisy. But dammit all, when he was sure, all hell would break loose.

"Pardon the intrusion," Dade said. "But Reid told me you'd found Daisy."

Daisy clamped both hands on Trey's shoulders and craned her neck to get a look at the brother she couldn't remember. "Is that him?" she whispered.

"Yep, it sure is."

Even in the dim light Trey saw Daisy's face leach of color. She shrank into the mattress and commenced buttoning herself.

"Dammit, Trey, where's my sister?"

Trey kept his gaze on Daisy and counted to ten, then twenty. Hell, it hadn't taken him that long to strip her.

He dropped a kiss on her mouth. "Brace yourself."

And when she smiled up at him, he shoved himself off the bed and rolled to his feet. His gaze locked with Dade's, and that old familiar pull of loyalty seeped into him. But oddly enough there was a stronger pull on him now, and it all centered on the golden-haired vixen who'd scrambled from the bed to stand beside him.

Beside him, not behind as he wanted her to do so he could protect her.

Yep, his Daisy had grit. She had shown it with Egan Jarvis and now she was showing it to Dade.

His foster brother was looking from Daisy to Trey like he was fit to kill.

Having Dade catch him between Daisy's spread legs with her bosom bared was not the way he'd thought to introduce the lost siblings. Shit, could it get any worse?

"You no-good sonofabitch," Dade said, face red and big fists bunched at his sides. "Outside so we can talk."

He swore under his breath, for the talking Dade surely aimed to do was with his fists. "Now calm down. It's not what you think."

Dade's eyes narrowed. "Your pants are unbuttoned, and her blouse is askew. Only way it ain't what I think is if you two are married."

"We're not," Trey said.

"You planning to be?"

Before he could think of a way to explain that one, Daisy spoke up again. "No."

"Then it's just what I thought," Dade said. "Talk's over."

"How dare you!" Daisy said, her tone as sharp as the glare she shot her brother. "You've no right to barge into my house, let alone my bedroom."

"I've got every right." He glared at Trey, who merely sighed in resignation.

How damned ironic that he'd tempted fate by sleeping with Daisy right under Barton's nose. He'd known full well that the man would flay him alive for touching his princess. Knew he would've had to light out or end up married if he was caught.

Now he faced the same thing with Dade. He knew he was in for a tongue-lashing and a whupping, and he didn't fault Dade for doing either.

"Get a move on," Dade said. "We need to talk outside."

He heaved a sigh and headed for the door, shouldering his way past Dade. "You better be right behind me."

"Right on your heels," Dade said.

Never mind the men likely knew she and Trey were cozy. This would bring it out in the open. Get tongues wagging. Daisy let loose an exasperated gasp. "Stop this, both of you!"

But Trey pounded down the stairs with Dade dogging his steps. As pissed as Dade was with him now, it was nothing compared to how furious he'd feel toward Trey if he heard the whole history between him and Daisy.

Not that he planned to enlighten Dade about their troubled dalliance. As she'd said, that was his and Daisy's business.

But he wasn't going to make Dade believe that his being in Daisy's bed was a one-time incident either. Nope, best thing he could do would be take his licking and agree to marry Daisy, which is ultimately what he wanted anyway.

Maybe this way he wouldn't have to bare his soul to her to get her to agree that they were right together.

"Will both of you stop and use your heads for something other than a hat rack?" she all but screeched at them when they reached the kitchen. "If you go outside spitting and fighting, then every man on this ranch will be privy to my private life."

Trey came up short in the doorway and turned. Dade had stopped as well, but his gaze was still fixed on Trey.

"Daisy's right," he said. "We take this outside and two things are going to happen. The men will jump you for attacking me, and Daisy's reputation will take a beating."

"Fine," Dade said. "We'll have it out in here."

"That's enough!" Daisy flicked Dade a glower as she made to breeze past him, but he caught her arm and held her fast, keeping her from going to Trey. "Let go of me."

"So you can run to him?" Dade asked. "You just stay out of this and let me handle it."

"There's nothing to handle," Daisy said.

Trey stepped forward. "Leave her alone."

"Back off."

"Look out, Daisy," Dade said, and gave her a tug to keep her from going to Trey.

She yelped and stumbled back toward Dade.

Trey swore. Now why'd he have to get rough with Daisy?

Before Dade shoved her behind him and straightened, Trey drove a fist into his face. But Dade always had been strong as a bull and barely flinched.

With a curse, he brought a roundhouse punch up that caught Trey under the chin and sent him stumbling backward. His back slammed into the wall so hard the plates in the cupboard rattled.

He moved his mouth to test his jaw and pushed from the wall. It'd been years since he and Dade had gotten into a fistfight. The last time Dade had been on his side fighting with him.

Now they were at odds over Daisy, circling each other in the kitchen with fists raised like pugilists. Didn't much matter that he felt Dade was in his rights defending his sister's honor. Trey wasn't about to sit still for a beating.

Daisy yelped again and scrambled around Dade, planting herself between the two of them. "Stop this nonsense!"

"Get out of the way," Dade said.

"Do as he says," Trey said.

She let out another weary groan but didn't budge. "No! Listen to me. Please! I won't have you fighting, but if you feel you must, then get out of here."

Dade pulled a dark face then started to the door. Trey heaved a sigh and started to follow.

"Once you leave, don't ever come back," she said. "Either of you."

Dade pulled up first and Trey damned near walked up his back. They both turned to her.

"You're serious," Trey said.

"Very," she said.

He caught the slight tremor of her lips and knew that drawing this hard line hadn't been easy for her. But she'd done it, proving she was indeed Jared Barton's daughter. Not blood, but a bond just as strong. A bond he understood, for he'd had the same with Dade and Reid.

"Now hold on," Dade said. "I'm family. You can't toss me out on my ear."

Her eyes swam with moisture but not one drop fell. For that alone Trey's respect for this little woman skyrocketed.

"I'm sorry but I don't remember you at all," she said.

Dade flinched, clearly not expecting that or taking it well. "How could you forget?"

She shook her head and cast Trey a pleading look.

"When Daisy was on the orphan train," Trey began, "she took a bad fall. Since then she hasn't remembered anything that happened before that day."

"Nothing?" Dade asked.

"I get fleeting images that make no sense, but I don't remember my parents or you," she said. "Trey is the one who finally figured out who I was."

Dade cut him a caustic glower. "Was that before or after you'd become cozy with my sister?"

"After," he admitted.

"Mighty damned convenient," Dade said, taking a threatening step closer to him.

Yep, they were going to throw fists. Not here. Likely not where anyone would see them. But they were bound to have it out just the same.

Trey almost looked forward to it, for he knew that was the only thing that would clear the fouled air between him and his foster brother.

"Don't blame him," she said. "Everything I know about you I learned from Trey."

Dade planted his hands on his hips and blew out a heavy breath. "Seems to me that your memory loss is more reason for you to need a man's help. A brother's help to be precise."

Trey just stared at him. For a man who'd been able to see both sides of any picture, Dade sure was blind when it came to his own life.

"Dammit, Dade," he said. "You're a stranger to her. How the hell can you expect her to trust you?"

Dade looked as confounded as he felt. "It's been years since you saw me," Dade said to Daisy. "But I promised you then that I'd take care of you. That's all I aim to do now."

She shook her head, her face pale and her expression troubled. "You must realize that too many years have passed and too much has happened for us to go back to that."

"I can see that now," Dade said, flicking a damning look Trey's way. "But you're a woman alone with a lot to manage. That's when kin pull together."

"You need to bear in mind that I'm of age, and I hold title to two ranches," she said. "My daddy left everything he had to me. Not a foreman or a friend. Not blood kin I may or may not have. Just me."

"You booting me out of your life then?" Dade asked.

"Of course not. I want to spend time with you. Get to know you again," she said. "But I won't hold with you running my life for me."

Dade nodded. "Fair enough."

She studied the two men in her life. Both sported fresh bruises, and Trey's face still bore cuts and bruises from his fight with Egan Jarvis.

The tension between them was real and disturbing. She didn't want to be the one who came between brothers. *Brothers!*

Likely the best thing to do would be to send them to the bunkhouse. But she still was uneasy staying here alone.

"Can I trust you two to be civil now?" she asked.

"I have no quarrel with him," Trey said, which earned a scowl from her brother.

"Well, he did at least send word to me that he'd found you," Dade said a bit grudgingly.

She sighed. Their animosity was still fresh. It likely wouldn't end until they'd talked things out. Again, that wasn't something she wanted bandied about near the hands.

That left the only sane solution. "There's a small room next to Trey's," she said. "You're welcome to it."

"Much obliged."

Trey frowned but didn't say a word. Not that he had to. She could read his expression clearly. He wasn't pleased that her brother would be living in the house.

That would stop any future dalliance with him like they'd enjoyed before Dade arrived. God knew she'd miss his touch too.

But this was for the best, because nothing had changed her decision. She wasn't going to marry Trey unless he revealed what was in his heart. And Dade would surely press the point and blame Trey if they continued being lovers.

She looked at the two men she'd come between. It

pained her to be the cause of this rift. Pained her more that she couldn't remember Dade, at least not clearly.

"Please, let's sit in the parlor and talk," she said.

Dade inclined his head, his eyes hopeful. "I'd like that."

She crossed to the parlor and stepped aside to let Dade pass. "Make yourself at home."

A saying she'd used before with little meaning, but the words seemed right this time. Her brother. Blood kin. And a lawman at that.

She was about to take her chair across from Dade when she realized Trey hadn't followed them. She looked through the doorway to him still standing at the back door.

"Trey?"

He gave her a crooked smile. "You two have a talk. I'll see to Dade's horse and be back in a bit."

"But there are so many things I'm unsure of," she said, earning a raised brow from Dade.

"I'll fill in any blanks for Dade later."

And with that he strode from the house, leaving her and the brother she didn't remember all alone. She turned to find him studying her, not with anger this time but concern.

"You rely on Trey," he said.

"Yes. He's helped me piece some of my past together, but so much is still cloaked in shadow."

He shifted on a scowl, as if uncomfortable with that admission. "What do you remember?"

She shook her head. "Pitifully little. Most of it comes in dreams. Just fragments of scenes or snatches of conversation that make no sense."

"Trey said you'd taken a fall on the orphan train?"

"I think so."

"You're not sure?"

She looked at him, such a changed man from the angry

one who'd been ready to tear Trey apart. He'd taken off his hat to reveal a head of thick brown hair.

His eyes were no longer in shadow. Soulful brown eyes that brought snippets of memories to mind of a young boy who'd seemed far too old for his years.

"You all right?" he asked.

She smiled and nodded, the unease she'd felt with him drifting away like a feather caught on the wind. "I remember seeing you as a boy. Remember you holding my hand."

He smiled then, and his broad shoulders lost their rigid lines. "I never let you out of my sight. They had to pull you from me at the orphanage."

That dredged a shiver from her. "The Guardian Angel's Orphan Asylum. I don't remember much of it at all, but Trey told me about that time. How you were always getting in trouble because you were trying to protect me."

His smile faded, and his gaze lowered. "That was the worst time in my life. I was lucky to make friends with Reid and Trey in the punishment shack."

"He told me." And she'd cried because it'd been her fault that they'd been punished.

"They put you on the orphan train soon after," he said. "I found the place where you'd been taken off it."

"In Texas?"

He shook his head. "Kansas. There was a bordello there and not much else. Ring a bell?"

She tried to remember it but couldn't. "I can remember being taken from the train. Standing with another girl and holding hands." That stab of old fear sank into her then. "The matron dragged me away. That's when I broke free and ran, but I fell. I've no idea what happened after then."

"You took a bad fall," he said. "Knocked you out."

Her gaze flew to his. "How do you know that?"

"Maggie told me. She was—"

"My friend on the train." Daisy lurched from her chair

and crossed to the sofa where Dade sat. Her fingers curled over his, and he turned his hand so he could hold hers.

The rightness that flowed through her warmed as nothing else had. But it was the affection that touch laid bare that brought tears to her eyes.

"You've talked with Maggie?"

He let out a small chuckle, but it soon built into a deep laugh that made his eyes crinkle and brought to mind the boy he'd been so very long ago. "It's a long story that I'll tell you later, but I married Maggie Sutten a month ago."

What a small world. "Where is she?"

"Back home and none too pleased with me for riding out without her," he said. "But I wasn't sure what to expect. Trey didn't divulge much in his letter, and I was too impatient to take the train."

She smiled at that admission. "That seems to be a universal trait with men. Daddy was that way. Trey's the same."

He turned serious again, and his fingers tightened a bit on hers. "When you say 'daddy,' you're not talking about our pa."

She shook her head. "I don't remember him at all. Or if I do, it's not clear."

"Reckon that's for the best."

She thought of what Egan Jarvis had said about Clete Logan and his gang. "Was our father really that bad?"

Dade heaved a sigh, then told her about the cruel man who'd treated their mother like dirt. That she'd died giving birth to another baby and that the baby had died as well. Of their pa not shedding a tear. He moved another woman into the house, and a few weeks later he packed his children up and took them to the orphanage because he didn't want the responsibility of a family.

Dade hadn't seen or heard from him until just a month or so back when the Logan Gang held up the bank in the town where Dade was sheriff.

"A bounty hunter tracked them down. They're all dead now." A sad smile tugged at his mouth. "We're the only blood kin we have left."

She didn't miss the "blood kin" part one bit, for it was clear that down deep he viewed Trey as his brother. But Trey March had never been her brother. He'd been the cowboy she'd taken notice of the first time he road onto the ranch.

He was her lover. Would have been the father of her baby.

"I'm glad that we've reunited after all these years," she said, choosing her words with care. "We have Trey to thank for that."

His smile vanished under a troubled frown. "How long have you two been"—he waved a hand as if trying to snatch the words out of thin air—"close."

She supposed that was a better word to use than *lovers*. "I was drawn to Trey the first time I saw him."

He nodded, his mouth set in a grim line. "Likely you remembered him from the orphanage."

"No, I don't think so. The only young boy I remembered seeing was you, and I didn't know at the time that I was recalling my brother." She laid her other hand atop his, sandwiching it between hers. "I didn't know for sure until I looked into your eyes."

They fell silent, and the beginnings of familiarity began to weave around Daisy. Holding his hand was a comfort. It gave her a sense of security like she'd always felt around her daddy that was far different from the protective passion she felt with Trey.

"I guess you never knew Barton adopted you?"

She sat back, breaking the physical contact with her brother but feeling that spark of connection with him remain. "Daddy never said a word about it, and I had no reason to believe that I wasn't his daughter."

Dade nodded. "Guess I can see where a man would do that, especially if he knew who you really were. He might've feared that if word got out, it'd bring the Logan Gang to his door."

"Maybe."

She supposed that could have been part of it, but she was more inclined to think that Jared Barton was simply a powerful, possessive man. Everything he owned bore his brand. It made sense that he'd see she carried his name as well.

"Barton know about you and Trey?"

"Yes, and he wasn't happy about it." He had been spitting mad when he learned that Trey had loved her and left her.

"Surprised he didn't put a gun in Trey's back and see that he did right by you."

She smiled at that, for it was exactly what Trey had said Dade would do. And he likely would still try to do that if she let him take over her life.

"Daddy would've if he could've found him," she said, earning a questioning frown from Dade. "I'll let Trey tell you the particulars of that episode. But because of me, he nearly died six months back."

She shivered just thinking again of what Ned had put him through. Not once but twice.

"He risked his life again for me just a few days ago."

"Sounds like he's got more history with you than I do," Dade said.

Most of it was troubled.

"Daddy protected me too much. But when he died, I wasn't prepared to take over the ranches, and Trey wasn't here to help then."

"But he came back."

She nodded. "He'd like to buy this ranch, but he's as cash poor as I am."

"He could marry you, which he ought to do anyway."

"He could," she allowed, ignoring the rest of his opinion. "All I ask for is his love, and he can't give that."

Dade pulled a face and downed his head. "Damn. The one thing a good woman wants and men like us have trouble giving."

"But you did find a way," she said.

"Wasn't easy," he said. "Reckon it'll be harder for Trey. He always was a stubborn cuss."

She hung her head, not knowing what to think anymore. "We're at an impasse. I'm not willing to take less."

He leaned back on the sofa and studied her with dark, unreadable eyes. "I don't know what all happened this past week, but I'll tell you one thing. If he didn't care deeply for you, he never would've risked his life for you."

"I know that, but it doesn't change what I have to hear from his heart."

"Could be that the worst is yet to come," he said.

"What do you mean?"

He leaned forward and rested his bent arms on his knees. "Mrs. Charlton, the wife of the man who bought the Crown Seven, thinks that Trey might be her long lost son."

She nodded. "Mr. Charlton has already paid Trey a visit. As you can imagine, it was laced with tension. He is coming back in a week with his wife. I'm worried how Trey will cope if he really is this lost son."

"Hard to say, but I'd guess he won't take it well." Dade rubbed his forehead, looking weary. "Reid's coming too. He thought it'd be best if Trey had his family close."

"A united front?"

He smiled. "Something like that." He took her hand and squeezed it. "Much as I want to stay here and get to know you better, I know if I don't head back home in the morning and fetch Maggie, there will be hell to pay."

"You'll come back and bring her?"

He laughed. "I won't get out of town without her. You're going to need a woman in your corner, little sister. An old friend."

"I'd like that," she said.

"Good. Now I'd best round up Trey and get some answers out of him."

"Promise me you won't bully him."

"You really are protective of him, aren't you?"

"Somebody has to love him."

He shook his head. "He's one lucky cowpoke. Hope to hell he realizes it soon."

So did she. But she was almost out of room to hope anymore.

Chapter 23

Trey March stood at the paddock and watched the horses cutting up in the pasture in the early morning mist. Most mornings he felt the same, with his first thoughts on Daisy and a hard-on that only she could ease.

He'd yet to wake with her in his arms and find that satisfaction, and it was looking like he never would. Unless he lied to her, told her he loved her.

He scrubbed a hand over his mouth and swore. He couldn't do that to her, and Dade's parting warning an hour ago to "get his shit together" had nothing to do with it.

By the end of the week, his brothers would arrive, and he'd find out what really happened with Reid over two years ago. Dade had only told him that the truth would make them stronger. That made him smile.

Since the day he'd driven these thoroughbreds to the Circle 46, he'd wanted to show them off to Reid. To brag a bit. To let his eldest brother know that he was well on his way to raising fine horses too.

He wanted to be on equal footing with Reid. He'd thought owning these horses and having a stake in land would do that. But now he wasn't so sure. Hell, he wasn't sure about anything, even who he was.

The scent of lilacs seeped into his senses. He turned just as Daisy climbed onto the fence and stood, so she was nearly eye level with him where he sat.

"Why didn't you come to breakfast with me and Dade?" she asked.

"Thought you two needed time alone."

He eyed her, thought she was the prettiest woman he'd ever seen in his life. Thought he'd surely never get tired of standing beside her each morning just like this, seeing her smile up at the sun. At him.

He could have it all if he could just say those words. But that's all they'd be. Words without meaning.

"Dade warned me that I shouldn't be surprised if you disappeared for a day or so," she said.

He nodded, knowing that's what he always did when tough decisions had to be made. He'd go off to think things through.

"'Sulking time is a waste,' Reid always said," he admitted. "Dade would always look me up and talk me into siding with him."

"Because he was right?"

He shrugged. "Sometimes he was, but I always ended up doing it just to keep peace."

That pattern had only served to set them up for the fall when Reid betrayed them. Except it hadn't been Reid at all. Kirby's cousin was the culprit, Dade said, but wouldn't tell him any more until they were all together.

"Are you nervous about seeing him again?" she asked.

"Reid? Hell, no. It's past time we talked things out." He needed to hear from him what had turned him. Why he'd been led to believe that Reid had betrayed them.

"Something's bothering you. What is it?"

Part of it was her and what she wanted from him, but telling her that would just be rehashing the same old thing. Besides, what was driving him away was himself.

"I've been thinking about what Charlton said about his wife looking for her son and thinking it's me."

"You sure that's all it is?"

"You got a better idea?"

"Yes, I do. You're hesitant about meeting Mrs. Charlton," she said. "You're afraid you won't be the son she's looking for."

He heaved out a breath. Hesitant?

"Nope, I'm scared shitless that I *am* her lost son."

Her big eyes widened, and her soft lips parted. "Why?"

Having a mother who wanted him could change his whole life in ways he couldn't imagine. *If* he was Mrs. Charlton's lost son. *If* she recognized the birthmark on his nape that Daisy swore he had. That Charlton had insisted on seeing.

He'd accepted the fact that he was a tumbleweed, likely a bastard not wanted by his family. Even on the Crown Seven, he'd never balked about being the youngest brother. He'd always felt he owed Reid allegiance for taking him under his wing in the orphanage. He'd accepted Dade as one of their own soon after that.

"I don't know how to be a son," he said. "Don't know how to be part of a family. Don't know much about those feelings you talk about."

She didn't say a thing. Just stood beside him clinging to the corral fence and watching the horses run wild. He thought maybe she was ignoring him, thinking he was crazy in his head for not understanding what she took for granted. But he couldn't just feel the same things she did.

"I guess I know more than anyone how hard this is for you," she said. "You can't change how you think and feel overnight. I sure don't expect you to. In fact I wouldn't believe you if you did."

He nodded. Blew out a relieved breath that she understood him better than he did himself. "What do I do, Daisy?"

"What did you do before when you were faced with a difficult decision?"

He hung his head and let out the beginnings of a laugh. "Like Dade said, I went off on my own. Holed up. Thought things through. Came back having an idea of what I had to do to be true to myself and whatever I was facing."

She smiled and gave his shoulder a teasing nudge with her own. "Did it work?"

"Most times," he said, liking her like that and feeling at ease, wishing they could stand here forever just jawing.

But that wasn't to be.

His past was fixing to descend on him. He had to take a good long look at himself before that happened. He knew only one way, even though leaving Daisy was the last thing he wanted to do.

"I'm going away for a few days," he said, his mind made up.

"Where to?"

Some place where folks were few and far between. Some place where he wouldn't be bothered. Some place where he could take that good, hard look at himself and see if there was a chance he could become the man she needed him to be.

"Think I'll head back to the JDB and hole up in the adobe," he said.

She didn't move. Didn't give any sign that she cared one way or the other.

"Will you come back?" she asked at last, and the worry in her voice sank into his soul and stirred that odd feeling again.

"You can bet on it."

No matter what he decided, he'd come back here, if only to tell her he was riding on. That she'd be better off with him being a memory than being her man.

"What should I tell Dade and Reid if they arrive before you get back?"

"Tell them I went off to think," he said. "They'll understand." Or at least Dade would.

He climbed off the fence and resisted the urge to help
her down, to slip his hands around her little waist once
more. To pull her to him and kiss her like there was no tomorrow. For there very well might not be one for them.

She didn't move from where she clung to the fence. She
just stared out at the pasture in silence.

Maybe that was best, for he didn't want to see any tears
as he rode off. Didn't want her sadness tormenting his mind.

Yet an empty feeling settled in his gut as he strode to the
corral. It was something he'd never felt before, at least not
this intensely.

Too much on his mind, he reasoned. Too much that
could go right or wrong.

He opened the gate to find Hollis carefully pouring a
bucket of water into a small trough set in the shade of the
barn. "I'll be leaving for a spell. Watch over Daisy while
I'm gone."

"You need supplies?" Hollis asked.

"Yep. Enough to last a couple of days." He kicked a clod
of rock-hard ground. "Daisy knows where I'll be, but if
something happens and you need me, I'll be at the JDB.
Keep that under your hat."

Hollis nodded. "I'll get your supplies ready.

By the time he saddled the calico gelding, Hollis had
filled his saddlebags with enough provisions to last a week.
Maybe the man knew him better than he thought.

He turned the horse south without looking back at
Daisy, without taking one last look at the Circle 46 that felt
like home with her here. His gaze fixed on the lonely plains
yawning ahead like an endless, dun sea.

He knew lonely. Had lived with it all his life even when
he was with his foster brothers.

Would it always be that way, or was he finally ready to

open himself up? That's what he had to find out, and he wouldn't come back until he had an answer.

On the afternoon of the fourth day since Trey left, Dade and his bride rode onto the Circle 46 in a buckboard that had a mound of valises and bandboxes tied down on the shelf behind the seat. Daisy wasn't surprised that her brother was the first of her guests to arrive. Nor was she shocked that it appeared their stay would be lengthy.

"This is my wife, Maggie," he said, his voice rich with affection. "She was on the orphan train with you."

Daisy smiled at the beautiful woman with the sparkling blue eyes and wealth of honey-colored hair and extended her hands to her. "Is it really you?"

"It's me," she said, their hands clasping in an age-old bond of sisterhood. "I've thought of you every day of my life."

Daisy wished she could say the same, but her memories of the tall girl on the orphan train were sketchy and troubling. And then her gaze fixed on the broach at Maggie's throat. A cameo broach of a mother and a child.

"Oh, my God," she said. "Where'd you get that broach?"

Maggie's fingers lifted to the piece, carefully unhooking it. She pressed it into Daisy's hands.

"You lost it the day they took us off the orphan train and a man took you in," Maggie said.

Flashes of that horrid scene tormented her, but none clearly enough to remember. Yet she knew this was hers.

"I remember this." She looked to Dade who was deathly quiet. "It was Mama's."

He nodded. "When Pa left us at the door of the orphanage, he pinned that on your dress."

Daisy closed her eyes as silent tears slipped down her

cheeks. Finally a memory of her real family. Blood kin standing beside her. And a family heirloom to cherish.

"For years I thought I'd made you up in my mind," she told Maggie.

"You poor dear," Maggie said. "When we found out you'd lost your memory, we were worried sick what had become of you."

Daisy looked from Maggie to Dade, whose cheeks had taken on a ruddy hue. "When did you find this out? Where?"

"In Kansas. Didn't Dade tell you about our adventure?"

She looked up at her brother standing so tall and solemn with just the tinge of red on his cheekbones. "No, he just said it was a long story and let it go at that. I gather it was an interesting one as well."

He shifted from foot to foot, looking mighty uncomfortable discussing his private life. "That's putting it mildly."

Daisy hooked her arm in Maggie's. "Do come in. I'm most curious about this adventure you took to find me."

"Believe I'll have a talk with Trey while you two are hashing over old times," Dade said.

Daisy stopped to face her brother. "He's not here. He went off to think things through and said you'd understand."

Dade swore and kicked at the ground. "Was afraid he'd take off."

"He'll be back."

But Dade's expression didn't reassure her at all. "I'll see to the buckboard and be in later. You two go on and catch up on old times."

Maggie stopped to get a parting kiss from her husband before joining Daisy inside. Daisy bit her lip, kicking herself for not kissing Trey before he left, for just standing on the fence staring at the horses through watery eyes.

My God, what if Trey didn't return? What if her insistence on holding out for love coupled with his fear over meeting the mother he'd thought had abandoned him were just too much to deal with?

Don't think that way. He had given his word. Only thing that would stop him from keeping it would be if he ran into trouble.

Like Egan Jarvis?

"You're worried," Maggie said when they were seated in the parlor.

She nodded, seeing no reason to deny it. "It's a troubling time for Trey, and there's nothing I can do to make it easier for him to bear," she said. "Now please, I am most interested to learn how you and my brother met."

Maggie laughed. "It all started with me running for my life and using your name. Your brother didn't take my deception well at all."

For the next hour, Daisy listened with rapt fascination as Maggie told her about the rich family who'd taken her into their home. Of the wild journey she and Dade embarked on to find Daisy, rife with danger and passion. How Maggie slowly fell in love with Dade but feared she'd never be able to have a normal life with him because of the man tracking her down.

"We were so sure we were closer to finding you once I recognized the place where the train stopped and you were taken away," Maggie said.

A hazy image of being herded from the train like cattle flashed in her mind's eye. "I remember the cold and the wind. The matron grabbed my hand and pulled me from you."

"Yes! It was horrible," Maggie said. "We were both crying, and you fought so."

She nodded, seeing that much. "I broke free and ran from her. But I fell." She shook her head. "I don't remember anything after that."

"You fell off the platform and knocked yourself out.

That man who arranged to have the train stopped there picked you up, put you in his buggy, and drove off." Maggie smiled. "Before we were put back on the train, I found your broach on the ground."

"I'm glad you kept it. Tell me, was Mama with Daddy?" she asked, hungry to know more about the woman who'd wanted a child so.

"No. He was alone, Daisy. And he wasn't the same man who raised you."

That surprised her, yet she'd had a flicker of memory of an austere man who'd scared her. "Do you know how I ended up being Jared Barton's daughter?"

Maggie looked away and bit her lower lip. "I don't know the particulars," she said. "But shortly after you reached Dodge City, Barton took you in. From there the trail led us back to Colorado. That's where it ended, and we had no idea where to look next."

"Hollis told me Daddy and Mama came back from Colorado with me. I thought he'd taken me off the train there."

She laid a hand on Maggie's. "Was he a good man?"

Daisy smiled. "Yes, he was a wonderful father and doted on me. All the boys were afraid to court me. Except Trey."

"He worked for Barton?"

She nodded. "For nearly a year. I was spoken for at the time, but all I could think about was Trey."

"Sounds like love."

"It is." One-sided. Doomed perhaps.

She rubbed her brow, then launched into the sad story of Trey disappearing by the foreman's hand. Of her finding out she was with child. Of losing the baby and then losing her daddy soon after.

"Damn him!" Dade said, his sudden appearance in the parlor startling them both. "I won't hold with him dallying with my sister. He'll marry you."

"No, he won't," Daisy said. "If he doesn't find he loves me, there won't be a marriage."

Dade opened his mouth to argue.

Maggie spoke up first. "You've butted heads with Trey over this already."

"Yes. He asked for my hand, but he couldn't give me his heart in return."

"He'll come to care for you deeply in time," Dade said, the heat gone from his voice now.

In fact her brother looked a bit white around the mouth, like the subject was one he tried hard to avoid as well. Maggie's knowing smile said she understood Daisy's stand all too well. Understood and agreed with her.

"Let it rest, Dade," Maggie said.

He huffed out a breath and pulled a face that was as close to a masculine pout as Daisy had ever seen. "That's why he went off to think."

"Partly, but he's also concerned that Mrs. Charlton could be his mother," Daisy said.

Dade nodded, looking grim. "This could go either way, Daisy. I say we take the decision out of his hands. He'll understand and thank us in time."

Daisy got to her feet. "He's always talking about how you were the levelheaded one. How you stuck by him. I suggest you do that, because I don't want this brought up now. And I surely don't want this mentioned around the Charltons."

"Fine. We'll all pretend nothing happened between you and Trey," Dade said. "But know this. I won't stand by and let him hurt you."

She nodded woodenly, fearing the worst hurt was yet to come if Trey convinced himself he was incapable of loving her.

* * *

The Charltons arrived the next day, and Daisy took an immediate liking to the small woman with raven black hair and deep eyes that seemed haunted. Like Trey's.

She welcomed them into her home while Dade volunteered to see to their bags. But there was only a small valise, and Charlton insisted on handling it himself.

"We hadn't intended to stay the night," he said.

Then they surely wouldn't take the news she had to share well. "Would you like a refreshment? I have coffee and tea."

"Coffee would be most welcome," Charlton said as he escorted his wife to an armless chair. "But my wife prefers tea."

"I'll see to it." Maggie slipped into the kitchen, leaving Daisy stuck with playing hostess.

"Where is he?" Mrs. Charlton asked her.

Daisy hated to tell her, for while Trey's mother might understand, she was certain Mr. Charlton would take a dim view of his decision. "He needed time to think, so he went off for a few days."

"I see," the lady said, disappointment etching deeper lines around her eyes and mouth. "We did arrive a day earlier than planned, so we can't complain."

Her husband snorted, living up to Daisy's image of him being disagreeable. "When did he leave?"

She hesitated, for this news wouldn't sit well with the gentleman. But there was no use in lying either, for the truth would surely come out.

"Five days ago," she said.

To her surprise, Dade spoke up in Trey's defense. "He tends to go off like this when something troubles him. He'll be back as soon as he gets it straight in his mind."

This time Daisy wasn't convinced that he would. Trey surely had more than this reunion with his mother to worry over.

Daisy had given him an ultimatum, and while she still wouldn't settle for less than his love, she realized now that she should have held off with such demands until he'd come to grips with his mother.

"And you are?" Mr. Charlton asked Dade.

"My brother," Daisy said and was rewarded with a wide smile from Dade.

"Dade Logan," he said and stuck out his hand. "I understand you bought the Crown Seven."

Charlton accepted the handshake. "Indeed I did. So you're the third foster brother. Reid told us about you."

Dade gave a short laugh. "I'm sure that didn't take long."

The man didn't so much as crack a smile. "He failed to tell us that Miss Barton was your sister."

"He wouldn't have known," Dade said. "I've been searching for Daisy for years, but Trey was the one who found her."

Charlton slid her a questioning look but didn't say more. The man was certainly more guarded than when he'd visited her and Trey before.

"Reckon I'll see to your horse and buggy," Dade said, and left her alone with the couple.

"How wonderful that Trey was responsible for reuniting lost siblings," Mrs. Charlton said.

"So we sit and wait for him to grace us with his presence?" Mr. Charlton asked.

"That's enough, Shelby," Mrs. Charlton said. "After waiting this long to find my son, a day or two wait is nothing."

"I'm not objecting to that," he said. "The boy could have had the decency to wait for you to arrive. One look at this birthmark would've confirmed if he is or isn't your son."

And that was the whole issue, Daisy thought. The uncertainty. The chance that he would be faced with an emotional mother who was a stranger to him.

"Please, tell me about Trey," Mrs. Charlton said, the longing in her voice so powerful that it brought tears to Daisy's eyes.

How to begin? "He's trustworthy. A hard worker and very knowledgeable about cattle and horses."

The lady smiled. "His father had a fondness for horses."

"Now Phoebe, you are setting yourself up for heartache should this man prove not to be your son," her husband said, and for the first time Daisy saw that his gruff exterior was simply his means of protecting his wife from hurt.

Charlton had told them before that they'd searched for years to find Trey. How many young men had Phoebe met, certain each was the one, only to discover the birthmark she remembered her son having was either different or absent?

"My husband told me you've seen Trey's birthmark," she said. "Describe it, please."

Daisy caught the warning look from Mr. Charlton, and for once agreed with the man. It'd be too easy for his wife to misinterpret Daisy's description.

"I think it would be best if you described it to me," Daisy said, and was rewarded with a barely discernable nod from the gentleman.

Yes, he was protecting his wife. She understood that and felt it was her duty to protect Trey as well. This way she could save them both grief if the mark didn't match the one she knew so well.

Mrs. Charlton frowned, and Daisy didn't know whether she was put out to have the tables turned on her, or if she was trying to find words to describe the birthmark. It shouldn't be that difficult, for the mark on Trey's nape was like nothing she'd ever seen before.

"It was reddish brown and in the shape of a teardrop," Mrs. Charlton began, her voice small in the quiet room. "Below the point there was one raised red mark."

Daisy sat back, trembling inside from the description of the mark Trey bore. "That's unusual."

"His father had one as well, but his was a bit lower. More on his shoulder." She tugged her handkerchief from her sleeve and dabbed her eyes. "I only got that one quick look at it before they took my son away."

Daisy held back the questions bombarding her, though it wasn't easy. There was surely more to tell here than the lady had divulged so far.

Charlton's gaze lifted to Daisy's. "Well, Miss Barton, does Trey March have such a mark?"

She couldn't lie, for she'd give anything if her own child had lived. If she could have any memory of that life taken far too soon.

"Yes. It's just as you described."

The woman broke down then in uncontrollable sobs. Daisy hovered closer, unsure if she should offer comfort or give the woman privacy.

Mr. Charlton decided it for her. "Come, Phoebe. You need to lie down and rest. This has been too taxing for you."

"Please. Take my room," Daisy said, facing a new worry. If the woman's health was that fragile, then seeing Trey could do her in.

She hoped Mrs. Charlton was simply overcome with emotion. She'd found her lost son. She was anxious to hold him in her arms, never mind that he was over six foot of strapping male.

To Mrs. Charlton, Trey March would always be the baby boy taken from her. She deserved her time alone with him, and he surely needed the same from his mother.

But how could Daisy possibly get her away from her overbearing husband?

Chapter 24

Trey had never spent a more miserable six days of his life. He'd sat for hours on end trying to dredge up those tender emotions that Daisy demanded. But he wasn't sure if he was closer to his goal or right back where he started.

He wanted her. He got sick just thinking about living without her. When he let himself dwell on her losing their baby, he damned near went out of his mind.

But the one question he couldn't answer was if he loved her.

On its heels came the worry of how she was dealing with her guests, for surely the Charltons and his foster brothers had arrived by now. They were likely chomping at the bit waiting for him to show up while he was trying to find the guts to saddle his horse and face his fate head-on.

Hellfire, cowpoke, just get your ass headed north. Take it like a man. And when that talking to didn't get him on his feet, he closed his eyes and saw Daisy needing him.

Trey was on his feet and to the door when the creak of wheels and the jingle of a harness reached his ears. His right hand hovered over his sidearm as he stepped back into the cool shadows of the adobe.

Somebody was coming by, and until he knew if he or she were friend or foe, he wasn't showing his hand.

The creak of wheels grew louder, mingling with the clomp of hooves. But his heart was hammering so damned loud he barely heard them.

Just shy of the adobe, his visitor stopped. He flexed the fingers of his gun hand, steadied his breathing, drove every thought but survival from his mind.

"Trey? Are you in there?"

Daisy? Forget keeping his breath steady and his heart from nigh on pounding out of his chest. He'd dreamed of her coming to him every damned night, and she was finally here.

He stormed out the door and came up short. It was his Daisy all right, handling the reins of her buggy with ease despite her small size. Beside her huddled a woman even tinier and more delicate than Daisy.

An older woman.

Shit! She'd brought Mrs. Charlton here.

He flicked a gaze up the road but didn't see anyone trailing her. "Where's your brother?"

"Back at the ranch, likely cussing up a storm when they realized I hadn't just taken Mrs. Charlton on a tour of the ranch." She smiled at him, and the anger he tried to hold onto popped like a soap bubble. "You two need to talk, and you need to do it in private. You wouldn't get that at the ranch."

"Anybody know you were heading here?" he asked.

"Just Hollis, and he wouldn't breathe a word."

"Oh, my, you are a handsome boy," the lady said, and just the sound of her voice jarred something buried deep inside him.

He sucked in a breath. Blew it out. And forced his legs to carry him to the buggy.

"I gather you're Mrs. Charlton," he said. "Pleased to meet you, ma'am."

The lady pressed a hand to her mouth. "You take after my side of the family, but you have his voice. Dear Lord, it is you."

Before he could remind the lady about the birthmark Daisy claimed he had, the woman was reaching for him. And dammit all, but he took that fragile little woman in his arms and set her on her feet before him.

He opened his mouth to spout some quip, but his throat was too clogged to utter a sound. Just when he'd swallowed enough air to blow up, she slipped her arms around him and just pulled him against her.

The rightness of her embrace seeped into him, stealing his strength to resist her. His eyes burned. His chest felt too tight.

He could no more brush this off as an inconvenience any more than he could will the sun to stop shining.

"Please. Let me see the birthmark on your neck," she said.

He took his hat off and went down on a knee before her. Her fingers moved like a whisper over his hair, parting it, touching a finger to his neck and setting off a skitter of sensations that he'd never felt before in his life.

Hell, there was no way a big oaf like him came from this tiny woman. Yet he felt the strength of will in her touch too. She was strong of spirit, but as much as he wanted to belong, the old hurt of abandonment wouldn't let go of him.

She let out a sob and clutched at him. "It's you. After all these years I've finally found my baby boy," she said.

His breath got trapped inside him, and his heart hammered so hard the world spun. "You sure, Mrs. Charlton?"

"Oh, yes, yes." Her voice trailed off, and she lost her grip.

He realized almost too late that she was about to faint and caught her up in his arms. She weighed hardly anything, he thought, as he carried her inside the adobe.

He didn't realize Daisy was right beside him until he bent to set Mrs. Charlton on his bedroll. "Mrs. Charlton? Ma'am? Can I get you anything?"

Her eyelids fluttered, then her gaze fixed on his. She smiled, a contented pulling of her lips that made her teary eyes sparkle.

"I don't know what came over me," she said.

"A bit too much sun." He glanced at Daisy, who merely smiled, her eyes sparkling with moisture too.

Mrs. Charlton lifted small hands to his face, the fingers delicately tracing the lines and contours as if memorizing them or assuring herself he was real. "Just finding you is all I needed, Thomas."

"It's Trey, ma'am."

"Of course you wouldn't know," she said. "I had decided if you were a girl, you'd bear my mother's name. If you were a boy, I'd name you after your father. Jeremy Thomas Warren, Jr."

He swallowed hard and let that name sink into him. His real name that had been passed down a generation already.

"Because your father went by Jeremy, we'd decided to call you Thomas." She wrinkled her nose. "I couldn't abide hanging the name Junior on you or any of the other Southern monikers to denote such."

"Can't imagine being called that either," he said, his voice sounding like sandpaper despite the deep breaths he took in. "How'd I end up in the Guardian Angel's Orphan Asylum?"

She shook her head, and her lips quivered. "The midwife took you there. You see, my father hated Jeremy for siding with the North. He hated him for surviving the war when his only son had lost his life. When he'd lost his plantation, his way of life, my father refused to let me marry Jeremy, even after I got with child."

He glanced at Daisy, who looked far too pale. Was she thinking how they'd fallen into a similar fate?

"Seems your pa got his way," Trey said.

She gave a short nod, her lips pursed. "The month before you were born, Jeremy was to get leave from the army to come get me. We were to be married right away."

Good God! He'd been wanted. Not just by a mother. But by his father as well.

"What happened to stop it?" he asked.

"My father was a horrible, bitter man who I am sure is burning in hell." Mrs. Charlton bit her trembling lower lip and stared at her hands, letting silent tears fall. "As Jeremy was leaving his post, he was murdered. Shot down in cold blood. I suspect by my father's orders."

"How terrible," Daisy said.

"I grieved so, but I clung to the fact I had you," Mrs. Charlton said, and she smiled up at him. "But Father had heinous plans for you as well, and the trouble I had giving birth to you aided his cause."

"How so?" he asked, taking her trembling hand in his.

She clutched his hand tightly, and the oddest warmth started to flow into him. Again, that sense of rightness took root, stronger this time. The feelings so new he shook inside.

"I held you for such a short time, then the midwife took you away so the doctor could tend to me," she said. "I heard you cry once, then no more. They told me when I woke again that you'd died."

"That was a damned lie," he said.

She gave a bitter laugh. "I didn't know that until ten years later when I happened upon the midwife in New York. She confessed to me then that Father had ordered her to take the baby and toss him in the river. But she couldn't do it, so she boarded a northbound train, and then left you on the steps of an orphanage. She thought there you'd be safe from Father."

"No name, just a note pinned on my blanket so they'd known when I was born. Trey March."

"She didn't tell me she'd done that," she said. "The midwife's memory was faulty by then, but she kept begging for my forgiveness. It was later that Shelby questioned the wisdom of believing her, for he suspected she'd done as my father wished and disposed of you."

He'd have been of a mind to suspect the same thing. "Why'd you keep looking for me?"

"Because I knew in my heart that you were alive. I knew if I kept searching that I'd find you." She smiled up at him through her glistening tears. "And I did. I've finally found my son."

He bobbed his own head, not trusting his voice any longer. His throat had closed up again with emotion he couldn't name.

Daisy shifted closer to him, laying her head on his shoulder and a hand on his back. He smiled at the two little women comforting him.

This felt right. Good.

Warmth stole over him, like he'd stood too close to the fire. A comforting warmth that made him feel like he belonged. That he finally had a past that was real.

He was Phoebe Charlton's lost son. Not the boy tossed aside like garbage because his mother hadn't wanted him. Not a bastard out of choice.

Nope, she'd hurt along with him all these years, and he hadn't known it. Now that he did, he didn't want this moment to end.

He wanted to savor this peace and sense of rightness for a long time. However he didn't want to get stranded here with the women tonight either.

"Much as I enjoy sitting here with you two," he said, feeling more light of spirit than he had in his life, "we'd best head back to the ranch."

Time to face the last obstacle in his life and make peace
with his foster brothers. And Daisy. He still had to give her the
answer she expected, the answer that was still eluding him.

Daisy, Trey and his mother made it back to the Circle 46
before dusk. Reid and Dade were just coming up the lane,
and the dark looks they wore were proof that they were
worried about Daisy's whereabouts.

"I knew you went to him," Dade said, seeming none too
pleased about it.

Daisy piped up before he could. "I thought it best that
he have a private reunion with his mother."

Dade and Reid shared a look. But it was Reid who
spoke to Trey.

"I'm glad you found out the truth," he said. "I know
how much it bothered you all these years. You all right
with it now?"

Trey nodded. "I'm getting there."

"Now that you're back, the three of us need to talk,"
Reid said, his commanding tone making it clear that it
couldn't wait.

Shit, all he wanted to do now was get Daisy aside and
talk to her. But that'd have to wait.

In too short a time, he went from having no family in his
life to having way too damned much. His brothers wouldn't
rest until they'd had this long overdue powwow.

"Take Mrs. Charlton on to the house," Trey told Daisy.

She gave each of them a pointed look. "You'll be along
shortly?"

"Soon as we can," Reid said, and Trey didn't gainsay him.

Daisy gave Trey one last longing look, then snapped the
lines and guided her buggy down the lane.

The three men sat their horses in silence, each taking the

other's measure. Reid looked his old self, assured and dominant of his surroundings.

Dade hung back, observant as usual.

"Charlton extended the deadline on the Crown Seven," Reid said. "If you want, you can buy back your shares. But know this. Erston sold off thousands of acres, reducing the Crown Seven to a third of what it used to be."

Trey barked out a laugh. "You expect either of us to forget that you betrayed us and Kirby?"

Reid winced, but held his gaze steady on his brothers. "I know it looked that way, but if I hadn't agreed to Erston's terms," he went on when Dade swore and Trey scoffed, "he would've ruined Kirby, seen me hanged for a murder I didn't commit, and swear you'd both been rustling."

"He tried to do that to us anyway," Trey said.

"So I heard," Reid said, then shook his head. "You can't imagine how damned much I regretted letting Kirby, and both of you, down. It took me years, but I found the true killer and cleared my name. I found a good woman, but I lost the only family I had."

"You didn't lose us," Dade said. "Kirby died believing that the three of us would stay strong. Stay a family."

"We still could be, if we can put the past behind us and join forces again," Reid said, staring first at Dade, then at Trey.

To Trey's surprise, Dade spoke up first. "Much as I enjoyed growing up there, I'll pass."

"You going to go back to being the sheriff?" Reid asked.

Dade shook his head, his gaze shifting toward the ranch. "Don't know what we'll do yet."

Trey knew. Dade wanted to be closer to Daisy, and he damned sure couldn't blame him.

"What about you?" Reid asked him. "Charlton bought the ranch because his wife was convinced you were her missing son."

"I'll have to think about it," Trey said, and that earned him a biting glare from Dade.

"Think damned hard, because Charlton will want an answer soon." Reid reined his horse around and headed back to the ranch.

Trey followed suit, only to be cut off by Dade. "Time for us to talk, brother."

He bit off a ripe oath. More than anything, he'd hoped to avoid this confrontation with Dade until much later.

"Maggie had a talk with Daisy and found out you'd knocked her up," Dade said. "What I want to know is why you dallied with her in the first place. You know a woman like her is the marrying kind."

He had known it, and he had tried to avoid her, but Daisy had come to him. She'd caught him when he was feeling sorry for himself, and too soon he got lost in her arms. Not that he aimed to tell Dade that.

"I offered to marry her," he said.

Dade's mouth thinned. "She wants more than that and you know it. I trust your time away helped you reach a decision."

He shook his head. "Wish it did, but I still don't know if I can give her what she wants."

"That's bullshit, brother. You either stand up like a man and tell my sister how you feel about her or you turn around and ride off."

"You can't make that choice for her."

Dade shifted in the saddle, sitting taller and giving the impression he wasn't one to be messed with.

"Then you make it for her," he said. "She's been hurt enough, you hear?"

"Loud and clear."

Dade whirled his horse around and cantered down the lane. Trey didn't budge, just sat there staring at the ranch he longed to call his own.

She'd be waiting for him to come any minute. She'd be sure he'd be able to confess his feelings to her now. But six days away from her had just left him hungering for her touch.

Dammit, Dade was right. He had to make a choice, and he had to do it now.

When Trey failed to arrive ten minutes after Dade, Daisy went outside to get a better look up the lane. He wasn't coming, and by the grim look on her brother's face, she suspected he knew why.

"Where's Trey?"

"Left him at the gate with the choice to act like a man and marry you or head out."

She stamped a foot, hands fisted. "You had no right!"

"I have every right as your brother."

"Damn you!" Daisy picked up her hem and started walking down the lane.

"Where are you going?" Dade asked.

She turned and faced him. "For a walk, and if you so much as come within fifty feet of me I'll have you horsewhipped."

With that, she whirled around and resumed walking. She heard her brother cuss. But he didn't follow her.

As soon as she was clear of the house, she lifted her skirts higher and ran. She was terrified he'd take it into his head to ride out. That he'd be gone before she could talk to him.

She saw the spotted gelding first, tied to a fence post. Then she caught sight of Trey.

He sat beneath the gate, his back leaning against the post and his long legs crossed at the ankle.

His head was down, like he was dozing.

"Trey!" She ran the rest of the way and fell beside him,

one hand resting on his chest. The other on his shoulder. "Are you all right? What did Dade say to you?"

He shook his head, his laugh brittle. "He cares for you, Daisy. He doesn't want to see you hurt again, and he's afraid that's just what will happen with us."

"Then don't leave me, because that will surely kill me if you do."

He slid her a heated look that made her toes curl and dragged her down onto his lap. "Relax, Daisy. He ain't running me off. Only you can do that."

"I wouldn't—"

He pressed two fingers against her lips, silencing her. "Before you say another word, think long and hard about what you might be hitching your cart to."

She slid her arms around his neck and smiled. "I'm looking, and I see a handsome cowboy who's too stubborn and too proud and too unsure of what he feels in his heart."

He tipped his head back and let out a sad laugh. "That's true enough. I don't know what to think. I tried hard to figure out what love was, but I still don't know for sure." He gathered her close and dropped a kiss on her lips. "All I know is I can't bear to live without you. Can't sleep without knowing you're at my side. Can't imagine having children with anyone but you."

She cupped his face and a tear slipped from her eyes. "You dear man. That is love or as close as a person can get to it."

Still he looked troubled. Unsure. "I've had a helluva bad start in life, Daisy. My grandfather hated my father so much he'd rather have seen me dead. He likely had my father killed and wanted the same for me. I grew up in an orphanage where folks came and went and none looked twice at me because I was sullen. A hard one to manage."

"You had every right to be sullen," she said. "I still can't believe what your mother went through. What you went through."

"Shit, the same happened to you because of me," he said, his features twisted with torment she could feel as well.

"That was Kurt's and Ned's doing."

He shook his head. "I should've suspected Ned would pull something. Should have gone to Barton right away and asked for your hand."

"Why didn't you?"

His mouth pulled to one side. "Afraid he'd send me packing. You deserved better than me."

She smiled and cupped his ruggedly handsome face. "Cowboy, all I ever wanted was you."

"You sure about that?" he asked, a mischievous twinkle in his eyes.

"There's no doubt in my mind that you belong to me, now and forever."

And under a waning West Texas sun, they sealed their vow with a kiss that went on and on.

Epilogue

One year later, Reid, Dade, and Trey threw a Fourth of July celebration at the JDB that made all the other barbeques in the county pale in comparison.

Cowboys, ranchers, and businessmen alike gathered near the barn to pitch horseshoes and shoot the breeze with the brothers who had united their three ranches: the Crown Seven, where Reid and Ellie would live, the Circle 46, which suited Dade and Maggie just fine, and the rebuilt JDB, where Daisy and Trey would call home.

The women found comfort under the wide porch of the new ranch house, sitting on fine wicker chairs, sipping sweet tea, and watching the children play.

Trey March finally tore himself away from the good ol' boys by the barn and headed toward the house, knowing he was late again and certain he'd get a chewing out from Reid.

They'd waited for this day for months. Now that it was here, Trey was beset with that old wariness again.

"About time you showed up," Reid said when Trey strode into the parlor.

"Hello to you too," he said and headed straight for his wife and his newborn son.

"We're ready to start," Daisy said and shifted their son into his arms.

His heart just puffed up with pride and that sense of rightness, but he pulled a face at the frilly getup his son had on. "Lace? You put my son in lace?"

"Hush," Daisy said in a low voice that had a sharp bite to it. "This is the christening gown your mother made for you, and you will not say another cross word about it."

"Yes'm," he said. But dammit all, his son had on more frills than Dade's baby girl.

By mutual agreement, Reid, Dade, and Trey had appointed Phoebe Charlton as the matriarch of their family. Trey's mama was tickled pink with her natural and adopted sons. But her husband was still trying to learn how to cope with three stubborn ranchers who all had an opinion yet stuck together as a united front most of the time.

"We finally ready?" Reid asked, cradling his son with one arm while keeping the other around his wife, Ellie Jo.

"I hope to hell so 'cause this bow tie is choking me," Dade said, jostling his daughter so she wouldn't start bawling again.

"Will the parents please gather around the grandmother," the photographer from San Angelo said.

The three couples stood behind Phoebe Charlton's chair like she was the queen. Hell, to them she was, Trey thought with a widening smile.

As soon as all six of them were standing like the photographer wanted, he took the picture that would hang in the parlor of the JDB ranch house for the next hundred years.

Trey looked at his brothers with their families, and his heart swelled with pride and love. Yep, he'd figured out what that emotion was when Daisy gave birth to little Jeremy.

Hard to believe that three urchins would end up cattle barons. That they'd forge a bond stronger than any blood.

Yep, they'd all found out that family was those you held close in your heart for as long as you lived. This dynasty was going to last.

"You seem mighty pleased with yourself," Daisy said as she snuggled up beside Trey and their beautiful son.

"Darlin', you've made me the happiest man on earth," he said.

**Don't miss the rest of the Lost Sons Trilogy
by Janette Kenny!**

It all started one snowy holiday
in *A Cowboy Christmas* . . .

Reid Barclay doesn't have time for Christmas,
not with trouble brewing at the Crown Seven Ranch.
He's got prize thoroughbreds to protect and a long-ago
wrong that he wants to make right. But the beautiful
cook who's taken over the ranch kitchen is a welcome
distraction, even if Ellie Jo Cade burns everything from
gingerbread to roast beef. Her sweet face
and womanly figure are pure temptation . . .

Cornhusk angels . . . bright berry garlands…
spun-sugar snow—everything about Christmas
holds fond memories for Ellie Jo. She's doing her best
to make peace with an ornery wood-burning stove
and make the old ranch house truly festive.
All she wants is to believe in Reid . . . and the
only-at-Christmas magic that makes hearts glow . . .

Maverick, Wyoming, 1894

Blinding light rode into the room on an icy gust of wind and rudely reminded Reid Barclay that he couldn't get rip-roaring drunk today. He shot a scowl at the newcomer who didn't seem to have the sense to know they were letting out what little heat the potbelly stove could belch out.

Damn, was he going snow blind? He blinked a couple of times just to make sure she wasn't a mirage. Nope, nothing wrong with his eyesight.

A lady stood silhouetted in the doorway, as if debating whether to come in or skedaddle. The answer was as clear as the big blue sky that stretched to the horizon.

A lady had no business stepping foot in this hole.

He ignored the inclination to stand up straight in her presence, preferring to hunker over his whiskey while she stood in the open doorway like an ice princess, gilded in white light and prim bearing—the exact opposite of what this place represented.

Any second Reid figured she'd realize she was in a bawdy establishment that made its money satisfying men's baser needs. Or in his case, trying to.

"Is this Mallory's Roost?" That sultry note in her voice was at odds with her prim appearance, putting lurid thoughts in his head that he had no call thinking about a lady.

"Yep," he said, in no mood to offer anything more.

She gave a shudder, but instead of hightailing it like any lady with a lick of sense would do, she stepped inside and shoved the door closed. Besides the wind that howled a protest at being shut out, the only sound in the Roost was the crackle of the stove and Reid's uneven breathing.

This lady oozed quality in a hovel that wouldn't know sophistication if it bit saloon keep Ian Mallory on his Irish ass. The tips of dainty black boots peeked from under her heavy tweed skirt. Fine-looking black gloves covered small hands that rested demurely at her sides. Her wrap hugged her narrow shoulders and didn't appear near warm enough for these environs.

He had just enough liquor under his belt to want to heat this lady up under a nice thick blanket. Dangerous thoughts for a man in his position.

He let his gaze drift up to her face, and her inquisitive eyes and lush lips hushed his heart a measure. He couldn't recall when that had happened to him last. To have a woman intrigue him so now—Hell, it was time for him to vamoose.

He'd heard the train chug in five minutes ago, and knowing he had a passenger waiting had chased off thoughts of getting drunk. Not that drink would solve his problems. But sometimes a man just needed to drown himself and his troubles in a bottle.

That would have to wait. It was time for him to collect Mrs. Leach's friend and head back to the ranch.

He would've too if that slight desperation he sensed in this woman hadn't stayed him. He couldn't pull himself away just yet, not until he found out why a young woman of quality would enter a grubby saloon.

He finished off his rotgut, then almost choked on it as the sweet scent of lilacs drifted over him, tempting him to forget the promise he'd made. He didn't have to look up to know the lady stood at his elbow, but he did anyway.

Dammit to hell but the uncertainty he glimpsed in those big brown eyes of hers had him wanting to reach out to her and tell her whatever was wrong would be all right. He knew better now than to make such promises.

He shot the lady a look that should've sent her running, but she hiked that pert little chin up as if telling him she wasn't one to bluff. If that chin hadn't trembled the slightest bit—Aw, hell, didn't she know it was dangerous for a woman to come close to a lone man swilling whiskey—a man who was wallowing in old regret and new longing?

"Was there a gentleman in here earlier?" she asked.

"Not that I recall."

She frowned and bit her lower lip. "Perhaps he left before you arrived—"

"I been here since yesterday, ma'am," Reid said and scratched his knuckles over the stubble he'd not bothered scraping off this morning. "Plenty of cowpokes and the like have come and gone, but nary a gentleman has passed through those doors."

"I see," she said, her mouth pinched in clear disapproval of his admission, and his appearance, if he guessed right. "Is the owner of this establishment here?"

Reid nodded in Mallory's direction, his curiosity hiking up another notch. "That's him propping up the far end of the bar."

"Thank you."

Yep, no doubt about it. She was the embodiment of the vision that had tormented Reid's dreams for as long as he could recall. True elegance with a throaty voice that hinted of naughty. So what the hell was she doing here?

She set off at a good clip toward the end of the bar where

Ian Mallory snored like a sawmill. Her boot heels clicked a jig, and her bustle swayed to the lusty beat pulsing in Reid's veins. Damn, but he'd sure like to see if her inviting backside was mostly padding or firm, natural rounding.

"Excuse me," she said to Mallory as she stopped a respectable distance from him.

Mallory answered her with a snore.

The lady tapped a foot impatiently on the floor and Reid bit back a smile, wondering what she'd do now. From what he'd seen so far, she wasn't the type to tuck tail and run.

She cleared her throat. "Sir, if I may have a moment of your time." She leaned close to Mallory, her voice louder and more commanding this time.

Like a schoolmarm. Or a general.

It took grit for a woman to walk into this place. A damn sight more gumption to stay. Just the type of woman who appealed to Reid.

Seeing his dream woman in the flesh brought all the old longing rushing back. A good dose of regret, too, though he rarely acknowledged it anymore. But what shocked the hell out of him was the beginning twitch of an honest-to-God arousal.

The past two years lust had been a stranger to Reid. God knew he'd tried to get back in the amorous saddle again as recent as last night, but nothing any woman did worked. Now, just being in the same room with this lady had nudged his cock awake.

About damn time. Now if only he were free—

She turned to Reid then, and indecision flitted over her inquisitive features. "Is he always like this?"

"He has his lucid moments, but they're rare."

Her mouth cinched up tighter than a banker's purse strings, but the gloved finger she slid between her neck and high ruffled collar was more telling than her tongue slipping out to dampen her full lower lip. That long-missed heaviness paid a teasing visit across Reid's groin again.

Yep, that part of him wasn't dead after all.

Reid gripped the empty shot glass in his hands, debating about filling it again. Drinking beat wishing to hell that he was holding soft womanly flesh, but he couldn't leave the old gal waiting at the depot much longer either.

She shook the sot. "Mr. Mallory. Please wake up."

"Uh, wha—" The old drunk roused from his stupor and stared at the lady, blinking like an owl.

Reid could well imagine what went through the shanty Irishman's head. Had he died and gone to heaven after all?

"And just how can I help you, miss?" Mallory asked as he straightened to his full five-foot-six height.

"I'm looking for Mr. Reid Barclay," she said. "The conductor at the depot said I could find him here."

Reid froze, his hand inches from grabbing the bottle of whiskey. Had he heard her right?

"Now what would a fine lady such as yourself be wanting with the likes of Reid Barclay?" Mallory asked, voicing the same question that swirled in Reid's head.

She slid Reid a dubious glance, before turning back to Mallory. "That's personal."

The whiskey Reid had swilled crashed like angry waves in his gut. He stared at her long and hard, but nothing about her stirred his memory. Why the hell was she looking for him?

"If that don't beat all." Mallory thumped a hand on the bar and let out a wheezing laugh.

"Well? Can you tell me where I can find Mr. Barclay?" she asked.

Mallory bobbed his shaggy head and pointed a gnarled finger at Reid. "That's your fine gentleman right there."

Reid pressed both palms on the sticky bar, more discomfited than offended by the Irish sot's mocking tone.

"Oh." She pressed a gloved hand to her throat and stared at Reid in clear disbelief.

Reid's mind churned with reasons, beyond the obvious one, why this lady had sought him out. Damn it all, but that one plausible cause wasn't reassuring in light of his physical reaction to her.

"Cat got your tongue?" Reid asked.

Again, that telling flush stole over her creamy cheeks. "Please forgive me. I was expecting someone more—I mean, someone far older and, and, and—" She waved a hand as if trying to catch words that had escaped her.

"Respectable looking?" he asked.

Her cheeks turned a fiery red this time. "Please don't take offense, but you don't look like the gentleman I'd imagined."

"None taken, ma'am."

She crossed to Reid, those sharp bootheels tapping out a lively ditty that had his blood pumping for a fare-thee-well. "I'm pleased to meet you, Mr. Barclay."

Reid inclined his chin a mite, his neck crawling with suspicion. "Barclay or Reid will do."

"Highly improper, but if that's what you wish." Her cheeks darkened a smidgen, and for the first time she looked as uneasy as he felt.

"Why are you looking for me?"

"I'm Eleanor Jo Cade," she said.

She couldn't be the woman he'd been expecting from Denver—the one his housekeeper had recommended for the job in her absence. "Mrs. Leach's friend?"

"Yes," she said.

"Why? What?" Reid scrubbed a hand over his face, annoyed as hell that she had him stammering for words. He sucked in a deep breath and wished he hadn't as he drew in her sweet lilac scent.

"Why didn't you wait for me at the depot?" he asked,

acting annoyed she'd come looking for him in this weather when he was really perturbed that she was a young, pretty and damned desirable woman.

Of course, the fact she was here in the saloon told him she was the type who took matters into her own hands. And dammit all for thinking that because his body jolted again at the thought of her taking him in hand. *Shit!*

"It seemed silly to wait when I could just as easily find you and we could be on our way."

There was more to it than that. The spark of panic in her eyes hinted she had another reason that she wasn't ready to divulge.

That alone was enough reason for him to send her on her way here and now and save himself a passel of grief. God knew he'd surely suffer misery in Miss Cade's company, for his thoughts were anything but gentlemanly around her. But he'd have a hellish time finding a suitable woman to replace Mrs. Leach at this late date and in this ungodly weather.

He blew out a disgusted breath at being caught between a rock and a hard place. "Then by all means let us collect your baggage and be on our way."

Her sigh was a fitting reaction, but the wide eyes glittering with relief, coupled with those soft lips trembling into a smile, went too far. Yep, this little woman roused feelings in him best left dead.

Reid shrugged into his jacket and motioned to the door. "Stay here while I fetch the sleigh from the livery."

"I don't mind walking with you. It'll save time." She click-clicked across the wood floor like a spirited filly and out the door into the bitter cold.

Reid tossed five bucks on the bar and started after her. He would have preferred to lose ten minutes and regain his equilibrium, but it was obvious Miss Cade would rather tramp through the snow than spend another second in the Roost.

"You've got your hands full with that one," Mallory said.

"She doesn't appear to be the troublesome sort to me."

"Unlike yourself, Mr. Reid Barclay. For all that cultured talk you spout on a whim, I know you've got the heart and soul of an Irish rebel."

"What if I do?" Reid paused at the door and stared at the man who'd watched him go from rebellious boy to respectable rancher.

"Her type won't give you a roll in the hay and then go her way with a smile on her face. Remember that."

Reid inclined his head. "I'll bear that in mind."

"Will you? You always were a cocky bastard. But then you have the blood of nobles flowing in your veins."

Mallory, the wily old goat, knew the truth Reid held close to the vest. He was an English nobleman's by-blow, disowned by his father long before Reid's mother died giving him life.

"I'm still a bastard, Mallory." If Kirby Morris hadn't cut a deal when he had, he'd be a dead one by now.

"Aye, you did 'em wrong, boyo. They ain't coming back."

His mouth stretched into a grim line. He'd given his brothers just cause to hate him, and damned if he knew how to right the terrible wrong he'd caused so long ago.

Guilt was a bitch to live with.

"Perhaps I'll have the luck of the Irish after all."

"More likely you'll have the devil's time of it," Mallory said as he splashed whiskey into a shot glass, "when your past charges into your life with guns blazing."

A possibility Reid hoped to avoid. He stepped out and let the wind blow the rest of Mallory's dire predictions back inside.

No matter how much he groused about his fate, he'd made

the right choice. Never mind it'd been the only one at the time. If his skin felt a mite tight for him at times, so be it.

He was ready to live up to his end of the bargain now. Or had been until he'd hired a fetching house cook that had him thinking of dishes best served warm in bed.

Reid squinted against a punishing sun, searching for Miss Cade. He spotted her easily down the street, thanks to a royal blue cloak snapping in the wind like a bullfighter's cape. He hadn't known her hair was the color of whiskey until now.

The back of it was caught up in an intricate weave of sorts and that touch of red glowed in the sun.

Reid headed toward Miss Cade, his blood running thick and hot with need. He had a fondness for fair-haired women.

She tugged the full hood up and ended his ruminations of taking the pins from her hair and running his hands through it. By damn, but the lady was a sparkling gem amid a blanket of white. She'd be living in his house, a constant temptation for him to take what he wanted and damn the consequences.

He paused to let a buckboard churn by, the bed laden with goods and squealing children huddled down in a bed of straw. He knew the whole family worked their behinds off on their ranch due north of his, yet he'd never seen a happier brood.

Simple pleasures.

He'd never known what it was like to have the love of family until he'd lost it. Now there was no getting it back.

Reid caught a glimpse of Adam Tavish plowing through the muck in the street. He, too, seemed arrested by the sight of Miss Cade.

Though the U.S. Marshal swore he was on the trail of the Kincaid gang, Mallory told him that Tavish had been asking an awful lot of questions about Reid. It wasn't the first time a lawman had inquired about his past.

The fact remained that Reid had left word everywhere, all but begging his brothers to come back to Wyoming. He'd also baited a trap for the man accused of killing Lisa True, letting it be known that Slim was at the Crown Seven as well. But so far the only one sniffing around was the lawman.

As for Ezra Kincaid? He'd likely be watching.

If the old outlaw was out there, he was holed up planning his move. That worried Reid the most.

Truth be, he was relieved Tavish was dead set on stopping the old rustler who surely must be drooling over Reid's thoroughbreds. But that didn't mean he wanted to be on close speaking terms with Tavish.

Considering his past, Reid was careful to keep his distance from the local sheriff and the marshal. But with Tavish reaching Miss Cade first and guiding her into the livery, he couldn't very well do that today.

Ice crunched underfoot as he made his way to the livery. He wrenched open the door, finding Miss Cade and Tavish squared off inside.

He knew the feeling.

Reid gave the livery boy a nod to ready his sleigh.

"I see you've met the marshal." Reid stopped beside Miss Cade, sparing Tavish a dismissing glance but feeling the man's curious gaze skewer him all the same. Was that annoyance he saw in her eyes?

"Yes, he was just assuring me that this is a quiet, lawful community," she said.

Tavish favored Miss Cade with his good-ol'-boy smile that didn't fool Reid one bit. "You never did tell me what brought you to Maverick, Miss Cade."

She flinched this time, a slight tremor Reid attributed to a case of nerves. Until he got a closer look.

The lady was clearly angry and her ire was directed at the U.S. Marshal. Damn, what had Tavish said to her earlier?

"I'm taking over Mrs. Leach's role of cook at the Crown Seven Ranch while she's away," she said.

Tavish thumbed back his hat, revealing a pair of observant green eyes that no doubt had saved the lawman's ass on more than one occasion. "Pardon me for saying, ma'am. But most cooks I've met tended to sample their fare a bit more than necessary."

It was the truth, but Reid took umbrage with the way Tavish looked at the lady, like she was a tasty morsel and he was starving. Never mind Reid had done the same earlier. She was his employee, and judging by her tight-lipped expression, she didn't wish to tarry in Tavish's company.

"So, where have you worked before, Miss Cade?" Tavish asked, his conversational tone at odds with his shrewd perusal.

A dull flush blossomed on the lady's cheeks, and the rigid set to her shoulders seemed an odd reaction, in Reid's estimation. "The Denver Academy for Young Ladies."

"Do tell?" Tavish's eyes took on a calculating glint.

"I fear I'd bore you with stories of teaching young ladies to acquire discriminating tastes," she said over the tinkling of harness bells. "Besides I am sure Mr. Barclay is anxious to be on his way."

"Another time then. Afternoon, ma'am." Tavish slid two fingers over his hat brim but stayed rooted to the spot. "Barclay."

Reid dipped his chin in farewell, then guided Miss Cade to the red sleigh. "You leave your baggage at the depot?"

"Yes. I have a small trunk and a carpetbag."

A rarity for sure. He'd warrant Cheryl would drag all manner of trunks and valises with her from England.

"After we retrieve your things, we'll stop at the mercantile. I suggest you select anything you need for yourself or the ranch now."

"I have everything I require with me."

"Fair warning, Miss Cade. We won't be coming into town for a week or more."

"I'm sure everything I'll need is at the ranch."

Reid expected she'd say that. So why did he have the sudden feeling he'd be going hungry this night—and in more ways than one?

And the passion continued with a warm embrace
In a Cowboy's Arms . . .

Colorado sheriff Dade Logan has waited twenty years
to reunite with his long lost sister, Daisy. But when she
finally turns up, they barely recognize each other.
That's because the beautiful stranger isn't Daisy,
but her childhood friend Maggie, on the run from an
impending marriage. Moved by this last link to Daisy,
Dade determines to bend any law that stands between
him, his sister—and the intriguing Maggie . . .

Maggie Sutten will risk anything to escape her fate,
though accompanying the broad-shouldered sheriff
in his pursuit of Daisy rattles her to the core. But as their
search—and desire for one another—escalates, the two
provoke a vicious bounty hunter, one who threatens
their hopes for a future together . . .

Colorado, 1895

It wasn't yet ten in the morning, and Dade Logan was already bored clean out of his mind. Other than locking the town drunk up every Friday night when he got a snootful, there wasn't much in the way of law to enforce in Placid, Colorado.

Not that he was anxious for trouble to come to this sleepy town that rested in the valley east of the Sangre de Cristo Mountains. Nope, he'd been waiting all winter for one person to return, and if she didn't show up soon he didn't know what the hell he would do.

The hiss of the locomotive and clang of the rail cars pulling out echoed up the main street of Placid. Two folks had boarded the Denver & Rio Grande, heading east to Pueblo. He hadn't seen anyone get off.

Maybe she'd arrive on the afternoon train. As the racket from steel wheels on rails grew faint, he heard his name being called out.

"Sheriff Logan! Sheriff Logan!"

Dade smiled. Raymond Tenfeather was pounding down

the boardwalk somewhere between the stable and the jail, hollering out his name like he did every day about this time.

When the liveryman's younger son wasn't trailing his elder brother Duane around town, he had taken to following Dade on the pretext of helping him look for lawbreakers. Dade had gently explained that wasn't necessary, but the boy took it on himself to be the town spy. God only knew what Raymond had seen this time.

Dade rocked back in his chair and stacked his crossed boots on the edge of his desk, awaiting the boy's imminent arrival. As always, his gaze narrowed on the wanted posters tacked on the wall.

Dammit all if the three outlaws staring back at him weren't smirking. His pa and uncles would find it amusing that Dade had taken an oath to uphold the laws that Clete, Brice, and Seth Logan had been hell-bent on breaking all their lives.

It'd been twenty years since he'd seen any of them, though their wanted posters had haunted him most of his life. There sure as hell wasn't any love lost between him and his kin.

Yet one question nagged at him right after they pinned a tin star on his chest. If his pa and uncles came to town, could he draw on them?

Part of him said yes. His pa had had no qualms about deserting him and his little sister. Yet when all was said and done, he wasn't sure he could turn on his blood. Hell, unlike Reid Barclay, he couldn't have turned on either of his foster brothers either.

"Sheriff Logan!" Raymond burst into the jail, his dark skin glistening with sweat and his scrawny chest heaving from his run. "I saw her."

"Just who'd you see?" Dade asked.

"The lady you been waiting for," Raymond said.

"Daisy?" he asked.

The boy nodded. "She got off the train, just like you was hoping she'd do."

Now how the hell had he missed seeing her?

Dade's heart took off galloping at the thought that sticking around here had paid off. His missing sister had finally come back like everyone in town said she would.

For the first time in months he visited that dream of buying a nice little farm for them to call home. He could run a few head of cattle. Do a bit of farming. Hell, he could find his brother Trey and bring him into the deal.

It was a damn sight better thing to dwell on than the idea of going back to the Crown Seven and having it out with Reid, the foster brother who'd sold them out when they needed him the most.

First things first. He'd waited twenty years to find his sister. He wasn't about to waste a second forestalling their reunion.

"Where is she?" he asked, heading for the door as he spoke.

"Mrs. Gant's boardinghouse," Raymond said, hot on his heels.

The place where Daisy and her crippled traveling companion had stayed before. Mrs. Gant had told him about their visit to Placid. How Daisy had caught the young sheriff's eye. How she'd promised to come back last fall and marry Lester.

But the sheriff was dead, spring was in full bloom, and nobody in town had any idea where Daisy Logan and her lady friend hailed from.

Dade figured she'd heard about Lester's murder and wasn't coming back to Placid. He feared he'd lost her again.

"Thanks, Raymond." Dade flipped the boy a silver dollar and headed out the door.

Long determined strides carried him across the dusty street. He wondered how much Daisy had changed. Would she recognize him? Would she be as glad to be reunited with her family as he was?

He'd find out damn soon, he thought, as he cut down the street between Hein's Grocery and Doc Franklin's house.

Mrs. Gant's boardinghouse sat the next street over, but the elevation made the walk seem farther. He bounded up the steps then paused at the door to steady his breath.

The climb was nothing, but the excitement pounding inside him made it hard to draw a decent breath. He blew out the air trapped in his chest, inhaled deeply, and stepped inside.

Mrs. Gant was in the parlor, serving tea to a lady seated on the stiff Victorian sofa. Neither seemed to have heard him come in.

That was fine by him, for it gave him time to study his sister. Her golden hair had darkened to a rich honey. Her features were still delicate and refined, but she didn't resemble their mother or father.

She wasn't a cute little pixie anymore. Nope, she'd grown into a beautiful woman with all the curves in all the right places. But it was the odd combination of grief and fear in her eyes that gave him pause.

"I am so sorry to be the one to tell you that Lester has passed over," Mrs. Gant said, verifying what Dade suspected had caused his sister's distress. "I didn't know where you'd gone, but when you didn't come back last fall like you said you would, I thought maybe you'd heard."

"No, I had no idea," Daisy said. "What happened?"

"It was just awful," Mrs. Gant said. "This ruffian came to town, intent on robbing the bank. Lester was there, and before he could turn and confront this no-account, the ruffian shot him dead."

Daisy pressed a hand to her mouth, clearly horrified by the news. Mrs. Gant's version was close enough to the truth that Dade didn't see the need to comment.

"I tell you truly," Mrs. Gant said, "I shudder to think what would've happened if Dade Logan hadn't stepped in like he did and ended the robber's reign of terror on our town. No telling who else would've been gunned down if not for your brother's courage."

Dade winced. The townsfolk had taken to embellishing the events of that day to the point Dade cringed every time he heard it. Now was surely no exception, for Daisy's face had leached of color at the mention of his name.

"W-what?" Daisy said in a voice that was way too high.

"Yes, indeed, your brother is a hero." Mrs. Gant launched into telling Daisy the details.

This surely wasn't the reunion he'd had in mind. A sound of disgust must've slipped from him for Mrs. Gant glanced his way and smiled.

Daisy, on the other hand, looked ready to bolt as her head snapped up and her gaze clashed with his. Instead of recognition lighting her eyes, they narrowed with suspicion and something bordering on dread.

Mrs. Gant patted Daisy's hand. "It'll be all right now, dear. You have family to help you through this difficult time."

Daisy shook her head. "No! I'm an orphan."

Dade scrubbed a hand across his nape, frustrated and more than a mite worried about his sister's increased distress. He wasn't surprised that Daisy hadn't recognized him after twenty years, but forgetting that he existed signaled something else entirely.

"You saying you don't remember me?" Dade asked.

She shook her head, her gaze focusing on his tin star before lifting to his face. He hadn't thought she could get any paler but he'd been wrong.

"Don't you remember that Pa left us at the Guardian Angel's Orphan Asylum?"

She shook her head and stared at him with troubled eyes.

"You recall being in the orphanage?" he asked.

She frowned. "Some. Mostly I was scared."

So was Dade, but it did him no good then or now to admit it. How could her memory be that bad?

She'd cried and screamed for Dade after their pa had dumped them there, and put up more of a ruckus when they'd been separated—boys in one wing of the drafty old building and girls in the other.

They'd seen each other precious little after that, but she hadn't forgotten him then. She'd pitched a fit when they took her away on the orphan train, to the point that they'd had to restrain him from going after her.

As the wagon pulled away, he'd vowed he'd find her and keep them together as family. But he hadn't been able to keep his promise.

"Reid, Trey, and I tried to find you," he said, but though they'd run away from the orphanage a few months later, they'd failed to pick up the trail of the orphan train that Daisy had taken west.

He'd failed his sister.

"Reid and Trey. Are they family?"

"They're as close as brothers to me." Or were. "But they aren't blood kin like we are."

Daisy didn't look the least bit relieved. In fact, she acted more leery than before as she turned to Mrs. Gant.

"Is he really my brother?" she asked the older woman.

Her trust in a stranger was a gut punch to Dade. It didn't ease his mind none that Mrs. Gant was giving him a long assessing look either. He knew trouble was coming before she voiced an opinion, which the lady always had on everything.

"Well, he says he is. But all we have is his word." Mrs. Gant pinned him with a squinty stare. "You have any kin in these parts?"

He hoped to hell not. The last thing he needed was for his outlaw pa and uncles to show their faces. He'd be lucky to get out of town without getting shot.

"No kin left but me and Daisy," he said, and he reasoned that could be true. Any day he expected to get word that his old man and renegade uncles had been gunned down.

He swore under his breath, damning his pa again for abandoning his family. Daisy had only been four years old when they'd arrived at the Guardian Angel's Orphan Asylum. She'd just turned five when she'd been put on the orphan train.

"Forgive me for being skeptical." Daisy swallowed hard and looked up at him. "But I was told that I had no family."

"That's a lie," Dade said. "You've got me."

Daisy grimaced and seemed not the least bit repentant about her aversion to him. "If you're telling the truth."

Dade scrubbed a hand over his mouth to smother a curse that ached to burst free. What the hell could he do to convince his sister of the truth?

"Well, this is quite an interesting turn of events," Mrs. Gant said. "You don't favor each other at all. Pity you don't have a photograph of when you were children. We'd likely be able to put all doubts to rest then."

Truer words were never spoken. "There was one," he said, barely recalling the day it'd been taken but knowing it had happened all the same. "Ma kept it in her locket."

Daisy was clearly uncomfortable with his recollections for her cheeks turned pink, and she began fidgeting with something at her throat. He gave a passing glance at the blue cameo broach pinned to her bodice, then just gaped at the locket.

"That's it, handed down to her by her ma." He could've sworn pure panic flared in Daisy's eyes. "Before Pa left us at the orphanage, he pinned that to your dress."

Her lower lip quivered as she turned to Mrs. Gant. "I don't know what to believe."

"Well, let's have a look inside that locket," Mrs. Gant said, taking the words right out of Dade's mouth.

Daisy squirmed, as if nervous over finding the proof of his claim. Finally she unclasped the cameo from her bodice, hesitated a moment, and then handed it to Mrs. Gant.

"My hands are shaking too badly to search for the clasp," Daisy said.

Not so for Mrs. Gant. The lady found and opened it before Daisy finished talking.

"There's nothing inside it," Mrs. Gant said.

Dade should've figured that'd be the case. And did Daisy just let out a sob? Or was that a sigh of relief?

The older woman closed the broach and pressed it back into Daisy's hand, then enfolded her in her arms. "There, there. You've been through too much, what with just hearing that your beau passed on. And now all this about having a lost brother."

"What happened to the photographs?" he asked his sister.

"I have no idea," Daisy said. "I didn't even know this was a locket until just now."

He snorted at that. How could she not know?

Mrs. Gant chastised him with a look that would've done a schoolmarm proud. But he wasn't backing down. Not now.

"Look at the back of the broach," he said, then stubbornly waited until she did as he said. "The inscription reads, 'Be true to yourself.' The initials *TL* are struck below it."

A frown marred Daisy's smooth brow. "Who's *TL*?"

"Our mother. Tessa Logan."

Her narrow shoulders slumped as she tightened her fingers around the broach in her hand. "That's it exactly. I guess that means you're telling the truth."

"It does. I've been looking for you for years," he said.

"Well now you've found me." She didn't sound particularly happy about it.

Dade couldn't fault her for that. He couldn't even grumble much about her hesitation now.

They were strangers. She'd lived a life apart from everything she'd known, just like him. She'd obviously lost her heart to Sheriff Emery and had intended to marry him. Or had she?

"Why didn't you come back last fall?" he asked.

"I couldn't decide if marrying Lester was the right thing to do," Daisy said, and avoided meeting his eyes. "By the time I knew what I wanted, winter hit and snowed me in."

That sounded fine on the surface, for he'd been stranded here as well. She'd gone back to wherever she'd called home, thought things over, and then returned to marry her beau. But Lester was dead, shot down by a young outlaw who was trigger-happy.

He reckoned it was better it happened now than after they'd married, leaving Daisy a young widow, perhaps with a baby. Yet Daisy didn't seem all that brokenhearted over Lester's death. In fact, she appeared more worried than anything.

"You never did say where you were raised," Dade said to break the awful silence.

Daisy fidgeted just enough to make him think she was uncomfortable talking about that. "A mining town west of the divide."

"This town have a name?" he asked.

She looked away. Swallowed. "Burland."

He'd heard of it. A couple of men had swindled claims out of many a miner, ending up rich while the rest of the miners went broke. Considering the way she was dressed, he had a feeling she'd been raised in one of the rich households.

So why marry a poor small town sheriff when she could likely have her pick of gentlemen? Now that Lester Emery was gone, why stay here with a brother she didn't remember?

"Will you return to Burland now?" Mrs. Gant asked.

Daisy's narrow shoulders went stiff. "There's nothing left for me there."

Mrs. Gant tsked. "Then you should stay right here with your brother. That'll give you both time to get to know each other again."

"Thank you," Daisy said, her smile as thin as Dade's waning patience.

He ground his teeth. She wasn't sticking around because she wanted to get close to her brother again. Nope, she had nowhere else to go. That wasn't a kick in the shins but it came damned close.

His little sister had been a delicate, fragile child who'd clung to him. She'd been unbelievably shy and prone to tears. But the Daisy before him seemed to have developed the grit to take off on her own across the Great Divide.

She also possessed an alluring womanly charm that called to some need deep inside him. Hell, if he wasn't her brother he'd have been drawn to her.

He shook off those disquieting thoughts and focused on the problem at hand. He still didn't know what type of folks had taken in his sister and raised her.

Not that it mattered. She had him to protect her now, just like he'd sworn he'd do twenty odd years ago.

If she'd let him. Right now that didn't seem too likely.

Dade blew out a weary breath. For damn sure he had his work cut out for him gaining her trust.

Maggie Sutten read the determination in Dade Logan's brown eyes and knew with a sinking heart that she had landed smack dab between a rock and a hard place.

She'd had no idea that Daisy had a brother. A brother who was waiting here in Placid for her to return. A brother who'd spent years trying to find his sister.

Heavens to Betsy! Now he believed he'd done just that. Could things get any worse?

They surely would if Whit Ramsey found her.

However, for now she'd do well to play along with Dade

Logan. That was the best way she could hide from Whit until she decided what to do next.

Yes, Whit would turn over every rock in Colorado looking for Maggie Sutten. He'd never dream she'd assumed another name and be living with a man.

And there was the advantage that Dade was a lawman. Though in truth she didn't think that would stop Whit from taking her.

A chill passed through her at the thought.

"Are you cold, dear?" Mrs. Gant asked.

"Just a case of nerves," she said. "It's a lot to take in at once."

Dade tucked his hands under his armpits and eyed her, and for an instant she feared he could look clean through her and see she was spinning a mile-long yarn. "You end up with a good family?"

Painful memories of the first family who'd taken her in threatened to torment her, so she blocked them from her mind and focused on the Nowells instead. "They treated me well enough, though it was clear I was just the companion to their crippled daughter."

As soon as the words left her mouth, she realized Mrs. Gant had put two and two together. "I had no idea that Eloisa Reynard was your foster sister."

Maggie forced a smile, for nobody here knew that Eloisa was in fact Caroline Nowell, the "Silver King's" daughter. "We thought of ourselves as best friends."

"You were fortunate," Dade said.

If only he knew the truth! But that was a secret she had to keep. Just like she had to keep up the pretense of being Daisy Logan.

"Eloisa was a delight, and that made living there enjoyable," she said, and that was the honest-to-God truth.

The hell didn't come into play until her foster father had

to pay up what he owed, and Whit Ramsey refused to honor the agreement of taking Harlan Nowell's crippled daughter's hand in marriage.

According to him, Whit Ramsey wanted Maggie.

If Whit had been a decent man and courted her, she might have considered his suit. But he was an overbearing snob and a lothario to boot.

She refused to marry him, but Harlan Nowell informed her she had no choice. She owed him for taking her in.

Maggie detested Nowell, and she didn't have much more regard for his wife. But she loved her foster sister and had hesitated over abandoning her.

"You can't marry him," Caroline had said after the last argument Maggie had had with Harlan Nowell. "Leave. Go far from here and never look back."

"I'm afraid what will happen to you," Maggie had said.

Caroline had laughed. "I'll grow old alone. No man wants to get saddled with a cripple."

"Never say never."

The long winter had proved true Maggie's suspicions about Whit Ramsey. He came to visit often though he usually ended up secluded in the library with Nowell, but even on those rare occasions when he stayed for supper he paid Caroline no attention at all. In fact, he'd often make some excuse and leave the room when she entered in her wheelchair.

So Maggie and Caroline planned out what she should do. Which, given the fact she'd told Lester she'd return to Placid, pretty much set the stage.

In the meantime, she went along with Harlan Nowell's plans for a big wedding this spring and suffered Whit's attentions.

The second the weather cleared and she found a chance, she ran away—ran here to Lester. Even then she'd backtracked and paid a painted lady to use her real name and take the train west. For if Whit got wind that Maggie Sutten was here, he'd come after her.

"You said there was nothing left for you in Burland," Dade said, bracing a shoulder against the doorjamb. He gave the impression that he was relaxing and exchanging idle chitchat, but Maggie wasn't fooled.

He was fishing.

"That's right," she said, and summoned up a sniffle.

"What happened to your foster family?" Dade asked.

"They came down sick with a fever over the winter," Maggie said, thinking that was the easiest way to keep her lies from getting too tangled. "Father survived it. Mother didn't."

Mrs. Gant made appropriate sounds of distress. "Did dear Eloisa pass over too?"

"No!" The thought of Caroline dying made Maggie sick, though as it had turned out she'd lost the only friend she'd had anyway. "No, her father sent her east to live with an aunt and receive treatment at a hospital."

Another lie, but again it'd divert attention away from Burland, the Nowells, and Whit Ramsey.

Mrs. Gant embraced her in a smothering hug again, and Maggie was just too weary to resist. "You poor dear, losing most of your foster family and your beau."

"It's been a trial," she said, and felt tears sting her eyes over Lester's death.

She'd genuinely liked him. But on the train ride here she'd finally decided she couldn't marry a man she didn't love. Not Lester Emery. And surely not Whit Ramsey.

"Now then I'm going upstairs and get your old room ready." Mrs. Gant smiled at them, and Maggie noted the moisture in the older woman's eyes. "For the first time in years this house will have a real family living in it."

Maggie forced a smile and hated that she lied to this kind woman who seemed hungry for family. As for Dade . . . Well, if lying sent a person to hell she was halfway there.

"I'd about given up hope of finding you," Dade said after Mrs. Gant took herself off, his voice going rough with emotion.

Maggie squirmed, truly bitten by guilt. "I'm sorry I don't remember you."

Sorry she didn't know what had happened to Daisy. And sorry that she was going to destroy his dream of a family without any explanation. But she couldn't keep up this charade.

She couldn't get too close to Dade Logan either.

The man was simply too big and too discerning for her peace of mind. And if she was honest, he stirred feelings in her that were best left sleeping. Feelings a woman would never feel for her brother. Feelings that would surely give her lie away.

No, she didn't dare get too close or too comfortable around Dade Logan.

As much as she wished otherwise, she couldn't remain here long either. Harlan Nowell would come looking for her, and he might do worse than drag her back to Burland and marry her to Whit Ramsey.

A chill tripped down her spine at the thought of being sold off like cattle. There had to be a trustworthy man she could confide in, a man who'd help her escape Whit Ramsey for good.

Her gaze flicked to the tall imposing man beside her. Dade Logan?

Those clear brown eyes of his had seen a world of trouble. According to Mrs. Gant's tale, he knew how to use that gun strapped low on his hip.

Yes, he was the type of man who'd risk his life to save his sister. But she wasn't his kin. She couldn't intentionally make him a target for Harlan Nowell's wrath.

For a few days she'd be safe here in Mrs. Gant's boarding-house. She could plan what to do. After she'd gained Dade Logan's trust and he let down his guard, she'd make her escape.

It was the only way. She knew Harlan Nowell was in a bind. He needed her to satisfy a debt, and he'd move heaven and hell to bring her back.

Or silence her.